Deeper ILLUSIONS

ANNIE JOCOBY

VINCI BOOKS

By Annie Jocoby

Illusions

Beautiful Illusions
Deeper Illusions
End of Illusions

Vinci Books

vinci-books.com

Published by Vinci Books Ltd in 2025

Copyright © Annie Jocoby 2013

The author has asserted their moral right to be identified as the author of this work in accordance with the Copyright, Designs and Patents Act 1988. This work is a work of fiction. Names, characters, places and incidents are the product of the author's imagination or are used fictitiously. Any resemblance to actual persons, living or dead, places and incidents is entirely coincidental.

All rights reserved. No part of this publication may be copied, reproduced, distributed, stored in any retrieval system, or transmitted in any form or by any means, including photocopying, recording, or other electronic or mechanical methods, nor used as a source for any form of machine learning including AI datasets, without the prior written permission of the publisher.

The publisher and the author have made every effort to obtain permissions for any third party material used in this book and to comply with copyright law. Any queries in this respect should be brought to the attention of the publisher and any omissions will be corrected in future editions.

A CIP catalogue record for this book is available from the British Library.

Paperback ISBN: 9781036707279

The EU GPSR authorised representative is Logos Europe, 9 rue Nicolas Poussion, 17000 La Rochelle, France
contact@logoseurope.eu

Chapter One

IRIS

It was the Friday after Ryan had asked me to marry him over breakfast, and Ryan and I made plans for Nick and his wife, Rielle, to join us for dinner at our house. Now that I had a ring on my finger, I finally accepted that the house was "ours." Funny, Ryan deeding the house to me as a joint owner didn't make me feel the house was "ours."

The ring made all the difference.

I was nervous, so I drank some wine before they arrived. Ryan noticed me looking nervous and put his arm around me protectively.

I smiled. "Don't worry, I'm fine. This is a first, though, I must admit."

He nodded. "Nick is a great guy. I promise you, you'll love him. And he, you."

"Does Nick, uh. Does he, uh." I blushed scarlet.

"Use your words," Ryan teased.

"Does he love you?"

"As a friend, of course. But I've a feeling that's not what you're asking."

I nodded.

"We've talked about that. We do have feelings for each other, I'm not going to lie. But it's different than how I feel about you and how he feels about Rielle. I hope that makes sense."

I nodded again, bringing the wine up to my lips once more.

"Does Rielle know?"

"Nah. She wouldn't understand." He looked at me longingly. "Most people wouldn't understand this. I admit, it's unconventional, but it's more common than you might think."

Finally, the hour was upon us. I heard the doorbell ring, and, taking another sip of wine, I answered the door.

Nick was just how I pictured him. Sandy blonde hair, blue eyes, a very muscular frame. Extremely handsome, like a young Robert Redford. He was the same height as Ryan. He smiled at me, giving me a hug. I noticed his dimples right away. I was always a sucker for a guy with dimples. "Iris, so good to meet you! And congratulations!"

His wife, Rielle, was a little cooler. She wasn't as friendly as Alexis, who was around less and less now that she and Todd were becoming more serious. Rielle was a rail-thin brunette with enormous brown eyes and alabaster skin. She wore little makeup, but didn't really need to. She reminded me somewhat of my former roommate in college who looked better without makeup than with it. At any rate, like everybody who I have met through Ryan, she was gorgeous and well-dressed.

She held out her hand and smiled. "I'm Rielle. I've heard a lot about you."

"Well, don't believe everything you hear," I joked. Rielle nodded and didn't pretend to laugh.

I had a feeling I would get along fine with Nick. Rielle, not so much.

Nick had a bottle of vintage Scotch in his hand. I saw him in the kitchen, putting his arm around Ryan as they poured out two glasses.

"What are you drinking?" Ryan addressed myself and Rielle. We were standing in the living room together, not saying a word. It was very uncomfortable.

"I'd like a mojito," Rielle called.

"That sounds good, I'd like the same." Beer than liquor, never sicker? I wondered if it was the same with wine. I guessed I would find out.

At that, Ryan went out the back door to pick some mint leaves. Nick motioned me to join him in the kitchen.

"So, you and Ryan."

"Yeah. Crazy, huh?"

"Sure. Let me see that ring." He looked at the ring, then gave a low whistle. "Leave it to Ryan to show the rest of us schlubs up. This baby is custom designed. Must've cost a pretty penny. A VERY pretty penny." He had a look on his face that I couldn't quite discern. Jealousy?

At that, Ryan was back with a bunch of mint leaves in his hand. He pummeled them with some sugar, poured the rum into a glass with the mint and sugar, with some ice, and added some club soda and lime.

The mojito was delicious, of course.

As was the dinner. Ryan prepared some filet mignons and I made the garlic mashed potatoes. The filets were grass-fed, as that was the only type of steaks that we ate, for ethical reasons. I had also steamed some green beans.

After dinner, we had some dessert and a few more drinks. I noticed the two guys sitting across the table, Nick's arm draped around Ryan's shoulders. I wished I didn't know what I knew about these two. They just looked like two best friends. I found myself silently cursing Alexis. *What I don't know won't hurt me.* But I *did* know, and I couldn't stop picturing them together.

"So, buddy. How about having it at my Lake Como home?"

I shook my head at Ryan. No way could my family afford tickets to Italy. *Oh, what am I saying? We can all just fly in the private jet.*

"Well, we can visit sometime. But I think Iris wants to have it right here."

"You can honeymoon at the house, then. And visit your winery. You haven't been there for awhile, you know."

Ryan looked at me. "Nick's Lake Como home is pretty magnificent. It has an amazing view of the Lake."

Nick addressed me. "You ever been to Italy?"

"No. I, uh, have never been out of the country." I felt like such a rube, again.

Nick raised one eyebrow. Ryan immediately changed the subject. "So, we were thinking about something pretty intimate. Nothing churchy, of course."

"What about the country club?" Nick asked.

"Nah. Too formal," Ryan said.

Ryan and I had actually discussed this beforehand. I didn't want the country club wedding, or the destination wedding. I just wanted something simple, in keeping with my nature.

Ryan was perfectly willing to go along with whatever I wanted.

"So, what were you thinking?" Nick asked.

"We thought about just having it here. In the backyard," Ryan said.

I nodded. Nick looked perplexed at this.

"Well, I agree your backyard is pretty bad-ass. But you have the choice of having it at the Lake Como house and you choose just to have it here?"

I was starting to feel more and more intimidated by Nick. I could feel a tension there, a dominance issue with him. It could have been just my imagination, but there seemed to be a subtle undermining of my relationship with Ryan.

I wondered if Nick really just wanted to be with Ryan and he was going to sabotage.

I shook that thought off. There was no indication this was the case.

I was just being silly.

Ryan was addressing the issue of the wedding again. "We appreciate the offer, Nick, but Iris has a lot of family here in town, and I can't put all of them on the private plane."

"Why not? Doesn't it seat like 30?"

"Yes, but not everybody can take off work, you know. And between the friends and family, there probably will be close to 100 people. How are we going to get all those people out to Italy?"

"You buy them first class tickets." Nick looked smug.

"Problem solved," Ryan said, rolling his eyes.

"Whatever. It's your wedding. I'm just along for the ride."

Ryan put his arm around me. "I admit, I'd like to stay at the Lake Como house for our honeymoon." Addressing me, Ryan said "I have a yacht out there, too, that I keep on the Mediterranean."

I smiled. *Yacht, schmact.* I really didn't care. I just wanted to be with him, even if it was in a shoebox.

Later on that night, I found out my hunch was true.

Ryan and Nick were in the living room, talking and drinking Scotch. Rielle had gone to bed early with a headache, and I, too, went to bed around midnight, after staying up with the guys. Nick played 20 questions with me. It wasn't entirely unpleasant, but he did seem to pry.

I was leaving my room to get a drink of water, and I decided to eavesdrop on the guys down below. They didn't notice me up above. They'd been drinking most of the night, so that probably had something to do with it.

Nick said "You mean to tell me she's never been out of the country? Ever?"

"Yes. So what, a lot of people have never been overseas."

"Nobody I know. Or you, for that matter."

"This just in - there are people out in the world who aren't rich."

"Buddy. Bro. I love you. You know that."

Ryan nodded.

"Well, then, I'll tell it to you straight. You can't marry that girl. She strikes me as a philistine."

"She's not a philistine. She's highly educated, very intelligent, and the nicest woman I have ever known."

"Educated at state schools."

"Jesus Christ, when did you get to be such a snob?"

"Ryan, you're slumming here. Whatever happened to Brigitte, the Dutch supermodel? She spoke five languages and could play the cello like Yo Yo Ma. Why didn't you like her?"

"Nick, you obviously don't understand."

"Try me. Iris doesn't even ski, for the love of all that is holy! How is she going to be on our vacations in the Alps?"

I sat, up above, wondering why Ryan was not offering a spirited defense of me. My heart started to sink, but I looked at my beautiful red diamond and felt comforted again.

Nick was continuing. "This isn't an Erich Segal novel here. You can have literally any woman you want." He shook his head. "I'm not seeing it here, buddy."

"Well, then, maybe you don't need to be my best man. Maybe you don't even need to be in the wedding at all."

"Easy, buddy. Sorry about the brutal honesty, but you know that's what I always give you."

"You've always been honest, I admit. But I didn't know you were so judgmental. Is that a new trait, or did you suddenly become an asshole while I wasn't looking?"

You go, Ryan! You tell him!

Nick audibly sighed. "You're right. She does seem nice, and she's kinda cute in her way. And, as long as you're happy, that's all that matters, right?"

To this, Ryan said, "There's something on your mind. I can tell."

Nick nodded. "Rielle and me, we aren't doing so good."

"What does that mean?"

"We're hanging by a thread, buddy. So, yeah, maybe I'm jealous that you found the one, right when my one is slipping away."

Ryan put his arm around him. "Sorry to hear that."

Then I saw them kissing. My heart started pounding. I mean, this was all good in theory, but seeing it in front of my eyes was something else entirely. I immediately went back into the room, and shut the door.

Oh, I didn't need to see that. I didn't need to hear that. Why can't I leave well enough alone?

I wondered what else was going on downstairs.

I could just imagine.

But I didn't want to.

I lay there, trying to get the spectacle out of my head. But, to my surprise, I also felt strangely titillated. After all, Nick was a very good looking guy. Seeing two hot guys together wasn't as bad as I thought it would be. I felt very conflicted about it all. On the one hand, Ryan was, technically, cheating on me. But, not really, because I had indicated I was ok with it. So, was he cheating, really? He wasn't with a woman downstairs, and we had discussed it beforehand.

I was very confused.

I opened the door again to spy some more. They were sitting on the couch now, side by side, Nick's hand once again draped over Ryan's shoulders. Nick was talking.

"Come on, Ryan, it's been way too long. Ever since you met her, you don't want to do it anymore."

"It just feels funny, that's all."

"It never did before."

"Well, for one thing, both of our girls are upstairs, asleep. That may change. Would you really want to be caught?"

"I don't really care anymore. I'm heading for a divorce as it is."

"You don't care? Don't you think Rielle might just use this against you, when it comes to custody issues?"

"Touché, buddy." He paused. "I just miss you, that's all. I miss us."

"I know. But it's different for me now. I've never felt like this about anybody else. I really need to minimize this," he said, motioning his hands from himself to Nick.

I saw Nick take another swig, then drunkenly place his hand in Ryan's hair, patting it. "Well, then, buddy, I guess I need my rest. I hope you don't mind if we just crash here. I really don't want to rouse sleeping beauty up there."

"Of course. I wouldn't want you to drive, anyhow."

"You mean, you aren't going to get Daniel out of bed to come and drive us?"

"Ha, ha. That would be totally rude, don't you think?"

"Joking, buddy. I'll see you in the morning."

At that, I leapt back into bed, realizing Ryan would soon be joining me. In a few minutes, Ryan actually was in the bed, crawling in next to me, fully clothed. I felt him stroking my hair. He whispered "You awake, beautiful?"

I lay there, pretending to sleep. I felt like it was the early days of our relationship, with me pretending to sleep, so that Ryan doesn't suspect that I saw and heard too much.

Ryan continued on, evidently soused. "I can't wait for you to be Mrs. Gallagher. You mean the world to me. I don't think I could love anybody as much as I love you."

He continued to stroke my hair. I lay perfectly still, and, after a few minutes, I could hear him snoring.

He was still fully clothed.

Chapter Two

The night before the wedding it was time to finally meet Sarah. She drove in from her home on Martha's Vineyard, where she lived with her husband and two children. The husband and the children stayed on the Vineyard, however. This was not explained.

She arrived in a brand-new Mercedes, a platinum blonde in a pair of big Louis Vuitton sunglasses and scarf around her head. Wearing a cashmere sweater set, a string of saltwater pearls, slim black pants and Tory Burch shoes, she looked like a cross between a wealthy housewife and Grace Kelley. She had a huge Mastiff in tow, who sat in the front seat.

When she pulled into the driveway, Ryan immediately went to the car and helped Sarah harness and leash the monstrous dog. She looked at me and held out a perfectly manicured hand. I shook it.

"I'm Sarah. I drove across the country for this affair, so you better be worth it." Then she smiled. I wasn't sure if she were joking or serious. I laughed anyhow. "Let me see the ring," she said, taking my hand and bringing it closer to her face. She raised an eyebrow and looked at Ryan. "He does really love you. Ryan, where'd you find that diamond?

"It wasn't easy, believe me," Ryan said, while trying to control the 175 lb. dog. "I found a connection to a South African jeweler who specializes in different colors of diamonds."

I didn't know that. I knew the red diamond was rare, the very rarest. But I didn't know he had to order it from South Africa.

"Really?" Sarah was interested. "Did you fly to South Africa to get it?"

"I did."

Huh? When did he do that?

He explained, addressing me. "While you were in the coma, I took a weekend off to get it. I prayed the whole time that I wouldn't miss you waking up. That was really the only time I left your side."

I nodded. "I had no idea you went to that kind of effort."

Sarah said "What, do you think you can just buy a diamond like this on the Internet? I mean, you *can* buy red diamonds on the Internet, but they're not perfect like this one."

Sarah was making me feel the way that Nick made me feel – like a total rube.

Ryan took the dog, Coriolanus – Cori for short – into the house, where he romped with Maximus and Brutus. They all apparently knew one another.

Ryan explained that Sarah always drove to his house, not flew, because she never wanted to be without Cori. And the dog didn't do well with flying, so she drove.

Ryan got out Sarah's Chanel luggage and the three of us went into our house.

Sarah looked around. "The place looks the same," she said, looking at me. "Where are you in this house, Iris?"

"I didn't really have much to bring over."

"Ryan, what's up with that? Don't you think this place should have some of Iris' influence here? After all, this house belongs to both of you."

"Really, Sarah, it's ok. I love Ryan's taste," I said.

"Sarah makes a good point," Ryan said. "We should really redecorate now that this will officially be our house."

Sarah smiled. I got the impression she had sway over Ryan.

We had dinner at the house, and, after dinner, Sarah politely asked Ryan if she could talk to me alone.

I dreaded this for some reason.

We got some brandy and took it into the den and sat down.

"So," Sarah said, patting her legs. "I'm not gonna beat around the bush, here. Have you signed a prenup?"

I somehow knew this subject would come up with somebody. I was surprised it never came up before. "No," I said.

Sarah smiled tightly. "Don't you think you better?"

"Ryan hasn't asked me to."

"He will. I'll make sure of it."

"Not a problem," I said, honestly.

"Good. Because you will not have the chance to do what that other witch did to him," she said, emphasizing the words "will not."

"Alexis isn't a witch. I really like her."

She snorted, which seemed odd coming from such a classy woman. "Has she got you fooled." She shook her head, and took another sip of her brandy. "You weren't there."

"I know, she's a piece of work sometimes. But she's very nice underneath."

"Nice? Bitch got him into drugs. She went to rehab so many times that her parents finally cut her off. She didn't have the money for her drugs, so she started running for a Mexican cartel." She shook her head. "That didn't last long. Ryan was in love with her. He didn't want her risking her life, so he supported her. Paid her tuition at Yale, paid her living expenses and thensome, and paid for her drugs. And his, of course." She took another sip of her brandy and stared at the fire. "Alexis was just one of a long line of people to take advantage of Ryan. He always lets them do it, though, because Ryan has one main motivation in life – to be loved."

I nodded. I got that from him.

"So now, here you are. Don't get me wrong. I'm happy he found someone decent. You'd think that someone like him wouldn't have a problem finding somebody real to love. But the ironic thing is, his looks and his wealth have always made it harder for him to find someone good." She shook her head, and looked at her hands. "You seem normal, though. Mom loves you, so that's something."

"Well, thanks for the support," I said, not sure if she really was giving her support.

"Listen, Iris, I don't want to be harsh here. But he's my baby brother and I was never able to protect him when we were younger. I look out for him now. He thinks you hang the moon." She smoothed her platinum blonde hair. "He would be devastated if you ever left him. But if you don't sign a prenup, there would be insult added to injury."

"It's not a big deal. I don't care about money and never have."

"Yeah, but you know the good life now. Private planes, red diamonds," she said. "Do you really think you can just go back to the way you were before? In a tiny apartment, working a job you hate?"

I was somewhat stunned that she knew so much about me. I guessed that she and Ryan were closer than I thought.

"I don't see why not. I got along fine for 33 years."

"You're so naïve." She called for Cori, who came bounding into the den. "Take Cori, here. He's a rescue dog. Lived on the end of a chain for the first two years of his life. It was the only life he was used to, so I guess he was ok. Now he lives with me. I baby him, take him everywhere with me, let him sleep in our bed." I made a face at that one – that huge thing sharing their bed? "It's a king-sized bed," she continued. "Hate to say it, but I like this dog more than my husband most of the time," she said with a chuckle. "And my kids for that matter." She threw her arms around Cori's neck, and he licked her face. "Anyhow, imagine if poor Cori had to go back to living on a chain. I'd think he'd be devastated."

"So, you think I'm like your dog."

"In a sense. Not literally, of course. I'm just saying that you have a taste of the good life. I would think that living in a tiny apartment, just getting by, would be tragic to you now."

"I'm not going to worry about that. Ryan and I are very much in love. There'll be no divorce."

"Yes, of course. That's what they all say. 'We're in love, nothing will happen.' Trust me, shit happens. If it didn't, we wouldn't have so many high-priced divorce lawyers." Taking another sip of her brandy, she continued. "Don't get me wrong, I don't want you left with nothing if you and Ryan break up. I just don't want you taking advantage of him."

"Give me the papers. I'll sign them."

"Don't be silly. There are no papers yet. But make no mistake, I'm going to exert my will on him to make sure there're papers drawn and you're forced to sign them. It's bad enough that you own half this house." She shook her head. "My idiot brother. I can never understand why he does what he does." She shrugged. "Then again, he doesn't get me, either, all the time."

"Not a problem. I'll sign whatever."

"Nothing personal, of course."

"Of course."

Later on, I was alone in the den. Well, not entirely alone. Cori, Maximus and Brutus were all snoring loudly beside me. I was sitting on the floor with them, my back against the sofa. I wanted January Jones, I mean Sarah, and Ryan to bond some. So I got out of their way.

I heard loud shouting, though, coming from the living room.

"Goddamn it, Sarah, I'm not going to do it! Now leave me the hell alone!"

"Fine. You want that girl to take everything you got, then go right ahead. Be a dumbshit."

"She wouldn't do that. She's not like that."

"God, you've always been so stupid when it comes to women. Wake up. She's not a saint. She had nothing before she met you, and, trust me, she won't want to go back to that. She'll take you to the cleaners, just like Alexis tried to."

"I had a prenup with Alexis." Ryan wasn't shouting anymore, but was talking loudly.

"Good. You see - if you didn't have a prenup with her, she would've taken you even more to the cleaners."

"Iris isn't Alexis."

"They all turn into Alexis when enough money is involved."

I peeked out the den door. They were now in the kitchen. They weren't shouting anymore. Sarah was getting a jug of milk out, and was pouring a glass for her and Ryan.

"So, tell me what the problem is. Why'd you give a prenup to Alexis, but won't with this girl?" Sarah asked, taking a sip of her milk.

"This is going to sound silly and romantic."

"You've always been silly and romantic. Go on."

"Iris is my soul mate. Alexis wasn't and I never felt that she was. That's all."

Sarah started laughing hysterically.

"What?" Ryan asked.

"Your soul mate. Oh, Lord. Mama raised a fool."

"Ha, ha. Mama didn't raise me, remember?"

"Then Nick's mama raised a fool. I got something for ya. There's no such thing as a soul mate. Now, don't be ridiculous and get to a lawyer's office pronto."

"No. The answer is no, and that's that. My foot's going down."

"Suit yourself. But when you guys break up a few years from now, and Iris is suddenly this greedy harridan who wants everything, don't come crying to me."

"Won't happen. We're in this for the long haul."

"Right. That's what every person in love says. They're in it for the long haul, until they're not. Be an idiot. What do I care? It's just that I helped you pick up the pieces every time that other witch pulled her crazy stunts. Every.time. I won't be there for you this time. You can handle your shit on your own."

"Thanks, Sarah. What a great, supportive sister you are."

"You don't take my sound advice, then you're on your own, buddy."

"You really are manipulative, aren't you?"

"What," she said with a shrug.

"I don't follow your advice so you're threatening to cut me off."

"Not cut you off. I just don't want to hear about her when she inevitably screws you over. We'll talk about any topic but her."

"Deal. I'm not scared of making this deal, because I know Iris and I will be 90-year-olds in a rocking chair together." He pantomimed having no teeth, then grabbed her around the waist and pantomimed biting her on the neck with no teeth.

She giggled. "Stop that, Peanut." Ryan had explained that "Peanut" was Sarah's pet name for him. When she was four, Maggie showed her a sonogram of her baby brother, and Sarah said he looked like a peanut. That had been Sarah's nickname for him ever since.

She ran off, with Ryan chasing her around, acting like he had no teeth. They ended up wrestling on the floor. Her perfect hair was getting messy and they were both laughing hysterically. Then Ryan started tickling and Sarah started shrieking. The dogs immediately woke up and ran into the living room, barking and growling at the two.

Sarah finally extricated herself from Ryan and the dogs. Her hair was pointing in every direction. She brushed herself off and sat down on the couch. Ryan got up off the floor and joined her.

Ryan said "I know you're just looking out for me and I appreciate that. But, trust me, Iris and I are in it for forever.

And, God forbid, if something happens, and we do break up, I always want her taken care of. You don't know how much that girl means to me."

"Wow. I've never seen you like this."

"Nobody has."

"Soul mate, huh? I gotta find me one of those."

They clinked glasses.

Later on, Ryan joined me in the den. "I suppose you heard that."

"Yeah."

"I will never make you sign a piece of paper. Not ever."

"I know. But I would be willing-"

"Of course you would be. But you're not going to."

And that was that.

Chapter Three

It was the day of our wedding. The backyard was decorated with twinkly lights and Chinese lanterns. I picked out the decorations myself, and Ryan and I worked together to put them up. We had rented some white chairs from a party planning company. The gazebo, which was where we actually would be married, also was decorated in pretty lights, and these lights were in the shape of little butterflies.

I prayed it wouldn't rain.

I chose a simple white sheath dress. No buttons, no bows, no lace, no bustle, no train, and no veil. I did, however, bother to put my hair up, with little tendrils framing my face, and I put a thin diamond headband in my hair. I felt thin and beautiful in my dress, glad that I had not gained back the weight I lost during my coma. I had started eating again and working out again, so I wasn't as skinny as before, but I knew I still looked good.

Ryan chose a suit in light grey, a silk lavender dress shirt underneath, and no tie. His collar was open.

He never looked more handsome.

As I walked down the aisle, strains of Beethoven's *Moonlight Sonata* filled the air. Ryan stared at me, his penetrating green eyes showing a vast reservoir of love for me. I took an enormous breath, but I didn't feel nervous. I only felt extreme happiness and peace.

Nick and Nate stood up for him, Debbie and my sister for me. One of my favorite judges performed the ceremony.

Ryan said to me "Iris, I felt like I was struck by lightning from the moment I met you. It wasn't just that you were quirky and dynamic, although those were definitely two words that I could use to describe you. It's just that I recognized you were my soul mate. My missing puzzle piece. You have brought me back to life, and I never want to be without you. So, I will love you, cherish you and protect you all the rest of my days. When you are sick, I will nurse you back to health. When you need me, I will be there. You are an inseparable part of me now. I really mean it when I say 'til death do us part."

I looked at my hands, which were holding his, and I saw that I was shaking. With a tremulous voice, trying to tamp down the tears and emotions that were threatening to overwhelm me, I began. "Before I met you, I didn't know what love really was. Now, since I have met you, I realize that love is unconditional and free. Love is something that is there when you are at your lowest point. You saved my life, in more ways than you will ever know. I know there will always be challenges ahead, but I vow to you that we will face them together. I love you, Ryan Gallagher, and I will be with you until death do us part."

Then we kissed for a long time, while everybody cheered.

Afterwards, we partied at the house. Ryan catered in pan-fried chicken from Stroud's, which was a rather famous local restaurant, known for its pan fried chicken, amazing mashed potatoes and gravy, and fried cinnamon rolls. The spread had a little of everything, and we served wine from his winery.

All in all, it was perfect.

As we made love that night, I thought I couldn't be happier. That nobody could be happier.

Thinking back now, I think about the saying that every story has a happy ending. It just depends on when you end the story.

And if the story ended here, this story would have a very happy ending.

If only the story ended there.

Chapter Four

"Mmmmm...Mrs. Gallagher, you are such a naughty girl," my new husband told me as I slowly and gently went down on him in his private plane. We were heading to Italy for our honeymoon. I had never been overseas, and to say that I was looking forward to this trip would be the understatement of the year.

"Don't stop, beautiful, please don't stop," he said, as I gently teased him, my tongue running up and down his enormous shaft, my fingers lightly massaging the opening of his sphincter. Then Ryan was suddenly begging me to stop - "stop, stop, stop, I'm too close. I want so badly to be inside of you." Then he pulled me up on the couch, unbuttoned my pants and said "are you ready to join the mile high club?"

I could do nothing but nod eagerly. He pulled on my hair, kissed me all over my face, lips, and neck, nibbled my ear, then plunged deeply into me as the plane ascended in altitude. It felt amazing, like it never had before. I now knew why the mile-high club was so popular. I couldn't imagine doing this in an airplane bathroom, mind you, but doing it here in luxury, and in private – there were no words. I orgasmed almost immediately as he filled me up, slipping in and out of me until I couldn't stand it anymore.

There was something about this scenario that made Ryan even friskier than usual, because he brought out a pair of handcuffs and a blindfold. "Lay down on the floor," he said, "on your belly." I obeyed. Then he handcuffed and blindfolded me, and got on top of me, kissing my back and neck. I felt the familiar shivers of anticipation. I could feel him rubbing something on my back. Something warm. Then he spent several minutes licking it off. Then he flipped me around so that I was on my back, and I felt the same warm liquid being spread on my stomach and my breasts, and he did the same thing. I could feel his hardness on my body as he slowly explored every inch of me, putting this substance on little patches and slowly licking them off.

I started to giggle a little, trying to guess what it was he was putting on me. It smelled like raspberries and chocolate. "What is that?" I asked.

"What is your favorite sundae?" he asked.

"The hot fudge and raspberry sundae at Sheridan's," I said. Sheridan's ice cream was a well-known place in Kansas City that didn't have any indoor seating, yet was constantly packed on every hot summer night. Their sundaes were the best I ever had.

"That's what I'm rubbing on your body. Are you jealous?" he asked, then gave me a taste of the concoction.

"Oh my god, that's so amazing," I said, as I ate the hot fudge and raspberry, while he continued to explore my body with his tongue. He smeared some on my lips, then slowly licked it off. Then his tongue was inside my mouth, exploring inside gently. He was, once again, inside me, thrusting hard and deep. Then, just as I was about to come, he withdrew himself from me. "Here," he said. "Have some Ben and Jerry's." At that, he put some ice cream on a spoon, and fed me some Chunky Monkey.

"Stop teasing me!" I said.

"Ok, then," he said, as he plunged into me again. I exploded at this point. "Mmmmm, what do you say we do this the entire way to Italy?"

"It's an 11 hour flight," I said.

"My point exactly. I think that we can make love the entire time. What do you say, Mrs. Gallagher?"

The thought of it made me titillated. "Oh, God, yes," I said.

So, for the duration of the flight, we explored each other's bodies, teased each other, and made love. This was the best flight I ever had, and, yet, I knew the best was yet to come.

We finally touched down at the Malpensa airport in Milan at around 10 o'clock their time. By then, I was driven crazy with lust. Somehow, I wasn't sated, even though we had just completed the sex marathon to end all sex marathons. We had always been known to make love for hours, but doing it for 11 hours non-stop was a feat, even for us.

"Whew," I said, feeling slightly dazed. "That was amazing."

"Oh, yes," Ryan said. "I can't wait to get you to Nick's villa, so that I can ravish you all over again."

I was so excited to see the place. But first, we had to go and get our rental car.

We arrived at the rental car place, which was open all night. Ryan spoke in fluent Italian to the clerk, who nodded and spoke Italian back. I had no idea what Ryan and this man were saying. I only knew that Ryan was smiling at me devilishly.

The man came back with the keys in his hand, and Ryan called to him in Italian, waving his hand. I only recognized the word "Ciao."

Oh, how I wished that I prepared more for this trip, language-wise.

"By the way," I said, "how do you still know your Italian so well?"

"Beautiful, I lived in Europe for several years and I spent summers here in Italy. It's not that big of a deal."

I smiled. I didn't know any other languages at all, and I was impressed with Ryan's fluency here.

I followed him out to the parking lot, then blinked my eyes in astonishment when I saw to which car Ryan was headed. It was a black Lamborghini.

Ryan raised his eyebrows, motioning to the car. "Get in, my lady," he said, as the doors opened up in their trademark upward trajectory.

I cocked my head. "Really? This the car we're going to be seeing Italy in?"

"We're in Italy, beautiful, we have to do as the Italians do." At that, he turned the ignition and I had never heard such a roar in my life.

Man, this was a car.

"We're doing as the wealthy Italians do," I said, with a hint of condescension. "I don't know about Italians, in general. I'm pretty sure that most Italians can't afford to cruise around in a car like this."

I was somewhat put off that Ryan was being so pretentious with the car.

But then I realized that he was just trying to impress me, which made me love him all the more.

Ryan just smiled and tousled my hair a little. "I have to take you on the Autobahn sometime in this car. Then you can see what it can really do."

We got to Nick's house on Lake Como just after midnight. I was exhausted by this time. The trip was catching up to me.

The house was gorgeous. It was behind a gate, and we had to travel up a long drive to get to it. It was situated on the shore of the lake, and it was an enormous Mediterranean-style home. The façade was a salmon-colored stucco, and the house was all porticos, turrets, arches and huge windows. The living room was impeccable – 20-foot ceilings, walls of windows, and a marble fireplace on one end of the room. The floor was marble as well. There was a large tree in a pot that looked like some kind of palm tree. The furniture was Italian leather, and the coffee table in front of the sofa was glass-topped with a marble pedestal.

I walked around the home, marveling at everything I saw. Above the fireplace was a Warhol original, and in the dining room were several Ansel Adams originals.

The entire house was like this. Cool, modern, impeccably appointed. There was an Olympic-sized swimming pool out back, framed by palm trees and African violets. A hot tub was attached to the pool, and the pool had a bar in the middle of it that one could swim to. There were waterfalls out back, as well.

I felt like I was in an episode of *Lifestyles of the Rich and Famous* with Robin Leach. This was especially true as I knew that Lake Como was the haven for wealthy celebrities. I went out on the balcony and looked at the stars in the sky and smelled the night air. It was a beautiful early fall evening and I was with the most mesmerizing and magnetic man on the planet.

Life was at its pinnacle.

Ryan soon joined me out on the balcony, two glasses of wine in his hands. He gave me a glass, and we clinked it. "To a long and healthy life together," he said, then kissed me. "Mmmm, you taste like wine," he said playfully.

"I wonder why?"

He kissed me again, longer and more passionate this time. "You ready to go again?"

"Always," I said.

"Get naked with me and let's get in the pool."

At that, we both stripped off our clothes and ran into the heated pool. I was glad that the pool was heated, because the night air was just a bit chilly. I certainly didn't want to be a baby about it, though.

Ryan picked me up and carried me around the pool, humming sweetly to me. "La, la, la, la, you're my beautiful wife," he sang. "God, that sounds amazing. Wife. You're my wife. You're no longer my girlfriend, but my wife."

I giggled, then he kissed me. "God, I want you," he said. "But I can't take you here in the pool. No lubrication." At that, he pulled me up and carried me over to the lounge chair that was by the pool, and entered me right there. Waves of orgasms floated through me. I felt like I was in heaven, like nothing could ever touch us. Nothing bad had ever happened to us, and nothing bad could ever happen to us. We were invincible, laying here on the chaise, under the stars, intertwined.

We were like this for the rest of the night, going into the house and making love in the enormous four poster bed. Nick's bedroom was just as gorgeous as the rest of the house, and it had a balcony attached. The arched windows opened up into the balcony, and the curtains billowed in the breeze. The zephyr felt amazing on my skin, because I was getting so warm with every single touch.

We couldn't get enough of each other for the rest of the night, so we slept in the next day, exhausted and happy.

We woke up the next day around noon, rented some bikes, and headed to Ryan's winery. The bikes wouldn't fit on the Lamborghini, of course, so we drove Nick's Jeep.

Ryan's winery was in the Lombardy region, which was close to Nick's home. We traveled some twenty miles to get there, through dusty streets. The building that housed the actual winery was built upon arches and porticos, and it had a more stylish look to it than many of the other wineries I encountered in the region. I walked in and saw enormous barrels lining the walls, and people milling about tasting the wine.

Ryan was greeted by the workers there, bantering back and forth with them in Italian. They were slapping his back, obviously thrilled to see him.

He brought me over to meet the manager of the place, Giuseppe. "Giuseppe, this is my new wife, Iris. Iris, Giuseppe."

"Ciao, bella," he said. Then, in broken English, he said "Congratulations to you both. Welcome to Italy." Then he laughed as he gave me an enormous bear hug.

Then Ryan turned to me and said "Let me take you on a tour, then you can get a glass of whatever wine you choose. I hope you don't mind sipping some wine while I talk to the people here. It's been a long time since I've been here, so we need to catch up."

"No, no, of course not," I said. "Here, just pour me a glass, and I'll sit right over there," I said, motioning to a small table and chairs that was just over to the side of the bar. "We'll take our tour later."

Deeper Illusions

I sipped my wine and watched them interestedly. Ryan fit right in, speaking rapid-fire Italian and gesturing with his hands. The conversation seemed to be light and non-serious – there was plenty of laughter and back-slapping. A few times, I saw Ryan look at me with an enormous smile on his face, gesturing while he spoke Italian, and I wished I had some kind of clue as to what they were saying.

It seemed that Ryan's Italian was perfect, accent and all. It was if he was a native speaker.

He came over to me with a wide grin on his face. "Everything's great, beautiful. It seems that the people running my place have it all under control. Let's take our tour."

He held my hand as we walked through the production room, then to the warehouse, and outside in the actual vineyard. It was beautiful and peaceful here, and remarkably busy. There were people everywhere, touring the vineyards, drinking the wine, chatting in a multitude of different languages. I hadn't heard so many different tongues spoken since I vacationed in San Francisco several years ago.

"You've done well here," I said. "Your place certainly seems to be a hot spot."

"Yeah. All the credit for that has to go to Giuseppe and his team. I own the place, but I really am not active in the day-to-day operations anymore. So the success of the place is directly attributable to them."

After we toured Ryan's place, we got the bikes off the back of the Jeep and pedaled through the Lombardy region. We stopped along the way at various wineries, sipping different varietals. Ryan explained to me the differences in the grapes, how they were grown, and how the different varietals were made. It was all very interesting to me, and he was a wealth of knowledge on the subject. I was starting to feel slightly drunk, and was a little nervous about pedaling while impaired, but went along, anyhow.

We got back to the Jeep around dusk, after biking around fifty miles through some of the most beautiful country I had ever seen. "I'm proud of you," Ryan said. "I don't think that we have biked this far together before."

I just smiled, feeling exhausted and a little drunk. "Let's head home, huh?"

We got home, and made love, but only once. After we made love, we were both zonked. We didn't even eat dinner.

That entire week was like that one day. Every day was an adventure. One day we took the rented Lamborghini to Milan to see *The Last Supper* in the Santa Maria delle Grazie, which is a church and Dominican convent. Ryan had booked this particular tour a month in advance, knowing this was a popular site. After we saw this most important painting, we drove to Venice to take a gondola tour through some of the Venetian canals. I laughed, telling Ryan that the closest I had come to such a tour was when I went to the Venetian hotel in Las Vegas. Now, I was doing the real thing.

Another day we traveled in our rental to Genoa, where Ryan's yacht, *The Maggie*, was moored. It was fifty feet in length and had luxury appointments inside. The main area, down below, was like a living room – spacious, with white couches, a large dining area, and a full kitchen with granite countertops and new appliances. The bedroom had a luxurious king-size bed and walk-in closet. We both got into our suits and sailed out into the clear blue waters of the Mediterranean. We anchored in the water, and jumped in from the deck. We also took out two jet skis and buzzed around in the water for a couple of hours, chasing each other around playfully.

Another day trip we took in our Lamborghini, slightly longer, was to Rome. I wanted to see Vatican City, so we did. I marveled at the Sistine Chapel. I had only seen the mural on television and in pictures before, and it was so much more magnificent in person. I couldn't believe the opulence and the wealth of the city, and was amused at the multitudes of cardinals and bishops who were walking around the grounds. We also rented scooters and visited the Trevi Fountain and the ruins of the Roman Coliseum.

And the food and wine! There were no words. I was glad that we did so much walking, because we were eating such rich food all the way through the country. Pastas, pizzas, cannolis, white sauce, red sauce. It was all so delicious. The seafood dish I got in Genoa was divine, as the fish was freshly caught. The pizzas were different than what I was used to in America, for they were smaller and had a red sauce made of crushed tomatoes. The cheese was also very light, compared to American pizzas. My favorite pizzas were the Margarita pizza, with the tomato and basil, and anything with a lot of vegetables.

I was feeling, during that week, that I had never been happier in my life. Each day I thought that nothing could ever top it, then the next day would come along and be even better.

Of course, I could never dream that anything would come along and shatter our perfect bliss.

I should've known better.

Chapter Five

It was on the seventh day of our honeymoon when it happened. I casually flicked on the television, looking for something to watch. Stretching and yawning, feeling sated after another night of love-making with my gorgeous husband, I flipped around the television.

"Beautiful! Come back up here!" Ryan was calling me. "I'm not done with you yet!"

Smiling, I tossed the remote aside, and started to head upstairs.

However, hearing my name on the television set stopped me cold. I spun around, turning the set up. A world famous attorney was talking to a generic blonde anchorwoman on one of the 24-hour news channels.

My blood turned to ice when I heard what he was saying.

Blonde anchorwoman was asking him "But wasn't Ms. Anderson caught in the act?"

"By her now-husband. He's clearly lying. Besides, he's a drug addict. He just got out of rehab, for the third time."

I was shaking. "Ryan! Ryan!" I screamed.

Ryan heard my tone, and came running out of the bedroom, completely naked. "What's going on?" he asked.

I said nothing. I could just point at the television. The attorney continued on. "He's a drug addict, he got her involved in drugs. He couldn't tell her parents that, so he cooked up this absurd story about her being kidnapped by Ms. Anderson."

Both of us watched, horrified.

"But she had all those marks on her body. Cigarette burns, whiplashes, deep gashes where she was slashed with a knife."

"The woman is a self-mutilator from way back. She was hospitalized three times for that. She obviously did those things to herself."

I could feel Ryan's eyes now on me, boring into me. I was shaking. I couldn't look at him. I could feel my face burning, red hot.

Ryan didn't say a word.

Blondie continued. "But why would they accuse Ms. Anderson of this? She is a very well-known socialite, with a lot of connections. Why not just get some random person involved in this, instead of somebody like Ms. Anderson?"

"Mr. Gallagher and Ms. Anderson had an affair when Mr. Gallagher was very young. It didn't end well. Mr. Gallagher apparently saw an opportunity for revenge and he took it. She is nothing but a scapegoat for Mrs. Gallagher's self-mutilation and accidental overdose. Or, who knows, maybe it was an intentional overdose. Wouldn't be the first time with her."

Again, I felt my face flush hot. I felt nauseated. Ryan was still staring at me, I could feel it. But I refused to look at him.

"I understand that he was only 14 when he got involved with her."

"Right."

"Isn't that a crime she can be charged with?"

"Statute of limitations has long since run on that one. There is no crime there to charge her with at this point."

"So let me get this straight. The theory is, as you understand it, that Ms. Gallagher mutilated herself, and overdosed on heroin. When Ms. Gallagher ended up in the hospital with an overdose, Mr. Gallagher cooked up this story to cover up the fact that she overdosed, because he got her involved with drugs. He implicated Ms. Anderson because he wanted revenge on her for seducing him when he was only 14?"

"That's exactly what I understand happened."

Blondie shook her head. "What a wild story." Then, looking at the camera, blondie said "We will have further updates for you as the story progresses. Now, for the top story...."

Ryan and I sat in silence, staring at the television. Neither of us said a word. My mind was surprisingly blank, and I had a preternatural calm, like when I was first kidnapped by Rochelle and thought I would die. The enormity of what was about to happen didn't yet enter my mind.

Finally, after what seemed like days, Ryan spoke. "Iris, is all that true?"

I nodded.

"Why didn't you ever tell me?"

I shrugged. Words couldn't come out of my mouth. However, I could feel hot tears coming out of my eyes. The thing I sought to bury, that I tried so hard to forget, was now on the international news, and God knows where else. If that station has it, then the possibility existed that this story would blow up. Then, I would never be able to get away from it. Ever.

I comforted myself a little bit, though, thinking that nobody died. Therefore, the story couldn't possibly blow up too big. Maybe it would be just a little story.

No, this story would be big. A socialite being accused of heinous things – torture, kidnapping, attempted murder. This was just too juicy.

My suspicions were confirmed when I switched the channel to another 24-hour news channel, and they, too, were talking about it. This time it was a dark-haired woman and a different attorney who was discussing the "facts" of the case. A new detail this time. "Mr. Gallagher was obsessed with Ms. Anderson. He was stalking her for years. When he couldn't have her, he decided to get back at her."

I looked over, and Ryan was on the phone, talking to Sheldon. "You need to do something about this. Slap them all with a cease and desist letter. They can't get away with these lies."

He paused. "What? She's an involuntary public figure? What does that mean?...That's ridiculous...I know, that will be the argument. But what the hell? What about the lies?" He shook his head furiously. "Rochelle hired who? Why did she do that?...Get on it. Do what you can. This is getting ridiculous." At that, he got off the phone.

"Sit down," he commanded, motioning me to a chair. I dutifully obeyed.

"There's trouble," he said, stating the brutally obvious. "Rochelle was none too happy when O'Donnell withdrew from her case. So she hired Greg Schultz as her attorney."

"Greg Schultz? *The* Greg Schultz?" I asked. Greg

Schultz was, to my mind, the most famous attorney in America.

"Yes, *the* Greg Schultz. So, now Schultz has his minions out there fanning the stories on all the 24-hour news stations. They're wanting the public opinion to be on Rochelle's side, for the purposes of tainting the jury, and the only way to do that is to spread absolute lies on these stations."

"But we can sue them for libel and slander, right? Right?"

"Of course. But how do we prove it? It's her word against ours."

"I don't understand. You were there. You know what happened."

"Yes, but who else knew I was there except Rochelle herself?"

"You called the cops, they came and picked me up at her house. They arrested her at her house, too."

"Yeah, but the lawyer is saying it was all a setup. I dragged you over to Rochelle's house after you overdosed yourself, then had her arrested, because I wanted revenge on her for leaving me. Or some such ridiculous story." He sighed and put his head in his hands. "The problem is that I was in rehab just recently. Rochelle doesn't have a spot on her record. She also owns the Kansas City social scene. I look like the derelict with a bone to pick. She's involved with every charity in the world, too. This will be tough."

"But Ryan, the story of your relationship with her when you were 14 is also out. Doesn't that tarnish her?"

"Of course. She's going to spin that, too, though. You just wait."

"How can she spin that? That's child molestation, plain

and simple." I was dumbfounded by all of it. Just when I thought that I was safe, and my ordeal was behind me....

I continued "what's this about my being an involuntary public figure?" I knew something about invasion of privacy laws, and knew that facts may be disclosed if they are a matter of legitimate public concern. Therefore, most people in the public eye can have their private lives exposed. I didn't feel I was a public figure, so I wasn't sure how my hospitalizations could be a matter of legitimate public concern.

"Sheldon just told me that, because you were a part of a crime that is a matter of public significance, your participation makes you an involuntary public figure. Because of this, the details of your life is considered to be legitimately newsworthy. That's why the stations can broadcast that information about you."

"But what about the lies? They can't just go on repeating falsehoods like they are."

"Let me talk to Sheldon again," he said. "I'll see what can be done."

He came back. "Sheldon is already on it. He is threatening them all with slander suits. He is also pressing an invasion of privacy issue with them, on the chance that a court won't find that you and I are public figures because of our involuntary participation in Rochelle's crime."

I sighed. It really didn't matter. The damage was done. So we win millions against them – so what? We had millions in the bank, more than we could ever hope to spend in our lifetime. What was a few million more? The point was that everybody now knew all of my deep, dark secrets. Plus, everyone now knew all the dirt in mine and Ryan's relationship.

He looked at me. "There is something else." I nodded.

Of course there was something else. There was always something else, it seemed.

"Rochelle is out on bail."

My breath quickened, and I felt my legs buckle as I collapsed on the floor. I was hyperventilating, and Ryan was rushing to my side. He picked me up, and laid me gently on the couch.

I finally found my voice. "How is she out? She was a flight risk because of her private jet and her house in Monaco. How could the judge let her out?"

"They don't call Schultz the miracle worker for nothing."

"I bet money changed hands. Who is the judge?" I hadn't asked that question before, surprisingly.

"Judge Reingold."

"He has a stellar reputation. I can't imagine him taking a bribe. So, how did Schultz convince a judge to let her out, I wonder. Also, how is Schultz taking this job? He isn't licensed in Missouri, I don't think."

Ryan raised his brow. "You know, the *pro hac vice* thing."

I nodded. Out-of-state attorneys can practice anywhere they wish, as long as they have local counsel overseeing them. I wondered which of my cohorts was willing to do that. Probably any one of them, if the money was right.

"Let me call Sheldon again. He might be able to fill in more of the details." At that, he went into the other room to call Sheldon. I could hear him talking through the door.

After about 45 minutes, he came out. "Ok, here's the deal. Rochelle has an electronic monitoring device. Sheldon thinks she got bail because she now has a plausible story for what happened. That wasn't true before."

"And? Isn't it funny that she's now changing her story?

"One would think. She's spinning, though. Get this –

she says she didn't tell her story before, because she wanted to protect me, because she loves me. Then, when I got married to you, she made the decision not to protect me anymore."

"Geez. Who's going to buy that?"

"That's the reason for the PR blitz. This story was buried before she got Schultz involved. Now it's exploded because of all the surrogates out there telling the story."

"And the tales grow taller on down the line."

"Right."

"And this story has all the elements of a juicy tale. The socialite, the son of a prominent billionaire, obsession, jealousy, drugs, suicide attempts, self-mutilation, child molestation. No wonder it's blown up."

"About that." Ryan looked at me expectantly.

"I don't want to talk about that right now."

He put his hand on my face, and tenderly stroked my cheek. "You can talk to me. You know all about my past. It sounds like you've had similar experiences."

"Maybe later. Right now, all I can think of is that woman is on the loose." I shivered. "I know that we're thousands of miles away from her right now, but her Monaco house isn't that far away from here."

"She has on a monitoring device. I don't see her coming this way."

I looked out the window. Press people with cameras and microphones were hanging around outside, just beyond the gate. "Whatever. Everybody knows that we're here, now, so Rochelle knows, too."

Ryan joined me at the window. "Looks like we'll be camping out here for awhile." He didn't look entirely unhappy. "Well, we might as well make the best of it, Mrs.-Gallagher."

"Not now. I'm sorry, but sex is the very last thing on my mind." At that, I ran into the bathroom and heaved my breakfast into the toilet. Ryan was kneeling on the floor next to me, stroking my back.

"It's going to be okay," Ryan said soothingly, stroking my back and playing with my hair. This was usually such a loving, comforting gesture to me, but, right now, his hands just felt like thorns on my back. Scraping my skin. I didn't want him near me.

"How can you say that? How're we going to get out of here? What am I going to tell people? God, all those people who know me, and nobody ever knew about my cutting and suicide attempt. Including you." The tears were burning in my eyes now. I couldn't look at him. I was so ashamed of him now knowing my secrets.

Now he was sitting next to me, still naked, his hands on his knees, his knees curled up to his chest. Still meltingly handsome, and I felt more inferior to him than ever. It was bad enough feeling that I didn't measure up to him when he didn't know these awful things about me. Now that he knew them, he had to think I was some sort of a nut. He probably wanted an annulment, I thought, miserably.

He just watched me, silently, my head still in the toilet. Nothing was coming out anymore and I knew nothing else would. But I still couldn't face him. I hoped that if I stared at the toilet long enough that he eventually would get up and just leave me alone. That was all I wanted at that point - to be left alone. But, still, he remained, watching me without a word coming out of his mouth.

I wondered why he wasn't getting the hint.

Finally, I spoke. "Hon, why don't you go and get dressed. Get me some clothes, too, please." *And take your time about it. I am in no hurry for you to come back.*

He got up without a word and returned not five minutes later wearing a pair of shorts and a button down. He wordlessly handed me a pair of shorts and a tank top, along with some underwear. I looked up at his pained eyes, then immediately looked away. I couldn't take those eyes, not now. I felt myself hating him for loving me so much.

At the same time, I wondered if he did still love me. His eyes said he did, but how could he? I did awful things to myself, and now the whole world knew about it. Everybody. And it would be a matter of time before all the sordid secrets of our life together was out for public consumption – Ryan's affair with Nick, all those sex parties where he was the guest of honor, his dad…his mother, for that matter. On and on and on, it was all going to come out, and how would I ever face anyone ever again? These kinds of things were fine behind closed doors, men having oral sex with men, but what happened when everyone I know thought I married a gay guy? I suddenly hated the world for being so judgmental about it all, just assuming there were no bisexual men. They were all going to think I was some sort of beard, because Ryan would never want to be with somebody like me otherwise.

Nobody would understand it.

Why did I care? I guess because I thought that I had finally attained respectability in the world. I had finally, after all my years of wanting and not having, found somebody who validated me as a special person. And everybody assuming it was all a lie was more than I could bear.

And, at the same time, the whole world would now know that I was some kind of a nut, a person who did things to herself to escape the mental anguish of being an outcast, a nobody, a misfit in society. The emotional pain of being invisible was always more than I could ever bear, so I cut myself to feel the physical pain, because the physical pain was so much better than the emotional pain. So much better - when I sliced myself, the emotional pain went away. Even for just that short period of time, then it became like an addiction. I felt embarrassed for doing all that to myself for my piddly little shitty problems, when there were people like Ryan in the world dealing with real shit. Yet he didn't hate himself nearly as much as I hated myself. He had the emotional resiliency that I could only dream about. People loved him. Everybody loved him. He was the golden boy I never thought would be attainable.

And there was another problem – there was something else that I had never told him about, and it was something for which I still felt a deep well of shame. It occurred to me that my cutting problems and suicide attempt were mainly due to this incident, even more than the invisibility issue. But I couldn't tell him about this. I prayed the media never picked up on it and ran with it. I would be absolutely devastated if it got out.

But I tamped down my feelings and decided not to bring it up.

He was still staring at me. I finally got up the courage to look at him right in the eye and not look away. I knew what he was thinking, without him even saying a word. He wasn't thinking about the horror that had befallen us – the paparazzi and reporters outside on the street, the world knowing his secrets at last, the fact that Rochelle was on the loose. He was thinking about me, about why I would never tell him how much I really hated myself. All that time, when he confessed one horrible thing after another, and I never said a word.

I simply stared back at him, willing him to speak.

Finally I spoke. "How're we going to get out of here?"

"I called John. He has a helicopter and he's going to take us from the roof."

"To where?"

"To the plane. Then onto…somewhere. We could stay with Nate for a few days. Nick wouldn't be safe. I talked to him and the pap are swarming him as well. They are being very careful not to be on his property, but are on the public street, waiting for him every day." He stared at the ceiling. "Whatta mess."

"The plane. You don't think the pap and reporters are going to be there as well?"

"Yeah, I thought about that. I'm going to have to call Giovanni, a friend from Harvard, to see if he doesn't mind taking us the next time he heads to New York. He makes business trips there all the time. That would probably be our best bet." He looked at me. "In the meantime, we have plenty of food and drinks here. But it looks like the honeymoon is literally over."

I nodded. "In the meantime, let's not watch any of those stupid news channels, huh?"

That night, I woke up in a start. Was it all a bad dream? I nudged Ryan awake. We had gone to bed that night without making love, wearing pajamas. Neither of us reached for the other in bed. I was on one side of the enormous, king-sized bed, he on the other. The distance between us was engulfing me. We were so close before.

Ryan awoke with a start after I nudged him.

"I can't sleep," I told him. I was shaking.

He immediately put his arms around me, and I felt comforted. I hoped we could fight this together, and not let it tear us apart. We were, after all, in this mess together – both of us were going to be humiliated, so we might as well lean on each other. If we could get through this, we could get through anything.

It was then, when I finally accepted his touch, his affection, that I was able to let loose with the tears that were threatening all day. I cried for hours in his arms and he held me silently. We were at the point in our relationship when each knew instinctively what the other needed at any given moment. And he knew that, right now, I just needed to be held, so this is what he did.

Chapter Six

The next day, we both knew that it was time to act. We had wasted the previous day with our shock and grief of what had intruded into our world. There would be plenty of time for crying when we figured out how to get out of this house and into a place that was safe for us. So, Ryan called his friend Nate that morning to ask if we could stay with him for a little while. Nate agreed, so the plans were set, as soon as Giovanni would be heading to New York. Giovanni agreed to take us there, so that end was set as well.

I sighed. "So what's the long-term plan? We're just going to be trapped at Nate's indefinitely?" And Nat's. Nat, who was in love with Ryan and didn't even try to hide that fact. Nat, with her perfect body and face and sweet demeanor. I suddenly felt insecure, which was an odd feeling for me in our relationship. I always felt insecure about myself, but I never felt insecure about how he felt about me. But that was changing with yesterday's devastating revelation.

"No, obviously that is not a viable plan. But I hope we

can think more clearly once we get to safety. I don't think that either of us is going to think clearly with those wolves outside the door."

Taking a deep breath, I said "Well, I might as well turn on my phone. God, I dread this." And I turned on the phone to see that it had, indeed, blown up. 166 missed calls in one day, 25 of them from my mother alone. I looked at my messages, and saw increasingly frantic messages from her. Also messages from my friends. But mainly the calls were from various news stations around the globe, and people calling for comments for the tabloids.

What was I going to tell everybody?

I called my mother. "Hey. Listen, and don't talk. I just wanted to let you know that I'm ok. I don't want to talk about it, so please don't ask me to."

"Well, I'm glad you are alright. That's all I really wanted to know."

"Thanks. Ryan and I are going to New York for an indefinite period of time."

"What does that mean?"

"Well, we won't be there too long. We're staying with one of Ryan's best friends, who's a Goldman banker. So obviously we can't move in there. We just need to stay there to figure out what to do."

"What is all this talk about you hurting yourself? I never knew about that."

"Nobody did. Listen, I don't want to talk about it, please."

She persisted in asking. She was always like that, can never leave well enough alone. I finally ended up hanging up on her.

I didn't call anybody else back who called me. I was drained enough talking to her.

Meanwhile, Giovanni contacted Ryan. He would be heading to New York in a week. A week! A week here, with *them* outside the door like hungry wolves. That seemed unbearable. And I could not avoid Ryan's eyes. Imploring me to open up to him. That has always been the problem in our relationship – I was always so guarded with him, and it took a long time for me to trust and break down the walls. Now, I was expected to bare my soul to him, something that I had, thus far, not been willing to do. But I knew that it was going to come out while we were here in this beautiful home, which had become our prison, because there was no escaping it.

We headed to the kitchen, and Ryan opened up a bottle of his wine. Pouring me a glass, he said "let's build a fire and drink this wine."

I nodded. The implication was clear – he wanted answers from me, although he didn't want to come right out and ask me for them.

We took our wine in front of the fire, and Ryan lay down on the blanket. I fingered my glass lightly, then gulped down the wine. I gave him the glass to refill, and he did so. I sipped this.

Taking a huge breath, I started. "Well, I guess you want answers."

"Only as much as you're willing to tell."

"Uh. Well, I have always had an issue with myself," I started. Then I thought better of it. "This is so embarrassing. I mean, you – you had real problems. Me, I don't have anything like that in my past. No sexual abuse, no schizophrenic mother, none of that."

"So, what does that mean? Just because you didn't have tragic circumstances doesn't mean you don't have a reason to have issues." He stroked my arm lightly. "So, please, stop being embarrassed. I'm your husband. I love you more than I've ever loved anybody. Nothing you can say to me will make me think any less of you."

I looked at my red diamond, and felt reassured. The red diamond was symbolic of how deeply this man felt for me. The very rarest diamond in the world, and Ryan made sure this was the stone that was set in the ring he gave to me.

I knew he loved me, so why was this so hard?

I gulped down the rest of the wine, and held out the glass expectantly. Ryan was still on his first glass.

I sighed. "Well, there really wasn't that much to it. I was pretty much invisible my whole life to just about everybody. No, that wasn't true. I was invisible to most everybody, yet was bullied as well. I just never fit in." Ryan was still looking at me, still stroking my arm lovingly, so I felt encouraged to go on.

"I never fit in," I repeated. "And the hard thing was, I wanted to fit in. I tried out for cheerleader, but was humiliated. The school play - humiliated. Always the last to be picked in gym class, the last to be asked to dance in gym class. God, on the day everybody was finding dance partners in gym class, I made sure I looked as good as I could. I'll never forget the look on the face of the guy who was stuck with me – he was stuck with me, because I was literally the last one picked. His look of revulsion..." I took a deep breath. "Never got invited to a party, never got invited to a dance, never had a date, missed my prom because nobody ever asked. A social zero." I smiled at Ryan. "Somebody like you, in high school, I could only dream about."

He was looking at me, his eyes penetrating. I still saw vast reservoirs of love in those eyes. He didn't seem revolted or horrified that he had ended up with such a misfit. So, I decided to keep going. "I got to college, and things changed.

I had freedom, and I took it. I drank myself into a stupor every night, and slept with way too many men. That's the way it was – the alcohol gave me courage and self-esteem, which I didn't have sober. And it made me way too easy. I was always craving love, always wanting somebody to validate me, to make me feel I existed, that I was not invisible. But all these men ever wanted was an easy lay. So, you see, there was a bit of cross-purposes there." I smiled ruefully. Then I suddenly remembered that this was, ironically, how I met Ryan – I went up and talked to him, liquid courage guiding the way, and we ended up in bed together that night.

So, the drunken one-night stand strategy finally paid off.

Ryan sipped his wine, then put his hand in my hair, smoothing back my bangs. He kissed me lightly on the forehead.

I continued. "So, I got depressed. I felt hopeless, and my depression became this deep well. The only thing that brought me out of it was cutting myself." I looked at my hand, which was shaking violently. "Uh, maybe we should switch to white wine. I'm afraid I'm going to spill this wine on the rug." At that, Ryan nodded, and was on his feet. He appeared in a few minutes, a bottle of Pinot Grigio in his hand. He poured me a glass and laid back down.

I continued. "I cut myself, and the physical pain took away the mental pain. The emotional pain. It felt – liberating. Freeing. For that period of time when the physical pain was excruciating, I forgot about how bad I felt inside. It became an addiction."

Finally, he spoke. "How did you end up in the hospital?"

"I slashed my wrists in my bathtub. My roommate found me when I was near death. I ended up in the hospital, of course, and I had all these other marks on me. There were cut marks everywhere on my body – fresh ones, older ones. Burns, too. I flicked Bic lighters on my skin."

Ryan's face remained impassive, although I saw a flicker of pain flash through his eyes. I could tell he was trying very hard to conceal his emotions.

Taking another gulp of the Pinot, I continued. "The doctors wanted to know about all of these marks, of course. It wasn't like I could claim that I was accident-prone. And I couldn't very well claim that somebody else was hurting me – that would have gotten an innocent person in trouble. So, I told them what I was doing."

"Did you get help?"

"No, actually. I was a poor college student without insurance. Nobody wanted to bother with me. So I was discharged after my suicide attempt without any help for me at all."

Ryan looked away. He looked angry.

I furled my brows. "What's wrong?" I asked.

Shaking his head, he said "That's such bullshit, how people are treated in this country. If you don't have money, you don't exist. I just can't believe that nobody tried to help you, even when you obviously desperately needed it."

"Yeah, I know." I paused. "Anyhow, I kept cutting and was hospitalized for it two more times. The other times were not suicide attempts, but I was hospitalized because it just got so bad that my roommates had no choice but to take me in."

"What finally changed? How did you stop?"

I shook my head. "I don't really know. It just got to the point where I didn't really want to do it anymore. I never got over my issues, I just stopped physically destroying myself."

He nodded. He looked pensive, sipping his wine. He

wasn't looking at me, but was staring at the coffee table across the room. I stroked his cheek. "What are you thinking?" I felt worried. He now knew that he was with a total loser. I faked my way into his life with just enough air of confidence that he could not imagine just how much of a misfit I was.

Now he knew. Would he stay?

He looked at me. Those eyes....

"I don't want you to think that I feel one iota differently about you because of what you just told me. If anything, I love you more than ever." At that, I realized that I was holding my breath, because I let out a long tendril of air after he told me that.

What was I worried about?

He continued. "I just wish you had the confidence in my feelings for you to have told me about this. I wish that it didn't take a news anchor to get you to open up to me." He looked hurt.

"I know," I said. "All that time, with you at Beverly Hills, and confessing to me all of your secrets, and I never said anything." I looked at him for a long time, then continued – "I just didn't want you to know how much of an outcast I am. I was afraid that you wouldn't love me if you knew."

I couldn't read those eyes. There were too many mixed emotions hidden behind them – anger, disappointment, hurt, mixed in with love and respect. They all seemed jumbled up, so I couldn't tell how he was feeling.

Finally, he sighed. "I guess I'll never convince you the depths of my feelings for you. Even now, after we're married. You never opened your heart to me, except now, when you're forced to. And that's what hurts."

I looked at my wine glass. "I suppose you want an annulment now."

He looked horrified. "What? Why would you ever, ever, ever, ever, ever think that?" His face changed to horror and then to pure mystification.

"Well, you know me now. You know I'm not good enough."

"Oh, hell no. Hell to the fucking no. You're not going to go back to that. I won't let you. That's bullshit and you know that's bullshit. I don't give a rat's ass about your social standing. All I know is that you are a beautiful, intelligent, fun and kind woman with compassionate depths that I could only dream of with my previous girlfriends, and wife. You aren't getting rid of me that easily."

"But, honey, everybody now knows that you're married to a self-mutilator who attempted suicide."

"And everybody now knows that you're married to a bisexual drug addict who was forced to participate in sex parties at the age of 13. As I see it, you have the shorter end of the stick here."

We sat in silence for awhile, both of us drinking our wine. Could we possibly see the humor in all of this? Maybe after awhile, but, for now, we were simply too much in shock to say much of anything.

Finally, I spoke "Yeah, but you have money and beauty. Society will give you a pass much more than they will me."

"Don't be so sure. It's *schadenfreude* to bring people like me to heel. No, trust me, the media will be harder on me."

I brooded a little about this. He was right, of course. People like Ryan – wealthy, handsome, educated –were the very people who the media always sought to bring down. They wouldn't give a frog's fat ass about me, except I had the standing of being his wife.

However, I knew that both of us would be in for this humiliation. We already were. Maybe the public, as a whole, would care more about the titillating details of Ryan's background, but the people I knew were sure to be snickering at me, and gossiping about me, behind my back.

It would be high school, writ large.

That night, we didn't make love. We didn't even sleep naked. Both of us put on formal pajamas before getting into bed. However, I did seek his body in the bed, as I moved towards him to snuggle with him. He reciprocated by taking my arm, and holding against his body.

I felt his warmth, and this was what I needed right then.

The week that we spent in our prison was tense like this. We couldn't go outside, because the media was surrounding us. It seemed that, with every passing day, more and more people descended on our street. We would never give them the satisfaction of a shot of us, not even a shot of us stating that we had "no comment" as we passed through the phalanx of reporters and paparazzi who were camped out. I used to think that those people who muttered "no comment" felt like they were pretty cool. After all, they were getting media attention.

I didn't think that anymore.

Chapter Seven

Finally, at long last, Giovanni was ready to fly to New York. John, the helicopter pilot Ryan knew, landed on the roof of Nick's estate, and we got in. As we ascended above the clouds, I couldn't help but give those reporters the bird. They were on the ground, hundreds of them, watching us fly away, as helplessly as the Vietnamese who watched when the last chopper from Saigon flew away from the American Embassy. I could see them down there, and I got some satisfaction in their helpless expressions.

They deserved not to get the story, if they were going to ruin our honeymoon by making us prisoners.

The chopper landed at the Malpensa airport in Milan, and it was there that we met Giovanni. Giovanni was a slight man, about 5'7", with tightly wound curly black hair and an olive complexion. He grinned as we approached.

"Ryan, my boy!" he shouted exuberantly. "How have you been?" His English was accented but otherwise perfect.

He and Ryan embraced. "Well, Giovanni, to be honest,

I've been better. But I have my Iris with me, so nothing can ever be all that bad."

Giovanni looked at him sympathetically. "Yes, I heard all about the story. It's all over the news here."

"Yeah, Giovanni, I'm afraid that we are embroiled in some intrigue here."

Giovanni raised his eyebrows. "That true about you? That you like the boys?"

"No, that's not true. I like one particular boy, but I do not like 'the boys.'"

Giovanni lightly punched Ryan on the arm. "Well, you know, it's no big deal."

"I know, it shouldn't be a big deal, but, somehow it is. I mean, who cares? I really don't know why this is even a story."

"Well, you know," Giovanni said. "You are one of the beautiful people. People are fascinated by people like you."

I was standing aside, feeling uncomfortable. I was the one who the story focused upon – it was my kidnapping, my assault, my false imprisonment at the hands of a very unbalanced woman. Yet Ryan was the one whose name was being dragged through the mud, because he was the one who had the most to lose.

It didn't seem fair.

"Anyhow," Giovanni said. "Welcome to my plane. Where's yours, by the way? I forgot to ask."

"It's here, and that's where it'll stay for now. I'd imagine the paparazzi are swarming that plane, just like they were swarming Nick's home for the past week or so."

"Oh, okay. Well, welcome aboard."

Giovanni's plane was nice, but not as nice as Ryan's. It was about half the size, and did not have the same luxurious appointments. Nevertheless, I was happy to be on the aircraft, because it would mean that I would be getting out of the hell-hole.

We spent the next 8 hours chatting. Giovanni did not pilot the plane, of course, so he was able to converse with us in the back. I snoozed part of the way there. And, it could be just my imagination, but Giovanni seemed rather intrigued with Ryan. He was downright flirtatious, but Ryan showed no interest. I long knew that Ryan's bisexual leanings only extended towards Nick, which made me think that most of the reason why Ryan was interested in Nick was because Nick helped him so much in so many ways. I supposed that it was true all over, that it was the person bisexuals were interested in, not the sex. In this case, Ryan was in love with me, and with Nick. In different ways, of course. But any guy is not going to interest him, anymore than just any woman would interest him.

So Giovanni was wasting his time

Three movies, and one long snooze later, we arrived at La Guardia airport. I half expected the pap to be there, waiting for us, but they weren't. I was relieved.

Nate was the only person there to greet us.

"Buddy! Just couldn't stay away, huh?" Nate said, taking my luggage.

Ryan rolled his eyes. "Trust me, Nate, I wish that we didn't have to meet like this."

"Man, you guys are really in it, huh? The media has been on this story like flies on shit."

"Oh? I didn't know. Iris and I have refused to watch the rags on TV."

"Well, let's just say they think that this has become a major story."

I piped up – "How can that be? Nobody died here."

"No, but you got that crazy bitch out there making both

of you look like you are just this side of being committed to the nut house. I feel for both of you."

I just bet you do. Why was I feeling this way about Nate? I liked him so much the first time I met him at the ice skating rink. Now he was just annoying me with his glib comments.

We got to Nate and Nat's place on the Upper West Side. Their apartment was a pre-war four bedroom place, with 20-foot-tall ceilings, crown molding, huge arched windows, hardwood floors, and a beautiful view of Central Park. I knew something about real estate in Manhattan in general, and the Upper West Side in particular, and figured that his place was worth at least $6 million.

"Where's Nat?" Ryan asked, looking around the apartment.

"Working. She'll be home soon enough to see her great love."

I sighed. Nat was in love with Ryan, and everyone, unfortunately, knew this. I wondered if there was going to be a problem with that while we were here. I hoped not.

Nat did return home around midnight, after working late at her job as an investment banker at Goldman's. Her eyes got wide upon seeing Ryan and me. She made a beeline for Ryan. "Oh, honey, I heard about what's happening to you guys. I'm so sorry."

"Not a prob, Nat. I just am glad that you guys are letting us crash here while we figure out our next move."

She looked at me. I looked down. I could almost feel what she was thinking. To my surprise, she grabbed my hand, and stroked it tenderly. "Iris, let's talk a little in the den, ok?"

I nodded, and she led me into the den.

She lit a fire in the fireplace. "Sit down," she said, patting the floor next to her.

I hesitantly took a seat next to her. Was she hitting on me?

"Uh, Iris, I heard about your, uh, problems. I wanted to see if there was anything that I could do to help you."

I looked at her quizzically. What could she do?

"That's all in the past. I'm better now."

She shook her head. "I know what it's like to self-destruct. I never hurt myself with a knife or anything like that, but I hurt myself in other ways." Then she mimed putting two fingers down her throat and nodded.

Nat was a bulimic? But why? She was the most beautiful girl I had ever seen.

"Why were you a bulimic?"

"For the same reason you cut yourself, I would imagine. I didn't like myself very much."

At that, I felt completely dumbfounded. Nat was indescribably gorgeous, Harvard educated, intelligent and sweet. Why was she filled with self-loathing?

"I don't understand."

"My sister died when I was 14. My parents always made me feel that they wanted it to be me, not her. She was so perfect – athletic, musical, always got straight As. She was always the good daughter. I never quite measured up to that."

"In what way did you not measure up?"

"I was rebellious, kinda a Goth kid when I was 14. Black eyeliner, black nail polish, black clothing, black hair. Everything was just – black. Not her, though. She was blonde, petite and perfect. Never caused trouble."

"How did she die?"

"Leukemia." She had little tears in her eyes. "When she died, I felt my parents looked at me and found me lacking. I was far from perfect. I was smoking pot, getting drunk, and sleeping with boys. So, I always felt my parents thought the wrong daughter died." She shrugged. "I was filled with self-loathing, so I puked my way through middle school and high school. Nobody ever knew except my dentist." She looked at me. "So, I guess I'm saying that I know from self-loathing. If there is anything I could do to help you, I would love that."

I put my hand on hers sympathetically. Yet I couldn't open up to her like she had just opened up to me. I admired her for being able to tell me these things. I wished I could be an open book as well, but I had always been pretty closed-off. That was probably a lot of my problem.

Nat continued. "Nate doesn't know about this. Ryan neither. So, please don't say anything to the boys. I'm only telling you this because I see a kindred spirit."

"Ryan has been through a lot, too, in his life. He used to also self-destruct. He would probably understand what you were going through."

She kept quiet for a bit. Then she finally said "Yes, but I never want Ryan to see me in that light."

The words she said left words also unspoken. The unspoken words were that she was still in love with Ryan, and she never wanted him to see her as anything but perfect.

It occurred to me that this house was a vortex of dysfunction, three of us recovering from destructive tendencies. Me a recovering self-mutilator, Nat a recovering bulimic and Ryan a recovering drug addict. I couldn't help but wonder if Nate had a similar dark secret.

I smiled. "Well, we certainly are a group of people in this apartment, huh?"

Nat laughed. "It seems that way."

I once again was reminded of the need to get beyond

the façade of beauty and wealth. You pull it back, and they are more vulnerable than anybody else. More vulnerable because they are expected by society to uphold their end of the bargain, as it were – they are given much, so they should be almost god-like. Then, when they fall, people like to pounce. *Schadenfreude* as Ryan says – that is what drives the media coverage about the beautiful people doing bad things. It's like the famous F. Scott Fitzgerald quote, where he said that he had never been able to forgive the rich for being rich. This was how society looked at the rich, a lot of times, and this was why people like Ryan and Natalie were vulnerable.

Ryan presently came into the den. "Honey, Nate and I have been talking. We can stay here for as long as we need to. I don't think the media will figure out we're here. But I want to get in touch with Nick back home, to see how he's holding up. I'd imagine he's getting it as much as we are. Alexis, too."

"Call him, and put him on speaker phone, if you don't mind," I said.

So, he did.

"Buddy," Ryan said when Nick answered the phone.

"It's about fucking time. Where the hell are you?" Nick asked.

"I'm so sorry about all this."

"What the hell? What's going on? My phone has been blowing up, and I have media people camped out on my doorstep, trying to get information about you two."

"What do you tell them?"

"No comment, of course. They won't go away, though."

"What about Alexis? You heard from her?"

"Of course. She's been calling non-stop, because she

can't get ahold of you guys. She's pretty sick of her private life blowing up on TV as well."

Ryan sighed. "The chickens have finally come home to roost. I knew they would, eventually. Now they have."

"When are you coming home?"

"I'm not sure."

"I really don't know why your job puts up with your constant absences." Nick seemed incredulous about this.

"Never mind about that. I have to figure out how to address this."

"Tackle it head-on. Talk to the media, give them your story."

"I hate to ask this…."

"Rielle wants a divorce, of course. She's not happy about any of this."

"How much does she know?"

"Enough. Put it that way. But, the divorce was a long-time coming. This was just the final straw, that's all."

"What about the kids?"

"I'm pretty sure that's gonna be a problem too."

"I'm so sorry about this."

"Hey, don't worry about it. It's not your fault. It's that psycho's fault. By the way, how is the new Mrs. Gallagher?"

He looked over at me. I simply raised an eyebrow.

"As well as can be expected," Ryan said.

"Well, come home. Don't keep dodging the issue. It's not going away. Every day you don't get on top of this is another day the lies are out there unanswered. You don't even want to know about the Tik Tok videos, trust me."

Ryan nodded his head. He knew that was true. I knew it was true, too. We were both running, trying to buy time, trying to have some kind of a happy life together. But we weren't living in reality. I knew this.

"Right," Ryan said. "Well, I wanted to check in."

"K. Talk later."

He got off the phone and came over to sit next to me. He took my hand. "We have to address this. He's right."

I nodded. It sucked that we had to do it, but there was nothing more that could be done.

Now it was just a matter of figuring out to whom we would tell our story.

Chapter Eight

The very next day, we met with a reporter from *People* magazine. They would be running a cover story on us. The reporter, Darlene Goode, came to Nate and Nat's apartment to meet with us. We decided that *People* would be the best magazine to give our story, because it had such a wide readership, and had a better reputation than any of the other pop culture magazines.

Darlene seemed eager to talk to us.

It seemed our story was a real scoop.

She was exactly on time, arriving at the apartment at noon on the dot. She was very professional, her dark hair loosely knotted, and glasses perched on her nose. Shaking our hands, we all sat down to talk in the den.

"Do you mind if I record this?" she asked.

"No, no, of course not," Ryan spoke. We had decided that Ryan would give his side of the story, and I would chime in when appropriate.

Darlene began. "I don't really want to beat around the bush here. I wanted to get your side of the story."

"Rochelle Anderson was my lover when I was 14 years old, and she was 34," Ryan began, then proceeded to tell the reporter the gist of what happened to me. He told her about Rochelle kidnapping me, torturing me, and shooting me up with black tar heroine. He told her about how I was in a coma for two months because of it, and my PTSD. He told her about how Rochelle was obsessed with him, and how she followed him.

Darlene turned to me. "Mrs. Gallagher, tell me something. I don't understand. You visited Ms. Anderson in jail, did you not?"

I shook my head. "We already tried to get tape of that meeting. They don't have it. They don't keep it for very long. Trust me, I wish that weren't so, because that bitch –" I composed myself. I couldn't afford to come off unsympathetic. "Sorry, that woman confessed all to me when I saw her in jail."

The interview went on from there. As we talked, though, I could feel my anxiety welling up. I had felt that I was over Rochelle's attack, but all of this was bringing it back up. By the end of the interview, I was shaking. Ryan held my hand tight, then put his arm around me protectively. We had laid it all on the table. Ryan's affair with Nick, Ryan's sexual abuse, my cutting, everything. We knew this was the only way to get our side of the story out there.

It was completely draining, yet liberating at the same time.

After about four hours, the interview was finally over. We then made an appointment to get our photos taken for the cover. I would imagine we would look odd together – his stunning beauty, and me.

I tried to set that aside.

Darlene looked at me before leaving. With a wry smile,

she said "It sounds like you're living a dystopian Cinderella story."

To this, I smiled. I never thought of it that way, but it was true – a dystopian Cinderella story was exactly what I was living. I was just the average girl, looking for love in all the wrong places, finding nothing but toads, until Ryan. Ryan, the sweet, handsome, rich guy who worshiped me, for whatever reason. Turns out that he was not only my savior, but the cause of my personal hell.

It occurred to me that if I never knew him, I would have been able to escape my past for the rest of my life.

But, then again, perhaps it worked out the way that it was supposed to. My past was brought to light, and I would have to examine myself once more to find out why I was filled with self-loathing for so long. At the same time, I was not only in love, but loved back, perhaps for the very first time in my life. Our life together was never perfect, and it wasn't even real – real people didn't experience the problems we were experiencing. Real people generally don't have their dirty laundry aired in front of the entire world. Yet, somehow, we were sticking with each other through this, supporting each other, helping each other through. It heartened me to know that we were in this together. I never in my life had a man who would stick by me through the crap that happened in my life prior to this.

Darlene finally left. I felt like a deflated balloon. I looked at Ryan, who was paler than I had ever seen him. He was very quiet.

"That was awful," I began.

"Yeah, but it's out there now."

"I guess we can probably go home now, huh?"

"Might as well," he said. "But I would like to see my sister before we leave."

At that he called her. After getting off the phone, he announced that we would be leaving in the morning to see Sarah on the Vineyard.

"We're going to have to fly there, huh?"

"Yeah. My plane is at La Guardia."

I felt a little disappointed. For some reason, I was thinking that Ryan and I would get the chance to fly like normal people for once. It didn't occur to me that he would have somebody fly his plane here to New York.

That night, we had one last dinner with Nate and Nat. Nat was doing her usual googly-eyes at Ryan. I felt badly for her, having such strong feelings for my husband. She was as vulnerable as anybody, and couldn't help the way that she felt. I knew that.

I felt nervous about seeing Sarah again. She was never all that warm to me, and I knew why – she thought I was a gold-digger, and could never accept that wasn't the case.

Nevertheless, I had to steel myself to see her again. Because it was about to happen.

Chapter Nine

Sarah's house on the Vineyard was just how I pictured it. It was a neo-Classical mansion, with four columns on the front porch. The home was made up of a light colored coral stone, with enormous windows and a gorgeous, and enormously solid, door. The garden out front of the house was perfectly manicured, with five different varieties of roses and African daisies. A circle drive was out front, and there was a six-car garage.

Ryan had explained that Sarah's husband, Gil, was a collector of classic cars. But the classic cars that he collected were unlike any other. For one, he owned a very rare Aston Martin and a Bentley. Gil also had a Duesenberg, which was among the very rarest of all classic cars. They were handmade, and sold for around $6,500 in the 1920s, and now sold for around a million dollars. That particular car was in mint condition, with white-walled tires, and was enormous, shiny and black. I somehow pictured Gil as a guy with a cigarette on the end of a long cigarette holder, like FDR.

Sarah and Cori appeared on the lawn. Gil appeared

next to her. He was a fortyish hedge fund operator, with greying temples and tan skin. He wore his dark hair slicked back, and he was just a little bit taller than Sarah, who was 5'7". Her two children, Alice and Henry, were at their private day school at the moment, but would be meeting us after school.

Sarah greeted us with a "Well, well, well. You two sure did get yourselves into a pickle, didn't you?"

"Great to see you too, Sarah," Ryan said.

Sarah's blonde hair was different than the last time I saw her. Before, she was a platinum blonde. Now she sported a darker blonde hairdo with highlights and lowlights. She was gorgeous as ever.

Genetics definitely favored this family.

"Well, come on in. How long are you staying?" she asked. Gil was mute, so far.

"For just a few days," Ryan said. "We have to get home and face reality."

She addressed me. "How you holding up there, kid?"

I smiled a little at her calling me "kid." Ryan was "peanut" and I guess I was now "kid."

"I've been better."

"You mean you don't like having all your personal problems aired for the world to hear?"

"Surprisingly not," I said. I was finding it easier every day to face the issues, though.

Then, addressing Ryan, Sarah said "You and me gotta talk. Alone."

At that, they went into the sun room and shut the door.

I looked at Gil. He raised his eyebrows.

"What's going on?"

"Sarah has to talk to Ryan about seeing their father."

Chapter Ten

"See Benjamin? What the hell? Why would Sarah want that?"

Gil just shrugged. "Something about Benjamin wanting to see them about what's going on in the media. He's really getting a lot of bad press, and he's losing all his friends. He's retired, so there isn't a job to worry about, though."

"Cry me a fucking river," I said. "Why would Ryan want to see that guy?"

"Well, there's something else."

"What?"

"Sarah and Ryan will tell you about it."

I could hear shouting coming from the den.

"Like hell. I don't care if he is sick, I'm not going." Ryan.

A muffled voice. Sarah.

"Not doing it," Ryan shouted.

The yelling continued for a bit. Then it stopped. However, the brother and sister remained in the den for the next hour.

Finally, they came out. He looked cowed. Sarah didn't exactly look happy, either.

"We need to talk," Ryan said to me.

At that, we mounted the winding staircase into the guest bedroom.

I looked at Ryan, who was sitting on the bed, his head in his hands. I sat down next to him, putting my arm around him, and holding his hand with my other hand. I stroked his hair for what seemed like a long time. He didn't react, just sat there with his head in his hands. I eventually put his head on my lap, as I continued to tousle his hair lightly. To my surprise, he started crying. This was the first time I had ever seen him cry. He grabbed onto my leg tightly, sobbing, his face in my lap, his entire body spasming. I just continued to rub his head and his back silently.

Finally, after what seemed to be an eternity, he stopped crying. But he still had his head on my lap, clutching my legs desperately. He was breathing hard, in and out, in and out, and started hiccupping. I just sat still, a perfect marble statue, except I continued to massage his back and shoulders. I buried my fingers into his neck, trying to ease his tension with my touch.

He finally lifted his head, and looked me in the eye. "I have to see Benjamin," was all he said.

I nodded. I knew that was coming. "When?" I asked.

"We're going to leave from here."

"I'm going, too, right?"

"Of course. I need you there with me, to keep me sane."

I sighed. "I hate to ask this, but why?"

"Benjamin has Stage Four lung cancer. He only has a matter of weeks to live."

"I see." I waited for him to say more. I knew him so well now that I knew just how to react to every situation. Sometimes it helped if I talked. Sometimes it helped if I was silent, and let him do all the talking.

This seemed to be the latter situation.

"So....I told Sarah that I didn't care that he was dying. I don't want to see him." He ran his hands through his hair, and started patting his legs nervously. "But she made the point that I would need closure. Otherwise I would regret it for the rest of my life." He paused for a long time, and tears came to his eyes once more. "She has a point."

I nodded. "I agree. You only have one chance to say your piece with him. I think it's wonderful that you're doing this."

"Maybe he'll finally tell me why he did what he did to me. That's my hope, anyhow. Deathbed confession and all that, you know."

"That would be perfect," I began. "But Ryan, don't expect it. I'd hate to see you get your heart broken if it doesn't come through."

He said nothing, just nodded.

I felt for him so strongly, especially at that moment. Once again, I saw him as a little boy, terrified of his father. At this moment, he wasn't a 33-year-old bank president. He was an 8-year-old boy who was terrified of being beat for the smallest transgressions, while he watched his mother slowly slip into oblivion. It must have been so hard for him, so very, very hard. I put my arm around him, and could feel him shaking all over.

I kissed his forehead. Then we were kissing, slowly, tenderly. We hadn't been physical like that since the day we found out that our story was breaking all over the world. There had just been way too much tension. There was still a lot of tension, but it was time to overcome that and give comfort to one another in the form of lovemaking.

He put his hand on my thigh, and I felt the familiar shivers. Somehow, his touch never got old. It always felt like the first time with him, no matter how many times we made love. His lips on my lips felt like they were touching for the first time. His strong, yet gentle, hand on my skin felt like it had never been on my skin before. As he ran his fingers through my hair, softly entangling his smooth hands in my rather thick mane, it was like he had never done this before to me. It was always the first time for me. I felt just as giddy inside as I did in our first meeting - my stomach doing cartwheels, my heart beating like a timpani, and my hands shaking a tiny bit.

I wondered if it would ever get old, feeling him touch me like this.

I certainly hoped not.

He slowly undressed me, unbuttoning my shirt, while kissing my shoulder lightly. I sighed, as his lips made their way to my breasts, then stomach. I was still quite thin, as I was forever monitoring my diet these days, so I wasn't in the least bit self-conscious about his mouth making its way to my nether region. He unbuckled my jeans, then slipped off my panties, his tongue slowly exploring inside me. Tenderly, gently, he kept me enthralled like that for almost an hour. For the first time since the sordid story broke, I was lost in his touch. Nothing else mattered in that moment, as I was brought to orgasm after orgasm.

And the best was yet to come.

I could hear him breathing in my ear, his breath feeling hot and sticky sweet. There was a faint smell of honeysuckle in his hair. His shirt was still on, but he had slipped off his shorts and boxer briefs, and he entered me slowly, kissing my breasts, neck and face, while his hands were intertwined in my hair. He nibbled my earlobe, while I stroked his back and bit his neck. I tongued the hollow of his collarbone, and grabbed ahold of his hand, and sucked his fingers gently. He sighed, and hesitated briefly, before his thrusting came harder, more insistent. All of our grieving and stress was being relieved in this cathartic experience. Both of us had been laid low and humiliated, yet, here we were, enchanted with one another, exactly as if nothing had happened to intrude into our perfect world.

In the back of my mind, I knew this moment was all we had, and that we would have to return to earth as soon as it was over.

I willed it to last forever.

As it was, it did last several hours, with us kissing passionately and slowly making love. It was all so…engrossing. Beautifully engrossing. Mesmerizing. We were completely in tune with one another again, and it was like nothing else was in the world but that. We didn't speak any words, just communicated with our eyes and our touch. That would have to be enough for now. It was our form of escapism, I knew. But it was just so loving and real, that it didn't really feel like escaping.

It just felt like love.

After we made love, we lay there on the bed, still not talking. I was afraid to say anything that would possibly break the spell. He kissed me lightly on the forehead, and spoke. "Thank you for that. It was just what I needed before seeing…him."

I nodded, not saying a word.

Then Sarah was knocking on the door. "Hey, you guys, it's dinner time," she said.

We made our way out to the sunny terrace that was on the side of the enormous home. Sarah was there with Cori and Alice and Henry. Henry was a mischievous looking scamp, with choppy dark hair and a slight weight problem. Alice was just like her mother, in looks, anyhow. Slender, blonde, precious.

They both eyed me suspiciously.

Henry spoke "Hi, Uncle Ryan. What's this I hear about you being gay? And why are you with a woman, anyhow?"

Ryan flushed scarlet. Sarah shot the kid a look, but he just shrugged his shoulders. "It's not a big deal," he said. "A lot of kids at school have gay parents and stuff."

Oh, geez. How to explain bisexuality to a child? I was well aware that kids in Henry's liberal school were learning tolerance for gay people, but, as far as I knew, they weren't learning much about bisexuals.

Ryan decided to tackle the issue as if Henry was an adult. "Henry, I am very much in love with Aunt Iris, here," he said, putting his arm around me. "But I also have a guy whom I love as well."

Henry narrowed his eyes. Alice stayed mute through the whole exchange, although I did see her kick her brother under the table. "How can that be?" he asked. "We haven't learned about this in school yet."

"Well, maybe you should," Ryan said. "You're what, 10? You're going to meet others like me, so you should just be prepared for that."

Then Alice finally chimed in. At 8 years old, she seemed wiser than her older brother, probably because she chose to keep her mouth shut. "Shut up, Henry. Let Uncle Ryan love who he wants and don't judge him about it."

I smiled. My first instinct was correct about Alice. She was precocious beyond her age.

Henry just shrugged, and started yammering about baseball. Neither kid seemed remotely interested in me, and who I was.

However, after the dinner, before they went to bed, Alice came up and gave me a hug. I hugged her back, and she looked up at me and said "You are so much better than the other one."

I smiled. "That's what I heard."

"Did you really rescue pit bulls?"

"I sure did," I said.

"That's so cool. I want one so bad, but mom just wants Cori. She says she doesn't need another dog, but I would really love one. Maybe you can drop one off the next time you're here?" The little girl was dead serious about this.

"Your mom wouldn't like that much."

"I know. It doesn't hurt to ask, though."

Henry was next. He was a little more standoffish, but he did approach me. "Sorry about embarrassing you."

"Not a prob."

"Do you like Drake?"

"I guess." Rap really wasn't my thing, but I would humor the kid. Who knows? Maybe if I gave Drake a chance, I might learn to like him. Too bad the kid didn't like Taylor Swift, who I adored with the passion of a thousand white hot suns. I really was a Swiftie at heart, but Henry, being a boy, probably didn't get into her. Alice probably did, though.

"You wanna come up and listen to him with me?"

"Sure," I said. "Let me go and tell Uncle Ryan first."

I found Ryan and Sarah out by the pool, talking quietly. They immediately stopped when I came out to see them. They looked very uncomfortable. The pool was illuminated by the tennis courts, but Sarah did not turn on the lights on the terrace, so they were sitting in the dark. Ryan had his familiar scotch rocks in front of him, and Sarah was drinking a glass of white wine. I saw she had the bottle with her as well. She poured a drink while I kneeled down to talk to Ryan.

"I'm going to listen to music with Henry," I said.

He simply nodded. Sarah was looking at him, not looking at me, and not saying a word. I could tell that I was interrupting a serious conversation. It was just in the air that they were talking about something engrossing.

I went back upstairs, but I heard a snippet of conversation as I was walking away from the French doors that enclosed the terrace.

"When are you going to tell her about it?" Sarah asked.

I groaned. *What now?*

I simply shook my head, and started towards Henry's room.

Henry's room was covered in movie posters and cartoon cells. He had a flat screen television with the latest X-Box attached, as well as a Blue-Ray player. His bed was a little racing car, with the comforter a NASCAR comforter, with pictures of various people I didn't recognize. NASCAR wasn't my thing, to say the least. The room was surprisingly neat, considering this was the room of a 10-year-old boy. Some of the books on the shelf were not put back, but were laying horizontally and scattered around, but, other than that, not much was out of place. Drake was streaming. Henry handed me a comic book, which was an old-school Superman issue. I flipped through it, becoming surprisingly fascinated by the stories in that issue.

After a little while, Henry asked me "so, do you have sex with Uncle Ryan?"

I knew that one was coming. "Yes."

"And did you know he gave another guy blow jobs?"

"Yes."

"What do you think about that?"

"This Superman comic book is pretty cool. You got any others?"

He looked at me skeptically, then gave me another comic book.

He persisted in asking more questions about it for the next half hour, when Ryan peeked his head in the door. "It's late, beautiful. I'm heading to bed."

I nodded. "I'm right there," I said, then said good night to the inquisitive Henry.

We got ready for bed, then climbed into the California King, snuggling under the covers. I ran my fingers through his hair, and touched his cheek. Then waited for him to tell me the latest bombshell.

Which he did. "Nick called me. He's actually in touch with Rochelle."

I nodded. "Go on."

He drew a breath, then let it out slowly. "And, well, you know she's out."

I felt the familiar chill and sick feeling. "Yes, go on."

He was silent for awhile, clutching my hand. Then he said "she's made threats against you."

Now my whole body felt the extreme freeze. "What do you mean?"

"Nick said she's told him that she wants to kick your ass for getting her first lawyer to withdraw from her case." He wrapped his arms around me. "But don't worry, I'm already hiring a bodyguard for you."

Good God. A bodyguard. That's all I fucking need.

"I don't need a bodyguard," I protested.

Ryan glared at me, narrowing his eyes. "Yes, you do. Do you really want a repeat of the last time Rochelle decided to teach you a lesson?"

At that moment, I once again started feeling disconnected from him. My mind started wandering, as I was realizing, perhaps for the first time, what a screwed up situation I had gotten myself into. I was desperate for love before I met him, and, for the longest time after I met him, I felt I was living some kind of dream. A good dream. Now, it had turned into such a nightmare, and I irrationally felt hatred for him. Hatred for what was going on, for what I was going through because of him and his fucked-up life and his problems. I would have been much happier with just some normal guy with normal problems. Instead I was a – what did that newslady say? A dystopian Cinderella. Perfect description for me. Now, on top of having all my dirty laundry aired to the world, I was in need of a bodyguard. Because of him. My life was once again threatened. Because of him. I almost died. Because of him.

And it struck me that there was a naked picture out there of me, in the hands of some random guy I hooked up with on Spring Break all those years ago. That was probably viral on the Internet by now. I hadn't checked on that, but I would imagine that would be the case. I mean, I was a notorious celebrity, and I did absolutely nothing wrong.

I was a celebrity because of him.

I was lost in all these thoughts, while Ryan continued to just stare at me. He was waiting for my answer on if I would willingly accept a bodyguard, or if he would have to force me to have one. I knew I really didn't have a choice in the matter, and that, too, made me angry.

I just shook my head. "No bodyguard. If she finishes me off, she finishes me off. I really don't care at this point."

His expression turned icy, like I had never seen it before. The green eyes were like two cold jewels, devoid of life and expression. Then he turned his head, and entire body, and, without a word, went to sleep.

I got up and out of the bed, not wanting to be there with him anymore. I headed down to the kitchen, looking in the fridge for something to eat. I found some hard salami and rolls, and brought them out.

Then was startled by the figure of Sarah sitting at the kitchen table, a cup of coffee in hand.

"Oh, I'm so sorry," I started, feeling embarrassed that I was just helping myself to food, like I lived there or something.

"What are you apologizing for?" she asked.

"For helping myself to your food. I, I, I will buy some more salami and stuff."

"Don't be ridiculous. God, you're weird sometimes," she said, but she was smiling, so I figured she said that at least partially in jest. Then, looking at me, she said "So, are you going to join me here at the table, or are you going to slink away and eat that stuff on the sly somewhere?"

I didn't want to join her at the table. I wanted to be alone. But, to be polite, I put the food down on the table where she was, and proceeded to make my sandwich.

As I prepared my sandwich, she was eyeing me interestedly. Then she said "so, what brings you here at this hour?"

"Couldn't sleep," I said.

"There are problems with you and Ryan, aren't there?"

I just shook my head. It was none of her business.

"I know better," she said, as I shot her a look that told her not to go there. But, she persisted. "Listen, I know my brother has had a pretty weird life. None of which was his fault. Well, the drugs were, but even those weren't really his fault, because our father drove him to it. Ryan was the victim for many years, and he came through it kinda a half ghost, half person. He was so checked out before he met you. He just went through life mechanically, from day to day, doing his job, dating his bimbos, and, when I called him, he was pretty laconic," she said, twisting her cloth napkin into a rope. "You know, 'yes,' 'no,' that sort of thing. When he met you he became, I don't know...flesh and blood again."

I sighed. I had heard this before, from Nate and from Ryan himself. It's almost like they all wanted to guilt me into staying, in case I had it in my mind to run.

I looked at her, wondering how much I could really confide about how I was feeling. She was his sister, and would probably tell him everything I said. Her eyebrow was raised at me, as she sipped her coffee through her full lips. Without a stitch of makeup, she still glowed. Her skin was flawless, her eyes a cerulean blue. She casually crossed one of her perfect legs over the other, still watching me behind her powder blue coffee cup with the words "Harvard, Class of '2010" printed on the front.

Finally, I decided to take the chance and do a few confessionals. "I know that Ryan has been through a lot," I began. "But I just feel that..."

She was still watching me, not saying a word, her expression very difficult to read.

I began again. "I guess I'm just frustrated that, ever since I met him, my life has been in danger. Well, I mean, ever since the incident with Rochelle. Now it's even worse. The whole world knows my name. I want to be anonymous and I never asked for any of this." My hand involuntarily went to my face, as I rubbed my eyes. "The bodyguard idea is the last straw."

To my surprise, her expression softened, and she covered my hand with one of hers, and patted it lightly. "I know it's been hard for you. But remember what I told you.

You have been his lifeline, and he would take a bullet for you if it comes to that."

"I know that. It's just…" I took a deep breath. "How do I keep from resenting him?"

"Only you know the answer to that. At any rate, there are going to be trials ahead. You guys have to face them together, because they're going to affect both of you," she said, as she got up from the table to put her coffee cup in the kitchen sink. "And seeing our father isn't going to be fun or pretty. You need to have enough strength for all of us, because there is liable to be some kind of break down coming from that. Fair warning."

I nodded.

"Now, get back up there with my brother. Don't try to sleep in a different room, or something cute like that. He needs you. I'm not trying to guilt you, I'm just stating a cold, hard fact. So, think long and hard before you have an urge to run. Just sayin.'" She washed her hands in the warm water, and Cori came in. She fed the enormous dog a bone, and he slinked away to enjoy it. "Besides," she continued. "The damage is done. Leaving him would accomplish nothing, and you wouldn't have an ally in all this. So, in other words, it would cause more problems for you if you leave than if you stay."

She made a good point.

I was trapped.

Chapter Eleven

The next day, we drove along in silence in Sarah's Mercedes SUV, with me in the back, and Sarah and Ryan in the front. I didn't talk much to Ryan when we woke up this morning, not really knowing what to say. I was trying to get out of my head, and out of my own way, so that I could be there for Ryan for this most difficult task of confronting his father.

We arrived at Ryan's plane, which would take us the short distance to Newport, Rhode Island, which was where his father had bought his mansion for his retirement. The plane ride was short but filled with awkward silence. None of us said a word. Ryan and Sarah just stared at the walls of the plane, and I flipped through a book I brought along with me – a memoir called *The Glass Castle* by Jeannette Walls, about a singularly dysfunctional family driven by alcoholism and homelessness.

We got to the Newport State Airport, a small general aviation airport, then rented a car. Driving around the city, I was in awe of the enormous homes on the seashore. Most of the mansions were built during the gilded age for everybody from Cornelius Vanderbilt to tobacco heiress Doris Duke to serve as their summer homes. There was "The Breakers," the 70-room Italian Renaissance style palazzo which echoed the 16th Century palaces of Genoa and Turin, commissioned to be built for Cornelius Vanderbilt II in 1893. There was "The Elms," which served as the summer residence of a coal industry magnate, modeled after the mid-18th Century French chateau d'Asnieres outside Paris. The "Marble House" designed for William Vanderbilt, brother of Cornelius II, with a façade that resembled The White House, with classical Greek pillars and arched windows, boasted 500,000 cubic feet of marble. "Rosecliff" was built in 1899 for a silver heiress, and was patterned after garden retreats in Versailles. "Rough Point," an enormous Tudor-style mansion on an oceanfront cliff, was the home of tobacco heiress Doris Duke.

And then there was Benjamin's home, which rivaled any of the other homes found in the area. I had no idea how many square feet it was, but was probably at least 50,000. The home was Mediterranean style, with a Spanish-tile roof, and enormous arches that formed the portico. Various windows had terraces and balconies, and the grass was perfectly manicured. An enormous fountain was in front of the house, with the sculpture of a maiden lady pouring water in the middle, and the house itself was on a bluff overlooking the Atlantic Ocean. Like Sarah's house, there was an enormous terrace that jutted out on the side, paved in marble, with a stone balustrade that enclosed it. This home served as Benjamin's retirement summer house and weekend retreat house, explained Sarah, as she rang the doorbell that echoed the chimes of Big Ben in London.

A servant opened the door, and I walked in to see two enormous staircases that led to the second floor. The ceiling was about one hundred feet from the vestibule where we stood. The foyer was paved in marble, with black and white tiles.

"How many rooms is this place?" I asked, looking around, half expecting to see an original Picasso or two on the walls. There weren't Picassos, at least not in this area, but there were original Titians and Rembrandts in the dining room, which was just off the main foyer area.

Sarah shrugged her shoulders. "Oh, I don't know. Probably 50 or so."

Turning to the servant, Ryan spoke in perfect Spanish, and the lady nodded her head. Remembering his fluency with the Italians on our honeymoon, I made a mental note that there were at least three languages that Ryan apparently spoke perfectly.

Seeing me staring at him, Ryan said "What? If you know one Romance language, you can learn all of them pretty well."

"Do you know French, too?"

"Maybe," he said, putting his arm around me, the first warm gesture from him of the day. "You will just have to find out when I take you to Paris."

The tension seemed to be easing just a bit, as evidenced by Ryan's light-hearted joke. But, when the lady came back down, and spoke Spanish, which both Ryan and Sarah understood, I saw Ryan's face color drain. He nodded to the woman, then grabbed my hand and Sarah's hand, and the three of us silently ascended the stairs. I could feel him clutching me tightly, and even Sarah looked as if she wanted to be anywhere else but there at that moment. I thought that if Ryan and Sarah had a choice between this home and a POW camp, they would both have eagerly chosen the POW camp.

We got to the top of the stairs, and Ryan politely excused himself and headed towards one of the bathrooms.

I followed him in to make sure he was ok.

He wasn't, of course. He was crouched by the bowl and dry heaving, because he hadn't eaten that day yet. I sat down next to him, gently stroking his back. For the moment, all the other issues had receded to the background of my mind. Ryan's mental health and well-being were all I was thinking about.

I ran my fingers through his hair, and put my hand under his shirt, touching the bare skin on his back. Ryan loved to be touched, and my touch usually calmed him down. His skin was quivering, and his heart was pounding so hard that I could feel his back pulsating rapidly. I put his head on my chest, stroking his hair, while he wrapped his arms around my waist. Both of us were still on the floor. He was crying softly into my chest, and he wrapped his arms tighter around me.

Sarah was soon in the doorway, and she, too, crouched down. "Peanut, we don't have to do this. I didn't think this would affect you this much."

He simply shook his head, which was still buried in my chest. "No, no," he said. "I have to do this."

Sarah tousled his hair a little, then said "Ok, when you're ready, I'll be right outside the bathroom door waiting for you."

He nodded silently into my chest.

Sarah looked at me meaningfully. Her look said "see how much he needs you?"

I just nodded to her, while I continued to stroke Ryan's hair.

After about a half hour, Ryan finally looked at me. His eyes were puffy red on the outside, and the green irises had turned fluorescent. I grabbed a Kleenex, and he blew his nose.

"Are you ready?" I asked.

"As I will ever be," he answered.

At that, the two of us got up from the bathroom floor, met Sarah, who was, as promised, right outside the door, and made our way to Benjamin's bedroom.

Chapter Twelve

Benjamin's bedroom was at the far end of the wing. The room was enormous and looked like a room out of a museum. The ceiling was about twenty feet tall and was decorated in a Venetian mural with gold inlay. An enormous chandelier hung from the middle of the room. Light was streaming in through the arched eighteen foot windows, which reflected upon the cherry hardwood floors. The walls were painted in faux finish gold, and an enormous red and gold oriental rug that covered most of the room matched perfectly. On one of the walls was a marble fireplace with two ionic columns on either side. Above the fireplace was another original from the Renaissance age, a Carvaggio portrait of two noble women. The room was furnished with a red couch on one of the walls. On another of the walls was an enormous four poster bed with a framed top.

And, in that bed, was a frail and pale man.

Ryan was standing in the doorway, his hand clutching mine. Sarah was directly behind us, like she was using us as a shield for her. We all stood there for a little while, staring at the man in the enormous bed, with an IV drip next to it, along with an oxygen tank. He looked at us, and motioned us to the bed.

I could see in his face and eyes a part of where Sarah and Ryan got their beauty. The eyes were crystal clear blue, and his face had the same chisel that Ryan's did. He was weathered and extremely thin, but he had a full head of salt and pepper hair.

I could imagine that in his day he probably turned heads as much as his son.

Now he was a mere shadow of a man, just over a hundred pounds, struggling to breathe.

But he was conscious, and appeared to have his wits about him.

"My son," he whispered. "My daughter." There were tears in his eyes. "Thank you."

Ryan simply stared at him and said nothing. I looked at Ryan's face, but his expression was inscrutable.

Sarah's expression was more readable. She looked extraordinarily sad.

Benjamin looked at me, then looked at Ryan questioningly.

"Benjamin, this is my wife. Iris."

I held out my hand, and he reached one bony hand and took it, covering it with his other hand. "Welcome," he croaked between rasps.

"Good to meet you."

He trained his eyes on Ryan and Sarah. "I would like to speak with you both alone," he haltingly whispered.

Ryan started to protest, but Sarah silenced him with a look. Then Ryan looked at me and nodded.

I got the hint and left.

For the next two hours, I wandered around the enormous house and the grounds. It was a beautiful October day, sunny, clear, and unseasonably warm, with very little wind. I ended up on the edge of the bluff, looking down into the ocean. I couldn't take my mind off Ryan. Thank goodness he had Sarah there with him.

I found myself talking to God, asking Him to help Ryan have the strength to get through this. There was something about this place, overlooking the vast ocean, that made me think about the creator of us all. I have always been somewhat spiritual but not religious, so I have, on occasions such as this, tried to connect to something larger than myself.

I also needed guidance. I loved Ryan, more than I had ever loved anyone. But I couldn't deny that trouble seemed to follow him like a shadow. And it was taking me down, too. I silently prayed for the strength to see everything through, to be able to have the strength to help Ryan and to know how to give him what he needs.

And the strength to stay.

After a few hours, Ryan came and found me. I stood up, and put my arms around his neck, and he wrapped his arms around me. He held me, silently, for what seemed like eternity, but was, in reality, probably only a few minutes. Then, I took his hand, and we both sat down on the rocks and watched the ocean for a little while.

Neither of us spoke for a long time.

Finally, I asked "how did it go?"

Ryan said nothing, just continued staring at the horizon for a few minutes. Then he said "Do you remember what it felt like for you to meet Rochelle for the first time? When you said that meeting her put a human face to her, which helped you to forgive?"

"Of course."

"Something like that happened to me in there. I haven't

seen my father in so long, not since I was a young boy. So, for all these years, I built him up into this monster. Now I see him lying like that, helpless, and, I don't know. I had the epiphany that he's not a monster. He's human. A very, very flawed human, but human nonetheless."

I had made a mental note that he referred to him as "my father," not Benjamin. So, that alone tipped me off that he was feeling differently about his father. It also seemed that this visit had somehow given him a sense of peace and closure about the past.

He went on. "He couldn't speak very well, because he couldn't breathe very well. But he apologized to us both." He shook his head, then brought out a letter with shaking hands. "And he gave me this. He gave Sarah one as well."

"May I read it?" I asked.

"Sure, go ahead. I read it twice already."

I opened up the letter and read.

Dear Son,

As you probably know by now, I have been diagnosed with terminal lung cancer, and I don't have much time left in this world. God has a funny sense of humor. At any rate, I guess that I am owed this manner of death. Cold, cruel and painful. You know what they say about karma being a bitch. Of course, the irony is that I never smoked a single cigarette in my life. I am not going to say that there is an injustice in this, because I know that whatever horrible thing happens to me, I deserve it after the way I lived my life.

As a consequence of my diagnosis, I have been taking stock of my life, and trying to figure myself out. I know that I was a cruel tyrant with you, Sarah and Margaret. I knew it then. But I was so filled with hatred and violence that I literally couldn't stop myself. That's no excuse, of course. All my life, I blamed all of you for my being unhappy. Then I realized, after I lost all of you, and I was still unhappy, that the problem was me.

But I still wasn't ready to face my own demons. So, for many years, I comforted myself with my pieces of silver, and became more and more ruthless in business. I was trying to fill a bottomless pit of need. I thought that if I stripped enough businesses of their assets, so that our company could acquire them for pennies on the dollar, I could be happy. I took satisfaction in liquidating pension funds for workers that were relying on them. I was delighted that thousands of people lost their jobs in the process. The happiness about all this was short-lived, of course, so I had to do some more raiding. That's what I did. That's how I found short-lived glee after I lost the ability to torment my family. It helped that my company was benefitting greatly from my cold-hearted ruthlessness, but that really was not why I was doing it.

It wasn't until I was forced out of my job that I began to realize what a sadistic monster I was. I was no longer able to get my short-term fix of making others miserable. I, of course, howled about how unjust it all was. The company was experiencing a downturn because the country was experiencing a downturn, and I was scapegoated. After all I did for them!

It turned out to be the best thing that ever happened to me. I decided to travel the world, and, after I traveled all through Europe, South America and Australia, I ended up in Asia. I found an Ashram, and spent several years there while converting to Hinduism.

It was there, through meditation and prayer, that I started to understand myself. I made peace with my own sadistic father, who regularly sexually abused me from the age of 5, and my mother, who knew what was going on, and did nothing to stop it. They, of course, were very wealthy, very old money, so nobody would have ever believed me if I said anything. So, I never did. I got some satisfaction in inheriting their billions after they died, but only because their money helped me perpetuate their sadism, by making their sadism my own. I also thank God that I was expected to go to boarding school at the age of 10, which means that I was able to get away from my father for good. By then, I was so filled with rage that I caused trouble wherever I went.

I did try to be good, though. Like Dorian Gray, there was always a seed that wanted to be good, but, like Dorian Gray, that seed never took root. When I met your mother on a trip to Ireland when I was 22 and fresh out of Yale, I thought that I finally found my key to happiness. She was so angelic and full of spit and vinegar at the same time. Of course, looking back, she was a possession for me, a beautiful possession. No different than the Van Gogh I acquired, or all the companies I looted. When she was diagnosed with schizophrenia, she became utterly useless to me, so I threw her away. As I would any defective possession. I am deeply ashamed of that mentality now, but that was how I thought at the time.

But you...It took me a long time, and many years of meditation while on the Ashram, to try to come to terms on why I treated you the way I did. You always had the kindness and beauty of your mother. And I hated you for that. I hated you because you were everything that I could never be. You were loving and compassionate, where I was hard and cruel. I wanted you to be hard and cruel as well, so that is why I abused you. That is why I forced you to take part in my sick games. I wanted you to be like me – filled with self-loathing, calculating, and ruthless.

Of course, I never did make you hard and cruel. I learned about your drug problem, and took some satisfaction in that. As sick as that sounds. But cruelty just wasn't in your constitution. I continued to hate you for not becoming like me, up until I spent those years finding peace in India.

Cruel irony. When I got back to the States, I was determined to make amends to you, Sarah and Margaret. It was then that I found out about my diagnosis. I had been losing weight, not eating, and coughing for a period of months. By the time I went to the doctor about my symptoms, I was already in Stage 4. I have not been responding to treatment thus far, and it seems that, barring a miracle, I do not have much time left.

I have sent for you and Sarah. I am very sorry for all of the publicity you have garnered, by the way. I feel responsible for that, as well, because I was responsible for your getting mixed up with that rotten Ms. Anderson in the first place.

So, it seems that I will not get my chance to establish a relationship with my family after all. These letters hopefully will help all of you find peace. I have written a letter to Sarah and Margaret as well, telling them different things. You may all share the letters amongst yourselves as you wish.

I just wanted all of you to know that I do love you all, and I am deeply sorry for all that I did to make all of your lives a living hell. I regret everything that I have ever done in my life, because it seems that all my deeds in this life have involved some kind of wickedness. I know that now. I wish all of you all the happiness in the world. All that happiness that I did not have, I wish for all of you.

There is not much more to say. I do not expect your forgiveness, but if I get it, I will be eternally grateful.

Love always,
Dad

After I read the letter a few times, I looked at Ryan. He was standing next to me, studying me, trying to gauge my reaction. He looked much different than before he saw his father. He was no longer pale, and his eyes no longer had the depths of hurt in them. He looked...serene. And sorrowful, but in a different way than before. It was more like he was sorrowful for losing somebody that he just realized he loved, as opposed to hurt because of everything that person did to him.

I didn't really have words. This was so profound, it seemed that anything I would say would be trivial. Ryan had gone through so much in his life, all of which was directly attributable to his father's behavior, and he finally got the answers he had always sought. And, by the looks of things, he forgave his father, as well.

This was huge.

Finally, I spoke. "This is perhaps the greatest thing that has ever happened to you."

He smiled. "Well, second greatest thing," he said, taking me in his arms. "Behind meeting you, of course." Then he kissed me.

One thing was certain. Even though I found myself wavering about my feelings for him, his magnetic attraction for me never dimmed. I felt that kiss as I have always felt all of his kisses. Every hair stood on end, and my body felt flushed and warm.

We ended up making love on the grassy area behind the bluff, both of us almost fully clothed. I was wearing a skirt, and he laid me down and slipped off my panties. Then he unzipped his pants, and lowered his underwear, and entered me right there, his pants and underwear around his knees, kissing me passionately on the lips the entire time. He raised my arms above my head, holding my wrists firmly in place while he thrust hungrily. We were in plain view of anybody who would be walking by, be it Sarah or one of the help, but neither of us cared. He evidently had a need for me right then, and I always craved him as well.

Afterwards, we were spent, and lay there on the grass after dressing ourselves again. I was on my side, and Ryan lay perpendicular, his head on my waist. I stroked his hair, as he talked.

"I feel like a 1,000 pound weight has been lifted off of me," he said. "All my life, I have felt this kind of suffocation. This anxiety. This fear. I have tried so hard to shake it, and I have to admit that meeting you helped me do that for the most part. But it was still always there, lingering." He hesitated, grabbing my hand, and playing with my fingers lightly. "Now, it is completely gone. Completely gone. I have forgiven my father for what he did to me, and I have even understood him. How broken he is. He wanted me to be like him, and I was in a way. Both of us broken, just acting out in different ways. Me with drugs, him with abuse and sex addiction. And raiding companies. The irony is, of course, that I was like him. He just didn't know it."

"I'm so happy for you. So very, very happy for you."

"Ah, life would be perfect right now. If there weren't for the little matters of Rochelle on the loose, our private lives being trashed, my job, which is about to can me, and having to make sure you're safe." He smiled. "You know, little things like that."

"Your job is about to can you?"

"Yeah. I've been gone for most of this year, you know. They've had an interim president in there, and they want me back, because I always did a good job for them. But they're losing patience with me. And the interim guy has been doing a stellar job, which complicates things."

"So, we probably have to get back and face the music, huh?"

"Well, maybe. Now that I've broken the ice with my father, I feel like I need to spend time with him before he dies. There is so much to say, so much catching up to do. He knows a lot about my life, because it turns out that he's had people keeping tabs on me and reporting back. But I really know nothing about him, except what he told me in that letter. And this whole thing has brought me so much closer to Sarah as well." He picked up a little daisy, and examined it thoughtfully before handing it to me, tickling my nose with it. "You don't mind staying here for a little while, do you?"

"No, of course not. That means I can put off the whole bodyguard situation for a little while, so that's all good with me." I smiled. "I'm joking, of course. In all actuality, I'm just thrilled you're re-establishing a relationship with your father."

So, we ended up staying at the Newport home for an entire month. Benjamin was actually getting better, because he was doing alternative medicines that were brought to him from some of the yogis he knew at the Ashram, and he also did Reiki therapy and acupuncture. This was in addition to his chemotherapy. By the end of the first week that Sarah and Ryan were there, Benjamin was sitting up in his bed and eating solid food. He wasn't exactly ready to play tennis again, but he was improving, and his doctor who came to visit him every day informed him that his tumors were shrinking.

By the second week, I would pass by the bedroom and hear laughter coming out of the room. Ryan and Sarah's laughter, and also Benjamin's. I kept my distance, knowing that I had nothing to add to their bonding experience and would actually detract from it. So, I made myself scarce - watching movies in the home theater, reading books by the indoor pool and in the Jacuzzi, wandering around the magnificent greens, working out in the gym. I worked on my tennis game with a pro Benjamin sent over to teach me every day. My hand-eye coordination wasn't the best in the world, but I was pretty fit these days, so that helped.

By the third week, Benjamin was dressing for meals and was able to slowly walk around the grounds. He was also ready to get to know me a little better.

"So, you're Peanut's girl?" he said. He had gained several pounds since I first met him, and his color was coming back rapidly. He looked more like the handsome man he no doubt was in his youth, with his thick salt and pepper hair, twinkly blue eyes and chiseled features. He was dressed in a white sweater and khaki pants, and was walking slowly with me along the garden path, using a cane.

I still felt creeped out by him, though. I knew that things were better, and Ryan and Sarah were bonding with him. But I couldn't get out of my head all that he did. I supposed that people could change, particularly if one has spent years in an Ashram and was presently facing a death sentence that appeared to be commuted for now. So I tried to shake off my bad feeling and get to know him as well.

"Yes," I said.

"I'm sure you know all about me."

I nodded.

"I'm a different guy now. The doctor actually says I'm getting better. He thinks it's because the chemo is working. My yogi thinks that my heartbreak is healing, because my kids love me again, so my body is getting stronger. Mind over matter and all that."

"I believe that," I said. "I am a firm believer in alternative medicine and the healing power of the mind. It wouldn't be the first time."

"Listen, I know about your troubles. I feel responsible for them. My abusive ways towards my son was like a tumbling rock that caused an avalanche. Everything that happened to him happened because of me. Including his sordid and cheap affair with that floozy socialite Rochelle."

"It wasn't a sordid and cheap affair. It was child molestation on her part," I corrected him.

"Well, that's what I meant. I just didn't come out and say it that way, but you're correct. At any rate, Ryan was mixed up with her because of me, which means she wouldn't have been coming after you if it were not for me. So, I owe you a debt, as well."

"In a weird way, though, Mr. Whitney, the mere fact that I know Ryan is probably due to you. So you have indirectly caused a good thing, too."

"I don't follow you."

"It stands to reason that Ryan's life would've been completely different if it weren't for the abuse and the sex parties. It would've been better for him, but I doubt he would've known me. He probably would've been married to a better woman than Alexis when he was young, and would be married to her today," I said, plucking a lavender stalk and smelling its fragrance. "It may sound selfish on my part, but I owe you a debt in a weird way, because if it weren't for you, I probably would've never known Ryan in the first place."

He stood looking at me thoughtfully, then shook his head. "I suppose you're correct about that, but I have to consider the bad consequences with the good. And the bad consequences for my actions, for you, are pretty bad. Now, I know people who have been trained governmental assassins, who are now working as private bodyguards. And I-"

"Ryan and I talked about that. I don't want a bodyguard."

"With all due respect, my dear girl, you do not know who you are dealing with. That woman has been unhinged since the day I met her. They say she murdered her first husband, and I do not doubt that for a split second. Not even for a hair of a second."

"What happened to her first husband?" I asked, remembering her telling me in jail that her husband had left her and taken her son away from her.

"She married him when she was 19, and had the kind of rare captivating beauty that drew men in like polar magnets. He was a prominent oil and gas billionaire, inherited from his father. He was only 33-years-old. Four years after they married, he dropped dead. Of a heart attack. At the age of 37, and he was fitter than a fiddle. He ran marathons, stayed away from junk, never smoked, and had no family history of heart disease. His parents died young, but they were in a car accident." We had arrived at a marble bench surrounded by flowers, and we sat down. "The rumors were fast and furious that she obtained some poison that was untraceable and put it in his food. They could never prove it, of course. Either that, or money changed hands, so the medical examiner magically couldn't find anything."

"If his death was suspicious, weren't there family members who would've demanded a second opinion from another medical examiner?"

"There weren't family members alive at that time.

Calvin was an only child, as were both his parents. I still think that's why Rochelle picked him, because there wouldn't be family members coming out like vultures after his death. Very clever girl, that one."

"With all due respect, Mr. Whitney, I do know what she is capable of. I'm sure Ryan told you that she almost killed me."

"Of course. I feel like I am almost completely caught up on my son's and daughter's lives, and I couldn't be more delighted. Delighted that we have bonded so much, not delighted about their trials and tribulations, mind you. But delighted all the same."

Talking with this gentleman was awkward and surreal. It was not a month ago that Benjamin's dark shadow lingered over Ryan's life, and the mere thought that he would be friendly with Benjamin would be beyond unthinkable. Yet, here I was, talking to Benjamin like he was my own long-lost father. But I still couldn't forget that he was a rapist and a child molester, and I felt self-conscious being so far from the house and away from everybody else. He didn't seem to be leering or inappropriate, and I supposed he really had changed.

I couldn't really trust him, though.

Benjamin was talking again. "So, my dear girl, as precious as you are to my son, you have to make sure you are protected at all times from that psychotic woman. Never think that she isn't capable of finishing the job she started at her house, that ended up with you in a coma for months. And, trust me, I know the best of the best when it comes to protection."

"I'll think about it," I said, trying to appease him without actually committing.

"Good. I'll be in touch with Andrew right now," he said, whipping out his smart phone.

I stood up. "Where is everybody else?"

"Sarah and Ryan are playing tennis."

"Let me go find Ryan and talk to him before you start calling anybody. Please?"

"Ok, but hiring you one of my bodyguards was his idea, my dear."

I nodded. "Would you excuse me? I need to find Ryan." At that, I practically sprinted towards the tennis courts, leaving Benjamin on the bench.

I got there to watch the two go at it. They were both amazing tennis players, evenly matched, although Ryan had the advantage, because he was obviously more powerful. I watched them for awhile. Ryan's forehand and backhand were tremendous, and he covered most of the court. Sarah, for her part, gave as good as she got, and used clever strategy to make up for her relative lack of power. Ryan was never quite sure where the ball was going to land, so she kept him on his toes in that way. At one point, Ryan stripped off his t-shirt, as he was drenched with sweat, and I admired, anew, his lean and taut frame. Wap! One powerful serve that was not returned by Sarah, and Ryan did a little victory dance – shaking his hips, and waving his racquet all around.

"I beat the Olympian. How do you like me now?" he sang. "How do you like me now?"

At that, Sarah came up to him and hit him lightly on the butt with her racquet, then pointed to me with it.

"Hey beautiful," Ryan said, coming up to the fence to give me a kiss.

"Hey sweetie," I said. I didn't feel like bringing up the bodyguard conversation just yet, because he was way too elated over beating his apparent tennis-pro sister. I never knew she was in the Olympics for tennis until now.

He put on his shirt, and gave Sarah a bear hug, then came out of the tennis court and grabbed my hand. "Sorry for the sweat," he said. "I've never played a game like that. None of my guy buddies can play like that."

"Not a problem," I said as we walked along, hand in hand, Sarah a few feet behind us. "She was in the Olympics?"

"Yeah, in the 2004 Summer Olympics in Athens. She was 18. She didn't medal, or anything, though."

"Impressive," I said. *Good God, these Gallaghers are over-achievers.*

We walked along in silence for a little while. Ryan could tell that something was on my mind.

"What are you thinking, beautiful?"

"Now that you mention it, uh, I hate to bring this up, but..."

"Let me guess. My father has talked to you about Andrew."

"Yeah. I told you I didn't want a bodyguard, yet you talked to him behind my back."

He dropped my hand, and crossed his arms as he walked. But said nothing. Then he halted. "And did he tell you about how she murdered her first husband. Huh? Did he? Believe me, you're just a speck in that sociopath's way. She would crush you with no more feelings than if she stepped on an ant. Now, you need to stop being so goddamned stubborn about this. My foot is coming down." His jaw was clenched, his eyes steely, his arms still crossed. "And don't give me that bullshit about how you don't care if she kills you. Because if she kills you, she might as well kill me too. If that's what you want, then have at it."

Deeper Illusions

I could only manage a feeble "But Benjamin said it was only suspected that she killed her first husband. Nothing was ever proven."

"Goddamn it. This is the woman who shot you up with so much black tar heroin it would've killed a 300 lb. man. You were goddamned lucky. Trust me, she wanted to kill you that first time. Don't think that because you managed to somehow get out of it that it wasn't her intent to murder you. She has no feelings. You were lucky to come out of that coma. I honestly thought you wouldn't. I honestly thought you wouldn't. I honestly thought you wouldn't."

Then he was sitting down on the grass, his knees up, with his arms propped on them. Sarah had long since passed us to go into the house. He looked up at me, the sun illuminating his piercing green eyes. "When you were in that hospital, a part of me died every day you were unconscious. Every day." He shook his head. "All I could think of was that I didn't think I would survive if I lost you. Everybody kept telling me the odds were against you, but I never stopped believing. If I gave up hope on you, then I would have given up hope on myself as well." He looked off in the distance, then back at me. "So, you see, your fate is tied in with mine."

I sat down next to him. I felt so defeated. "Ok, then. But a retired government assassin? Really?"

"Andrew is the best of the best."

"When do I get to meet him?"

"Say the word and my father will give him a call."

Andrew appeared later on that day. I eyed him suspiciously, hanging back a little, still not crazy about the whole idea, and feeling intimidated by him. He was around 5'7", probably around 65 years old, but very compact and muscular. He was also completely bald. He approached me and shook my hand, his dark eyes flashing.

"Hi, I'm Andrew. Benjamin hired me to protect you from your would-be assailant."

"Iris," I said, looking at Ryan with an expression that said "I really don't want to do this!"

Andrew looked from myself to Ryan, and immediately surmised the situation. "I know you don't want me to protect you, but, from what I understand, it's for your own good. I have intelligence on Rochelle Anderson, and, from what I understand, it's not just Ms. Anderson who is threatening your life, but she has hired other people as well."

I suddenly felt horrified. I looked at Ryan, and his expression was the same as mine – mystified, panicked, terrified. He grabbed my hand tightly.

"Do not worry, though. I have the information on at least two people who have been in touch with her."

I suddenly realized that this may never be over. Even after Rochelle was imprisoned, if Rochelle was imprisoned, I would always have to be looking over my shoulder. I would have to have Andrew, or somebody like Andrew, with me at all times.

Well, not at all times. Ryan explained that he only wanted the bodyguard to be around when he, himself, couldn't be around to protect me – he was going back to work as soon as we arrived back home, so Andrew would be around when he wasn't around, and when he would have to go on his business trips. He had explained to me yesterday that he had one lined up to go to Tokyo in less than a month, and he would be gone for two weeks. He made sure that I was mentally strong enough to lose him for that long, and I assured him I was.

Now I wasn't so sure.

There was also the issue with the pap, if they would be stalking the house when we got home. However, it appeared, for now, that the pap would no longer be an issue. Everything appeared to calm down after the *People* interview, as we gave all the dirt there was possible to get, and the 24-hour news cycles had long since moved on. Of course, as it got closer to trial, that would all change, but, for now, everything seemed to be calmed down on that front.

In other words, things would be returning to normal once we got back. Aside from the fact that the world now knew about us, our faces were on the cover of a *People* magazine, and our lives were fodder for public consumption, everything would be normal.

Oh, and there was the little matter of my being marked for death.

Other than that, everything would be normal.

Other than that, how'd you like the play, Mrs. Lincoln?

Chapter Thirteen

We got back, and I started to brace myself for Ryan finally returning to work. He had been off work for about nine months now, because he was taking care of me, then we were on our honeymoon, then at Sarah's house, then Benjamin's house. We were together constantly during this time, during a period that I would say was among the most stressful of my entire life, yet we were still very much in love. After the grief about our private lives going public had passed, and we had returned home, we got back into our usual routine of love-making, eating out, watching television, going on bike rides and long walks, seeing movies, hanging out with friends, etc.

I even got back into doing some more pit bull rescues.

But D-Day was soon to come. I felt like whining when I saw Ryan getting dressed in his mega-dollar suit, silk shirt and Italian shoes, his leather briefcase in hand. He had a new haircut, as his hair was getting ever so slightly shaggy and unruly while we were on vacation, and he was wearing aftershave that gave him a slightly musky smell.

He approached me as I was sitting on the couch. I was trying not to be a wimp. I knew his job was important to him. He was not the type to be a trust fund baby, and I knew this as well. As much as I secretly wanted him to just quit his job and stay with me 24/7, that wasn't reasonable.

I really had zero plans for my own life. The mere thought of going back to law nauseated me, not to mention the fact that everybody would be poking each other and laughing behind my back because of what was now public knowledge about me.

So, for now, I was a Country Club wife. Only I didn't have children to take care of, I really didn't fit in with the other Country Club wives, and I had a bodyguard to babysit me during the day.

I was going to have to find a new path in the world, and I really didn't know where to start.

Ryan came next to me, where I was sitting on the couch. He tousled my hair a little. "Beautiful, you're going to be okay, aren't you?"

I nodded and smiled, feeling tears threatening.

He kissed me on the forehead. "You're safe here with Andrew. That's what's most important to me." He looked at me for several seconds. "I'm going to miss you. We haven't been apart for any period of time for around nine months. But know that I will be thinking of you throughout the day, and I will check on you several times a day, when I get a second."

I nodded my head, trying not to cry.

At that, he stood up and walked out the door, with one last glance at me before leaving. He blew me a kiss, and he was off.

Then Andrew walked in the door.

"Don't mind me," he said. "Just go about your business like usual."

Which I tried to do except...I didn't really know what my business as usual was anymore. I was the only person I knew now who wasn't working during the day. These past few months, there was nothing at all on my mind, except being with Ryan, then thinking non-stop about the horrible invasion of privacy we were facing.

I found myself wanting the pap back, just so it would give me something to do.

Because now all I could do was to sit and stew about my own thoughts and my own life. I hadn't had a minute to really think about all that had happened, because it all happened so fast. I was attacked, I was in a coma, I went through PTSD, I got engaged, then married, to Ryan, we went on our honeymoon, the pap attacked, we saw Benjamin, we hired me a bodyguard. Boom, boom, boom. Never a dull moment.

Now I had to consider what it was that I wanted from my life. I had Ryan, and that was great. But that couldn't possibly be all there was. I would soon become boring to myself and to him. Going back to law was...I felt nauseated just thinking about it. Maybe it was because I was attacked at my law office, and maybe it was because I was completely unhappy there. I really didn't know.

I knew where my passions lie. With animals. I always got great satisfaction out of my pit bull rescues. The beautiful thing was that I could practice law without getting paid now. So I contacted the Animal Legal Defense Fund, and inquired about what I could do to help.

But a part of me didn't feel exactly ready for that, either. I loved animals, but didn't feel strong enough to deal with full-time activism. Knowing, affirmatively, what happened to animals on a daily basis would be enough to spin me back into full-on depression.

Ryan got home that evening somewhat early, around 6, and I couldn't be more relieved. He arrived bearing a bouquet of roses and orange chicken from Bo Lings, our favorite Chinese restaurant. He kissed me passionately.

"How was work?" I asked, taking his jacket from him and walking back to the bedroom to hang it up.

"A nightmare. Charlie, the interim president, was not nearly as competent as I thought. He screwed a lot of stuff up, and I spent the better part of the day trying to fix his mistakes. I didn't have a lot of spare time, which is why I didn't call. I'm so sorry about that. I was thinking of you, though."

"Not a problem," I said.

"How was Andrew?" he asked.

"Fine. A little boring. Which is okay, I guess. I'm guessing that he really shouldn't be getting too chummy with his charges."

Ryan brought out the dinner, which was orange chicken and eggrolls, bringing out chopsticks for us to use. He seemed a little different – he was distracted, which was really to be expected. He was once again in his role of bank president, and somewhat out of his role as full-time protector.

Without looking at me, he said "I have something kinda bad to tell you."

"Worse than the fact that there is Rochelle and untold minions out there threatening my life?" Andrew had given me the low-down on three of them, but he didn't seem too impressed. He said that they struck him as the gang that couldn't shoot straight.

I was surprised Rochelle didn't get people more professional.

He looked me in the eye, putting his hand on mine. "The Tokyo trip has been pushed up, because of some of Charlie's screwups."

My heart was in my throat. I had hoped that I would have some time to get used to not having Ryan around for half the day, then I could wean myself off of him, to where I could get used to him not being around for two whole weeks.

"When do you have to leave now?" I asked.

"Tomorrow."

I nodded, looking at my shaking hands that were gripping the chopsticks.

"Beautiful, I'm so sorry about this. I wish it could be helped. I know that Andrew will keep you safe, but I do worry about you just the same."

"I'm a big girl," I said. "And Andrew is going to teach me how to shoot a gun."

He nodded. "I asked him to do this for you. You need to know how to defend yourself. I hope you don't mind, but I also have asked him to give you other self-defense lessons."

"Do you know how to shoot a gun?"

"Of course," he said. "As f'd up as my life has been, knowing basic self-defense and knowing how to use a weapon has been a must for me. Now it's time for you to learn as well."

I examined my orange chicken at the end of my chopsticks and said nothing. But I knew Ryan was reading my mind, as always.

Sure enough, Ryan said "Again, honey, I can't tell you how sorry I am that a self-defense course and a weapon shooting lesson is even necessary for you. It's because of me. Sometimes I'm sorry we met."

I looked at him, feeling horrified and startled that he would say such a thing.

"I mean, I'm really glad we met, for my sake," he said. "You have been the missing puzzle piece for me. But, for your sake, I wish we hadn't met. Your life would be so much simpler now."

"The sacrifice has been worth it," I said. "100% worth it."

We made love that night with tender passion, knowing that it would be our last night together for at least two weeks, maybe more. Ryan wasn't sure when he would be getting back from Tokyo, but hoped that it would not be too terribly long of a business trip. He made love to me right after dinner, and we went on through the night, both of us exploring each other's bodies in the most sensual manner possible. Ryan said that he didn't mind making love all night, reasoning that he had a long plane trip ahead, on the corporate jet, and he could sleep on the plane.

"And I have to make sure that we make every minute count," he said, while he thrust hungrily, his head buried in my shoulder.

Once again, I willed the love-making never to end, so that we might put off the inevitable.

Little did I know that this would be the last time we would be making love for a long, long time.

Chapter Fourteen

Ryan had been gone for about a week when it happened. He had called me as much as he could from Tokyo, Zooming with me for hours in the evening. I told him all about my self-defense classes and target shooting exercises. To my surprise, I was getting rather handy with my .45 pistol that Ryan bought me before he left, although I still wasn't a great shot. I also was able to flip Andrew when he "attacked" me, and pin him.

Andrew told me that I was a prize pupil.

I was gradually getting into life again without Ryan around, feeling less depressed and more like I wanted to actually engage with the world.

I had Richard and Debbie over for dinner one night.

"So, doll, how are things going without hunky boy around?" Richard asked me.

"Great. Married life is great."

"Uh, huh," Richard said. "Tell me the truth."

"Well, I'm a Country Club wife," I said.

"Don't tell me you actually joined the country club," Debbie said.

"God, no. Like I would ever fit in there," I said.

"So, what are you going to do with your life?" Richard asked.

"Not sure yet. Right now, I'm concentrating on learning self-defense and how to shoot a weapon. I never thought that I would be in the position where I would be so bored with my life."

Debbie offered helpfully that I should "take some classes, find out what you want to do."

To which I said "Yeah. Do you guys want to play a game?" I had no desire to engage in a conversation about my future, because I didn't know what to say about it just then.

At that I brought out some board games, and we had fun with that for several hours.

They went home, and I got ready for bed, changing into my pajamas. I was in the kitchen fixing myself a little snack, the dogs having been kenneled for the night, when Andrew emerged from the downstairs. I hadn't told anybody that I had a bodyguard, not really wanting them to worry about me even more than they already were, so I asked Andrew to stay downstairs while I had my company over.

Andrew snuck up behind me, and put his arms around me from the back. I figured that this was my opportunity to flip him again, so I put my hands on his arms, and made the maneuver like he taught me.

To my surprise, however, he didn't flip, just started gripping me tighter.

It was then that I felt him slipping a belt around my neck.

I still thought it was all a game, but I hadn't yet learned what to do when somebody puts a belt around my neck.

"Ok, Andrew, this is my lesson for today. What do I do now?" I asked.

He said nothing, just pulled it tighter. I started to panic, as I was losing consciousness. I desperately grabbed the belt, trying to loosen it, then he loosened it on his own.

I spun around and faced him. He still had the belt in his hand.

"Lay down," he ordered.

I was quizzical. What kind of game was he playing? He must just be trying to scare me, to simulate a real-world situation.

"Lay down," he ordered again.

I lay down on the tiled floor of the kitchen. He pulled the belt around my neck tighter still.

Then he started to unbuckle his pants.

My heart quickened. The belt was tight enough that I was starting to lose consciousness again, but he loosened it just when I was about to pass out. He did that several times more, then ripped down my pajama bottoms and my underwear.

He was now without pants, having unbuckled them and thrown them aside. I, too, was half-naked, lying on the floor, going in and out of consciousness with every tug of the belt. I started to struggle, then he tightened the belt.

"If you keep struggling, I won't loosen this belt," he said. "Hold still."

At that, he thrust into me. His manhood was huge, as large as Ryan's, and I wasn't wet because of my fear, so the pain was excruciating. He jackhammered me for about five minutes, but every minute seemed like a year. All the while, he kept tightening the belt and loosening, tightening it and loosening it.

I started to scream.

As soon as I started screaming, he pulled on the belt violently. I gasped for air, not able to make a sound, clawing desperately on the belt. "You scream again, and I will tighten this belt so hard that you won't get any air at all." Then he tugged even harder to make his point. All I could do was open my mouth, and nothing came out. Then he grabbed one of his socks, rolled it up, and put it in my mouth. I bit down on the sock, feeling hot tears running down my face.

He was still on top of me, thrusting over and over and over, not stopping for even a second.

Then he flipped me over, violently putting a handcuff on one of my wrists. He dragged me over to the bar, like a dog, leading me by my leash, which was the belt around my neck. I crawled on my knees and one hand, my other hand desperately gripping the belt. Then he pounced on top of me, dragging my handcuffed wrist to the leg of the barstool, then dragged my other arm, then handcuffed that wrist as well, so that I was securely handcuffed to the solid leg of the barstool.

I was breathing in and out, in and out, from my nose. My mouth still had a rolled up sock in it, so my nose was the only breath that I could get. Then I muffled a scream as he penetrated me anally. This was pain like I had never experienced, not even when I was being tortured by Rochelle. He was ripping up my insides, not bothering with lubrication, and he pounded me for what seemed like hours, although it was probably only minutes. I could feel hot tears running down my cheeks, as my legs were violently kicking, but he tugged on the belt violently, then said "you keep kicking like that, and I will have to do this to you while you are unconscious. And I'll just leave you here, handcuffs on, to fend for yourself."

In other words, either I stopped kicking, or I was going to die.

I stopped kicking, then willed myself away from the reality of what was happening. I just lay there, my mind focused on my honeymoon with Ryan. The last really happy time. We were in Nick's villa, making love non-stop, going on bike tours through wine country, seeing the sights. I was posing for him while he made a portrait of me, sticking my tongue out at him playfully. We were on his yacht, the *Maggie*, while we looked into the deep blue Mediterranean, watching the dolphins and the waves. On and on and on my mind drifted, and I felt myself relaxing.

Then he was once again penetrating me vaginally, but, at this point, I was only vaguely aware of what was happening. My mind was a million miles away.

After what seemed to be days, it was finally over, and he got up, without a word, as he pulled up his pants and fastened his belt. Then he produced a key, and removed the handcuffs.

"Not a word about this," he said. "You know how I am trained. You won't stand a chance."

I lay on the kitchen floor, too shocked to say anything.

Then he left the house, leaving me all alone.

I was in shock, dazed, and feeling like I had been dreaming. I lay on the kitchen floor for what seemed to be an eternity, lying motionless, curled up in the fetal position, not crying or screaming. Just lying there. In a pool of blood. I got up to use the bathroom, and wiped more blood off me. Then cleaned up the blood in the kitchen.

Then I threw on a heavy coat, gloves and a hat, and wandered out of the house. I walked several miles until I found a bus stop.

I lay down on the bus bench, turned off my phone, and waited for the bus to arrive.

Where I was going, I knew not.

Chapter Fifteen

RYAN

I was having drinks in a Tokyo Bar, with some of my colleagues, but I couldn't feel further away. Iris felt she was most affected by what has happened in the last few months, and, in a way, she was right about that. But I wished that she knew how paramount she was on my mind, even now that I was on this trip that was necessitated by Charlie's screw-ups. Well, the trip was pushed up because of this, but the trip was originally scheduled because our bank was looking into acquiring some struggling Japanese banks. I was the face of our bank, so I sent to represent the company, along with the CFO and the CEO, and various management team leaders.

It had been a fruitful trip, but I had to admit that I was worried. I called Iris at 8 PM her time, 10 AM my time, just like I promised, but it went straight to voice mail. I called several times after that, straight to voice mail. After not getting her for several hours, I gave up, knowing she probably was asleep.

Then, I waited until 8 AM her time, 10 PM my time.

Straight to voice mail.

Yet, here I was, entertaining the Japanese business men with my colleagues, and my mind was literally thousands of miles away.

We were all making small talk, and making plans to go to a strip club later on. The very last thing I wanted to do at that point, but I obliged like a sheep.

"Before we go to the next place, do you mind if I make a phone call?" I asked them.

"No, no, of course not," Hirohito, the point man for the merger, said to me, bowing his head a little.

"Thank you," I said, then went outside and called Nick.

It was around eight AM there on Saturday, ten PM here, and Nick was at work, as he always was on every other Saturday. He was the lead architect for a large firm in town and was often away from the phone.

I prayed that I would get him.

To my surprise, he did answer the phone. It turned out that he was in his office doing some drafting of a major project in town.

"Buddy," he said, his familiar greeting for me. "How's Tokyo?"

"Fine. Listen, I need for you to do me a favor," I said.

"Anything."

"I need for you to go our house as soon as you can and check on Iris."

"Sure," he said. "But she has a bodyguard there. I'm quite sure she is in capable hands."

"Even so, I need you to check. I can't get ahold of her, and I'm worried."

"Isn't she kinda an airhead?" he asked.

"She tends to be kind of forgetful. So what?"

"Well, she's the type who would let her phone run out of a battery, then forget where she placed her charger."

"I know that," I said, feeling impatient. "But I have a bad feeling. So, please, do this for me?"

"If you say so."

"Call me when you find out?"

"I get off at noon, I'll swing by there before I go home, then call you."

"Call me immediately," I said.

"That'll be around 2 AM your time," he said.

"That's fine." I just hoped that I wasn't still at the strip club at that time.

Then we headed over to the strip club. I was laying off the alcohol that night, so far. I was drinking club soda, and waiting for the phone to ring.

Jackson, one of the management team that was also on this trip, came up to me. "You having fun?" he asked flirtatiously. I knew that the boy was gay, which wasn't a problem, but, since everybody in the office now knew that I swung both ways, it seemed that men were coming out of the woodwork to ogle me. I never cared about that, though. People were people, and it was flattering, if anything, but I let them all know that I was happily married, thank you very much.

It was bad enough getting the female attention constantly, now I had to put up with the male attention, too.

"Sure," I said, looking at my phone anxiously. It was only 1 AM this time, around 11 AM Nick's time, but I was hoping that he would get off early and give me an answer. Not that I expected it, I just willed it.

"This trip has been the time of my life," the boy said. "I've only been out of college for less than a year, and here I am, sitting in on takeover negotiations halfway around the world. Who'da thought?"

I nodded, distracted. I saw Hirohito motion to me to tip the dancer, and I gave her a hundred dollar bill from my wallet. I felt a little showy doing that, but impressing these people was the name of the game here, and whatever I could do to facilitate the best asking price for this bank, I would do it.

We were still at the club at 2:30 AM, when I looked at the phone and saw that Nick was calling.

"Excuse me," I said to my companions. I answered the phone in the loud bar, then made my way outside to talk to him. Outside, the night air was warm, unseasonably so, seeing as this was December, and the parking lot was full. There was a loud group of people entering the club, so I walked a bit further, under a barren cherry tree, and sat down on the grass. I could still barely hear him.

"Did you go by the house?" I asked.

"Yes," he said.

"And?"

"Her car is there. But she is not."

My heart was in my throat. I knew something was wrong. I just knew it. Iris and I had almost a psychic connection, and I knew somehow that she was in trouble.

"What about Andrew?"

"Nowhere to be found."

"What about Daniel? Maybe he drove her somewhere?"

"I called him already. He hasn't seen her either."

My mind started searching, wandering. "What about the other cars? Maybe she took the Jag, the Porsche, the Rivian, the Escalade?"

"All the cars are at the house."

"What about Maximus, Brutus and Madison?" I asked,

knowing that Iris would never, ever, just abandon the animals.

"They were there, looking pretty hungry and thirsty. The dogs were kenneled. I gave them food and water, then brought them to my house to care for them."

Shit. She just left the animals there? Now I was really starting to panic. "Thanks," I said. "I need to make some other phone calls."

"Sure. Do you need anything else?"

"No, just please be on stand-by?"

"Of course."

Good old Nick. There wasn't anything he wouldn't do for me, nor I for him. It was nice to know that there was somebody who always had my back, no matter what.

Besides Iris, I mean.

I called Charlene, her mother. But I didn't want to panic her, so, when she answered the phone, I asked for Iris as casually as possible.

"Iris isn't here," Charlene said.

"Oh, I'm so sorry. She said she might be paying you a visit today, so I wanted to call and wish her happy anniversary."

"Anniversary?"

"We met a year and a half ago today," I said, which was actually true.

"Well, I'll be sure and tell her that you called when I see her," she said. "I guess you couldn't get ahold of her?"

"No, but you know how she is," I said, trying to sound as light as possible, disguising the panic in my throat, "she no doubt lost her phone charger."

"She should wear that thing around her neck," Charlene said with a laugh.

"Right," I said, trying to fake a laugh of my own.

We hung up, then I called her two best friends, Richard and Debbie, repeating the same light-hearted scenario, panic rising with each time I heard that nobody knew where Iris was.

My phone calls made, I went back into the club, and tried to take my mind off of the whole thing for now. There were a few women in the club, and they came onto me, which I was more than used to. I was always polite with everybody who hit on me, because I hated to hurt people's feelings, but I was not in the mood for sexual advances. So, I rather rudely rebuffed them.

I sat back down, and drank a beer. Somebody was talking to me. Hirohito. I had to charm him - he was the point man for the takeover - so I mustered up my actor energy, flashing a smile, and laughing at the jokes he was making. I had taken some acting classes at Harvard, just because I thought they would be fun, and they were. I learned a lot, and I used what I learned to fake my way through much of my life, putting on a brave face for the world, when I was dying inside all those years.

It was really only after I met Iris that I no longer had to fake anything, because I was finally happy and at peace with my life.

Now, here I was, digging into my repertoire once again, the comedian disguising the deep well of hurt. Only now I was disguising a rising sense of panic. My gut told me something was wrong.

Something was terribly, terribly wrong.

Yet, here I was, laughing at jokes, talking about American popular culture, telling jokes of my own. Drinking scotches, which I started ordering after I got back into the club, knowing that I had to drown my sense of panic in something, and also knowing that my familiar crutch, heroin, could not be accessed. Not that I couldn't find it. It was always easy to find, if you look. Rather, I knew that I couldn't do it, even if I could find some. That road led to ruin once before, or near-ruin. I barely escaped with my life, then was sure that, the second time I became addicted, after I met Iris, it would lead to ruin once more. I had something to live for, more than I ever had before, and that something was Iris. That helped me clean up my act the second time. And it was what kept me from turning to the drug this time. Iris would be disappointed in me. She might even leave me. She had shown remarkable patience and resilience through everything that she had gone through since she met me, but I knew her patience and resilience were not boundless.

And I had no desire to push it.

So, I drank my scotch, and turned on the charm full force.

Then, after the evening was finally over, and we all turned in around 4 AM, I started to panic again.

I called Iris' phone. It was now around 2 PM her time.

Straight to voice mail.

Chapter Sixteen

I didn't sleep a wink last night. I kept calling Iris' phone, every fifteen minutes, then every five minutes, until I was calling it every minute. I was willing her to pick up her phone, talk to me, tell me she was okay.

But I knew she wasn't. I knew it the very first time I called her, and her phone went straight to voice mail.

How was I going to get through this next week? I would be here in Tokyo for one more week, as we finalized our negotiations for taking over this bank. Yet, Iris was out there somewhere, in trouble. And Andrew, the person who was supposed to be protecting her, was nowhere to be found, either.

I felt so impotent, so helpless.

Who could help me find her?

I tried to get into her mind, willing myself not to think the worst, which was that Rochelle had nabbed her, somehow, under Andrew's nose.

I called the police in Kansas City.

They answered the phone, and I said "I would like to report a missing person."

"Ok, sir, who is missing?"

"My wife, Iris Gallagher. Could you please give me an e-mail address, so that I can send a picture of her?"

The dispatcher gave me this information, and I sent a picture of Iris immediately.

"How long has your wife been missing?"

"About two days. There have been threats against her recently, so that's why I'm so worried."

"Does she have a history of running off?"

"No."

They took down some more information, then told me that they would call the hospitals and morgues to check on her. They also would assign a detective on the case.

My blood ran icy when I heard the word "morgue."

I wasn't satisfied with just the police looking for her, though. I didn't feel they would do enough to find her. So, I paced the floor, and decided to call my father.

"Dad," I said, mystified anew that I ever would be calling him. He was remarkably getting better - now the doctor was giving him several years to live, as opposed to weeks, which is what he had when I first arrived to visit him.

"Son," he said. "What can I do for you?"

"Iris is missing."

"Impossible. She has a bodyguard, you know."

"He's missing as well."

"Oh. Let me put my people on it and find out where he is."

"Put your people on it and find out where she is, first."

"Andrew is the best, you know. He wouldn't let anything happen to her."

"Even so, I need an APB on her."

"Right. I'm on it as we speak."

We hung up. I shrugged off, for now, the oddity that I would be calling my father for this, then made another phone call. To one of my underworld connections that I made when I was an addict all those years. I kept in touch with a few of them, knowing that sometimes having friends in low places could be the very best thing in life.

"Gino," I said, after calling several other connections, and getting nothing but voice mail.

"Ryan?" Gino said. "I never thought I'd hear from you again."

"Listen, I need a favor."

"Ah, a favor. Well, you know, I am in serious need of a fix, and I can't seem to find the funding for it. You know of anybody I might ask about this?"

"You still got the same bank account?" I asked.

"I do."

"I'm wiring $10,000 to your account as we speak," I said, tapping on my phone, and wiring him the money. It probably would be going down the drain, but I really couldn't care less. It was pocket change, especially compared to the life of my beautiful wife.

"Just a second," he said, and I heard him tapping on his phone, and checking his account. "Ok. Now, what favor do you need?"

"I'm going to send you a picture of my wife. I need for you to be on the lookout for her," I said, sending him her picture.

After a few seconds, he said, "cute girl. I'll look out for her. But why would she be hanging around here?"

"Just a hunch," I said.

"Ok. What should I do if she shows up?"

"Call me. Detain her somehow. I need to find her. If

you find her, there's another $100,000 in it for you. That would keep you set up for awhile."

He gave a low whistle. "I'll be looking for this cat for sure."

"Oh, and Gino?"

"Yeah?"

"If you fuck me over, you're cut off for good."

"Don't worry. I got your back," he said, one drug addict to another.

I felt my bases were somewhat covered. I had the police and my dad's team looking for Iris, and I had also had my underworld connection looking for her. Now, all I had to do was try to concentrate during these interminable meetings that were coming up this week.

I called Iris' number.

Straight to voice mail.

Chapter Seventeen

I was like a ghost that week, sitting through meetings, then calling Iris during every break. I called my father, the police, and Gino every night, being sensitive to the time change, knowing that I was a good 14 hours ahead of them. This meant that I had to call around 10 PM every night, so that I could get them around 8 in the morning. They always answered the phone when I called, and always told me the same thing.

They got nothing.

Still, I kept up my acting job. Nobody knew there was a thing wrong. Typical. Nobody ever knew there were things wrong with me, all my life, except Nick and Alexis. Everybody else saw the charmed boy who rowed, played football, and got straight As. All the while, I was dying inside from all my trauma. Now, it was acting time again, and I managed to help guide our takeover for the best possible asking price and the best possible terms.

My hell week was finally over, and I boarded the corporate jet for the 15-hour flight from Tokyo to Kansas City. In-flight movies were playing, and my seat mate, Harry, who was the CEO of the company, was trying to make small talk, but I was exhausted from all the acting I did that week, and really needed a break. So, I shut my eyes and pretended to sleep, and Harry eventually gave up talking to me.

We finally arrived in Kansas City, and I drove my Porsche to my home. I prayed for a miracle, that, somehow, someway, Iris would be there waiting for me.

I realized my prayers were not answered when I arrived to my empty house.

I did such a good job with the takeover negotiations that my work allowed me to take the rest of the week off. Which was amazing to me, considering all the time I took off before this trip, but I really needed the break, so I was grateful.

But I wasn't sleeping, at all. I found myself up all night, every night, calling Iris' phone every five minutes, and mindlessly going through Internet pages. I also ended up in the seedy parts of town, combing the streets, showing Iris' picture. I had a hunch that I would find her there, among the dregs of society, which was where I myself used to haunt, back in my drug days. I never used to hang around here, except to buy my dope, but I still knew people on the streets. Gino was still on the lookout as well.

I also went to Rochelle's house, in a much tonier area, and banged on the door.

She opened the door, then smiled like I had never seen her smile before. "Well, well, well, handsome, imagine seeing you here."

"Where is she?" I demanded.

"Where is who?"

"You know very well who. My wife."

"I don't know."

"Bullshit. Where is she?"

"I have no idea what you are talking about."

"You've made threats against her, and now she's missing. Coincidence?"

She just shook her head. "I'm all talk, you know that."

"Bullshit. All talk, my ass. Were you all talk when you almost murdered her? And what about your minions who also have it out for her?"

"What minions?"

"You know. The people you hired to come for her."

"Are you alright? Why would I do that? I'm out on bail, don't you think that I would be put right back into my tiny little pen if I did something like that?"

For some odd reason, I ended up believing her. I had a keen ability to read people. That had always been a talent of mine.

And I read her as being completely above-board.

"Sorry for bothering you," I said, then turned and got back into my car and went home.

I was completely jet-lagged, and, night after night, I stayed awake, getting no sleep. I was a ghost again, like before I met Iris, only worse this time. I was vaguely worried about my lack of sleep, knowing that not sleeping causes strange things to happen, like hallucinations, and my body seemed to be shutting down. But every night, I tossed and turned in the big empty bed, then ended up back on the streets, driving around, looking for her. I talked to every vagrant I saw, and even ran into a few people I knew from before.

Then, one day, at the end of the week, when I had gone about five days without sleep, Iris arrived.

Chapter Eighteen

My beautiful girl arrived after I had a particularly harrowing experience in the shower. I was exhausted and spent, not having slept for around 5 days, and I slipped and hit my head, hard, on the edge of the tub. I passed out, only to come to sometime later, being awakened by the licking of Brutus and Maximus. I looked at the clock, realizing that I was unconscious for the better part of the hour. I patted my head, and found that I was bleeding. I then tried to call Daniel to come and take me to the hospital, but, for the life of me, I couldn't remember his phone number. I couldn't even remember 911. I remembered that there were three numbers that you are supposed to dial when you have an emergency, and I dialed 711, 611, 311, then gave up in frustration after dialing these numbers and getting nowhere.

I finally decided just to go to my bed and try to sleep it off, but my head was throbbing. Then I saw my father, as plain as day. He was in my bedroom and talking to me. Only he looked different – his head was blue, his body orange. Not a fake tan sort of orange, but more like an Oompa Loompa orange. He was also very fuzzy.

"Dad," I said. "Have you heard any word about my wife?"

He just shook his head and said nothing.

"Where is she, dad? Is she still alive?"

"I don't know, son. I wish I did."

Then I passed out again, and, when I came to, Iris was standing by the bed. I rubbed my eyes, not sure that I was actually seeing what I was seeing.

I touched her, and felt flesh and bone.

My heart leapt out of my throat. She was finally home! Relief coursed through every cell of my body.

"Oh, my God! Beautiful! You're back!" I shouted, wrapping myself around my one true love.

"I don't understand. What do you mean?" Iris asked me.

"What happened to you? Why did you shut off your phone? Why didn't you call me? I was so worried," I said to her, my face in her hair, my hand on her back.

"Shut off my phone? I don't understand. This isn't Iris, this is..." Iris hesitated. Then she said, "of course, I'm back. I love you. I've always loved you."

"I love you too. Oh, God, I was so worried."

Then I kissed her full and sensuous lips. Her lips met mine hungrily, her hands clawing my back. "I love you so much," she said. "I've loved you for so many years."

There was something in the back of my mind that was telling me that it wasn't right, but I ignored that inner voice that was trying to remind me that Iris and I had only known each other about a year and a half.

I carried Iris to our bedroom, and lay her down on the bed. I stripped off her clothes, and stripped off mine as well, and hovered over her for a few seconds. Then I kissed her passionately and thrust deeply into her, over and over again. I was so hungry for her, I couldn't get enough. She was telling me, over and over again, how much she loved me, and how much she had always wanted this to happen. I put her face in my hands, and kissed all around her face, my hands in her hair. Her legs were wrapped tightly around me as I thrust, deeper and deeper into her. Then I came inside her, and, feeling completely spent, I laid down next to her and stroked her hair.

And, since the first time since I found out she was missing, I was relieved of my stress, and I found the sleep that I needed for so long.

Chapter Nineteen

I woke up in my bed and looked at the clock. It read 8 AM, which meant that I had only been asleep about 5 hours. I think that I fell asleep around three in the morning, after making love to Iris for hours after she came home to me.

I made my way down the stairs.

Natalie was in my kitchen, helping herself to some orange juice.

"Nat," I said, confused. "When did you get here?"

She was startled by my presence. I also noticed that she was wearing one of my button down shirts, and seemingly nothing else. Her face turned bright red.

"I got here a couple of days ago."

"A couple of days ago? Where's Iris?"

"Sit down," Natalie asked.

I sat down at the kitchen bar, feeling disoriented and confused. Natalie had been here a couple of days? I didn't remember her coming here at all.

"I did a terrible, terrible thing," she began.

"What terrible thing did you do?" I asked, although I was starting to realize what, exactly, she was referring to.

"Uh, the other night, I came into town. I called Nick, because I couldn't get ahold of you. Nick told me what you were going through with Iris missing, so I flew into town because I wanted to help."

"Go on," I said, becoming increasingly suspicious, and feeling that my confusion was clearing up with every word she spoke.

"I came in the door, and you thought I was Iris. And I -"

"Pretended to be her," I finished.

"Yes."

I just stared at her for a few minutes. Then said "well, Nat, looks like you got your fucking wish." Then I looked away.

"Ryan, I'm so sorry. You made love to me thinking I was Iris."

"I know exactly what happened now. I finally got some sleep, because I thought Iris had come home. Now my mind is totally clear, and I can't believe that you would pull a stunt like that. On top of it all, Iris is still missing." Natalie was shaking a little, pulling on the ends of her hair, and examining it carefully. "That's why I said you finally got your fucking wish."

"I know," she said. "But I do love you, Ryan. I love you so much, I can't stand it."

"Go home, Nat. Go home to your husband. Get out and leave me alone, and never, ever, say a word about this to anybody. Do you understand?"

She started crying, and hung her head. "I'll see what flights I can catch, but, since this is Sunday, there might not be much available."

Wait, Sunday? Sunday? I asked Nat "how is it Sunday? How long have I been asleep?"

"For over a day," she said. "You've been asleep about 30 hours. I was about to call the ambulance, if you didn't wake up soon."

"30 hours. I haven't slept in more than a week, which is why I was hallucinating. And I hit my head." I shook my head. "You completely took advantage of my mental state. I just can't believe you would do something like this."

She was crying again. "Why can't it be me? What's so wrong with me?"

"Nat, nothing's wrong with you. You're beautiful, you're bright, and you're sweet. But you're not Iris."

"I loved you for years before you met Iris," she said.

"I know," I said. "Bad timing, I guess."

Then I sat down again on the bar, and put my head in my hands. When was Iris going to come home for real? Where was she? Did Rochelle get to her? She said she didn't, and I believed her, but was I being naïve? What happened to Andrew?

Then Nat said, as if it just dawned on her, "you hit your head? Oh, shit. When did that happen?"

"Sometime. I'm not sure. I fell in the shower because of my exhaustion, and knocked myself out. All I remember was that I was talking to my father, but he looked weird. Then you came in, and I thought you were her."

"I better get you to the ER right away."

At that, Natalie drove me to the nearest hospital so that I could get checked out. The doctor finally saw me after about two hours in the waiting room, and gave me a neurological exam, including a CAT scan. He announced what I already knew – I had suffered a severe concussion when I smacked my head, and that, combined with severe sleep deprivation, is what caused me to hallucinate.

"Are you still having the hallucinations?" the doctor asked me.

"No. My memory issues have resolved as well."

"There probably is not any reason for further treatment, then. Just monitor your symptoms, and come back in if you start suffering severe headaches, more hallucinations, memory lapses, nausea or vomiting, dizziness, vision problems, slurred speech, confusion or clumsiness. We can't be too careful," the doctor said, handing me a brochure on concussions. "It sounds like you also hallucinated because of severe sleep deprivation. Five days without any sleep can cause a variety of neurological impairments. It is somewhat unusual to hallucinate, even after a lack of sleep and a concussion, but not unheard of. Especially since the two risk factors were combined."

"Thanks," I said.

On the way home, I laid into Natalie again. "Natalie, first of all, thanks for taking me to the hospital. I want to get that out of the way. Now I have to ask – what the fuck were you thinking? You completely took advantage of my mental state."

"I told you, I love you. I don't know. You thought I was her, and I...well, I had to feel you inside of me again. I've never gotten over that feeling of having you inside of me. I'm ashamed of what I did, but it was almost worth it to have that feeling again."

"As I said, Nat, not a goddamned word about this. Not to Nate, not to Nick, not to Alexis, and certainly never to Iris. Got that? You breathe a word, and I will never speak to you again. Ever. We clear?"

She nodded her head, tears spilling down her cheeks. "I just want you to love me, that's all."

"I have to be blunt here. You're a good friend. Like a sister. Nothing more. I know that we used to be friends with benefits back in the day, but that can't happen anymore. I'm married to my soul mate. I'm sorry if that's an inconvenient truth, but there we are. Now you have to get on my plane and go home."

I sent Nat on her way, putting her on my private plane, so that she couldn't use the excuse that she was unable to find a flight home on such short notice.

Then stayed awake all that night.

I got into work the next day, and put on my acting face once more.

Around five, I was working away, trying to focus and throw myself into my projects, when my secretary informed me that I had a call from a Cindy Johnson.

I groaned. Cindy was the prosecutor for Rochelle's case, and she no doubt was looking for Iris to ask her some questions prior to Rochelle's trial as a part of the discovery process.

"Ryan Gallagher," I spoke into the phone.

"Hello, this is Cindy Johnson. I've been trying to get in touch with Iris because I need to talk to her about the Rochelle Anderson case."

"Actually, Ms. Johnson, Iris is missing," I said in as professional tone as I could possibly muster.

"I don't understand?"

"I haven't seen or talked to my wife for over two weeks now." Just saying the words made me die inside, but I had on my actor persona again, and I was sure that I was coming off cold.

"Over two weeks? That's about when I spoke with her."

Chapter Twenty

I was stunned when Cindy Johnson informed me that she had spoken to my wife. "What? What do you mean?" I asked her anxiously.

"She called me and negotiated a plea deal with me a little over two weeks ago. I haven't been able to get ahold of her since, and I need to ask her some important questions before I depose Ms. Anderson."

"A plea deal. With whom?"

"His name is Shaun Jefferson. It was a plea deal on a drug case."

"Where does Shaun Jefferson live?"

"Just a second," she said. "2615 Montgall Ave., KCMO."

"Thanks," I said, "I'll have Iris call you as soon as I see her."

After getting off the phone with her, I immediately bolted out the door, and headed down to 2615 Montgall Ave.

I got to the house, which was a shirt-waist house in the

run-down area of town. The other cars that were parked on the street were older-model cars, most with hubcaps missing and sporting various dents. I knew my Porsche was probably not safe here, but I figured that if I was jacked or rolled, I could always call Daniel to come and get me.

I approached the creaky porch, and knocked on the door.

A pale blonde-headed boy of about 22 answered the door, and just looked at me expectantly.

"I'm looking for Shaun Jefferson," I said.

"That's me," the boy said. Then he looked at my car, and looked back at me. "You a cop or a dealer?"

"Neither. I'm looking for my wife, Iris Gallagher," I said, holding up her picture on my phone.

His face lit up in recognition. "Ah, yeah. Yeah. She's real cool."

My heart started pounding. "Where is she?"

"I dunno. I met her when she knocked on this door. She said she was an attorney and she could get me out of a drug charge if I gave her, uh, money."

"Did you give her money?"

"Yeah. She worked a good deal for me, so it was worth every penny."

"Where is she now?"

"Shit. You better not be a cop."

"I'm not. Where did she go?"

"There's a house up the street. It's abandoned. Not sure of the address."

"Where? Exactly where?" I tried to contain my excitement, although I could feel myself breathing heavily, and my heart was pounding a mile a minute.

"Three houses up, on this side of the road. It's a big old house, like this one. It's been taken over by squatters."

"Thank you," I said, feeling like kissing him.

Then I ran up to the house to which he was referring, and tried the door. The door wasn't locked, so I walked in and looked around.

There were no lights, and, this being wintertime, it was almost pitch black outside, even though it was only around 5:30, so I could see very little. A cat came up to me and rubbed on my leg, purring loudly.

Somebody turned a flashlight on me.

"Who are you?" that person asked, then brought out a pistol and held it up to my face.

I put up my hands, and looked around, my eyes adjusting to the dark. There were people everywhere, in corners asleep. Some of them were not asleep, but were holding their arms and staring into space. A few were crashed out in sleeping bags in the middle of the floor. Somebody had a boom box, and the strains of Beethoven's *7th Symphony* was wafting through the air.

Good taste.

Nobody paid attention to me except the guy who held the flashlight and gun up to me.

I started feeling the shivers of familiarity, knowing that I was once one of these people, even if I never actually lived in an abandoned house. I wanted to get out of there because the temptation to use was still strong.

But I had to get Iris out of there first.

"I'm Ryan Gallagher. I'm looking for my wife," I said, holding up my cell phone and showing him her picture.

"She's here. She's upstairs," he said, motioning to the ancient staircase.

My heart leapt with joy at the thought of being so close to my beautiful Iris. I could barely contain my excitement as I hurried to the staircase.

However, flashlight boy beat me to the staircase, and stood in front of it, crossing his arms. "You look like a rich boy," he said.

"I am a very rich boy. What do you want?"

"That looks like a Rolex," he observed, looking at my watch.

At that, I took it off and gave it to him.

"Thanks," he said. "Lemme see your wallet."

I gave him my wallet, which had about a thousand dollars in it, which is the amount I usually carry with me. "Take it all," I said. "Just let me find my wife."

"Thanks," he said, taking out all the money out of my wallet. "Follow me," he said.

I followed him up the creaky stairs, with him leading the way with his flashlight. He went into the second bedroom, with me following closely behind, then flashed his lights into the figures lying down in the room. There was about six people in this room, some of them sleeping on the floor, others sleeping upright. As with the people downstairs, none of them reacted to our presence or to the light.

My pulse quickened as he shined the light on an alabaster-skinned red-haired girl who I barely recognized. She was dressed in oversized sweats that went well past her ankles, and a man's t-shirt. Like everybody else in the room, she had a vacant stare. Her hair appeared that it hadn't been combed in two weeks, and she apparently hadn't bathed in that time, either. She was extremely skinny, and, when the guy shined his light on her arms, I could see track marks on her skin.

I felt tears running down my cheeks.

I had found Iris at last.

Chapter Twenty-One

I walked over to Iris. She looked at me with her dead eyes, and I gently picked her up off the floor. She was limp, like a rag doll, and I couldn't get her to hold on to my neck. She just lay in my arms, her head swinging as I walked, so I slung her over my shoulder, my hands wrapped around her legs. I could feel her arms and head on my back.

As I approached the staircase, I knew this would be tricky at best. Flashlight boy illuminated the staircase, but it was narrow, the stairs were very steep, and I was extremely nervous about falling with Iris in my arms. I sat down at the top of the stairs, and gently set Iris down next to me. She went limp on my lap. I gently stroked her hair while I tried to think of what to do. I knew she couldn't walk - she was way too high. Since this was December, the sky was pitch black outside, as was this house. There was no way I could make my way down this staircase safely, with Iris in my arms.

Flashlight boy was standing at the bottom of the steps, looking at me expectantly. "You coming or not?" he asked.

I gently tried the railing to see if it was solid. It was unstable and threatened to give way if I were to lean on it. So, bracing myself on the railing while taking Iris down the stairs was out of the question. Maybe flashlight boy could help me? Nah, he was probably high, and I didn't trust him not to drop her.

I sighed and said to flashlight boy "I better not. The staircase is too dark. I'll just have to stay here until it is light."

"Suit yourself," flashlight boy said. "You can sleep on one of the beds in that first bedroom. Nobody will bother you."

"Thank you," I said, carrying Iris into the first bedroom. There was a single bed up against a wall, with very thin sheets and a tattered pillow. I was wearing a heavy coat, and I knew that Iris wasn't feeling the cold now, but might be by the time it was light outside. So, I took off my coat, and put it on her, and gently lay her down on the bed. The bed was more like a cot, with a light mattress and no box spring, on a rickety metal frame. I lay down with her on the bed, covering her with my body and stroking her hair.

She was unresponsive.

I knew there was a very slim chance that my car would still be out front in the morning, so I called Daniel and asked if he could be on standby to come and pick us up.

"Sure," he said. "But what are you doing in that neighborhood in the first place?"

"I'll explain later," I said.

Then I fell asleep, holding Iris in my arms.

Even though I was on a flimsy cot, in the middle of a dilapidated house without heat, I felt comfortable and safe for the first time in over two weeks.

I slept better that night than I had since Iris went missing.

When I woke up, Iris was apparently coming down. She was twitching violently, and I saw goose pimples on her flesh. She was also visibly shivering. Her head was shaking and twitching, over and over. She looked at me and appeared not to recognize me.

However, it was now light, so I felt more confident taking her down the stairs.

This time, however, when I picked her up, she was able to put her arms around my neck. I could feel her entire body convulsing, which also made me nervous with regards to our flight down the stairs, but I knew that I had to get her out of there and get her into a hospital as soon as possible. I took a deep breath, and negotiated the stairs carefully, taking each step one at a time. When I got to the bottom step, and the floor below, I let out a sigh of relief.

Flashlight boy was nowhere to be seen, but I did see other people lying around, and some were starting to twitch like Iris.

I walked out the door with Iris in my arms. She was twitching violently and shivering. To my surprise and delight, my Porsche was still out front. When I laid Iris on the passenger's side seat, I discovered the interior was intact, much to my further surprise and delight. I honestly thought the interior would be stripped of the GPS and satellite radio, but that was not the case.

Then I drove Iris towards St. Joseph's Hospital, which was a hospital across town, and was the hospital where Iris lay for months in a coma.

Oh, Iris, what drove you to this? I knew she was in real trouble, and I was right, but the question was why? Why would she go off the grid like this and live among the junkies? Iris was never a drug abuser. Never a drug abuser.

But she was shot up with black tar heroin. That made her more susceptible to doing something like this. She seemed fine. She recovered from that. She moved past that. I thought she was safe. I never, in my wildest dreams, could imagine that she would do something like this.

Why?

Next to me, Iris was now twitching violently, her entire body and head going into what looked like convulsions. I thought about taking her to a closer hospital, but the closest hospital was one I didn't trust to give her the best care. And I knew that what she was going through right now were the normal symptoms of coming down off a powerful heroin high.

My heart broke with every twitch and every shiver. I was kicking myself for not being more prepared with a heavy blanket for her. I was coming down in this area looking for her. I should've known this was a possibility. Why didn't I bring a blanket? The heat in the car was turned up as high as it could go. This made me feel uncomfortably warm, but she was all that mattered right now. Her comfort was all I was thinking about. I knew the cold was coming from within, that nothing I did would make her warm, but that knowledge didn't stop me from beating myself up about not being more prepared.

I finally got to the hospital and checked her in.

Only to be informed there would be a 9-hour wait for an available bed.

Screw it. We could be in Los Angeles in a little over three hours, and she could be checked into the best facility in the country. But could she fly in this condition? At least here, she could have an Emergency Room bed, and they could give her fluids and monitor her vitals.

I could fly her out to LA once she is stabilized.

So, Iris was given an ER bed, and they hooked her up to a saline tank and gave her methadone to help ease her withdrawal symptoms. I sat next to her, holding her hand. I stroked her hair and talked to her soothingly. She probably was aware of my presence, even if she couldn't show it.

"There, there, my beautiful girl. You're back safe, if not sound. And I love you, and will never leave you again." I bowed my head, realizing that there would be yet another long leave of absence from my job, as I helped Iris recover from this.

I started to reconsider even being there at all. What harm would there be if I simply became a trust fund baby, and spent all my time with my lovely wife?

I answered my own question - the harm would be that I would be leaving a job I was good at. I had the business acumen of my father, without the cold-blooded ruthlessness. I was able to finesse negotiations, like the one in Tokyo, and that made me valuable.

At the same time, perhaps it was time to move on. There wasn't a reason why I should be working for somebody else. I could buy my own company, start it from the ground up. I could choose passion projects, something that could do some real good in the world, as opposed to simply acquiring pieces of silver.

I called my job and told them what happened. They understood, of course. They really didn't want to lose me. They told me to take all the time that I needed.

Inwardly, though, I knew. I knew that it was time to move on. When Iris gets better, I could make my next move in life, and it should be something that would include her.

Opening up an animal sanctuary was something that I could do, and we could do it together. When she gets well, I will bring this up to her.

But, for right now, her getting better is what was most important. Period.

Chapter Twenty-Two

IRIS

I was laying down at the bus stop, waiting for a bus to pick me up and take me to parts unknown. My mind was a blank, except for focusing on how I could get away from what happened to me in that house. I couldn't go back into that house. But my thoughts were jumbled, incoherent. They didn't make much sense, even to myself. I didn't have a plan, I only knew I had to get away.

And yet...there was a vague memory in my brain. The memory that was in my cells of a euphoric sensation that I had never experienced before or since. The mental and physical pain that I was experiencing right then was excruciating, worse than anything I'd ever experienced.

I was desperate to get back to that euphoria.

The euphoria I was remembering was the feeling after Rochelle shot me up with all that heroin. That was what I needed right then. Euphoria.

Which gave me a plan. I needed to find a drug house so that somebody could give me what I started to desperately crave. The voice inside my head was at top decibel now, telling me that I somehow deserved what just happened to me. That I really never did escape my misfit situation, I just got into a new one. And all I could think about was the feeling of the belt tightening around my neck, and the threats that every protest, every kick, and every scream would result in death for me, as that man would strangle me and leave my body right there in the kitchen.

And the physical pain was more than I could bear.

But I really didn't know exactly where to go to get some drugs that would help me ease my extreme mental and physical pain. I knew that I was very naïve about all of that, never having been in that world. I just figured that I would be able to go to the seedy part of town and go on a street corner and find somebody who would deal to me.

That wasn't going to work.

I could go to a rape crisis center. But they might expect me to tell them who did this to me. It was a retired government assassin. I wouldn't last two minutes in this world if I ever breathed a word about him.

And Ryan...lovely Ryan. He wasn't here. I couldn't rely on him to fix me this time. Besides, this was his fault. I told him a million times that I didn't want a bodyguard, but did he listen? If he just would've listened to me, this never would've happened.

I just needed to get away. I needed to find a way to get back to that extreme euphoria that I experienced before. My cells had memory. They remembered what it felt like to float above the world, as if I were in heaven. I had to stop my physical and emotional pain, otherwise I simply didn't know what I would do to myself. I knew what I was capable of when I was experiencing extreme emotional pain – I was capable of hurting myself so badly that I was at the point of death. Now I had something to really give me pain, and I didn't want to go down that road again.

I lay at that bus stop until the sun came up and the bus came around to pick me up and take me downtown. I had actually formulated a plan in my head for how I could find some drugs. It was such a simple plan it was genius.

I simply had to find out the names of people being charged with drug distribution.

So I decided to sit in on some initial appearances, which were the first appearances that defendants have in court, where the judge reads them their charges.

I needed to find some addresses of drug dealers.

I entered the courtroom. I didn't even think about how I looked. In reality, I was dressed in Hello Kitty pajama bottoms and a t-shirt, and my winter outer-wear, not bothering to change after my...attack. I couldn't bring myself to say the R word, even in my head. It was simply an attack, like what happened to me with Rochelle.

Every time I started to think about how I was sexually violated, a huge swell of panic threatened to engulf me.

I went right up to the prosecutor and asked to see his files.

"Iris," the prosecutor, Randy Davis, said to me. "You, uh...how've you been?"

"Fine," I lied. "Listen, I have a client on your drug docket here. You're doing the initials for the drug docket, right?"

"Yes," he said, still looking at me strangely. "Did you just get out of bed?"

I wondered why he was asking that. I wasn't thinking about my attire. I was only thinking about how I could score a name from this guy.

Then he said "I didn't think that you were practicing anymore."

"I'm not. But I got a name from somebody. I didn't want to be completely out of practice."

"What's the name?"

"Oh, shoot," I said. Then pulling a first name out of a hat, I said "his name is Shaun. That's his first name. I can't for the life of me remember his last name. I'm so sorry."

He looked at me skeptically, then reviewed his files. I prayed that there was somebody with the first name of Shaun in there.

He handed me a file. "Here. Shaun Jefferson. Is that the guy?"

"Yes, yes. That's him," I said. "What's he charged with?"

"Possession with intent to distribute. First offense."

"Thanks."

"You gonna represent him in your pajamas?"

"Well, I'm going to represent him. But I'll let the public defender handle the initial appearance."

"Yeah. Looks like you probably better go back to bed."

I smiled, not even feeling humiliated. After what happened to me on the kitchen floor, nothing could touch me.

I took the file, making sure that Shaun didn't already have a private attorney, then borrowed a pen and wrote the address for Shaun Jefferson on my hand. Then gave the file back to Randy. "Thanks, Randy."

"Yeah. You take care of yourself, Iris. No offense, but you're not looking so good."

"Filter, much?" I said.

"I call them as I see them. Get in touch with Cindy, she's the prosecutor for this case."

"Thanks, I will."

Then I went out the door to catch another bus that would take me to the neighborhood of one Shaun Jefferson.

Chapter Twenty-Three

The bus dropped me off within a few blocks of Shaun Jefferson's home. I knew that it was a first offense for him, so he was probably out on bail, if there even was a bond for him. He probably had a signature bond, which meant that all he had to do was sign his name and an oath that he would appear for his court appearance.

I waited around after having been dropped off. Shaun wouldn't be at his home just yet. He would be in court, at his initial appearance. Those dockets sometimes take hours, so I hoped that wouldn't be the case today.

I walked around the neighborhood in a daze. I only could think about getting ahold of some drugs, some way to ease the pain I was feeling.

The neighborhood was not one that I had ever really been in, although I had hung out in similar neighborhoods when I was a kid. My aunt used to live around here somewhere. We used to visit her back in the day. Some evenings we held séances, trying to contact the spirit of the dead guy who used to live in that house. Other times, I would wander around the neighborhood with my cousin Lynn. One time, we were gone the entire day, but never told anybody where we were going. We walked all the way to the Hyatt Regency, riding the glass elevators up and down, and generally making trouble. When we arrived back home after several hours of being "missing," my mother was frantic and had almost called the police. She was like that, anyhow, but, to be fair, two young girls alone in this rough neighborhood, just wandering around – I didn't blame her for being panicky. I would've been as well.

This was the sort of neighborhood where many of the houses were boarded up, and the ones that weren't had overgrown weeds in front of them, and cars that were on blocks. There were very few vehicles that didn't have some type of major dent, and also very few cars that were newer than 2000.

Most of the houses were bounded by a front fence, and behind many of these fences were ferocious-looking dogs. A house in this neighborhood could be bought for under $15,000, and these homes were pretty large, considering their price. Most of them were shirtwaist, a particular style of Kansas City home. Popular around the turn of the century, the shirtwaist was characterized by a first floor made of brick or stone, and the second floor made of siding, wood shingles or stucco. These homes had two and a half stories, which means that the first and second floor were typical box-style, and the third level is more of an A-frame style, with slanted ceilings and picture windows. A shirtwaist could be a beautiful old home, with bay windows, a well-constructed stone porch, and lots of room. That is, if the home is well-kept. These homes were not. Most of them had stripped siding, roofs with holes, and crumbling foundations.

I wandered around this neighborhood for a couple of hours, looking at all the houses, saying hello to the barking dogs that abounded, and encountering more than a few friendly people sitting on their porch and drinking.

I stayed around in that neighborhood because I was determined to find some drugs. I found that, while I was concentrating so hard on finding some drugs, I was able to put the incident behind me. Still, it was bubbling just below the surface, along with the Rochelle attack not nine months ago. It was threatening to overwhelm me, but I fought it down as I finally, after several hours of walking around, approached the house where Shaun lived.

I knocked on the door.

A thin blonde kid answered the door.

"Hello," I said, not really sure how to approach this perfect stranger to ask him if he had any drugs available.

"Yeah," he said. "What's up?"

I suddenly realized that my appearance would help me in talking to Shaun. I probably looked the part of a druggie looking for a fix.

"You're Shaun Jefferson?"

"Who's asking?"

"My name is Iris," I said, then decided that I would just be honest and let the chips fall where they may. "I need drugs."

"Who sent you here?"

"Actually, I'm an attorney, believe it or not."

He stood there looking at me with a very puzzled expression, apparently trying to decide if I was there to trap him, or if I really was an attorney who just randomly showed up at his house, asking for drugs.

Finally he said "come on in."

I went into the house. The furniture was second-hand

and run down, and the house had a musty smell to it. There was a Barcalounger with several holes in the seat cushion, and the sofa was not on legs, but was resting on the floor. Nothing matched – the Barcalounger, which was probably left out on the curb by somebody, was a dark red, and the couch on the floor was an old-lady gold with old-lady patterns. There were not any curtains up – instead, there were bed sheets held up with thumb tacks. There were several cats running around, and two of them were friendly and greeted me. The rest scurried like roaches away from light. There was a rickety card table that apparently served as a dining room set, with four folding lawn chairs around it. On the table was a roach and a pipe, and a baggie that evidently contained pot. The hardwood floors had seen better days, and were probably original, which meant the floor was more than 100 years old, which was about the age of the house.

There was also a 72" plasma screen on one of the walls, which was probably worth more than the entire house and all the contents in it.

Shaun motioned for me to sit down, and I did so, on the couch.

"What you looking for?" he asked.

"Horse," I said.

He nodded.

"How much?" I asked, then realized I didn't have a single penny on me, after using all my money on the bus fare. I had my debit card for one of the bank accounts in my wallet, which was in my pajama pocket, along with my red diamond engagement ring, and my simple gold wedding band. But no way would I take money out of the bank. That wasn't my money, as far as I was concerned, and I certainly wasn't going to use Ryan's money for this.

"$1,500 for a gram." Then he looked at me. "That'll last you awhile."

"I don't have any money," I said. "Can we do a trade?"

"No offense, but I'm gay," he said. "You can work off some with my roommate, though. He'll be home around 7 tonight."

"No, no, no," I said, shaking my head. "Not that kind of trade."

"Sorry. What were you talking about?"

"You need an attorney, right?"

"Sure. But you don't look like an attorney."

At that, I brought out my wallet from my coat pocket, and showed him my driver's license and Missouri Bar ID.

"Ok," he said. "What kind of a deal can you get me?"

"First offense...drug court maybe."

"No drug court. I'm not going to bother with shit."

"Ok, then, an SIS." "SIS" meant suspended imposition of sentence, which basically meant probation without a record if the probation is completed without incident.

"SIS? Really?"

"Yeah. I'm good friends with the prosecutor." This wasn't entirely a lie, as Cindy was a friend. A good friend she really wasn't, but we had been known to hang out some before I met Ryan.

He looked skeptical. "How much you charge for that?"

"$3,000," I said. "So, you can give me a gram and another $1,500 in cash, and we can call it even."

He nodded his head. "That sounds like the best deal I've heard all day. I was calling around, and everybody was quoting me $5,000 on up." He looked at me skeptically one more time then said "wait right here."

I continued to sit on the couch, and a black and white cat leaped on my lap and started purring. There was something buried in the back of my mind that was setting off alarm bells upon seeing the cat, but I quickly hushed that voice and waited for Shaun to reappear.

He came back with a bag of white powder with him and a roll of cash.

I looked at the white powder in the bag, not really knowing what to do with it. I seemed to remember something about a melting it on a spoon. At least, that was how I seen them do it in the movies.

"Thanks, Shaun," I said. "I'll give Cindy a call and I'll let you know." At that, I asked to borrow his phone, and I called Cindy right there for him.

Cindy answered the phone. "Cindy Johnson," she said.

"Hi, this is Iris Snowe, uh Gallagher," I said.

"Iris? This is a surprise. I didn't know you were still practicing."

"Well, I have a drug client," I said. "Could you work a plea over the phone?"

"What's his name?"

"Shaun Jefferson. First offense."

"Hang on. He had his initial this morning."

"I know."

"The file's right here." She was quiet for a few minutes. "No priors. Go 3 year SIS."

"Let me call you back," I said and hung up.

"What did she say?"

"3 year SIS."

"What does that mean?"

"You're on probation for 3 years. You walk down your probation, you have a clean record. You mess up, and get revoked, you can face up to 10 years in prison. However, what probably would happen is that the first time you get revoked, you probably would get what's called an SES.

That's probation, still, but it carries with it a felony record."

"SIS means no record, right?"

"Sure. If you walk it down."

"In other words..."

"Watch your ass," I said. "I can't put it any plainer than that, because I know you're going to go on dealing. Just get better at it."

"Ok," he said. "When do I plead?"

"I can schedule one on the next docket," I said.

Crap! I had no clothes to wear. This entire scenario was becoming more and more complicated. I also didn't have good transportation.

Then I remembered an attorney who owed me a "cover," which is when one attorney shows up for another one. I called him, after calling Cindy back to schedule the plea, and he agreed to cover for me on the plea docket for Shaun.

Then I took a deep breath and looked again at the package of white powder. I saw salvation in that package. I saw euphoria and a way to forget all that had happened to me in the last year between Rochelle and...that man. That bad man. Who attacked me. Not raped me. Attacked me.

"Do you know how to do this?" he asked.

I shook my head.

"Here," he said, taking out a spoon, then putting a dab of the white powder on the utensil. Then he put a lighter under the spoon, and the powder liquefied. Then he showed me a syringe, and showed me how to put the liquefied substance into the syringe.

I nodded my head. "That's what I thought. Thanks for the demonstration. And thanks for everything."

"Do you have a place to go?" he asked.

I shook my head.

"I would offer you to stay here, but..."

"No, that's ok. I don't want to put you out."

"I was going to say there is a place you can stay. It's two houses up. There's lots of people there, and they're pretty cool."

"It's a drug house?"

"Yeah."

And that was how I ended up at the drug house with my drugs and a small wad of cash. I honestly planned to live there and never go home. The forgetfulness that this house offered me sounded just like heaven.

Chapter Twenty-Four

After talking to Shaun, I went up to the house he told me about. I was very careful to put my red diamond in my underwear, along with the wad of cash and my simple wedding ring. I hoped that, at the very least, the red diamond and the band would be safe there.

There was still a large part of me that would be beyond devastated to lose these treasures.

The house was a shirt-waist, like Shaun's house, but it had boarded-up windows. I doubted that it had electricity. Still, I felt that I had no choice but to stay here for the time being. I didn't know anyplace else that I could safely do what I was about to do.

I knocked on the door, but nobody answered. Then I opened the door.

I immediately felt uncomfortable. This was all so foreign to me. The ironic thing was that, between Ryan and me, I was the one who grew up broke, and Ryan was the one who grew up privileged. Yet Ryan would, no doubt, feel much more comfortable in this setting than I ever would.

A guy with dreadlocks looked at me. He was a white guy, ghostly pale, very slight frame, wearing a Green Day T-Shirt that was full of holes, as were his jeans. He was also wearing a heavy coat, gloves and a hat. He was one of only three conscious people in this enormous house. The others were lying in sleeping bags, or sitting on the floor, holding their arms with a vacant expression on their face. Two guys were sitting back to back, both of them unconscious. A guy in the corner was injecting himself. Another guy was eating a sandwich from his position on the floor.

The dreadlocks guy spoke. "Who are you?" Then he looked me up and down. "You don't look like a cop, but you never know anymore. Those undercover cats can look pretty good these days."

Should I give them my real name? Sure, what the hell. "Iris. Iris Gallagher. And yours?"

Still looking slightly suspicious, the dreadlocked kid held out his hand "Brad. Brad White. Now, why are you here?"

"Shaun sent me from down the street. He said that I could, uh, maybe stay here for awhile."

Brad narrowed his eyes. "Let me see those arms. You don't look like a junkie."

"I'm not. At least not yet," I said, showing him my arms.

"Then why are you here?"

"I...something happened to me. Well, a few things have happened to me. And I need some way to forget them for awhile."

He nodded. "Sounds like a familiar story." Then he motioned his hand in a sweeping motion. "You can stay here for as long as you need. There's no electricity here, and no running water. But we got a guy bringing us food every few days and soda from the 7-11 around the corner."

"I hate to ask this, but—"

"Where do we do our business?" He apparently was trying to be at least somewhat delicate to my sensibilities.

I nodded.

"Well, let's just say that after a little while you're not going to care about that, and leave it at that."

"Meaning?"

"Come here," he said, taking my hand. He led me up the creaky stairs, which included a missing stair, and into a room with a closed door. There were several newspapers stuffed into the crack underneath the door. Then he opened the door, and I almost fled right then and there. There were newspapers on the floor, and, on these newspapers, was where the people in the house did their business.

I looked at him and asked "how does this get cleaned up?"

"We have designated people to do this every day. You get to earn drugs that way, so it is actually a popular job, believe it or not."

"And the food runner, what does that entail?"

"We take turns doing that. Sometimes the food comes from the convenience store, other times the person dumpster dives. It doesn't really matter. If you're hungry, you eat it. If you're high, you don't care about it. Sometimes the dumpster dive is pretty good shit, though. Jackson over here," he said, motioning to an unconscious young black guy with a bald head, sunglasses, low slung jeans and baseball t-shirt, "gets some good shit. He takes the bus over to a pizza joint a couple of miles away on a Wednesday, and finds about five pies in the dumpster behind the place. Wednesdays are good around here," he said, rubbing his slender belly.

I nodded, already looking forward to Wednesday. What

day was this? Monday. Two more days until pizza day. That is assuming that young Jackson climbs out of his present stupor to get the promised pizzas. Then I asked "I notice that you seem to be the only person around here who is conscious. How does that work?"

"In this house, there is always one person who agrees to not get high on a designated day. My day is Monday. Penny over there," he said, motioning to a slight blonde girl in a t-shirt dress under a heavy coat, "is Tuesday. Jackson is Wednesday. Etc. We always have to have somebody around with their wits, in case the cops come, or there's an emergency, or something like that."

"I guess if I stay here, I'll get a designated day, too, huh?"

"Sure. We may be a bunch of junkies, but we also have a kind cooperative society around here."

I took a deep breath, then looked at the white powder in my little baggie. How much should I use? How do I find a vein? The only drug that I had ever done was pot and, once, mushrooms. I looked over at Brad, who was eyeing me with an interested expression, while he munched on a bag of potato chips.

"First food I've eaten in three days," he said. "You look like you might need some help."

"I do," I said, fighting back tears. "I've never done this before."

"Ok. Let's see, you're, what, a buck oh five, buck ten?"

"Somewhere around there."

"Here, let me fill the syringe for you." At that, he put a tiny dab on the spoon and lit it, just like Shaun had showed me. Then he filled the syringe to the right CC level. "Look here," he said, taking out a sharpie and making a tiny black line.

"This is how much you need to do. Anymore than that, and you might have problems. Any less, then you might not get a very good high. It's like Goldilocks – you gotta get it just right."

Then, he brought out the rubber tourniquet and tied my arm off with it. I started to feel panicky upon feeling the tourniquet on my arm, as the memories of Rochelle and her attack started to flood my brain. I fought it down, though.

Brad said "here, feel your vein." I did, putting my finger into the position where his finger was. "Ok, now, you get your needle, and stick yourself right there." I did so. "Now, push down the plunger."

I felt nauseated and terrified, but I did as I was told.

At first I didn't feel a thing. But then, after a few seconds....there were no words. I had never in my life felt this way. Rochelle and the bad man receded into the background. It was paradise. I literally hadn't a care in the world. I had the most vivid dreams about myself and Ryan. He was here with me, and nothing bad had happened at all to me, nor to him. We were perfect, whole and happy. So happy. So very happy....

I had no idea how long I was in this state of bliss, but it was better than anything that I had ever felt before. Well, maybe not better than making love with Ryan, but it was the equivalent.

But when I started to crash, it was horrible. Sometimes I got hot, so hot that I walked out into the December air and stood outside, and was still burning up. I walked up and down the streets with no coat or hat, still in my Hello Kitty pajamas and tank top. I even had taken off my shoes. I wanted so much to take an ice cold bath, but the house didn't have running water. I was halfway tempted to go and pay Shaun another visit, and ask him if I could take a cold bath there.

Other times there were shakes and chills. Suddenly, there was no way for me to get warm. I piled my coat, hat and gloves on, and stood by the stove, which was woodburning. I would stand by that stove for hours, not feeling the heat at all. I was still chilled to the bone.

Then came the violent twitches, pounding headache, nausea and vomiting.

All this was cured with another hit, though, and paradise began anew.

I did this for days, and didn't think anything of it, because everybody around me was doing the same. They were all going through the same thing.

I started to get to know some of the people also staying at the house. Jackson, I learned, was a performing arts college grad who once performed on Broadway. He was a music major at a prestigious college, so he always had a radio with him that played his classical music CDs. Nobody seemed to mind, and it was relaxing to hear Vivaldi and Rachmaninoff, to tell the honest truth.

It sure as hell beat rap.

Penny was a girl who grew up much like Ryan, with a silver spoon in her mouth. From what I could tell, she did drugs for much the same reason Ryan did them – to forget about some serious sexual trauma in her youth, perpetrated at the hands of her father. She left home at age 14, same as Ryan, but didn't have a benevolent mentor like Ryan. Instead, she started living on the streets, prostituting herself and getting high. At age 25, she looked around 50. She told me that she had been living at this house for six months after having been thrown out of her last home by her pimp.

There were several others who lived there as well. There

was Lakisha, a thirty-something black girl who was the sometime girlfriend of Brad. There was Terry, a former computer geek. He graduated from a tech school and went to work in Silicon Valley in California before his drug habit got the best of him. There were also various transient people who came in and out, sometimes when I was conscious. Other times, I would wake up and they were just there.

At some point, I needed a change of clothes, because I was getting ripe. A nice guy with extra pairs of sweats and t-shirts gave me one of his pairs of sweats and one of his t-shirts, and I put them on. "You didn't come prepared, didya, little one?" he said. To this, I merely shook my head. I changed in another room, being very careful about the rings in my underwear. Those rings were my connection to my real world, which was frightening. But, they were also my connection to Ryan, and this made me feel elated and depressed all at once.

There was a nagging voice that told me I needed to call him, but I couldn't bring myself to do so.

I also wasn't thinking about what would happen when that gram was used up. I didn't want to face it.

I ate and drank water when the designated runner brought food and soda from the convenience store down the street, which was every few days. As promised, Jackson brought pizza on Wednesday, but I was unconscious that day. When I came to, on Friday, all the pizza was gone. So, I didn't eat much, nor did I want to.

All I wanted was on this spoon.

Then, one night, to my absolute horror, Ryan appeared. My mind knew what was happening. My body couldn't react, though. My mind was somewhere else, but I was vaguely aware that he was picking me up and slinging me over his shoulder. Then he put me down on the floor next to him. Then I was being picked up and put into a bed, a heavy coat being draped over me. Then his body was covering mine on the rickety cot. Then it was morning, and I was once again being picked up and carried down the stairs and into his Porsche. By then, I was more conscious about what was going on, but the twitches, chills and shakes were starting, and I was in serious need of another fix. My mind started to get desperate as I realized that a fix was not going to be coming now that Ryan had found me.

How did he find me? I was trying not to be found. I didn't want reality. He was going to take me back there, where the bad man...attacked me. Inside my head, I was screaming, I was freezing, and I was feeling ready to puke. And I couldn't quit twitching. The car was making me more and more sick.

Please, please, please Ryan, just give me what I need. I'll do anything, just give me what I need.

But I couldn't talk. I just kept twitching, and panicking.

Then I was in a hospital bed, an IV in my arm. I could feel myself convulsing on the bed, and Ryan's hand on my hair, stroking it as he was talking to me.

On and on and on it went, for days. I shivered, convulsed, and shook, and was transferred to the drug floor as soon as a bed opened, then shivered, convulsed and shook there. My head was splitting, my ears ringing, and the feeling of dry heaves was constant. I had nothing in my stomach, so dry heaves was all there was. I felt like I was dying. I wanted to die. Anything would be better than this. Burn me at the stake, boil me in oil, bury me alive. Anything would be preferable to this.

Finally, after days of the constant feeling that I wanted to die, I was able to sleep.

Then I came to, apparently days later, although it seemed like only minutes. Ryan was sitting by the bed.

He took my hand. "Hello, beautiful."

I looked at him, then looked away, feeling more than ashamed. I suddenly realized that I was now going to have to face what happened to me on the kitchen floor.

I couldn't possibly get away from it now.

"Ryan," I said weakly. "I'm so sorry," then started crying.

"Beautiful, don't cry. I was worried sick about you, but I found you. We'll get through this together. What happened to you that made you go off the grid like that...we'll get through it."

"You don't understand. You don't understand. You don't understand," I said through tears.

He took a long breath, and rubbed my hand thoughtfully. "I know what happened to you."

"How do you know?"

He stared at me, his beautiful eyes sorrowful. "The doctors examined you," he said quietly.

Then I turned my head again. I could feel myself shaking.

"Beautiful, you can talk to me when you're ready. I need to know who did it."

I shook my head, the tears now coming fast and furious. I started sobbing uncontrollably, and he climbed into the bed with me, holding me and stroking my hair. I felt like I would never, ever stop crying uncontrollably. I was finally accessing the emotions of what happened to me with Andrew raping me. I was re-living it all. The tightening of the belt, the searing pain, the humiliation, the feeling of extreme violation. And it coming so closely on the heels of Rochelle's attack.

It was too much, too much.

I was sobbing so hard that I was hiccuping. I needed something, I needed a fix, I needed something to push this awful pain out of my head. The emotional pain was excruciating.

Ryan just sat there in the bed with me, stroking my hair and my back. He kissed me on the forehead. "I'm going to lie here with you. I'm here, and I will never leave you again."

I cried for the rest of the night. At first my face and body was turned away from Ryan. Then, at some point, I buried my face in his chest and cried and cried and cried.

Chapter Twenty-Five

After I stabilized, Ryan checked me out of the hospital, and informed me that he was taking me to Los Angeles, to the rehab facility where he stayed. "That place is world class, beautiful. You'll get what you need there."

I sighed. I was starting to get a little bit better, but the emotional issues were still like a 1,000 pound elephant sitting on my chest. "Ok," I simply said. There was no arguing with him, I knew, so I didn't even try. Plus, I was feeling the familiar feeling of exhaustion and depression. I remembered this feeling from after the Rochelle attack, only now it was 1,000 times worse than that. I realized that I never mentally recovered from the Rochelle attack, at least not to the extent that I would be strong enough to survive something even more devastating.

"Really? You aren't going to fight me on this?"

"Ryan, no offense, but I have no fight left in me."

So, we took his plane out to Beverly Hills. I stood there, on the tarmac, waiting for the plane in the cold, feeling resentful and pissed-off. Ryan had his arms around me, but

I felt like screaming. Christmas was coming, and I was going to be in this place. Nobody knew where I was going – I told my family and friends that Ryan and I were going to Jamaica for the holidays.

Well, I was going someplace warm, but a sunny beach in Jamaica wasn't it.

At the same time, I felt badly for Ryan. He, too, was going to be spending the holidays away from his mother and best friend. Sarah even invited us to spend Christmas with her.

On the plane, Ryan was trying his best to make small talk, but I politely ignored him. I wasn't in the mood for his chipper observations. Plus, I was feeling extremely nauseated, and had been for awhile. Ryan told me that was normal with the drugs – my body was getting rid of the nasty poisons, so feeling sick was a good sign that my body was doing what it was supposed to.

Still, Ryan talked. "So, I've been thinking about us. I know that what you want to do most in the world is to have an animal sanctuary. When you get better, I'd like to take you to some property I found just out of town. It's perfect – lots of trees and tall grass. I've also been in contact with some people who can help me in setting that up. I have to have a team of veterinarians working there, of course, and I'm in the process of finding out what else it entails. That will be an exciting project for us to work on together."

I just huddled beneath a blanket and said nothing. There was a movie playing on the big screen television, and I pretended to be watching it. I didn't want him to talk to me anymore. But I really couldn't think about the television, either. I found that I had to have my mind a perfect blank, because if I started to think of anything at all, I could only think of...him. Andrew. He was in my thoughts obsessively.

So, I simply willed all thought away and found that to be better. I watched the screen with a blank stare and tuned out Ryan and everything else.

I wanted that plane ride to be over. I wanted some peace and quiet and some alone time.

We arrived at LAX, then took a limo straight to the facility, where he checked me in.

Betty, the woman who was there the last time, when Ryan was here, was sitting at the receptionist area again. She gave me a warm smile, but I didn't smile back. Ryan, did, however. "I called ahead of time. My wife needs to be checked in."

"Of course," she said. "Mrs. Gallagher?"

I nodded and said nothing.

I got a room which was similar to where he stayed. Meaning that it was cozy and beautiful, and even had a little meditation area.

I lay down on the bed and Ryan lay next to me. "Beautiful, I want you to tell me your needs. I want to hold you, and touch you, but you need to tell me if you feel uncomfortable at all."

I looked at him quizzically. My mind was slow to process his words. "I don't understand," I simply said.

"You seem to flinch when I touch you. You don't say it bothers you, but I see the face you make."

I nodded. "I'm sorry about that. I really don't want to be touched right now," I said, then turned my back on him and attempted to sleep. We were both on top of the covers, fully clothed. Then, I turned back to him and said "Actually, I hope you don't mind. I really need to be alone."

He looked briefly stricken, then his face was completely composed. "Of course, beautiful. I'll be staying at the

Wilshire while you're here. I hope I can visit you tomorrow during visitor hours."

"I'll call you and let you know," I simply said, turning my back away from him again. I was fully clothed, including my shoes. I heard him leaving, then I sat up in bed and wondered what I would do until I was able to see somebody.

It turned out that I didn't have to wait long. A Dr. Bassey, a blonde woman about 45, with a very compassionate demeanor, came into my room.

"Mrs. Gallagher, I need to go over your treatment plan with you."

"Yes, thanks," I said. I was an automaton.

"Now, I understand that you had already gone through detox before you arrived here."

"Right."

"Our program is a holistic program. You will see a psychiatrist every day for two hours, and be a part of group therapy every day for four hours. We also have outlined a diet and exercise program that we would like for you to follow while you are here."

"Ok."

"We have also worked with your husband to design a unique alternative medicine approach that you will take, in conjunction with the other steps. It will include acupuncture, yoga, massage, meditation, and equine therapy."

"Equine therapy? You mean, I get to play with horses?" I finally felt that I was coming to life. Just the thought of being around those gentle animals was giving me a sense of peace.

"Yes. Your husband thought this would be the part you would love the most. We have a horse for you. Her name is Polly. You will work with her for as many hours as you like, but a minimum of an hour a day. You'll be grooming her, feeding her, leading her, riding her, and haltering her."

I felt a smile creep on my face, the first smile I'd felt in awhile.

Inwardly, I also felt an overwhelming sense of love for my husband. Leave it to him to know exactly what I would need in this place.

But I couldn't get past the other feeling. The feeling that, if Ryan weren't so damned stubborn about getting me a bodyguard, none of this would've happened. Well, maybe Rochelle would've gotten me, and finished me off, but even that would be better than what actually happened.

"Thanks, Dr. Bassey," I said. Then felt nauseated. "Excuse me," I said, running to the bathroom to throw up. I came back in. "How long do I have to put up with puking my guts out every five minutes?"

"It should be easing up any day now," she said.

"Thanks. When do I get to meet Polly?"

Dr. Bassey laughed. "This evening, I can take you out there. Tomorrow, you begin your routine. It's very structured. You have to make your bed every day at 7, then you have breakfast. Your husband has given us a list of healthy foods you like, so the meals that we offer you will be based upon that. According to your husband, you can tolerate most vegetables, and you like tomatoes, asparagus, broccoli, squash, zucchini, pumpkin, spinach, kale, and carrots. You don't care for white onions that aren't cooked, and you love artichoke hearts. Is this correct?"

"Yes, that sounds like a pretty exhaustive list. What else did Ryan tell you?"

"He gave us a list of dishes that you like to eat as well. We have a chef here that will prepare your meals according to what you like. We have prepared a sample menu for you as well."

At that, she gave me the sample menu. Everything on the menu was organic, including the meat, and the meals seemed very well-rounded.

I was looking forward to eating here.

"I hate to ask this, but how much is this place costing?"

"It's $80,000 a month, and you are scheduled to be here for two months."

I nodded. In my former life, one month here would be equivalent to two year's earnings. Now, it was just a drop in the bucket.

Still weird.

Dr. Bassey went on. "You will have a personal trainer, and you are scheduled to exercise with your trainer every day for one hour."

I started to panic a little. "A personal trainer? Could I please have a woman?"

Dr. Bassey nodded. "Of course. That is a given, considering your situation."

I relaxed some. "The group therapy, what does that entail?"

"It is four hours a day, six days a week. Sundays are the only day that you do not have therapy scheduled. But you are still expected to make your bed and keep your room tidy," she said, looking at her chart. "The group is led by a trained professional and everybody is encouraged to talk openly."

I felt that I wouldn't care for the group therapy. I had a hard time talking to anybody, even Ryan, about what happened to me. And I was expected just to talk to perfect strangers?

"Individual counseling is two hours a day," she continued. "And your husband has requested the possibility of couple's counseling as well."

"How often are we to have couple's counseling?"

"He asked for that to be one hour per day, Monday through Friday. But this is only if you agree to this. It is strictly optional, of course."

I nodded. "That would probably be a good thing, actually," I said, realizing that I was feeling extremely resentful and hateful towards my wonderful, patient husband. I hoped a therapist could help me get past these feelings.

Dr. Bassey continued. "You are expected to keep a journal, as well. You may structure your journal however you wish," she said, handing me a journal with a Matisse painting on the front. "You can write in there whatever comes to mind. But your therapist will give you a topic to write about every day as well."

"Thanks," I said. "When can I meet Polly?"

"I'll call your equine trainer to see if she can take you right now," she said. Then she called somebody "Ms. Watts? This is Dr. Bassey. We have a client here who would like to meet her horse this evening. Are you free?"

I was relieved that the equine trainer was also a woman. I wasn't quite ready to be alone with a strange man just yet.

"She will be here in a half hour," Dr. Bassey said.

We chatted until the trainer showed up. Ms. Watts, first name Jamie, was a tall and lanky brunette who wore her hair in a long braid down her back. She was dressed in riding crops and high riding boots, with a plain white shirt that fit tightly around her non-existent chest. She had chiseled cheekbones and flashing dark eyes. She held out her hand "Hello, I'm Jamie Watts."

"Iris Snowe, uh, Gallagher," I said, taking her hand.

We walked to a golf cart, and Jamie drove the cart to

the stables. There, in one of the stables, was my horse, Polly. Polly was an enormous dappled horse, with sad brown eyes and a black mane. I looked into those eyes, and immediately saw a kindred soul. Jamie gave me an apple to give to her, and Polly eagerly took it, snorting her approval. Her head was bobbing to and fro, back and forth. She whinnied softly.

I pet her nose while she chomped the apple. Then I looked at Jamie. "Polly. Where did you find her?"

"She's a rescue horse. All of our horses are rescue horses. We got Polly from a farm in Kentucky. She was neglected and starving. The owner lost the farm, and left the animals there. She was also abused."

I nodded. I knew I had met a kindred soul in kind Polly. Jamie just confirmed this for me.

"How much do I get to see Polly?" I asked.

"As Dr. Bassey said, a minimum of an hour a day, with me. But you can come out here whenever you like. You just need to call for a golf cart driver to bring you out here, whenever you need to come."

"And what are you going to have me do?"

"Groom her, bridle her, lead her, and ride her. It's pretty structured when you are with me, but if you come out to visit her on your own, you can do whatever you like."

"I take it that this evening is not actually a therapy session?"

"Right. This is just a get-acquainted session."

I stroked Polly while I talked to Jamie. "How much do you know about me?"

"I've been briefed about your situation."

"Then you know that I lived in a drug house for a couple of weeks?"

She nodded and said nothing.

"Do you also know that I abandoned our animals in

our house?" This was one of the things that shamed me the absolute most. More than anything else, I couldn't live with myself for doing that. After all the times I rescued dogs from that type of situation, and after all the traumatization I saw in those animals after being abandoned, how could I do that to my own animals? They would've died if Nick didn't come when he did. If they would've died because of my stupidity, then I didn't think that I would've survived.

Jamie looked at me with sympathetic eyes. "Iris, people do things when trauma happens to them. Everybody reacts differently."

I looked at Polly. "How could I do that? Thank God Nick came by on time. To think what would've happened to them if Ryan hadn't have called him, though. I don't think that I could've lived with myself if something had happened to them because of my stupidity."

Then Jamie stood on the other side of Polly's nose, and stroked the horse's ear gently. "At some point, Iris, you have to stop beating yourself up. Maybe you can make amends to your animals by treating Polly here extra special."

I found myself crying, leaning my head into Polly's. "I'm so sorry, Max, Brut, Maddy. I'm so very sorry. I'll never do that again," I said, over and over again, while I sobbed. Jamie put her hand on my shoulder and squeezed a little. I clutched Polly's neck and stroked her mane.

When I got back to the room after seeing Polly, I called Ryan.

"Beautiful," he said. "I'm so glad you called."

"Where are you?"

"Just sitting here in my hotel room, watching a little television. How are you doing?"

"Good. I, uh, wanted to thank you for all you're doing

for me to help me get better. I haven't been very kind to you lately, and, for that, I'm sorry."

"Hey, that's not a problem. You haven't gotten to the making amends part of the program yet, so why are you skipping ahead?" he asked, with a joking tone to his voice. "Kidding, of course. Really, beautiful, you haven't offended me. I know that you are going through a lot. I just want to know the best way to help you through it."

"You've helped a ton, just by getting me here. It's really like a resort more than a rehab facility." I tried to sound cheerful, even though I was dead inside. "We had talked about going to a resort for Christmas, so I guess this is the next best thing, huh?"

Ryan was quiet for a few seconds. "You don't have to put on a brave face," he said. "Not with me."

"I know." I didn't really have any other words. I wasn't quite ready to invite him to come and visit me, even though it was visiting hours.

"So....are you lonely there?" That was his way of asking if I wanted him to keep me company.

"I'm pretty tired, actually," I said. "Maybe you can come and visit tomorrow."

"Sure, honey, whatever you need."

"Well, I just wanted to call and thank you for everything you are doing."

"Of course. I love you."

"I love you, too." It took me a long time to ever say those words, and they were, once again, difficult to say. I did love him, more than he could ever know. I think that I loved him from the first time I saw him in my office, waiting for me after our first encounter, which was a rather sleazy one-night stand. Since then, it had been a roller-coaster, and it seemed that we were on the down-slope at the moment.

We hung up the phone, and I lay in my bed, staring at the walls. Willing my mind to be a total blank before I fell asleep.

The next day was regimented, as promised. I made my bed at 7 AM, then went down for my breakfast of scrambled cage-free eggs with spinach, organic strawberries and a homemade bran muffin. I hung my head, hoping that nobody would try to talk to me and make friends with me. It seemed that everybody was in a clique, anyhow, and nobody noticed me.

Kinda like in high school.

In our group therapy, I didn't contribute much, choosing to pass when it was my turn to speak. I saw at least one person staring at me like she knew me, which might have been possible. The media attention on my case had died down quite a bit, but I found that, on occasion, people still came up to me to ask me about what was going on with Rochelle. I knew that if the case went to trial, the publicity would gear up again. I hoped that it wouldn't be televised. But, for now, it seemed that my fifteen minutes of fame were over, thankfully.

In my meeting with the psychiatrist, Dr. Knight, things didn't go much better.

"So, Iris, how are you feeling today?"

"Fine, thanks."

"Fine. Meaning?"

"Fine," I said with a shrug. "Everything's great. My husband's great. This place is beautiful. Those grounds are so manicured, and that reflecting pool — I've never seen anything like it. I'm scheduled for a massage and acupuncture treatment this week, too. What could be bad?"

"Tell me about your husband. How are you really feeling about him?"

"Ryan? Oh, he's the most magnificent guy in the entire world. He's so kind, gentle and funny. He's my best friend. We're best friends," I said, as I twirled my hair, not looking the psychiatrist in the eye. "So, that's it, can I go now?"

"You're angry with him. Tell me about that."

"Angry with him? What makes you say that?" I asked, piling my hair on top of my head, and patting my legs, which were bouncing up and down a mile a minute. Then I started biting my nails.

"Your body language. Tell me about your marriage."

"Our marriage is fine. He's the love of my life." That last part actually was true.

The doctor tried a different tact. "Why are you in this place?"

"I don't know."

"You were addicted to drugs. Why did you turn to the drugs?"

"I don't know." This session was becoming a waste of time. "Listen, doc, everything's fine. I don't really know why I need to talk to you. Everything's fine."

"Our sessions are two hours long. Now, I need for you to write in your journal tonight about why you turned to drugs and lived in a drug house for two weeks."

The doctor was becoming more aggressive, and soon would be pinning me down about my feelings about Andrew. It was time to cut the shrink part of the session short. "I know that I am supposed to talk to you for two hours, but maybe we can talk about other things."

"What would you like to talk about?"

"My honeymoon," I said, bringing out my iPhone. "Let me show you some pictures." So, for the remainder of the time with Dr. Knight, I showed her pictures from our honeymoon - Ryan's yacht, Nick's house, Ryan's winery,

Lake Como, the locals, the Vatican, and the ruins in Rome. "And here's where we took our scooters over to the Trevi Fountain and made wishes. Here's where we went to the Roman Colosseum ruins, and this is where we visited The Pantheon," I said, showing the pictures as a slide show. Dr. Knight nodded along, but didn't really say much.

The session was finally over after about an hour and half of my show and tell about our wonderful honeymoon.

I went back to my room, and I was eager to see Polly. To tell the truth, Polly was all that was on my mind all day long. The beautiful horse with the soulful brown eyes. Abused, abandoned Polly, who was my kindred spirit. I longed to see her and begin my first session with her.

So, I called the golf cart driver, Max, to come and get me and take me to the stables. I knew that Jamie wouldn't be able to meet me for our actual therapy session until around 5, so I could have a couple of hours just to commune with beautiful Polly. I went to the cafeteria to pick up several apples and carrots, and carefully put them into a bag as a treat for her.

Max pulled up in front of the facility, a skinny young 20-something with a mop of unruly brown hair, and teeth like an Osmond or a Kennedy. "Hello, Mrs. Gallagher," Max greeted me.

"Hi, Max. Thanks for picking me up."

"Not a problem," he said, as I got into the front seat with him. I tamped down the anxiety that was welling up in my throat about being alone with a strange guy, as we sped along the road that led to the stables. *Stop being paranoid, Iris. This guy is harmless.* Still, I found myself gripping the iron bars of the golf cart as Max zipped along. I could feel myself shaking.

"Is there anything wrong, Mrs. Gallagher?"

"No, no. I'm fine. Call me Iris." 'Fine' appeared to be my word of the day.

We finally arrived at the stables, and Max dropped me off. I told him that he wouldn't need to come back for me, as Jamie would be bringing me back.

I got to the stable where my Polly was housed. I couldn't do much with her, yet, as I had not yet learned how to lead her or anything else. I longed to have a brush for her, and get in the stable and groom her. But that was also a lesson that was reserved for later. All I could really do was stroke her nose, and pet her mane, while she whinnied softly in my ear.

"Sweet Polly, girl," I said, giving her an apple. "You're a beautiful girl." She neighed, bobbing her head up and down, and stomping her hooves in her stall. She nuzzled my ear. "So, Polly, you were abused and abandoned. Looks like we have a lot in common."

I continued stroked her mane as I said "I have to bring my husband out here. He'll love you too. He loves me, you know, Polly. He loves me more than anyone ever has." I put my arm around her nozzle, and stroked her.

"He loves me, Polly. So why do I hate him?"

Chapter Twenty-Six

I admitted to Polly what I couldn't admit to anybody else. That I hated my beautiful, sweet husband. "I'm really screwed up, Polly. He has never been anything but kind to me. Good to me. Yet, I feel that my life has just become so fucked up because of my association with him. Rochelle, the media, Andrew, all of that is associated with him. Not that my life was so great before him, but I at least had my sanity. Now, I'm not so sure."

Polly snorted in my ear. "Polly, you know, girl, I never wanted to face my past. Now, I'm forced to. I'm forced to face it, while dealing with horrible stuff that is happening right now. It's only a matter of time before people find out what happened to me when I was a seventh-grader. I'm surprised the media never picked up on it. It's stuff that I can't tell anyone, not Dr. Knight, not Ryan, not my parents, not my friends, nobody. Just you, Polly. Just you, 'cause I know that you won't tell anyone."

I looked into the distance, and saw the figure of Jamie walking towards the stable. I looked at Polly. "Well, for now,

Polly, we'll just leave it at that," I said, waving to the lanky figure heading my way.

We went through our first lesson with me and the horse. Jamie taught me first how to lead Polly, demonstrating, then letting me take the reins. I led her around the dirt road directly outside of the stable, Polly prancing behind me, whinnying and snorting the whole way. After I led her around for a little while, Jamie told me that it was time to put her back in her stable. Then she gave me a brush, and showed me how to groom her.

"That's our lesson for the day," Jamie said. "Tomorrow, you'll get to bridle her, and maybe ride her if you're up for it."

I nodded, looking forward to the next lesson already. Then the two of us headed back to the main facility.

I decided to call Ryan and see if he would come and visit me.

"Of course, beautiful, I can't wait to see you," Ryan said, eagerness in his voice.

He was over in record time. I imagined that he flew over here, like George Jetson. "I got lucky and didn't hit any red lights," he said, as he met me at the receptionist's desk, slightly out of breath. He leaned down to hug me, and I could feel myself stiffening up. I immediately felt bad for my reaction to his touch.

What was wrong with me?

Ryan, for his part, appeared not be ruffled by my obvious rejection. Still, he looked uncomfortable and unsure of what to do. "What would you like to do, beautiful?" he asked.

"Maybe walk on the grounds," I said. "Wait here, I'll be back with my coat." The sun was going down, so I knew that I would need some kind of warmth if we were going to be outside for a spell.

I got back, and the two of us walked along the grounds, onto a little nature trail. He didn't try to hold my hand, and I really didn't want him to, so that was ok. "So, how are things going so far?" he asked.

"Fine," was all I said.

We walked along in the uncomfortable silence. I knew that he was trying to open me up, but I wasn't ready. I was still struggling with my irrational feelings of loathing for this beautiful and kind man.

But I couldn't tell him that.

"Have you thought any more about us doing counseling together?" he asked.

I nodded. "Maybe next week. I'm still trying to get adjusted here."

"Sure, beautiful. Anything you like. You're the boss."

"Yeah. I wish I was the boss when I told you I didn't want a bodyguard," I blurted out.

Ryan said nothing. I didn't look at him, but I could imagine he looked stricken.

We got to a little stream, and both of us sat on the ground on the banks. "I wish I knew what to say to you," Ryan said. "I want to help you. How do I do that?"

I just shook my head and said nothing. Then "We better go back. It's getting really dark."

Then we headed back in silence.

Chapter Twenty-Seven

The days flew by. Make bed, eat breakfast, go to group therapy, see the shrink, then see Polly. I was starting to talk a little bit in group, but about nothing important. I only talked because the counselor was starting to get impatient about my passing every time. So, I made stuff up to satisfy them.

"I'm really fucked up because I'm a part of the Phelps family. You know, God Hates Fags and all of that," I said to the group one day.

The rest of the group nodded, then some guy said "What a wack job, huh. Are you a grandkid to that Fred Phelps guy?"

"Sure," I said. "So, now I'm a fugitive from there."

"Bullshit," said Candace, a recovering meth user. She was the one who was looking at me with a funny expression when I first got into the group. "I didn't want to say anything, but you're that girl who's married to that hot rich guy. The hot bisexual rich guy. Goddamn, if you don't want him, give him to me. I'll share him with my boyfriend anytime he wants."

"Candace," the leader said. "That's against the rules, calling people out like that. We're supposed to remain anonymous in here."

"Sorry, but she can't go around saying that she's part of an anti-gay cult when she's married to a guy who swings both ways."

At that, the group started getting into a heated argument about me, my life, and how much of my life was supposed to be brought up to the group. I really didn't care. Ironically, the argument took the focus off me, as everybody was arguing about me, without paying much attention to any input I wanted to add.

But, now that my cover was blown, I knew that I couldn't get away with any more lies about my past. So, I just resorted to shutting up and not talking, much to my group leader's chagrin.

Fuck him, he can't make me talk if I don't want to.

I only looked forward to every evening, when I could see Polly. I was riding her now, and, every evening, Jamie and I took her out. I bridled her, led her, then rode her along with Jamie, out into the woods. I was very tentative at first, never having ridden a horse, with the exception of the very slow horse rides that were offered at Benjamin Stables in Kansas City. But I soon got used to her, and she to me, and we galloped for miles through the woods. One evening we ended up on one of the beaches, galloping through the sand and surf.

I also visited her whenever I could, because she was the only company I really wanted during this time. After the awkward evening with Ryan, where we walked along in silence, I started putting him off and making excuses for why he couldn't come and visit me. I would tell him I was tired, or had a headache, or was nauseated.

Actually, the nauseated excuses were often true. I was often extremely sick to my stomach and found myself throwing up. I didn't tell anybody, though, because I didn't want to have to undergo any medical tests. I wasn't detoxing anymore, so I surmised there was something wrong with me. And I had too many blows for there to be one more, so I kept quiet. I was in denial, I knew, but what else was new?

But I was never too tired for Polly. I talked to her for hours.

Then, one night, I finally let her in on my secret. The secret that I had been keeping for 22 years.

Chapter Twenty-Eight

It was an unseasonably warm evening, about three weeks after I arrived at this place, when I finally decided to let Polly in on what was going on with me. "Polly," I began. "I told you when I first came here that I had a secret about what happened to me in the seventh grade. Well, now you deserve to know," I said, as I brushed her, and stroked her ears. "There was a gym teacher. A very handsome gym teacher. The girls were googly-eyes about him, including me. I was 12. I had crushes on all types of boys, and men, too. He noticed me, Polly. He noticed me."

Then I looked at my hands on her neck and mane. They were shaking uncontrollably. "I miscarried his baby, Polly. He and I had sex behind the bushes in the fields behind the school. It was only the one time, but I know that I miscarried his baby. I passed clots, huge clots, when I got my period after we did it. I never told anybody about this."

It was then that I finally figured out the source of my self-loathing. The gym teacher, of course, kinda forgot about me after that incident in the bushes. There were rumors that he was doing the same thing to a lot of other girls. Then he was transferred out of the school for mysterious reasons, a few years after the incident between us.

I put my head into Polly's neck and mane, and wept uncontrollably. I ended up spending the night in the stable with her, laying down in the hay, not caring that I was probably laying on horse pee. The horse poop was dug out of the stall, so that wasn't a problem.

I couldn't move. I just lay down on the hay, and cried myself to sleep.

Chapter Twenty-Nine

After I had my cathartic experience with Polly, I was finally ready to have Ryan come with me to some therapy sessions. Our first session was scheduled for that Monday, with Dr. Bryan, a forty-something woman with corkscrew blonde hair and thick black Elvis Costello glasses.

Ryan seemed more than eager for this session. I dreaded it, but I knew that it had to happen. I had to get past my animosity for Ryan. I had to know that we weren't broken, just bent, like the song said. The only way to do that would be through these therapy sessions.

Ryan met me in Dr. Bryan's office that Monday. My breath caught a little when he walked through the door. It was like I was seeing him for the first time. His dark, wavy hair. His perfectly chiseled face. His long, incredibly thick eyelashes, and his beautiful green eyes. His sensuous mouth, and perfect teeth. His rock-hard body.

I sighed, feeling giddy, like a schoolgirl.

Did this mean I was falling in love with him all over again?

I hoped so.

He sat down next to me and I took his hand. Those beautiful green eyes got huge at my gesture, then he broke into an enormous smile. Tentatively, he put his hand in my hair, gauging my reaction to his touch. I smiled big, then he stroked my cheek and kissed my forehead. The words were unspoken, but we both knew.

We were going to be ok.

I was finally ready to open up.

Dr. Bryan observed us for a few minutes then addressed me "Mrs. Gallagher. Can I call you Iris?"

I nodded, smiling.

"Iris. I notice that the two of you seem to have come to some new kind of understanding of each other just now. It seems like there was a degree of tension when Mr. Gallagher came into the room, now that tension seems to have passed. Could you tell me what you are feeling right now?"

"I love my husband. I really, really, love my husband."

"Ok," she said. "And, is that different than the feelings you felt before?"

I hesitated, looking at Ryan. He was still watching me, those beautiful green eyes full of passion and love. Then I looked back at Dr. Bryan. "Yes. I have felt....contempt, and irrational hatred for him."

"I see," she said. "Mr. Gallagher, do you know why your wife would have felt this way about you?"

He nodded.

"Why, Mr. Gallagher, do you feel that your wife hated you?"

"Please, call me Ryan," he said, then squeezed my hand. Then he hesitated for a few minutes, looking at me, then said, quietly, with his head down "It was my fault that she was raped."

"Why do you feel that way, Ryan?" asked Dr. Bryan.

"I was trying to protect her. I was going away on a business trip, and, even while I was in town, I was going to be working long hours in the office. I'm a bank president, and I had taken an extended leave of absence that was ending. And Iris was being threatened by a woman from my past. So I wanted to protect her while I was gone." Then he broke down a little. "I wanted to protect her. Instead, she was raped. If I didn't hire that guy, she wouldn't have been raped."

"Is that true?" Dr. Bryan asked me.

"Yes, that's true," I said. "I've been journaling about it since I've been here, and I have this horse that has really helped me. I wasn't ready to face my rage about what happened to me. I wasn't ready to admit to myself that such a thing even happened at all. So, I think that I channeled my rage at Ryan, instead of where it should be."

"Have you talked about this to Dr. Knight?"

"No. I just kinda had an epiphany last night when I talked to my horse. I've been punishing Ryan not only for Andrew, but also Rochelle, and...Mr. Green." I changed the name of the gym teacher. I was still afraid of getting him into trouble.

"Who is Rochelle, and who is Mr. Green?"

At that, I told her about Rochelle's attack. "Rochelle is a woman from Ryan's past. She kidnapped me from my office a little under a year ago. Then she tortured me and shot me up with black tar heroin, enough to kill me. I was in a coma for about two months because of it."

Dr. Bryan nodded, scribbling notes in her pad.

Then it was time to talk about Mr. Green.

I saw Ryan looking at me with a very interested and worried expression.

I took a deep breath and said "Mr. Green was my first, uh, sexual experience. When I was 12. He was a very handsome and flirtatious gym teacher. He used to come up to me when I was standing on my head, and rub his hands up and down my leg. I had to admit that I had quite the crush."

"Ok," said Dr. Bryan. "So, he touched you inappropriately while you were in class."

"Yeah. You know, we used to have to do headstands and that, and he would rub the back of my legs while I was standing on my head. And I used to fantasize about him. Everybody did."

"You said that he was your first sexual experience. Tell me about that."

"Excuse me," I said. "I have to use your bathroom." At that, I ran into her bathroom, and hurled.

Ryan was immediately by my side, rubbing my back. He helped me up, and gently ran some water, and got a cool rag to put on my face. "Sorry about that," I said to Ryan. "Guess this story is making me really anxious."

I didn't want to tell him that my puking was still a daily event, sometimes an hourly one.

I came back out. "Yes. Uh, he used to ask me to stay late after school. To help him put stuff away – jump ropes, balls, hula hoops, that sort of thing. I told my mother that I was at band practice, because I knew that she would never let me stay after school if I she knew that I was helping a man all alone," I said, shaking my head ruefully. "Mothers always do know best after all."

Dr. Bryan nodded. "Go on."

"Well, he and I were in the closet one day, the apparatus

closet, where they keep all the gym stuff. And he kissed me. The next day, in the same closet, he kissed me again, and he unzipped his pants and made me give him oral. Pretty soon, this was a daily event. I started to think that he loved me, and that we would end up getting married after I became an adult."

Now Ryan was looking at me with his best poker face. I could tell that he was covering up what he was really feeling as I told this story.

I went on. "We had intercourse one day after school. He asked me to meet him in this clearing behind the school, so I did. Then he had sex with me behind the bushes."

Ryan was trying to cover up shock and rage, but he was having a hard time of it. I saw him clench his fist, then pound it on the arm of the chair.

I continued. "After that, he never asked me to help him after school again. He never paid any attention to me at all. I was crushed – I thought that he was going to be my husband one day. I kept asking him if I could help out after school, but he always said no after that. He started having a different girl help him out after school. I was so jealous of her, I couldn't stand it."

Dr. Bryan was noticing Ryan's reaction to my story. "Ryan, I see your face. Tell me what is going through your mind."

He shook his head. "You don't want to know," was all he said. His fists were still balled up tight, then one of his hands involuntarily went through his hair. Then he hung his head, both of his hands on his neck. "Finish your story, beautiful," he said.

"Well, I think I had a miscarriage that year. I had just started my period, and it was always super-light. Kinda like it is now. But, one month, it was super, super heavy.

And clotty. I've never had a period like that before or since."

Ryan couldn't hide his reaction to this particular revelation. He just looked stunned, and I saw, in the depths of those eyes, rage. Not at me, of course, but at Mr. Green. Ryan was still so protective of me, which is one of the reasons why I loved him so.

I took a deep breath and continued. "Uh, what happened with Andrew made me realize that what happened to me with that gym teacher was also a rape. I never thought of it that way. I always thought that it was some kind of love affair gone bad. Now, I realize that I was violated then. So, the Andrew thing is cumulative on top of that, and on top of what happened with Rochelle last year." I looked at Ryan, who had a stress ball in his hand, and was squeezing the life out of it. "I've come to realize that I don't have Mr. Green, Andrew or Rochelle handy to take out my rage, so I took it out on my husband."

Dr. Bryan looked at Ryan. "What would you like to say to this?" he asked.

Ryan took a few minutes to compose himself, then took my hand, and rubbed it thoughtfully. Looking me in the eye, he said "I want to apologize, from the deepest part of me, about Andrew. I feel totally responsible for what happened. But, at the same time, I can't apologize for wanting to make sure you're safe. You're my world, beautiful. That's why I forced you to have a bodyguard. So, I have mixed emotions about it."

I nodded. "I know. You couldn't have known what was going to happen with Andrew. I've come to terms with that. And I love you more than I ever thought I could love anybody. You're my world, too."

That night, Ryan came and spent the night with me. We

didn't make love. He knew that I wasn't ready for that. But he held me close, both of us under the covers, fully clothed in our pajamas, ready for bed. Then he said "we missed Christmas together."

I didn't realize that Christmas had come and gone. How I managed to miss Christmas altogether, I didn't know. Christmas was always a very special time for me – not because of the gifts, but, rather, because of the gaiety of the season. The childhood memories for me were always very strong around this season, whether it was my delight in discovering Rudolph, the anticipation of presents, or the memories of family gatherings. Yet, this year, I managed to avoid it altogether.

"Anyhow," he said, "I've been thinking about it. I know how much you are in love with Polly, your horse. And, you know how I was thinking about buying some land and creating an animal sanctuary?"

I nodded eagerly, knowing where this was going.

"I've made arrangements to buy Polly when we get our sanctuary open. That way, you can see her whenever you want. I feel like that would be the best present for you that I could give."

I felt tears coming to my eyes. How could I have ever hated this man? How could I have ever felt rage towards him? He was the one really great thing in my life, besides my family and friends. He had been the only man who had ever treated me with love and kindness, instead of anger and disrespect.

He smiled when he saw my tears. He knew me so well by then, so he knew when my tears were happy or sad, and he knew that these were very, very happy tears. I smiled and nodded mutely at him. "I love you," I said.

"I know that this is late, but Merry Christmas, beautiful."

We lay in the bed, fully clothed, and I put my head on his chest. This was more intimacy than I had been able to manage with him since the rape, and, although I was sorry that we couldn't do more, lying there with him was as comforting as anything that I could've possibly imagined.

Chapter Thirty

I stayed at the resort, I mean facility, for another month after my breakthrough with Dr. Bryan and Polly. I was much more open with Dr. Knight, so I was able to tell her more about my feelings about what happened to me. She was able to understand that I not only had issues with Rochelle and Andrew, but that I also had severe issues from my past that resulted in my overall feeling of low self-esteem. So, in addition to the talk therapy, she also put me through a regimen of cognitive behavioral therapy, aimed at eliminating negative self-talk. The goal was to change my thought process through changing my behavior.

The CBT process involved helping me to reconceptualize negative situations, because I automatically tended to think the worst of any given situation. Skills acquisition was the next phase, and this was where I was taught to catch my negative thoughts and replace them with positive ones. I was required to keep a journal and jot down any negative thoughts that I had throughout the day, then, the next day, I was taught about how to replace these specific negative thoughts with specific positive ones.

I was also given a course of treatment called eye movement desensitization and reprocessing. This was for my specific traumatic issues regarding Rochelle, Mr. Green, and Andrew. In this treatment, I was asked to recall what happened to me while the psychiatrist asked me to focus on their hand gestures. I followed these hand gestures with my eyes. I was also asked for positive thoughts, and the therapist did the same thing with the gestures. The goal, as was explained, was for my brain to process the memories of what happened to me differently. The treatment was somewhat controversial, as it had evidence that showed that it worked, and also evidence that showed that it didn't work, but I was willing to try anything to overcome my traumatic incidents.

I also continued my therapy with Polly and my group therapy for four hours a day. Acupuncture treatments were daily, as were massages. The acupuncture was geared specifically for my drug addiction. I didn't particularly feel that I needed drug addiction treatment, as I really didn't feel like I was addicted. I had severe trauma, two severe traumas within a period of nine months, so I went ape-shit. That was really all there was to it, so I felt that the psychotherapy was effective. I felt that the therapy aimed at my drug addiction to be superfluous.

Nevertheless, I found both the acupuncture and the massage therapy to be incredibly relaxing, so I looked forward to these sessions.

Ryan and I continued with our couple's therapy, as well. We were becoming closer through the therapy, as I was able to express my feelings about my life being turned upside down after meeting him, and I was helped with processing these emotions and feelings.

By the end of the two months, I was feeling myself again. Better than myself. I had the tools to help myself whenever negative thoughts crept into my head, and I felt that I had a handle on all that had happened to me with Rochelle, Andrew and Mr. Green. Ryan and I were closer than we had ever been. We still were not making love, of course. I still wasn't ready for that, but I hoped that I would be, with time.

I also hoped that I would stop being so afraid of strange men.

Ryan, for his part, got me set up with a psychotherapist, Dr. Brammell, in Kansas City, so that I could continue regular therapy.

The only issue that we were having was the matter of pressing charges against Andrew. Ryan was adamant that I needed to call the police and tell them what happened. I was just as adamant that this would never happen.

"Not doing it, Ryan."

"Listen, beautiful, I know that you're scared – "

"Scared is not the word. He threatened to kill me, and I believe he will. Or, worse yet, maybe he'll come after you. If anything happens to you, I might as well be killed as well. I couldn't survive it."

"But, beautiful, he might do it to others."

"I know that, and, trust me, that weighs heavily on my mind. But I just can't do it. I'm sorry, it may seem selfish to you, but I have to keep you safe. And, I admit, I'm thinking of my own safety as well. No, no, no. I won't do it. Please don't make me."

Ryan didn't push.

Aside from that issue, though, Ryan and I were doing

better than we ever had. I had high hopes that the worst was behind us. I lived through trauma and drug addiction. He lived through seeing his father, and making amends with him.

But the worst was not past us. Not by a long shot.

And the next blow would be, by far, the most devastating of all.

Chapter Thirty-One

On the plane on the way home, Ryan informed me that he had a special surprise waiting for me.

"What is it?" I asked.

"It wouldn't be a surprise, now, would it, if I told you what it was."

Upon landing, and driving in the city, I soon found out what it was.

Ryan had bought a brand new house.

This was an even more beautiful house than the Tudor mansion we had before. This house was huge, in a classic Greco-Roman style. Ionic columns were on the enormous front porch, with a beautiful terrace that jutted out from the side, with sculpted balustrades bounding it, and arches opening onto the terrace. The house was a stucco grey, with enormous arched windows, and the roof was a Spanish tile.

I knew why he bought that house, and I never loved him more than I loved him right at that moment. Once again, he understood my needs perfectly, without my saying a word.

"You like,?" he asked.

"Of course!"

"I have another surprise."

When we walked in, I saw what the surprise was. The house was empty, aside from our bedroom, which had our bed in it.

I looked at him questioningly.

"We're going to decorate this house together. The last house didn't have you in it at all. Sarah was absolutely right. This gives us a chance to start completely fresh, and the house will be truly ours at last."

At that, I jumped into his arms. He kissed me passionately. But I pulled away. I still wasn't ready to be touched like that. I wondered if I ever would be. Still, this was a wonderful surprise, and I was feeling like I was getting back to my old self.

So, for the next few weeks, we were busy hiring interior decorators. I had more of a jazzy, modern sensibility. Ryan's taste was more elegant and masculine. We had plenty of room in the new house, so we talked about making the den to reflect my taste, and the living room to reflect his taste, and the bedrooms to have a marriage of tastes. The home theater would also have a marriage of tastes. The wine cellar would reflect him, while the sun porch would reflect me. We also worked together to build our vegetable and flower gardens, looking at different flowers – Roses, Geraniums, African Daisies, Gerber Daisies, and Peonies. In the vegetable garden, we chose thyme, rosemary, basil, mint and oregano for the herbs, and, for the vegetables, we planted kale, spinach, tomatoes, cucumbers and bell peppers.

For the den, which had enormous windows that streamed natural light, I chose a multi-colored sofa with one cushion light green, another cushion dark blue, and the third cushion stripes of various colors. The lamps in the room would be Chinese lanterns of various colors. The walls would be painted in accents of bright yellow on every other wall. The big screen television would find a home in this room as well. And, since the sofa would be so colorful, as would be the walls, we chose to leave the floor hardwood with white rugs. The de Kooning would be the centerpiece of this room, as it was brashly colored in yellow, red and blue hues. We would also decorate the walls with some of Ryan's original paintings, some of which were abstract, others that favored the surrealist movement. Salvador Dali was evidently an influence on Ryan's work in this regard. There was also some cubist work that was experimental for him, and these were some of my favorites. At any rate, there were three or four paintings that I thought would look perfect with the rest of the décor, so I selected them, and we consulted the decorators for the best way to show them off.

After giving our vision for the den to the interior decorator, we decided to go with a more traditional look for the living room. Dark leather couches were selected, accented with sculptures that Ryan picked up in South Africa when he got my engagement ring. The throw pillows would add a pop of color to the couches, and the rug that we selected for the cherry wood floors was a piled white. Above the enormous fireplace would hang his Thomas Hart Benton mural that I marveled at the first day I saw his old house.

I had to admit that I was having the absolute time of my life with the interior decorator. It was always my dream to be able to have a house that was decorated the way I wanted it, and I loved that I had an entire room that would reflect my vision. Plus, I had input on the living room, because Ryan was interested in how I could put some of my touches on "his" room as well. The sun porch would also reflect me, and I went about looking for the right wicker furniture with cushions I loved, the best plants and flowers that would thrive in the sun porch environment, along with a mosaic tiled table that I had to have. Never in my life had I had the opportunity to decorate a home where money was no object.

Contentment was not the word for how I was feeling. Ryan was on another extended leave of absence from his job and I selfishly was overjoyed about this. And he brought up, several times, the idea of opening an animal sanctuary with me. That would be our next project, and Ryan even hinted that he might leave his job to manage the sanctuary with me full-time.

I was feeling better about myself than I had in a long time. The CBT was really helping me banish the negative thoughts, which also helped me feel much more in control of my life. My self-esteem was higher, too.

At this point, I thought that nothing could touch us. After all that we went through, how could anything else go wrong? Fate wasn't that cruel.

How wrong that turned out to be.

Chapter Thirty-Two

So much had happened to me in the past few months that I never noticed that I failed to get my period. I should've been paying more attention to this, considering how nauseated I was for a long time, when I was supposed to be over the drugs. In the back of my mind, I thought maybe I was sick. Maybe something serious.

That would be a good way for fate to come in and snatch our happiness away.

So, one morning, with shaking hands, feeling completely nauseated, I finally took a pregnancy test.

It was positive!

At first, I was over the moon, excited to tell Ryan the news.

Then a dark cloud immediately rolled in.

What if it wasn't his?

The thought of possibly carrying Andrew's baby made me want to hurl some more.

I couldn't tell Ryan. I didn't know if I was going to keep it. I would know by looking at the baby who the father was, and I knew that, if I had Andrew's baby, it would bring on a lifetime of abject depression.

So, I kept quiet, and made a doctor's appointment. I had to know how far along I was, but Ryan and I hadn't had sex since the rape, so there really would be no way of knowing who the father would be. My cycle had always been screwy, with my periods coming in a haphazard fashion. Sometimes the cycles were three weeks, sometimes four, sometimes six. So, just because the doctor would give me an estimated conception date, that would mean nothing. I had made love with Ryan only one week before Andrew raped me, so seeing the doctor would give me no peace of mind.

If I kept the baby, I would just have to pray it was Ryan's. But I was not at all sure that I was going to keep this child, because I couldn't live with him or her if I knew that he or she belonged to Andrew.

So, after taking the pregnancy test, I went downstairs to see Ryan, and tried to conceal my feelings about the positive result.

Because I honestly didn't know at that point what my feelings were.

Ryan was sitting at the makeshift table. He looked extremely pale and his hands were shaking. He looked like somebody had died.

I immediately thought that something had happened to Maggie, or even to his father. His father was actually in remission the last I knew, but I also knew that when the cancer comes back, it comes back with a vengeance.

I went over to him and put my arm around his back.

He had a glass of scotch and he was drinking it with shaking hands.

"What's wrong?" I asked, alarmed.

He just shook his head, his shaking hands attempting to

bring the scotch to his mouth. He failed at this, then put the scotch back down. Then he put his head in his hands.

"What's wrong?" I asked again. "Is it Maggie? Something happen to Nick? Your father?"

He just shook his head, over and over, putting his head in his hands.

"Then what is it?" I demanded.

Between heaving breaths he said "It's Nat. She, she, she's pregnant."

"That's great!" I said. "Good for her. I didn't realize that she wanted children, but she'll make a great mother." I didn't understand why that would upset him so, however.

"You don't understand," he said. Then he hesitated, looked at his glass, then threw it against the wall. "You don't understand," he repeated.

"What don't I understand?" I asked.

After a pause that seemed interminable, he simply said "She says the baby is mine."

Chapter Thirty-Three

I wasn't hearing him right. I was hallucinating. Perhaps those drugs somehow reactivated in my system, and I wasn't hearing things right at all.

There was no way he just said what he said.

No.way.

Calmly, I asked him "I'm so sorry, I don't think I heard you right."

"Sit down," he said.

"No, I'm ok right here."

"Please, beautiful, sit down."

"Don't call me beautiful."

He was now breathing harder and harder, and his hand went sweeping on the makeshift table, crashing a vase onto the floor. Then his head was in his hands, and he was sobbing more than I had ever heard. Even more than when he was going to confront his father.

I merely stood there, my arms crossed. "Repeat yourself. Repeat yourself, goddamn it. Repeat yourself."

He looked at me with those green eyes, and I saw more

pain in those eyes than I had ever seen. I was scared about the amount of pain that were in the depths of those eyes. He shook his head. "She came over when you were gone. I hadn't slept at all for five days, and I was also completely jet-lagged. All I did was haunt the streets, all night long, looking for you, asking everybody I saw about you. Night and day, night and day, that's all I did while you were gone."

I clenched my jaw, not liking where this was going. "Go on."

"She came over to help me out. Nick told her what had happened, that you were missing, so she hopped a plane. She hopped a plane, and came into the house after I hadn't slept for five days. Not one wink. Wasn't hardly eating, either. And I was so desperate to find you. So desperate to see you. And I hit my head hard, on the edge of the bathtub. I started to hallucinate – I saw my dad by the bed, with a blue head and orange body. I spoke to him."

I raised an eyebrow. I saw my fist was clenched, and I knew that I was two seconds from hauling off and hitting him.

"She came in the door, and, I swear to God, I thought she was you. My mind was so desperate to see you, and I only thought of you, so when she came in, I was obviously hallucinating that it was you."

My fist was still clenched, waiting for the ending to this story.

He got up, and started pacing the floor, rapidly. "I thought she was you. I was so happy. God, I was so happy. I was so terrified while you were gone. I knew that there was something wrong, something terribly wrong. I knew that you were in trouble, so when she came in, I never felt such happiness and relief."

"Go ahead. Go ahead and tell me that you fucked her

thinking she was me. Go ahead and tell me that. See how far you get with that fucking story. See how far."

He said nothing, just stopped pacing and looked at me.

At that, I walked up to him and pummeled him with my fist. It hurt like hell, because his body was still so hard, and it was like hitting steel. But I kept pummeling him, on and on and on, and he just stood there, not even trying to protect or shield himself. It was as if he thought he deserved it, so he wasn't going to stop me.

While I was hitting him, I was screaming "You fucked her. You fucked that whore while I was missing. You bastard. You bastard. You bastard. You fucking goddamned worthless bastard. You fucked her, and I was raped because of you. How could you do that? How could you do that? You fucking ruined my life, then didn't even care enough about me not to fuck her while I was in a shithouse getting high, trying to forget about a rape that happened BECAUSE OF YOU. I hate you. I can't stand the sight of you. I hate you. I hate you. I hate you."

There were tears streaming down his cheeks, but he wasn't making a sound. He just took my fists and my words, and, when I was worn out, and collapsed on the floor, he sat down next to me, and put his arm around my back.

"I'm so sorry," he said.

"You know what, fuck you!" I apparently wasn't done with my rage.

Then I was sobbing, my body pouring out more rage and grief. The rage and grief seemed to come from endless sources. Some before I met him, most after I met him. I thought that I had recovered from the rage and grief about the intrusive news stories, the Rochelle attack, the rape, Mr. Green. I thought that my stay at the hospital had helped me process all of that, yet this latest thing was literally the last straw, and it reactivated all of it.

All of it.

I was back to square one.

I was vaguely aware that Ryan was literally covering me with his body, and he stayed silent while I sobbed. Then I said "a bucket, I need a bucket, now." There was a baby inside me now, too, but now I really wouldn't tell him about that. He dashed into the kitchen, and brought me a bucket, and I vomited everything that I'd eaten that morning. I heaved long after there was nothing less to vomit, dry heaving into the bucket while sobbing.

At some point, I just lay down on the floor. There was nothing left. No more tears, no more puke, no more rage. There was just...nothing.

I had no more feelings.

"Iris," Ryan was saying. He hadn't said a word for hours while I raged about. "I love you more than I could ever love anybody. You're my soul mate. My other half."

"Do I complete you?" I asked.

"Yes."

"Am I the sunshine of your life?"

"Yes."

"Got any other clichés you can bring out? How about telling me that it's always darkest before the dawn? Or, I know a good one – what doesn't kill you makes you stronger." I shook my head. "I should be fucking Hercules by now." Then I smiled. "not literally fucking Hercules, but you get the idea."

He chuckled too, thinking that the worst was over. "We'll get through this."

"Like hell we will."

Then he looked devastated. He obviously had some

hope that because I made a little joke that I was ready to let bygones be bygones.

He couldn't be more wrong.

At that, I whipped out my iPhone and called Richard. "Hey. You know how you wanted to rent out that room?"

"Yes."

"I'll be over in fifteen minutes." Then I thought better. "Sorry, could you pick me up? I don't have a car."

"What do you mean? You have that Volvo. And are you saying you want to move in?"

"I don't have a car," I repeated. "That car doesn't belong to me anymore," I said, looking Ryan right in the eye.

"What do you mean?"

"I'm leaving Ryan."

Chapter Thirty-Four

After I made that phone call, I went upstairs to pack. This was a familiar scenario, as I packed up the cat and a bag while Ryan stood in the doorway, pleading with me.

"Don't go, don't go, don't go, please don't go. I love you, I can't live without you."

"You can live without me. You got Natalie now. She'll take real good care of you. You were the one she has always wanted anyhow. And now she has her wish. I sure feel sorry for Nate, though."

"I don't love her. I love you. I've always loved you. I knew it from the second I saw you that you were meant for me. Please don't go."

"You already said that. Think of something new. It's sounding like your greatest hits now," I said. "Please don't go, please don't go. I love you. You're my soul mate," I said in a mocking voice. "Is that really all you got?"

He just said nothing, but continued to plead with me with his eyes.

I looked out the window. Richard had just pulled up in the driveway.

"Well, it looks like I'll be off," I said. "There are still a lot of clothes and shoes here and stuff. You can let Natalie have those. I mean, she's taller than me, but she can wear some of my blouses at least. Not sure about her shoe size. At any rate, whatever she doesn't want, please give to the Goodwill."

Then I remembered something else. I took off my red diamond and my wedding band and put it on the windowsill "Here. I don't need a thing from you. You can also give these to Natalie. She'll appreciate them one helluva more than I will."

Then I ran down the stairs and into Richard's waiting car.

Chapter Thirty-Five

In the car, Richard asked "Doll, do you want to tell me what happened?"

I just shook my head, and stared out the window.

My iPhone was blowing up. Ryan was calling me every minute it seemed.

I finally just turned it off.

We got to Richard's house, which was a four bedroom home in a nicer area of town. It was a newer area, with spindly trees and not much shade cover. The house was colonial style, with a small veranda, and a staircase just inside the front door. Richard lived there with his partner, Mark, and the place had the definite air of a gay man's taste – immaculate, tasteful, with perfectly matched furniture, embroidered throw pillows, and large indoor trees.

"Uh, I hate to say this, but I might be short the first month. I have to find a job," I said, upon getting into the house and putting my bags down by the front stairs.

"Doll, you have a megabucks husband. How can you be short?"

"Had a megabucks husband. Had one. Every penny he has is his own, not mine. I did nothing to earn any of it."

"That's not how it works," he said.

"That's how it works with me," I told him. "So I have to find a job. Thanks to him, I am no longer financially independent."

"What's that supposed to mean?"

"I lost my law practice because of that psychobitch from hell attacking me. Or did you forget about that?"

"Doll, you weren't financially independent before you met him."

"Thanks for rubbing it in."

"You know what I mean."

"How much is the rent here?" I asked.

"$400."

I scratched my head. "I can swing that. I wonder if Whole Foods is hiring?"

"Whole Foods? With your education, you want to work there?"

"Yeah. Why not? It always looks like fun and the people there are so cool."

"Doll, you aren't in your right mind."

"I'll be ok making whatever Whole Foods pays. At least until the baby comes."

"Baby?"

"Yeah. I took a pregnancy test this morning, and it was positive. Ain't that the shits?"

His eyes were wide. "Are we....happy about it?"

"No. Considering that the father is either dumb or dumber, and I have no idea which one," I said, shrugging. "Let's just say it's not the ideal situation. Then again, I have no idea if I'm going to even keep it." At that, I tapped on my iPhone, looking at my personal bank account. It was probably either a negative balance, or had been closed because the balance was too low. I probably had to open up a new one.

"Mother fucker!" I yelled after logging on to the site.

"What?"

"That asshole put a million fucking dollars into my personal account. How in the hell did he transfer that amount of money this fast?"

"Megabucks boys can do whatever they want these days," he said. "What an asshole, huh? How dare he make sure you're taken care of, especially when you're carrying his child?"

"Number one, he doesn't know about the kid. Number two, I told you, I don't know if that baby is his."

"You said that, but I didn't know what you meant. What do you mean the baby could have either dumb or dumber as its father?"

"Oh, I didn't tell you about that. I was raped. Brutally raped," I said, taking secret delight in the look of horror on Richard's face. "Vag raped, ass raped. He used a belt to strangle me until I was at the point of passing out, then he raped me. He forced me on all fours like a dog along the floor by pulling at the belt like it was a leash, then he hand-cuffed me to the barstool and raped me some more." I felt myself smirking. "So you see, he is dumber, and Ryan is dumb. Ryan and I made love about a week before the rape, so I literally have no idea who is the lucky sperm donor."

"Oh, doll," he said, putting his hand on my shoulder. "I don't know what to say."

"I do. How about congratulations! It's not every day that you get to carry around a rapist's baby."

He just stood there, looking at me mutely.

"And the kicker is," I said, suddenly laughing so hard I

couldn't speak. Richard started to laugh along with me, obviously not sure what was so funny. "Ah, the kicker is that, get this. There's another baby!"

"What do you mean?"

"Ryan impregnated another woman while I was living in a drug house trying to forget dumber's rape."

"You lived in a drug house?"

"Try to keep up. I went cuckoo for cocoa puffs and shot up my veins for a couple of weeks before Mr. White Knight came riding in on the cavalry to rescue me again. He should've just left me there. Anyhow, he neglected to tell me that he fucked another woman while I was gone. That would've been nice to know." I continued to laugh, but Richard was no longer trying to laugh along with me. "Boy, I tell ya. My life...I really should write a book. A memoir. Nobody would ever believe it, though. Could you imagine? Average girl meets gorgeous rich guy, and her life becomes a never-ending nightmare from then on. Dystopian Cinderella, indeed."

"Doll, you aren't making sense."

"No, I'm making perfect sense. You just have to listen to me and know that I'm not joking about any of this."

"I know you're not joking about this. What can I do to help you?"

"I'm not sure. I have to buy a car, but my credit is shot. So if you could let me borrow your car if I need it, just a few times, that would certainly help. At least until I can earn enough for a down-payment. I'm thinking maybe I could try my hand at some free-lance writing projects, so I don't have to have a car for work. Then, once I earn enough from the writing projects, I can buy my own car," I said, ignoring the increasingly incredulous look on Richard's face. "At any rate, I'll need a car for going to the store and a baby doc.

Because I can't terminate, of course, due to this backward-ass state's abortion laws." Then I raised my eyebrows. "Then again, Kansas has laws that permit termination up until 20 weeks. I think I can come in under the wire on that one."

"Doll," he said. "You're account has -"

"No, it doesn't. I'm opening up a new account. Fuck him and his money. If I could transfer it back right this second, I would."

That night, I tossed and turned. How far along was I now? In my first trimester, at any rate. And with the drugs I was doing, and the fact that I hadn't even thought about nutrition or pre-natal vitamins, the baby was liable to come out with three heads. And I was going to be a single mother now, with little visible means of support. So I better not be selfish and work a minimum wage job.

On and on I tossed and turned, willing myself not to think about my overall situation and just to think about the baby. Baby Dalilah. Baby Dalilah with the three heads. Baby Dalilah who might have rapist's genes. Or she might have Ryan's genes, in which case she would be a lucky girl indeed. As long as she doesn't get stupid and sleep with some other dude while married, she would be fine. She can even be bisexual. That would be fine, too.

Just as long as she's not a cheater.

That week, there were different things coming through the front door. First, there were 120 red roses, in ten vases, with cards attached to each of the vases. One said "I'm sorry if this sounds cliché, but I can't live without you." Another said "I'm bleeding from a thousand tiny cuts here." Still another said "Please come home." Another said "The bed's too big without you." All of the cards had similar sentiments – sweet, but cliché. Then again, it was difficult to express sentiments that weren't cliché, so I gave him a pass for this.

Just the same, I put every rose in the composter, after carefully snipping off the buds.

When Richard got home that night from work, I told him "Good news. You have a full composter now!"

Then "Can I borrow your car? I need to go to Goodwill and donate some vases."

The next day after the roses came a handwritten card. On the front was a Matisse painting, who was one of my favorite painters, and I read the card once before retiring it to my drawer.

Something couldn't quite bring me to throw it away.

The card read:

Beautiful,

I know that Nat being pregnant looks bad, but you have to believe me when I tell you that I never would've have done that if I was in my right mind. You are my world. I refuse to use the past tense in describing my love for you, because I refuse to believe that our love is over. So, I say that you are my world, not you were my world. Are. You can push me away, and you can be angry with me. I understand. But know that, no matter how long it takes, I will be right here waiting for you. Nothing can deter me from believing that you are my wife now and forever. I have known from the moment I met you that I wanted to be with you for eternity. I will never give up. And I will always fight to be with you.

Love,

Ryan

My heart thawed a tiny bit, then I remembered that he impregnated another woman while I was in trouble, and my resolve went up anew.

Still, I didn't throw away the card. I simply hid it in the drawer of the nightstand.

Meanwhile, I had to decide soon what to do with baby Dalilah. Either I was keeping her, assuming it was a her, in which case I better see a doctor quick, or I was going to not keep her. This was the most impossible decision, because I knew that if she belonged to Andrew, and I would know this immediately, then I would always have the reminder of what happened to me on that kitchen floor. And if she belonged to Ryan...I would cross that bridge when I come to it, I guess.

I sighed.

And made an appointment to visit Planned Parenthood the next day.

Chapter Thirty-Six

I sat in the waiting room of the Overland Park, Kansas, Planned Parenthood clinic, after taking several different buses from Richard's house. The waiting room was sterile and white, with pamphlets in little plastic holders on the wall about STDs, pregnancy, abortion services, pap smears, mammograms, pelvic exams, and the like. On the table there were *People* Magazines, along with magazines about parenting and a few other women's magazines. I prayed that "my" *People* magazine was not in the stack. I couldn't deal with that, on top of everything else I had to deal with today.

There was a woman behind a glass partition, who handed me a clipboard with forms for me to fill out. They were forms about my medical history.

"What services are you needing?" the girl, Prentiss, asked me.

"I'm not sure. I'm pregnant. That's all I know."

She nodded knowingly. "The doctor will discuss all your options."

"Thanks."

I tried to relax by looking at some magazines, and it seemed to be an eternity before my name was finally called.

A young girl with a sandy blonde pony-tail and Winnie the Pooh scrubs took my vitals, and gave me a gown that opened in the back. I sat on the edge of the table, my feet dangling over the edge, and found another magazine and read.

The doctor came in about 45 minutes later. A man. My heart started beating fast and hard.

"Is there something wrong?" Dr. O'Neill asked, seeing that my face was probably white as a sheet.

"Uh, I'm so sorry. I forgot to ask if I could have a woman. No offense, but I-"

"Not a problem at all," he said kindly. Then he left, and I waited another hour for Dr. Morgan to arrive. She finally did arrive, a 5-foot-tall woman with a greying ponytail and wire-rimmed glasses. I immediately felt comfortable with her.

"Now, Ms. Snowe, what are we doing today?" she asked.

"I'm pregnant," I said, taking a piece of my hair and twisting it. "And I've had....trauma."

"Sexual trauma?" she asked.

I nodded.

"This is a very delicate question, but -"

"I don't know if the father was my rapist. I was married at the time, and we had sex about a week before it happened. And my cycle has always been so erratic that I would think it would be hard to get a handle on exactly when I conceived."

It was her turn to nod.

Putting my hand in my hair, twisting it up into a knot on the top of my head, I said "so, I wanted to know my options. I mean, I know my options, but just wanted to hear what they were."

"Well, here at the clinic, we can offer you pre-natal care. That would include sonograms, vitamins, and examinations. And we also offer pregnancy termination services, as you probably know. As long as you are no more than 20 weeks along."

"Let's start with the prenatal care."

"We'll start with a sonogram," she said, as she wheeled the machine over to the table. I lay back, and she put some gel on an enormous wand, and put the wand inside of me. She pointed to the screen – "There's the cervix, and there's your little one," she said. I looked at the screen and saw a tiny object floating there, and I could hear the heart beating rapidly. "Everything looks good," she said.

I nodded. "I guess you don't know if it's a boy or a girl," I said.

"No, it's too soon to tell," she said.

"Doc?"

"Yes?" she asked.

"What would you do if you were me? If you were raped and pregnant and unsure if the baby's father is the rapist or your husband?"

"Well, we're two different people," she said. "What is your situation?"

"I'm not with my husband anymore. I also don't have a job." I neglected to mention that said husband was a gajillionaire.

"It's completely your choice," she said, stating the obvious. "Don't forget to pick up a card on the way out with our information," she said. "And call when you decide what to do. In the meantime, I'm going to send you off with a month's supply of pre-natal vitamins, a list of foods that you should eat and a list you shouldn't. Stay away from the sushi," she said with a smile.

"Uh, one other thing before you leave," I said.

"Yes?"

"I, uh, had a drug problem when she was conceived. Heroin. I was addicted for a couple of weeks. Is that going to cause problems?"

"It might," she said. "But, believe it or not, harder drugs are not as likely to cause fetal damage as more common things like alcohol and cigarettes. At any rate, I wouldn't recommend that you use that as a significant factor on whether or not to terminate. Chances are that your baby will be just fine."

I nodded, relieved.

Then I took my vitamins, gave the receptionist my insurance card, and went out to catch the bus to get to Richard's.

When I got to Richard's, I saw Ryan's Porsche on the street in front of the house.

Chapter Thirty-Seven

There was a large part of me that wanted to walk on past Richard's house when I saw Ryan's car in front. But I knew that I would have to confront it sooner or later.

Might as well get it over with.

I walked in and Ryan immediately stood up. He was apparently sitting in the living room prior to my arrival, talking to Richard and Mark, and casually drinking a beer. He had a hopeful look in those beautiful eyes. I had to admit that seeing him gave me the usual reaction of heart pounding electricity, and oh, how I wanted him to simply take me in his arms and tell me that everything was going to be ok.

I loved him so much it hurt.

I wanted to tell him that I would go home with him, that he was the love of my life, that I couldn't live a single day without him, and that I wanted to be with him forever.

Instead I said "What the hell are you doing here?"

His face immediately fell.

I shot a look at Richard and Mark, and said to Ryan

"Would you please excuse us? I need to talk to Richard and Mark alone."

He nodded, and went out on the back patio and shut the door.

I looked at the two men "You didn't tell him about-" and pointed to my stomach.

"Of course not," Richard said. "That's your job, not ours."

"Good," I said, pointing at both of them, then pointing two fingers at my eyes and pointing the two fingers back at them in the universal symbol of *I'm watching you*. "Keep it that way. Now tell him he can come back in."

At that, Richard opened the patio door, and Ryan stepped back in.

"Well," Richard said. "Mark and I are going to get something to eat." And they got their coats on and left.

After they left, I stood there glaring at Ryan with my arms crossed.

Ryan spoke first. "I'm not leaving here until you come with me."

"What, are you going to force me to come home? Like you forced me to get a bodyguard? That turned out really well, didn't it?"

He looked stung at my words.

"And, by the way, I mean, I know that I didn't want to press charges against the guy. But I really expected you to have more emotions about the whole issue than you did. That has always bothered me. I figured that you would want to kick his ass, or something."

He went white as a sheet. "I did want to kick his ass," he said quietly. "Trust me. I wanted to kill him. After I found what happened to you, I found out where he was hiding. My father tracked him down. And I got my gun and was going to go straight to where he was and gun him down." His face was contorted, and I knew that he was dead serious about this. "Nick found out what I was about to do and told me that there probably wasn't any way that I could win against a retired government assassin, and that, even if I did, I would be put into prison for the rest of my life." His hands ran through his beautiful hair, as he spoke. "I said I didn't give a shit about that. All I cared about was ripping his lungs out of his body. But Nick talked me down as usual."

"How did he talk you down?"

His beautiful eyes looked directly into mine as he said "Nick told me that if anything happened to me, it would be devastating to you. If I was killed trying to kill Andrew, or if I was put into prison because I killed him, you would be the one who would suffer. And he was absolutely right."

"Oh, honey. You never told me this." I suddenly realized that he was suffering, right along with me. He always hid this so well. "I love you."

Now he looked hopeful. His eyes suddenly lit up, as did his entire face. "Then you're coming home?"

I shook my head. "No. I'm not really angry anymore, which is why I can admit to you how much I still love you. But I can never trust you again. I always thought that you could never cheat on me. But now you have. We haven't been married six months, and you have already impregnated another woman. And not just any woman. Someone who is also madly in love with you." I looked at his face, which was now back to being crestfallen, his head down, and his hands shaking. "I can't come back. Not when there is a baby on the way with somebody else. I'm sorry."

And I *was* sorry. I realized that I, too, was devastated, just as much as him.

"Iris. Please. There must be a way to get through this. Please don't do this. Please," he said, as a tear ran down his cheek. "You're a part of me. If you leave me, you will rip out my soul."

"Then your soul must be already ripped out. Because I have already left."

"No, no, no, no, no. This can't be. There has to be a way."

I just looked at him. Then I quietly said "I think you better go."

He just stood there, shaking his head. "I'm not leaving without you."

"Then I'll leave," I said, getting my coat and walking out the front door.

He chased after me, grabbing my arm. "No. You can't leave, I won't let you."

I looked at my arm, which was being gripped by his hand, and simply said "I want a divorce."

Chapter Thirty-Eight

"A divorce? God, Iris. No. You can't do this."

"Listen to reason, here. You need to make an honest woman of Natalie. You can't just be with me and have a kid across the country. That kid has to know his father. You don't want the kid to grow up in a broken home like you did. Well, not the same thing, of course, but the shit is going to hit the fan when Nate finds out what happened, and Nat will be out on the street. Then what? The kid needs a stable home." I found myself thinking what a hypocrite I was, because I, too, was carrying a child that had a fifty-fifty chance of being his. And that kid was going to grow up without him. But it was the other fifty percent chance that it wasn't his that made me have resolve about what I was saying.

And in my speech, I never once considered the fact that perhaps Natalie also didn't really know who the father was.

He looked pained. "Uh, Nat was already kicked out of the apartment."

"There, you see. She needs you."

"She's living in town now."

I nodded my head. This was getting worse by the millisecond.

"So, what are you doing here? You need to make your family with her and leave me out of it."

"I don't love Nat. I love you. And you are the only woman I will ever love."

"Don't be dramatic. You have everything. Enjoy it. She looks better with you anyhow. And the kid with her will be guaranteed to be gorgeous. Any kid with me would-"

"Would what?"

"Would have a fifty-fifty chance of being gorgeous, that's all."

He got his familiar pissed look that he always got whenever I put myself down, but said nothing.

He obviously didn't pick up on the real reason I cut off when I talked about having a kid with me.

And I left it at that.

"Anyhow, please forget about me and be happy with Nat. I can never be yours again, because I can't trust you."

At that, I ran back inside the door and locked it. He stood outside the door, pounding on it, yelling my name over and over and over, but I shut out the lights, put earplugs in, and went to bed.

Chapter Thirty-Nine

Ryan continued to pursue me constantly, with daily phone messages and regular roses, all of which I ignored.

I had to form my plan on how I could manage to divorce him without him knowing about Dalilah, then make a new life with just her and me.

I had a chance to think about what I wanted, really wanted, after Ryan was forced out of Richard's house that day. He finally gave up and went home at some point during the night. And I lay there and realized that I could never be with him, because I could never trust him not to hurt me again.

He talked about his soul being ripped out.

So was mine when I found out about Nat.

He talked about a part of him dying.

The same thing happened to me when I found out about Nat.

After everything that had happened to me, I didn't need anymore pain in my life.

So, all I wanted was to carry my child, and hope that we

could make a little family that would never leave me or hurt me.

With a heavy heart, I prepared divorce papers.

I didn't need a lawyer. I literally didn't want anything from him. Just my maiden name restored. That was all that I wanted, so I figured that it would be easy as pie to get through it. And I had to do it quick, before I really started to show. As it was, I was seeing a little tiny pooch that was getting bigger by the day. If he knew about the baby, there would be no divorce by law. And it would complicate matters after the baby was born. There would be a custody battle, and I would always have him in my life, ripping out my heart every time I saw his beautiful face. Every time I saw him with Natalie and their no-doubt beautiful child, a part of me would die.

I couldn't have that.

I needed a clean slate.

It occurred to me that I would be committing a major fraud when I made the allegation that I was not currently pregnant, which was an important part of every dissolution of marriage petition. But I would simply go off the grid again. Start a new life somewhere else, somewhere he could never find me. I always wanted to live in San Francisco.

But I wouldn't have money.

At that, I made an online application for a Visa. I figured that, at that moment, I had a million dollars in my account, so getting approved would be a snap, bad credit or no.

In a matter of minutes, my hunch was correct. I had a $20,000 limit.

Enough to get me started someplace new, to tide me over until I found a job.

My divorce petition prepared, I took a bus downtown to

file it with the fee. Ryan would be served at home. I couldn't do that to him at his work.

Chapter Forty

Ryan was served at his home, and he started blowing up the phone again. I refused to take his calls, but I did call his lawyer to schedule a meeting where we would hammer everything out. That way we could simply walk the divorce through on the uncontested docket, and get the judge to sign off on it.

This meeting happened about a month after I filed the papers. Ryan had finally given up in defeat, and we agreed to meet at his lawyer's office. Sheldon would be handling his divorce, as he apparently handled all of Ryan's legal matters.

Of course, Sheldon's office was in a high-rise downtown. We met in the enormous conference room with floor-to-ceiling windows, and legal books lining the shelves. I smiled looking at the legal books. They were all for show, of course - no lawyer ever looked at a book. There's no need to, when absolutely everything is on-line. Still, it looked nice.

Ryan walked into the room, and I almost didn't recognize him. He had lost a considerable amount of weight, he was pale, there were dark circles under his eyes, and his hair had become unruly. It had a tendency to become unruly anyway, as it was super thick and wavy, but he always kept it trim and tamed. Now it was just growing out and looked a bit wild. He also had a full beard and mustache, which actually suited him. He was dressed down in shorts and a rumpled button down. I didn't think that it was possible he could look so disheveled.

Even so, he was still the most beautiful man I had ever set eyes upon.

My heart broke.

We sat there, just looking at one another, waiting for Sheldon to come in. His eyes were pleading with me, and it was all I could do to not leap into his arms and kiss him as passionately as ever, to tell him to forget this divorce nonsense, and that we would get through the Nat crisis together. That I never wanted to be apart from him, ever, and that I wanted us to be the two old people in the rocking chair, just like he told Sarah.

Instead, I looked away. I felt self-conscious about my little belly, so I was wearing a loose-fitting shirt. I hoped that he just thought that I was gaining weight from eating too much from depression.

Finally, Sheldon came in. He was a short man, about 5'7", chubby, bespectacled, and with a receding hairline. He wore suspenders and a pin-striped shirt.

"Ok, Mrs. Gallagher. Here is our opening offer," Sheldon said, sitting down, and giving me a piece of paper.

"No need. I just scheduled this meeting because I want to get everything finalized. I don't want a thing." I was trying so hard to be courageous and I felt I just came off as being cold.

At that, Ryan looked pained.

"Mrs. Gallagher, that's not an option. Please review our offer."

It was some opening offer. Ryan was trying to give me $50 million and the Cezanne, along with the Volvo and the red diamond ring. My mouth dropped open when I read on the offer sheet that the Cezanne was valued at $120 million. The red diamond ring was valued at $2 million.

"With all due respect, I don't want anything," I said, pushing the paper back in rejection of the offer. "This is all very well and good, but I really don't want anything."

"Mrs. Gallagher, this is our offer. You need to take this, or there will be a trial."

"That's good with me. In a trial, that judge won't give me much. We were married for about a minute. Now, please don't be ridiculous," I said, addressing Ryan directly. "I didn't earn any of this, so I'm not taking any of it."

"Mrs. Gallagher, that's not how it works. You are entitled to-"

"Half of all earnings and increase in property value during the marriage. I know. I was a divorce attorney, so please don't talk down to me. What I am entitled to isn't what you are offering me, and you know it," I said, again addressing Ryan directly. "You're offering me half of everything you have, essentially, and I'm not taking it. I'm telling you I don't want anything. Those divorce laws are antiquated, anyhow, made during a time when a woman couldn't live without support from a man. I can make my own living."

"Be that as it may, Mrs. Gallagher, we are not withdrawing our offer."

"If you try to force me to take this offer, I swear to God, I will give every last penny to charity. I'll sell that Cezanne and give every nickel to the ASPCA, and every last penny from the cash I am getting."

To this, Ryan finally spoke. "Good. Those animals need protection."

My heart was being ripped out, as I remembered that those were the exact words Nate said to Ryan at that dinner just before Christmas of the year before last. God, that was a little over a year ago, and it now seemed like it was decades ago. That was such a happy time....I fought back tears remembering that wonderful memory.

But I didn't tell him what I was thinking, how my heart was breaking with every glance I made at him. Instead I said "Well, if you aren't going to be reasonable, I will take my chances with the judge, and tell the judge that I don't want anything. Hopefully the judge will listen to me more than you will, Ryan."

I was bluffing, of course. The trial would be set out too far in the future, and, by then, there would be no hiding Baby Dalilah. And the last sonogram did show that the baby was a she, so I didn't have to change the name I had picked out for her.

"That's my offer," Ryan said. "Take it or leave it."

I shook my head angrily. I was being backed into a corner, and I didn't like it. I had to take this offer, but there was no way I was going to take it lying down. It would be drastic to give it all to charity, but I could always just pretend it didn't exist. I would continue to live on my own wages and my own gumption, and pretend it all doesn't exist.

"I don't want your money. I don't deserve it, and I don't want it. Please listen to me. I don't want anything from you." Inside I was screaming *I love you, I love you, I love you. Please don't leave me. Please don't leave me. I'm dying inside.*

Ryan and Sheldon were now whispering amongst themselves. Then Sheldon said "Fine, Mrs. Gallagher. We will see you at trial."

No. No trial. "Ok. I'll take the offer."

Ryan looked like a deflated balloon. I thought that I saw a little bit of life in his eyes when he first saw me, but that flicker was gone. Now he just looked dead inside.

Like myself.

With shaking hands, I signed the paperwork.

Then got up and left without a word.

Chapter Forty-One

"Doll, what are you going to do now?" Richard was asking me, as he watched me packing my suitcase.

"I'm leaving. I can't be here. There are too many bad memories here, and, besides, Ryan can't know about Dalilah."

"How can you just keep that from him? That's his child, too."

"50-50 chance it's not his, remember?"

"50-50 chance it is his, too. Besides, what are you going to do when Rochelle has her trial? You are the star witness."

"Hopefully that will plead and I'm not going to have to worry about it."

"Fat chance. The news stations are already gearing up for it."

"By then, Dalilah will be here, and I'll put her in day care or something. I'll think of something."

I always do.

"You still aren't thinking rational, Doll."

"Richard, I haven't been thinking rationally since the

rape. And I really haven't been rational since the whole Nat business. Do you know that she's living with him, now?"

"How did you figure that out?"

"I've been doing drive-bys. Her car is there night and day." I held back tears. "Anyhow, I always knew that my whole life with him was too good to be true. He's too good to be true. I never deserved him anyway. I never deserved him anyway." At that, the tears came, and Richard held me close to his chest while I cried.

"I'll miss you, Doll," he said. "We all will."

I said nothing, just nodded my head. "I'll miss you too."

"Well, we can't just let you leave without having a goodbye party. I'm going to throw you the most fabulous bon voyage imaginable."

"You always do throw the best parties," I said.

So, the going away party was set for the next day, an impromptu shindig. The short notice for the party was necessitated by the fact that I, well, wanted the hell out of town.

I felt awful breaking the news to my parents. "What?" my mother asked me after I invited her to the party. She was astonished. "Why are you leaving?"

"I just feel the need to get away," I said. "I can't face the fact that I might run into Ryan here in town."

"Don't be ridiculous," my mother said. "There's over a million people in the area. Chances are that you never will have to see him again."

"I can't take that chance," I said, not telling her that there was a grandchild on the way.

The party was a success, in spite of the short notice. I helped get everything ready, and the boys used their good China. Over 40 of my closest friends and family showed up to wish me well. I was touched that they were able to make the party with only a day's notice. The spread included lasagna, garlic bread, pizza, cheesecake and lots of alcohol. I didn't partake in the alcohol, of course, but everybody else did. Everybody stayed until around midnight, then they headed home, pretty much *en masse.*

Debbie stayed late to help clean up. "So, what are you going to do once you get out there?"

"I have no clue," I said. "Get a job, I would imagine."

"Are you going to take the bar?"

"I doubt it. I didn't like law here, so why would I want to practice it out there?"

"Because that's what you know. That's what you are trained for. That's what you spent 7 years of your life getting an education for."

"Yeah, that's played. I'll just have to figure something else out."

She was disapproving, I know, but she said nothing. She was very good about not pressing the matter when it became clear that I didn't want further discussion. This was a learned skill for her, but she mastered it well. Yes, I was screwing up my life. I was well aware of that. But I was determined to follow through with my plan, come hell or high water. I didn't care that the plan was stupid, or not viable. Debbie knew this, understood this, so she said nothing more.

She did, however, admonish me about the baby. "You can't just keep that baby away from him forever, you know. Sooner or later, you're going to have to tell him."

"I realize that. But I need to feel a little more sane and stable before doing that. Right now, with my hormones so out of wack, and with my feeling so betrayed and traumatized, I just cannot face him. I'll recover, I always do. I'll get stronger, and then I hope to come back and make things right."

The next day, I got my suitcase, and packed Madison in her carrier. Then I cried in Richard's arms for what seemed to be an eternity, and said "drive me to the airport?"

At that, we got into his car and headed to the airport so that I could catch the next flight to San Francisco.

Chapter Forty-Two

I was now in San Francisco, the city by the bay. I had a cash advance from my Visa, and put the money into my new account. I pretended that the other money didn't exist. I also got a new phone and a new phone number.

I checked into a low price hotel that was by the Pier 39, hiding the fact that I had a cat, and walked down to watch the sea lions frolicking on the dock. I stood there for hours, just watching them bully each other and bark. Then I took a bus through China Town and over to Ocean Beach. Since it was now early spring, it was freezing, and I had wrapped myself up in a winter coat, hat, gloves and a scarf. The beach was deserted, but the ocean was comforting. There was no way that I could possibly get in the water, but I, once again, felt the presence of God. The ocean always made me think of Him, for some reason. There was no other times when I felt His presence but when I looked at the vast depths of water.

I closed my eyes, trying to forget about Ryan and I on the beach of LA, and Ryan and I on the cliffs of Rhode

Island. But the memories could not be fought, and as I lay down on the sand, the tears came once again. It seemed that I had never really stopped crying since I found out about Nat. I just could never show Ryan that.

I lay there by the ocean for hours, my tears flowing as much as the ocean itself. The waves were crashing, again and again, and the seagulls were shrieking. This was a beautiful moment, and I prayed that Ryan would be happy with Nat. All I wanted was for him to be happy and find peace in his life. It devastated me to see him at Sheldon's office, because seeing him at all ripped my heart out, but it was more than that. I realized that the way that he looked at the office meant he was severely depressed. Because of me. In my own weird way, I was trying to do the right thing. Trying to make sure that Nat's baby has a father.

But I had devastated him in the process.

I spoke aloud "God, are you there? If you are, please hear me. Please help Ryan find happiness with Nat. Please keep him off drugs. Please help him find peace. Please, God. He deserves it. He deserves it. He deserves it. He deserves it. He deserves it."

Then I got up off the sand, and wandered along the shore for hours, picking up seashells and poking little jellyfish that had washed ashore. The sun was finally setting, and I made my way to the nearest bus and headed to my hotel room.

Chapter Forty-Three

I couldn't live off of my credit card money forever. I had to find a job. I thought for about a half second about taking the California bar and pursuing some kind of attorney job out here. But I realized that I had been out of school for so long that I couldn't remember much about all of those areas of law – contracts, torts, constitutional law, property law, and criminal law. I had a pretty good working knowledge of many of those areas, but detailed knowledge was what I would need to pass. The passage rate was quite low, and I barely passed the bar in Missouri and Kansas.

Plus, law didn't make me happy.

So, I set my sights low, having very little energy for a demanding job. I walked into the local Whole Foods and asked for an application.

A tattooed guy of around 25 was clerking, and I asked him about how to apply at the store. He directed me to a kiosk, and I filled out my information.

"So what's next?" I asked.

"Your app will be looked at, and hopefully we'll call you for an interview. What kind of qualifications do you have?"

"I know a lot about organics and the importance of buying local, and the advantages of buying meat that isn't factory farmed." Truth be told, most of my knowledge about these topics came from listening to Jillian Michaels on my iPod while I exercised or walked.

I didn't tell him that, though.

"What's your background?"

"I was actually an attorney back home in Kansas City."

"And you want to work here?"

"Yes, actually. You won't believe me if I told you this, but I've wanted to work in a Whole Foods ever since I stepped foot in my very first store. It just has such a cool vibe, and seems like a very relaxed place to work. Don't get me wrong, I know that there is a lot involved to the job, but I really want to work with people with a laid-back attitude."

He nodded. "You've come to the right place, for sure. You'll probably get an interview."

"That's all I can ask."

At that, I went home to my hotel room and willed the phone to ring. I didn't know what I would do when the Visa money ran out, which would happen sooner than I thought in such an expensive city. I didn't go out much, except to wander around the city on foot. I couldn't afford a car, so I got around by street car, bus and cable car. I also went for long walks, wandering all around the city. I must have walked six miles a day or more – there was just so much to see and take in. This city was really the most beautiful place I knew. I couldn't afford to go out to eat, so I usually packed a small brown-bag lunch, consisting of fruit and a peanut butter and jelly sandwich. I was also very cognizant that I needed to feed Dalilah, so I started every day with a protein shake mixed with spinach and other veggies. I really wasn't all that hungry, though, so I had to force myself to eat.

I didn't know if my lack of appetite was because of Dalilah or because of my depression, which was threatening to overwhelm me. I tried very hard to work my program that I learned through my CBT, but it didn't seem to be working. Everywhere I saw Ryan. There weren't too many guys who matched him as far as how he looked, but I sought out men who had his kindness, intelligence and humor. But I really didn't find men who matched him in these areas, either.

I despaired that I ever would have that kind of love again, and I really didn't want it.

But I wanted companionship, and that was what I really missed the most about Ryan. From the start, I felt that I had known him forever. Our rapport was always so easy, never forced. We laughed at each other's silly jokes, could get into endless political discussions, and he was always so…interested. In me. In what I thought, how I felt, what my dreams were, and my nightmares. The thought that he wasn't in my life anymore was more devastating to me than Rochelle, Andrew and Mr. Green put together.

Every evening I took the bus to the beach and just sat and watched the waves and cried. It didn't help that my hormones were going haywire. I thought about just going into the ocean like Virginia Woolf, weighed down with rocks. The only thing that stopped me from doing that was Dalilah. She was what kept me from harming myself with alcohol or drugs as well. I couldn't rely on any of my old crutches, because I couldn't do harm to her.

And just the thought that I could possibly have a part of Ryan in her gave me great comfort.

About a week after my application process at the Whole

Foods I was granted an interview. I must have impressed the hiring manager with my personality, because I, amazingly, got the job. I would start clerking, and rotate to other departments while I worked there.

Since my Visa money was starting to get slightly low, because the hotel was so expensive, I had to find a cheap place to live, which was not easy in San Francisco. The place also would have to let me have Madison, which complicated matters. Poor Madison – cats hate change, and she was having a tough time adjusting. Plus, it seemed that she was absolutely traumatized by the plane ride. I was able to store her under the seat, so she didn't go cargo, and I did give her some tranquilizers. But, still, she didn't seem the same.

Yet another creature whose life I destroyed.

I did find a small room for rent in one of the Victorian mansions for $1,200 a month, which just about cleared out my bank account each month, as my take home pay was only around $1,800 a month. Still, I got good discounts at the Whole Foods, so that helped. Everything helped.

Dalilah was growing inside me. I could feel her kicking me now. It started out as little flutters, now it was as if she was fighting to get out. I was about six months along, and everything was going fine. I was keeping up with my prenatal visits with a gyno I found, taking my vitamins, and trying to eat right.

I started to feel not so alone when she kicked, because it reminded me that she was there.

Even so, I was a shell. I was dead inside. I prayed that I would come to life when Dalilah arrived. I had to come to life when she arrived. She couldn't have a mother who was dead inside.

Every night when I went home, I was alone with my

thoughts. And I realized that I would gladly have suffered everything again – the rape, the Rochelle attack, the splashing of my private life across the news channels – if I could have one more moment with Ryan. I was dead inside because I lost the love of my life. Everything else that had happened to me paled in comparison.

I did my work dutifully, learning more about organics than I ever thought I would. There was even a guy there who evidently had his eye on me, burgeoning belly and all. But I politely declined to go out with him. He was cute and seemed nice, but I had already made the decision not to pursue anybody else, ever again. It would only be me and Dalilah forever. And when she grew up and left me...I didn't want to think that far.

I had Richard do the drive-bys for me at home, and he agreed. He always reported back, and it seemed that Natalie was still living there with Ryan. This pained me beyond measure, but also made me happy.

Maybe he was finding his peace and happiness with her.

That was still all I wanted.

Every night, I had the same dreams about Ryan. He and I were always together and happy. In my dreams, we were always laughing and teasing each other. We were always holding hands, and holding each other. We were always making love. Then I would wake up, and feel the devastation of an empty bed.

Then, one day, my water broke, right there in the Whole Foods.

Chapter Forty-Four

"Oh, shit," I said. "My water just broke."

"Well, come on, girl, let's go." Lena, who was a lesbian hippy, was more than happy to take me to the hospital. "Hey, Chaz, I gotta take this lady to the hospital. Can you find people to cover for us?"

Chaz, a dreadlocked boy of about 22, appeared and agreed to call people to come in to cover.

"Thanks, Chaz," Lena said, as I panicked a little, breathing in and out, in and out, in and out.

"This is your first?" Lena asked.

I simply nodded, and kept breathing in and out.

"Don't be too afraid of the pain. It's not that bad. Well, I lied. It is that bad. But don't be afraid," she said, as we made our way to her 1997 Datsun.

I shook my head. She had no idea how much physical and emotional pain I had been through. No earthly idea. No matter how much pain this would cause me, it would be cake compared to everything else.

She sped to the hospital, with me in the passenger's side

doing my breathing like I was taught in my Lamaze class. Then the hospital orderlies got a wheelchair for me, and pushed me into the ER. I immediately was admitted to the OB/Gyn unit, where there was a team of doctors around me telling me to push. I pushed harder and harder. The pain was excruciating, but not as bad as the pain from the rape and Rochelle attacking me, and my emotional pain from losing Ryan, which was the most excruciating of all.

As I suspected, this pain was nothing compared to everything else.

Finally, after about an hour of my bearing down and pushing, at the urging of the doctors, I heard a cry. I was exhausted and spent, but when the doctors brought me Dalilah, all the pain in birthing her was forgotten.

I looked in her face, and I knew. I knew exactly who she belonged to. She had a delicate little nose, and precious rose-bud lips.

And the greenest eyes I had ever seen on anybody.

With the exception of her father.

Chapter Forty-Five

With the baby here, I found that it was going to be a problem trying to make ends meet. The money from the Whole Foods would no longer stretch, so I had to think of something else. Day care alone would cost some $1,200 a month for the very cheapest place, so Lena and I decided to move in together and watch each other's children while we alternated shifts.

We talked about the deal over dinner one night. The Whole Foods gang went out to a restaurant in China Town to celebrate a co-workers birthday. I brought my newborn daughter along, and put her in her carrier next to me. She dozed while I had fun with my new friends.

"So," Lena said, "how are you liking this city so far?"

"Great. It's really expensive, though. It's kinda discouraging, really."

"You don't know the half of it. Try to find a house to buy here. No, really, try. Do you know that the median home price for this town is around a million dollars?"

"I believe it," I said.

"So, what's your story? We've all been curious about you, just popping up out of the Midwest, without a real job that would require you to leave your home."

"No story. I just needed a change, that's all. I really had a desire to live by the ocean. That's always been my thing."

"This city isn't really known for its ocean. Way too cold on the beaches, and the water is absolutely freezing year-round. If you wanted a coastal town, you probably should've looked further south, like in Los Angeles or San Diego."

"That doesn't matter," I said. "I just like being close to the water. The beaches here are actually very peaceful, just because they are so deserted."

Somebody got up to order some dim sum for the table, and we all dug into the bite-sized entrees eagerly. It was delicious. "See," I said, holding up a dumpling on the end of my chopstick, "this is why I moved to this city. I don't think that I can find Chinese food this good in my hometown."

Then I asked Lena "what about you? How long have you been living here?"

"All my life," she said. "My parents lived in the Haight-Ashbury district when I was growing up, and I got involved with all kinds of social justice projects. I would never want to leave this city, no matter how much it costs to buy a home, just because no other city has the same vibe. I've visited many different places, and I have come to find out that there really is no place like home for me."

Frank, another co-worker, asked me "so, you're a single mother. Are you looking to date anybody? I mean, a lot of times a woman doesn't really want to date when she has a child, because she doesn't want a revolving door."

"I haven't thought about it," I said.

"I hate to pry, but where is the father?" he asked.

"Not sure. It was kinda a one-night stand type of deal. I never got his name."

"Ah," he said, looking at Dalilah. "Well, from the looks of things, you chose your one-night stand well. Your daughter is absolutely stunning."

"Yes," I said. "That she is."

Another co-worker looked at Dalilah and exclaimed "look at those eyes. You rarely see an infant with eyes that color. Usually they're blue."

"Yeah," I said. "She is unusual. She was actually born with eyes that color."

"Well, she's beautiful, that's for sure."

I smiled and took a sip of my green tea. "Thank you," I said.

Then Lena got up and did an impromptu belly dance to some of the music that was playing. She was actually quite good. She convinced me to get up with her, while she showed me some moves. The rest of our party was cheering us on and laughing. I guessed that they were drinking a bit, but I was completely sober, so I was feeling self-conscious.

I found myself having a good time, perhaps for the first time since I found out about Natalie. Lena was a lot of fun, and she invited me over to her apartment to watch some movies. So, after dinner, Dalilah and I headed over to her tiny studio apartment, and I sat on a bean bag on the floor and prepared to watch *Shaun of the Dead*.

Lena brought out some popcorn. "So," she said. "Are you having problems making ends meet, what with day care and all?"

"God, yes," I said. "I mean, I haven't gone back to work yet, but, when I do, I'm gonna have to use my Visa cash advance money to pay for it. I don't know what I'm gonna do."

"I have a plan, then," she said. "Just wait right here, I need to go next door and get my son."

At that, she went out the door and came back in a few minutes later with a beautiful half-Asian child who was a few months older than Dalilah. The little boy, like Dalilah, was fast asleep, his little hand curled up towards his mouth. "This is Samuel," Lena said. "His father was a turkey baster."

"Aw," I said. "How cute. How does the turkey baster thing work?"

"That's just a joke. Actually, I convinced one of my best friends to father Samuel for me. He doesn't want custody or anything, he just did it so that I could have a kid."

"Do you get child support?"

"No, I couldn't do that to him. He did it as a favor to me, that wouldn't be right to make him pay like that."

"So, then, we're kinda in the same boat," I said. "Neither of us are getting child support, and both of us are single mothers," I said.

"Right," she said. "So, I was thinking that maybe we could help each other out, here. I thought that we could find a place to live, and be roommates. We could get the store to give us different shifts, so that I could watch Dalilah when you work, and you could watch Samuel when I work."

I thought this was a great idea. I was lonely and starving for adult companionship anyhow, and I needed to cut my cost of living and find somebody to watch Dalilah. It seemed that all of these wishes were fulfilled with my proposed living arrangement with Lena.

So, we found a small two-bedroom bungalow for $2,600, which would still be a stretch for both us to make, but we put together a workable budget that would presumably help us make ends meet. What would happen when our kids got too old to stay with us in our respective bedrooms was an open question.

Everything was going good with this arrangement, and I felt a bit recovered from my Ryan emotional devastation, because I had a part of him in my beautiful daughter. I saw Ryan in everything about her, even in her newborn state. She was beautiful, docile and happy.

Just like her father.

Lena even agreed to watch her while I went on my first date with Brent, who was a guy I met while checking at the Whole Foods. He was nice enough, was around my age, and it was a plus that he was at the Whole Foods, because it meant that he was at least somewhat sophisticated.

I really didn't want to go, but I was lonely.

But, when I started getting ready, I started to panic at the very thought of going out with somebody new. It wasn't just that I was still passionately and completely in love with Ryan, although that certainly didn't help matters. There was the matter of intimacy. I hadn't let Ryan intimately touch me, even before the Nat thing. He didn't even try. He knew how broken I was because of what Andrew did to me. I despaired that I would ever let somebody touch me like that again. If I wouldn't let Ryan, the love of my life, do that to me, I certainly wasn't going to let this Brent person, or anybody else for that matter, touch me like that.

Of course, this was our first date. I hoped that something like sex wouldn't come up, and, if it did, I would address it directly. I would tell him that I was raped and I couldn't think about doing something like that.

Then watch him run.

He showed up right at 6, to take me to dinner someplace on the Pier. I told him that what I really wanted to do was to watch the sea lions. Those animals were absolutely fascinating to me, and I found myself watching them for hours on end. I even took Dalilah down there, although she was far too young to appreciate them. They were there by the hundreds, barking, preening, and forcing each other off the pier. I found them hilarious, and I found that I could lose myself watching them. I was especially fascinated with the babies, with their protective mommas there. I felt the same about Dalilah – a protective momma sea lion. I had always loved sea lions, even when I lived in Kansas City – when I went to the zoo there, all I wanted to do was see the sea lions and the hippos. Here they were in their natural habitat, and they were my greatest form of escape.

My only form of escape, really.

So, we made a date to go to the Sea Lion Café, which was no doubt going to be bustling on a Friday night.

When he showed up, he looked dapper in a button down shirt, jacket, sandals and jeans. I wasn't digging the sandals so much. I hoped that I could overlook it - I had dumped people for less, I was ashamed to say. Well, not really. I had dumped people because the chemistry wasn't there. Ryan could wear as many sandals as he wants, but that wouldn't matter because he was, well, Ryan. Gorgeous, yes, but more than that. He was…my soul mate.

Brent had dimples when he smiled, which usually are a major turn-on for me. Usually.

I smiled back, but I wasn't feeling the smile inside.

I wasn't feeling anything but polite.

"Have fun, you two!" Lena called from the living room.

"Thanks, Lene, I owe you one."

"Yeah, I'll take you up on that in the 12th of never." Lena was having problems finding a suitable partner herself.

Over dinner, Brent tried to get to know me. "So, you went to school at Ol' Mizzou. What brings you out here?"

I figure it would sound pretty stupid for me to tell him that I came for the sea lions, so I said "I just think it's the most beautiful city in the world. The last time I was here, I saw the city on foot. I must've walked ten miles that day from the Pier, through Japan Town, over to Haight Ashbury, and up through Pacific Heights. I have never seen a city with such old-world charm."

He raised his eyebrows. "And you were a lawyer back in Missouri?" He was obviously suspicious on how I went from lawyer to Whole Foods checker.

"Yes."

"And you moved out here on a wing and a prayer? This is a really expensive city to live in, you know."

"Yeah, so I'm finding out."

"I see. If you don't mind my asking, you said that you have a daughter who is just a few months old. What's the story there?"

I started to panic. How would I explain any of it? My story is just too weird for anybody to understand. So I said "that was a turkey baster conception. I really wanted a child, and figured I'm not getting any younger, so…"

Now he was looking incredulous. "You're just kinda a play by ear kinda gal, aren't you? Just go where the wind blows, bring a child into the world without knowing how to support her."

"Are you judging me?"

"No. But you strike me as somebody who doesn't think about the consequences of the decisions she makes."

Truer words were never spoken.

But he doesn't know the half of it.

"Uh, perhaps this date wasn't such a good idea," I said.

We ate in silence for the rest of the meal, and I insisted on splitting the check afterwards.

I wouldn't have to explain my rape to Brent after all.

I didn't try to date anybody else after that. To tell the truth, getting up the courage to even go out with him took a lot out of me. So, I decided just to do my work, and raise my child, and be happy with that. Nobody would ever compare to Ryan, anyhow, so it was no use even trying to find somebody who could take his place.

Then, one day, Lena came home from her shift at the Whole Foods and simply said "Why didn't you tell me?"

I was sitting on the floor with her child, Samuel, playing blocks with him, while Dalilah was in her crib above my head. I somehow knew just what she was talking about.

Still, I played dumb. "Tell you what?"

She shook her head. "Is this your husband?" She had the old *People* magazine in her hand.

"Well, what do you think? That's me there, isn't it?"

"Why didn't you tell me you're rich?"

"Because I'm not rich, that's why."

"Bullshit." At that, she gave me another article that she printed off the Internet. It was story about my divorce from Ryan that also appeared in another issue of *People*, but was not the cover story. "Says here that you own a painting that has a value of $120 million, and you also got a $50 million cash settlement."

"That's not my money," I said, simply.

"Then whose is it?"

I never thought that I would have to explain this to anybody. Why I thought that, I don't know. Naive, I guess.

"Well, it's technically my money. But I want no part of it. I didn't earn it, and I don't want it."

"Nevertheless, it's your money. Good God, you mean that we could be living it up in the Pacific Heights, instead of living here in this dump?"

"Lena, drop it. I'm sorry I didn't tell you about it, but that money doesn't belong to me."

"Whatever," she said. "Why would you lie? You told all of us that the father of Dalilah was some random hookup. He's not some random hookup, he's the son of one of the richest men in the world."

"Benjamin Whitney is considered to be one of the richest men in the world?"

"Yes," she said. "How do you know so little about your child's heritage? It says here that the Whitneys are old money shipyard tycoons."

"I don't know why I know so little about Dalilah's grandfather. It's probably because I just met the guy not even a year ago, and my ex-husband never talked about him very much. I did Wiki him when I first started dating Ryan, but I pretty much skimmed through a lot of that." I didn't tell her that I was looking for information about Benjamin's personal life at the time, not about his business interests.

"Jesus Christ. After that old man croaks, your daughter is going to be rich beyond belief. What do you think about that?"

"First of all, Benjamin is not old. He's like not even sixty. Second of all, why do I care about that? Since when does money ever make anybody happy?"

"Since always," Lena said.

"Money is kinda like intelligence," I said. "You want to be smart, but you don't want to necessarily be a super-genius, because mental issues tend to accompany that. Look at all the people with bright minds who committed suicide. It's the same with money. You want to have enough, but when you start talking about billions, it's just too much. You start running into people like Reginald Vanderbilt who was a wastrel and an alcoholic, and the Getty family that had all kinds of problems over the years. They say that the great fortunes of the super wealthy are depleted by the third generation. Shirt sleeves to shirt sleeves in three generations is the old saying."

"Maybe so, but, come on. You're not doing your daughter any service at all by pretending to be some broke clerk who is living hand to mouth. Maybe you don't want her inheriting billions, but I would think that you would want a better life for her than what you are providing."

Lena made sense, but it was still frustrating. It seemed that my past would never really leave me. It always had a way of bubbling up. As long as my face was on that *People* magazine, there would always be people like Lena, demanding that I come clean. I would never be able to truly escape who I was before.

The following week, I discovered just how right that was.

Chapter Forty-Six

I was waiting in line at the Starbucks in our neighborhood. I had taken Dalilah out for a little walk before work, and ended up there. Then I turned around and...of all the gin joints, in all the towns, in all the world, he walks into this one.

Nick O'Hara was coming in the door.

I immediately turned my head, and started to try to push Dalilah as I attempted to make my way out the door.

"Iris?"

Shit, shit, shit, shit, shit.

"Nick. Hello."

"Hi," he said, looking at Dalilah. He was fixated on her.

"This is my roommate's child, Dalilah."

"Bullshit. That's your child with Ryan."

I gave a look as if to say *what are you talking about?* "No, it's not. I don't know what you are talking about."

"Come on. I got eyes. That kid is the spitting image of him and Sarah."

I just shook my head.

"Whatever. Hey, listen, meet me on the patio. I have to talk to you."

I sighed, wanting to get away as quickly as possible. But, never mind, I was caught. Even getting 1,500 miles away apparently wasn't enough. Shit, I probably would've been caught if I lived in Taipei.

Fate obviously wanted me to confront what I had done.

I sat outside on the patio and waited for him to come out.

He sat down. "I'm glad I ran into you. I tried to call you many times, but it seems that your phone was disconnected. I now know why."

I nodded. "I got a different number when I moved out here. It's easier that way."

"Right. Listen, I'm not going to beat around the bush. You have to get back to Kansas City. Ryan is not doing well at all."

"What do you mean? He's living with Nat."

"Yeah. But you know what? They may be living together, but they have never had sex. Ever."

"Then why is she living there?"

"Hello? You know Ryan as well as anybody. You know that he's not the type to just a leave a woman high and dry if she's carrying his child. What did you expect he would do when she was kicked out by Nate?"

I did know that about him. If nothing else, Ryan was a stand-up guy. Then I said "They did have sex, though. That's why she has his baby now."

"Aside from that, he hasn't touched her. Listen, you have to get off your high horse about that. You're the reason that happened in the first place."

"Don't tell me that you believe that nonsense about him thinking she was me."

"Your goddamned right I believe it. Ryan told me, and Nat did too."

"Nat told you?"

"Yeah. I finally got her to confess about it, about the same time that she told me that Ryan refuses to touch her. She was upset because she imagined that if she was living with him and having his baby, that they would naturally become a couple. When that didn't happen, she called me and poured her heart out to me."

"Why aren't they having sex?"

"Duh. There is only one woman for him, and it ain't Nat."

My heart started to melt just a little. "They'll get used to each other and become the family they're supposed to be."

"Listen, Iris. You're either going to come to Kansas City the easy way or the hard way. The easy way is that you get on a plane willingly and face the music. The hard way is that I will report to the judge who did your divorce that you lied when you said that you weren't pregnant at the time of the divorce. At any rate, that divorce is null and void."

I hung my head. I knew what he was saying was the truth.

And a part of me really wanted to go back home. Go back home to the one person that I wanted to be with for the rest of my life.

"I-"

"Easy way or hard way. Your choice."

"Nat told you that she tricked him into bed?"

"Yes. I told you that, didn't I?"

"How is that possible?"

"The mind does funny things when deprived of sleep, and when the person is stressed out and suffering from a concussion. And, if you ask me, I don't think Nat's baby is

Ryan's. This one looks just like him," he said, looking into the little bassinet at Dalilah. "But Nat's baby looks like Nate to me."

"Hasn't there been a DNA test?" I asked.

"Nat hasn't allowed it so far. Wonder why?"

"So, Ryan gets a court order. Simple."

"Iris, you don't understand. Ryan is a ghost of a man. He hardly does anything anymore. He walks around in a daze most of the time. I don't think he's exactly on drugs again, but I wouldn't be surprised. At any rate, he has no spirit left in him. So, he hasn't fought for a DNA test, and Nat sure ain't going to offer it."

"Is he back at his job?" I asked, concerned.

"Yeah. He's still good at that. He says that throwing himself into his work takes his mind off you, so that is the only thing keeping him going. Other than that, though, there's no life left in him."

My heart went out to him. And I was finally starting to believe that maybe, just maybe, Ryan was telling me the truth about Nat and how she conceived. Plus, Nick thought that the baby wasn't Ryan's after all.

"Ok."

"Ok, what?"

"Ok, I'll go back the easy way."

"Good. I'll have Ryan's plane flown out here to pick you up."

"No. I'll fly commercial. There's no need-"

"Would you shut up? Goddamn, sometimes I have no idea why that guy is so in love with you. Go to the San Francisco Airport and meet me at the private jet hangar."

"Where exactly do I meet you?"

He drew me a map of the airport, then pointed "Right here."

"When will the plane be here?"

"I'm going to call Tim right now to charter it," he said as he got on his smart phone. He talked a little, then got off the phone. "Done. We're leaving in four hours."

"We? You said to meet you there," I said. I actually had the devious plan to stand him up and run. Of course, running was not as simple as it might have seemed, seeing as I was short of cash. But my mind was thinking desperately that I could hop a Greyhound to Los Angeles or somewhere, then try to figure things out from there. Poor Lena would be left high and dry, which would mean that there would be one more victim of my bad decisions, but I was only thinking of myself and Dalilah.

And how much I still couldn't face Ryan.

Yes, Nick said that Ryan and Nat aren't exactly a couple, which was ridiculous to me. Gorgeous, sweet Nat, and he doesn't want her? Well, I used to think she was sweet, anyhow, before she slept with my husband. Ex-husband.

Nope, current husband – Nick was right, that divorce was null and void.

Nick was looking at me, with a pissed-off and incredulous expression. "Yes, I know I said meet me there, but I immediately thought better of it. I don't trust you to meet me there, and Ryan would kill me if he knew that I found you and let you slip through my fingers."

"Why are you here, anyhow?"

"Business. I've been hired to design a building out here, and, lucky you, I've already had our meeting, and I was prepared to go home this afternoon. Stopped in to this Starbucks for a cup of coffee, and, boom! There you were."

"Yeah. Lucky me."

Fate was stalking me in the guise of Nick.

"Well, now, let's get into my rental car and head up

there, shall we? We have about four hours to wait for the plane, so we can use this time wisely."

I immediately felt threatened. What did he mean by that? I used to be so trusting of people, but after Andrew raping me, and Ryan cheating on me, my faith in the male gender was faltering.

He was looking at me and smirking.

"Nick, I can't go. Please let me just meet you there in a few hours. I have to pack and everything."

"Nope. You're coming with me."

Another pushy guy.

Just then, Dalilah started screaming, and I picked her up, bouncing her up and down. I reached into my diaper bag for some bottled breast milk, and she took the nipple and started sucking hungrily.

While I fed her, I said to Nick "I do have a job, you know. I have to be there in about a half hour."

"Baby, you aren't coming back here, so you might as well tell that job that you quit."

"I have a roommate, too. What's she going to do? I agreed to watch her kid while she worked, and she watched mine while I worked."

"Set her up. Give her the money for day care and rent until she can find something else."

I sighed. That was probably what I would have to do, to make things right. Which would mean that I would have to get the money out of the bank, the money I swore I wouldn't touch in my lifetime. Or I could just get a cash advance on the Visa card. I had about $10,000 left on it. "I guess I'll have to do that," I said. "I wonder if $10,000 will do her for awhile?"

I was sounding like Ryan now, throwing away money like water.

"Whatever you gotta do to make things right."

"Well, we signed a 12-month lease. I can't just leave her high and dry."

"I don't care what you do. All I know is that you're coming with me. And we have four hours to get things straightened out. Because, trust, I have a lot to tell you."

"Let me call Lena," I said, digging out my cell phone. Dalilah was still sucking hungrily on the bottle, so I balanced her with one hand, while calling with the other.

"Let me take her," Nick said. I nodded, and handed her to him while she cooed. He cradled her in his arms and continued to feed her. He seemed mesmerized by her. "Goddamn, she's the spitting image of her dad," he said, raising her above his head.

"That she is," I said, calling Lena. She answered the phone. "Lena, it's me, Iris."

"Iris the gajillionaire who acts like she's a bum?"

"I said I was sorry about that. Listen, there's been an emergency."

"What kind of emergency?"

"I have to go back to Kansas City for awhile."

"How long is awhile?"

"I might not be back."

"Thanks. Now I'm stuck with the entire rent and will have to pay for day care. Thanks a lot."

"About that. Um, would $10,000 tide you over until you can get out of your lease and find somebody else to watch Samuel?"

"You're just going to give me $10,000?"

"Yeah. I figure that will cover my half of the rent for half a year, plus some of the day care for half the year as well."

"What's the catch?"

"No catch. I just need to make things right with you."

"You're not so bad after all. Sure, I'll take that."

"So I need to transfer the money into your bank account."

"Ok. You better not be a scammer," she said, giving me her Venmo information.

"Thanks Lena. Sorry it didn't work out. I thought it would be pretty fun to share a place with you," I said, while I worked on getting my cash advance, then transferring the money into her account.

"No, thank you," she said. "You take care. Why are you going back, anyhow?"

"I need to fix the mess I made. That's why I'm giving you this money – it wouldn't be fair to leave you in a mess as well. I should have a motto of only screwing up one person at a time."

She laughed. "I have to admit, that's a good motto to have in life."

"Take care of yourself."

"You too."

I got off the phone and watched Nick, who was enchanted with baby Dalilah. He was cooing to her, baby-talking her, and rubbing her round belly. She laughed out loud as he tossed her a little bit into the air. "I'm your Uncle Nick, your Uncle Nick," he said, picking her up and down. I looked at him expectantly, and he finally turned his attention to me. "We good?"

I nodded, feeling resentful. I knew that I would eventually go back when I was ready, but I wanted to go back on my own terms. And when I was ready. That was key. At that time, I was still in la-la land - working my job, trying to adjust to being a single mother, and trying to forget about Ryan and his new family in Kansas City.

Also, I was trying to forget his awful betrayal. His awful betrayal.

Now I was going to have to face it, and I just wasn't ready.

"So, how old is Dalilah?" he asked.

"I would imagine she's the exact same age as – what is the name of Nat and Ryan's baby?"

"Christopher."

"She's the same age as Christopher."

"So, about four months, huh?"

I nodded, suddenly realizing I had been out here for about eight months. Eight months since I last saw Ryan. I had to admit that he did look like a ghost of himself when I saw him. I wondered how he looked now.

"Oh, crap," I said, suddenly remembering Madison. "I can't go until I get my cat."

Nick rolled his eyes. "Where is your place?" he asked. "I'll call one of my buddies out here to bring you the goddamned cat."

I gave Nick the address, and he got on the phone. "Yeah, Jack? I need you to do me a favor...I need you to pick up a cat and bring her to the Starbucks here on Market Street." Then he gave the guy my address, and looked at me and gave me the thumb's up. "Thanks, man," he said. "I owe you one."

Then, not fifteen minutes later, I saw a dark-haired man in a leather jacket and sunglasses approach us with a carrier in hand. I could hear Madison yowling. Nick got up and took the carrier, giving the guy an iced coffee that he ordered before Jack came on the scene. He patted him on the shoulder. Then he looked at me. "Here she is," he said, giving me the carrier. "Now, let's move."

We walked to Nick's rental, Nick carrying Dalilah and

me carrying Madison. The car was a spanking new Ferrari. "Crap," Nick said. "We can't take this car with Dalilah and the cat." At that, he called somebody to come and pick up the Ferrari and take it back to the rental place. "We're going to have to hail a cab," he said, getting off the phone and motioning for the cab that was approaching. It stopped, and we got in after I fastened Dalilah's car seat. Nick sat up front.

We got to the airport hangar, where there was a bar, and Nick got a scotch, which was what Ryan always drinks. I got a glass of iced tea. Dalilah was still nursing, and I was trying to do everything right. I was feeling stressed about the poor cat, but I hoped that she could calm down some and fall asleep. As it was, she was still mewling and crying in her carrier, and my heart broke a little.

"So, go ahead. Give me all the dirt of what has happened since I've been away," I said.

"What's there to tell? Ryan is devastated. He barely talks to me anymore. Nat does, though, all the time. She's good friends with Alexis, so she hangs out with us a lot."

"Alexis. You're hanging out with her?"

"Yeah. I'm living with her now."

I raised my eyebrow. This was getting more like *Days of Our Lives* every second.

"When did that happen?"

"The shit hit the fan after my soon to be ex-wife found out about Ryan and me. As I knew it would. Fuck her, though. I shouldn't make any apologies for that." Nick motioned for the waitress. "At any rate, it was bound to fail. We were just too different."

"But Alexis? Really?"

"Yeah. Listen, I'm sure that Ryan told you that the three of us used to be together?"

"He said something about that."

"Anyhow, we spent a summer in college at a Hampton's house. We all messed around with each other, and Alexis and I started to have a thing for each other. Just each other. It was kinda a mess, to tell you the truth."

"*Kinda* a mess?" That was an understatement.

"Yeah. Word to the wise – never get into a three-way relationship with your best friend and his girlfriend. It never ends well," he said, shaking his head.

"Thanks, I'll take that advice."

"Anyhow, Alexis and I hooked up a lot behind Rielle's back over the years. Alexis was always in love with Ryan. Always."

"Sounds familiar," I said, thinking of Nat.

"When he married you, she finally gave up, and, well, we were single at the same time. We always liked each other. And, most importantly, she's perfectly fine with my bisexuality. I can be exactly who I am around her. So now we're together."

I sighed. Why did I foresee a messy quadrangle between Nick, Ryan, Alexis and Nat in the future?

"Thanks for catching me up. But what about Ryan?"

"As I said, he doesn't talk to me much. I call him all the time, but he is very laconic."

I remembered that the word "laconic" was what Sarah said about Ryan before he met me.

"So what I know about him I hear from Nat," Nick continued. "Poor Nat doesn't know what to do. Nate actually wants her back. He told her that he doesn't care if Christopher is Ryan's, he wants her back. But Nat doesn't want to go."

"And why not?"

"I don't think you realize how much that girl is in love

with Ryan. She makes it out like it's a little crush, but it has always been far more than that. So, even though she can't get Ryan to touch her, and she can barely get him to talk to her, she's sticking it out."

Sticking it out. With my husband.

"So, what does Nat tell you about Ryan?"

"That she thinks he hates her. He does blame her for what happened to him and you. He has a point."

"But he keeps her there."

"Well, of course. His presumptive child is there, although, as I said, I highly suspect that. He has told Nat that they are basically roommates who are raising a child together. Nothing more. She won't accept that, though. She always thinks he'll come around."

"I take it he's not coming around, though?"

"No. He has told her, point blank, that he will never love her. When she asks why not, he always just says that he's still in love with you and he never sees that changing."

My heart melted still further. "He says that? That he's still in love with me?"

"Have you not been listening to me at all? He's told anybody who will listen that you're his soul mate. Ryan isn't the type to take that sort of thing lightly."

"What about his, uh, relationship with you?"

"What about it? Listen, I really don't consider him bisexual. Yeah, he and I get into it, and I know we have feelings for each other that go beyond bros. But he doesn't get around with guys. I do, though, and I still do. I make no apologies for that. As James Dean said, why would I want to go around with one hand tied behind my back?"

I would imagine that the men he gets were as smoking hot as the women he gets.

I was afraid to ask the next question. "You said earlier

that you didn't think he was back on drugs. Are you sure of that?"

"No, not sure. But Nat doesn't think so. He doesn't sleep much and doesn't eat much, so he's starting to take on the junkie look he had in college. But she checks for track marks, and doesn't see any, so she doesn't think he's using. Oh, and there's one other thing."

"What's that?"

"Nat says he paints rather obsessively. I mean, he's at work a lot, but when he comes home, he really doesn't pay attention to Nat, or Christopher, for that matter. He goes into his studio, and he paints portraits of you."

"He does?"

"Yeah. She said he must have 50 portraits of you in that studio. Oh, and by the way, there still isn't a stick of furniture in that house. Aside from the baby room, that is."

"What? Where do they sit and eat and stuff?"

"Orange crates and TV trays. They sit on the floor. Except, of course, for the baby room, like I said. Nat got that decorated, but he refuses to get furniture for any other room in the house."

I wondered where Natalie slept.

I didn't want to know.

But I asked anyhow. "Where does Nat sleep?"

"She has a bed in the baby room. It's a nice queen-sized bed."

"Why no furniture?"

"Because he thinks that you will be home at any minute, and he promised you that the two of you would decorate the house together. Are you starting to get the picture here?"

"But Nick, he doesn't know about Dalilah. How I lied to him. He probably will never forgive me."

"I don't think he should've forgiven you for the stupid stunt you pulled when you went off the grid like that. Jesus fucking Christ, why would you do that? Don't you see that your actions were the snowball that started the avalanche that resulted in all of this bullshit happening?"

"I wasn't in my right mind."

"I know that, and I'm sorry for what happened to you, but you made some really poor decisions there. Any normal woman would've called a friend, or gone to a rape crisis center. But no, not you. You decided that the best course of action would be to go to a drug house and get high." Then he looked thoughtful. "Come to think of it, that was Ryan's reaction to trauma, too, so I guess you guys do have something in common." Then he looked at me again. "But not calling him and turning off your phone was inexcusable. And just plain stupid."

"I didn't want to be found. I didn't want to go back into that house."

"Don't you think for one second that Ryan is sensitive enough not to make you go into that house again? As much as he protects you and takes care of you, and you think that he would just go 'la la la, I think I'll make my wife re-live her trauma every time she looks at the kitchen floor?'"

"How did you know it was on the kitchen floor?"

"I found some blood there. I didn't tell Ryan that, though, over the phone, when he called from Tokyo. He would've gone absolutely ape-shit."

Dalilah started screaming again, and I picked her up and put her on my lap. I put a pacifier in her mouth and felt her bottom. "Would you excuse me? I have to change her."

"Sure," he said.

When I got back, I put Dalilah back in her bassinet.

Nick continued. "Anyhow, I had never seen Ryan so

enraged as when he found out what happened to you. He immediately knew it was Andrew who did it, and I literally had to talk him out of finding him and killing him. He literally would have. Ryan may be a putz when it comes to women, but he's not a pussy. He's been around tough people in his life, and he felt he could take him." He shook his head with a smile. "A retired government assassin, and he thought he could take him. That's Ryan for ya."

"Ryan told me something about that. He told me that you talked him out of killing him."

"Yeah, I had to. The only thing that brought him to his senses was that I told him what impact it would have on you. It took him less than a second to realize that you would suffer even worse for his actions, so he put the gun away. But I had never seen him so devastated and angry as he was at that point."

Nick confirmed what Ryan told me about his feelings about my rape. I was reminded, anew, of how much Ryan was affected by what had happened to me.

"Now, of course, Ryan and his father are strained again," Nick said. "The father was the one who hired Andrew, although Ryan had him checked out independently. Andrew was clean. Turns out he was far from clean, and he had a target for you."

"Target for me? What does that mean?"

"It means that the bastard lied about Rochelle hiring people to come after you. Rochelle did no such thing. Andrew lied and said that she did, so it made it seem that you really needed his protection. He was apparently concerned that he wouldn't get the job unless he made it look like there were a bunch of people out there, gunning for you."

"How did you find that out?"

"It's hard to prove a negative, but Ryan hauled Rochelle in for a lie detector test about it. She passed with flying colors."

"Sociopaths usually can beat those tests."

"Yeah, but Ryan can also read people extremely well. Or haven't you figured that out by now?"

"Of course. That's one of the many reasons why I am so madly in love with him still."

"Anyhow, he believes she is telling the truth. And there never were any names forthcoming from Andrew about who was after you. That was pretty suspicious."

"Ok. So Andrew lied to get the job. You said he had me as a target. What did that mean?"

"It means that Andrew wanted you, specifically. Not sure why. But he wanted to be your bodyguard, and we think he intended to rape you all along."

My hand involuntarily flew to my mouth. "Why?"

"We're trying to figure that out. That's the other thing that Ryan does with his time. He paints, he works, and he obsessively looks into Andrew's background, trying to find out anything he can about him. He still wants revenge, he just doesn't know how to go about it."

Dalilah was crying again, so I picked her up and bounced her. She sucked on her fingers, and I gave her a pacifier and one of her stuffed animals.

"Anyhow, Ryan's theory, from what Nat tells me, is that Andrew's mother is red-headed. Which she is. And he is angry with his mother for something, so he took it out on you. You know, the classic killing the mother over and over thing."

"Why does Ryan talk to Nat and not you?"

"Because sometimes he gets in spurts where he starts talking. Nat says that the only thing he talks about is you.

He is still trying to figure out why everything happened the way it did. You really fucked him up."

I sighed. I had made some really poor decisions. Poor decisions that resulted in all of this. This is why Nick was here. He was the boulder that came crashing through the window, telling me that I had made a serious wrong turn in life. They say that, when you make bad decisions, the universe tries to tell you to make a U-Turn. At first, it's a pebble thrown at you, as the universe gently tells you to get back on track. Then, if you don't listen, the universe sends a boulder that you cannot ignore.

Nick was my boulder.

But what was my pebble?

Dalilah. She was the pebble. The universe was telling me, by my being pregnant, that I had to stay with Ryan. I ignored it, went to San Francisco without telling him he had a daughter, and now here was Nick. It wasn't a coincidence that he was in the same Starbucks as me. No, sir. He was the boulder I needed. I was too stupid to see it on my own.

Finally, the plane appeared on the runway. I got on, and strapped Dalilah in. Nick sat across from us.

I was, at long last, going home.

Chapter Forty-Seven

Nick and I chatted a bit on the plane while I attended to Dalilah. She was, remarkably, doing fine with her very first plane ride. Probably better than her stupid mother. Madison was another story, of course. I could still hear her whimpering and mewling. I tried to talk to her soothingly, but, of course, that didn't help.

"So," Nick was saying, once the plane was in the air. "If I didn't happen to run into you, would you just have kept on running?"

"I really don't know. I haven't exactly been myself for the past year or so. Before Rochelle, I doubt that I would've made such poor decisions about my life. It's no excuse, of course, but I think I'm still shell-shocked. Nat's pregnancy was just the last straw."

"So the answer is probably yes."

"I don't know. Would you believe me if I told you that I feel that the universe brought you to me to try to make me do the right thing?"

"Yeah, I'd believe that. Although it sounds pretty New Agey to me."

"I guess what I'm saying is that running could never have been a long-term choice for me. Something, somewhere would've brought me back to Kansas City. It's just that running into you is bringing me back before I'm ready."

"Sorry you're not ready," he said sarcastically, "but you made your bed."

"I know," I said. "I know."

We didn't talk much more. After a few hours, I looked out the window, as I started feeling the plane start to descend. I saw the familiar squares and itty-bitty cars below me, and extreme anxiety started to well up, until it became more like a panic. Ryan probably hates me, I thought. He will see what I did, taking his daughter and hiding her, and all his love for me will be gone. He wouldn't be able to love a woman who would do such a thing.

I started to do some deep breathing through my nose and mouth, trying to calm down. Nick was looking at me with his familiar smirk. I was quite sure that he was enjoying this spectacle of me feeling anxiety and panic. After all, I devastated his best friend. Nick had no compassion for me, nor should he.

One of Nick's cars was waiting for us at the airport hangar when we arrived. Like Ryan, Nick tended to drive only the best, and his car was a top of the line Mercedes CL-Class sedan. I was glad that he had a sedan there waiting for us, because, otherwise, I had no idea how Dalilah, Madison and I would be getting home.

"So, should I give Ryan a warning that you're coming home, or should I surprise him?" Nick asked, looking in his rear view mirror at Dalilah and me in the back seat.

"Surprise him."

"Suit yourself."

My anxiety rose to a fever pitch as the car drew closer and closer to Ryan's home.

We finally reached the home, and I could hear yelling inside.

"Well, you can take it from here," Nick said, leaving me on the front porch. "I'm not getting into the middle of that."

"But you want me to," I said, incredulously.

"As I said, you made-"

"My bed. I know, I know."

"See ya," he said, his back turned as he was walking back to his car.

I tentatively knocked, but nobody apparently heard me. After hearing snippets of the fight, I knew why.

Ryan was yelling "What do you want from me? I'm letting you live here, aren't I?"

Nat was yelling "I want us to be a family. Please, Ryan, please let's be a family."

"No offense, Nat, but you aren't my family. Christopher might be, although I doubt that, but you aren't."

"What's that supposed to mean?"

"It means that I don't love you and I never will. And Christopher doesn't look much like me."

"Are you saying that you think Christopher isn't yours?"

"That's exactly what I'm saying."

"So why would I still be here?"

"Nat, I don't know. I'm too nice of a guy just to let you be out on the streets. I wish that you would just go back to your husband, but, since you've said that if I kick you out, you still won't return to him, I don't see what choice I have."

I remembered what Nick had said about Nate wanting Natalie back. And Nat being out on the streets? She's an investment banker, for the love of God. I doubted that she ever would be on the streets.

This whole scenario was starting to become ridiculous.

"So, it's her, isn't it? She's the reason why you can't love me?"

"Yes, and I've told you that 100,000 times. Yes. It's her. It's always going to be her. Only her. Accept that, or move out."

I looked at Dalilah, and wondered if he would feel the same about me once he found out what I had done.

Then I heard Nat crying.

I picked up Dalilah in her car seat, and Madison in her carrier, and prepared to find a way to leave the scene. I didn't have car keys anymore, so taking my Volvo wouldn't be possible. Anyways, it would be like stealing. I prepared to call an Uber, thinking I didn't need to be in the middle of that drama and would come back at a later time.

However, right when I was about to call the Uber, the door opened, and I was face to face with a shocked and startled Nat.

Chapter Forty-Eight

"Iris?" she said. "What are you doing here?" She looked shocked and more than a little befuddled. Her beautiful blue eyes were puffy and her face was streaked with tears, but she still would look right on the cover of a magazine.

"What?" I heard Ryan inside. "Nat, who are you talking to?" Then he was immediately behind Natalie at the front door.

I felt sheepish as I said "surprise!"

Ryan looked even more shocked than Nat. He looked different than the last time I saw him. His hair was back to normal and he no longer had a beard and mustache, but he still looked pale, thin, and tired. Like Nick said, he was taking on a junkie appearance. This was no doubt how he looked in college.

He still took my breath away.

He looked at Dalilah. Then back at me. In those beautiful green eyes I saw befuddlement, anger, and pure love. He never could hide the love in his eyes, no matter how irritated he was with me.

He stood there with his mouth open, and Nat stood there looking at me with an increasingly pissed-off expression. Her pissed-off expression became even moreso as she eyed the child that was so obviously Ryan's. In her arms was apparently Christopher in his carrier. I looked at the child and saw what everybody else saw. Dark curly hair, blue eyes, dimpled chin. Mini Nate. Beautiful child, but I didn't see Ryan in him at all.

I tried to make light of the situation. "Well, is anybody gonna invite me in?"

"You can't be here," Nat told me. "You don't live here anymore."

"I know that. Hence my asking for an invitation as opposed to just barging on in."

Ryan pushed Natalie aside a little bit, then put his hand on my shoulder. "Come on in, Iris," he said, giving Nat a look. "Of course, you're welcome anytime."

I flinched at his calling me by my name instead of calling me "beautiful," and his invitation also seemed just a bit cold. But what did I expect, showing up here with his four-month-old child after having gone off the grid for eight months? Not to mention the fact that I divorced him.

I didn't blame him for not rolling out the red carpet.

I entered the spacious home which, just like Nick had said, had not a stick of real furniture in it. There were orange crates in a circle, but, other than that, there wasn't anything in this home. Natalie came in as well, even though she was apparently leaving before. I immediately opened the carrier, and Madison dashed out and ran into another room.

Ryan was in the kitchen. "Well, this is quite a surprise. I'm embarrassed that I don't have a place for you to sit. I probably should make you something to eat, but there really isn't much here."

"I haven't gone to the store this week," Nat said. "And Ryan never goes to the store."

"Don't start," Ryan said.

"Well, it's true. You never go to the store. You never cook. I don't understand that at all, because you were always an amazing cook in college."

I was a little taken aback by that. Ryan always had a full fridge of everything you could think of and he loved going to the store. And one of the many things that made me fall head over heels for the guy was his cooking ability.

Ryan looked sheepish as he brought out some cheese, crackers and hard salami. "I'm so sorry, Iris. Short notice."

"No, no. I'm sorry, I should've given you notice."

Nat said, "Alright, since nobody else is, I'm going to address the 800 lb gorilla. Who is that?" she said, pointing to Dalilah.

"This is Dalilah," I said, looking at Ryan. He now had his full attention turned on her, and I saw his eyes go from angry and befuddled, to love and adoration. "Dalilah is my daughter."

Ryan looked at me quizzically. "Your daughter?"

I looked back at him. "Our daughter. I wasn't sure until she was born, but, as you can see, she's definitely yours."

Nat now had a look on her face that clearly said "Oh, crap."

Ryan motioned to her. "Can I hold her?"

"Of course," I said. I watched him as he picked her up gently, then looked at her with wonder. It was like he was a cartoon figure who started out with a white face, then gradually took on more and more color. His cheeks were becoming more flushed, and his eyes were becoming brighter.

He was coming back to life before my eyes.

He just held her without saying a word. He put his finger on her nose, and gently rubbed her bald head. He brought her close to his face, and I saw him inhale a little bit, then close his eyes. For her part, she reached for him and put her hand on his nose as she gurgled and cooed.

Meanwhile, Nat was standing aside, glaring at me with an expression that clearly said *you bitch*.

"That's enough of that," Nat snapped. "Iris just said that she's not sure this kid is yours. So you better not get too attached."

Ryan just laughed. "Look at her, Nat. She looks just like Mia. No, Nat, I've no doubt who she belongs to. Now Christopher is another story."

"Well, even so," Nat said, "I'm quite sure that Iris isn't welcome in this house anymore. Aren't you even going to ask her what the hell happened to her? Aren't you even going to confront her on where she has been, and why she hid that child from you?"

Then Ryan looked at me. And the hurt in his eyes was renewed. "Good point, Nat. Iris, what did happen to you?"

Oh, where to begin?

Chapter Forty-Nine

"Where do I begin?" I said to Ryan.

"You can start by telling me how you have a baby here, when you clearly said when you divorced me that you were not pregnant."

"I was pregnant, of course, at the time."

"Did you know it at the time?"

"Yes," I said, quietly.

"So you committed fraud."

"Yes," I said, glancing at Nat. She was looking happier and happier by the second.

"Why?"

"I wasn't in my right mind. That's all I could figure. I was afraid the baby wasn't yours."

It was then that Nat got into the act. "What? You mean, you were cheating on Ryan? Ryan, are you just going to sit there and take that?"

Ryan shot Nat a look that said *drop it*. Then he turned to me. "I understand."

"Ryan, what do you mean you understand?" Natalie

whined. "You dropped Alexis like a bad habit for cheating, why-"

"Nat, if you don't be quiet, I'm going to have to ask you to leave." Then he turned to me. "Go on."

"I thought the baby wasn't yours and I was scared. And betrayed. So betrayed. You ripped out my soul, Ryan, you and Nat. Absolutely ripped it out. I mean, I was attacked by Rochelle, then raped, then was on drugs, then found out about Nat in such a short period of time. I plead temporary insanity."

I looked at Nat, who now had a look of understanding on her face. "Raped? Oh, Iris, I'm so sorry." She was, once again, sweet Nat.

"Yes, Nat, I was raped."

"By the bodyguard that I forced her to have," Ryan said quietly to Nat.

She just looked at me with a bit of a shocked look on her face, then looked at Ryan. "Why did you force her to get a bodyguard?"

"Because I thought Rochelle would be coming after her. I was going to be gone in Tokyo and I wanted to be sure she was safe."

"Ironic, huh?" I said to Nat.

Ryan turned to me. "Go on with your story beaut, uh, Iris," he said.

"What is there to tell? I didn't tell you about the baby, then ended up living in San Francisco with a lesbian I met while working at Whole Foods. That wasn't a long-term plan, I know, but it was all I could come up with at the moment."

Nat was incredulous. "You're a lawyer. Why would you be working at Whole Foods?"

"I wanted something low pressure and kinda fun. Law

work is the diametrical opposite of those two qualities. Anyhow, I had trouble making ends meet, but I managed."

"I know you haven't touched the money I gave you," Ryan said.

"True."

"So, what brought you back?" Ryan asked.

I hesitated for a moment, then said "Nick. He ran into me at Starbucks. I was in there before work. It's in our neighborhood, so I was taking Dalilah here out for a walk, and stopped in there to get a cup of coffee. Then he comes through the door, as big as you please. He informed me, in no uncertain terms, that I had to come home," I said, seeing Ryan's face become pale once more. He no doubt surmised that I was only here because I was forced, not because I wanted to come home. At least, that was what his face was telling me. "So, I felt bad about leaving Lena high and dry. I gave her $10,000 to tide her over until she could find another place and good day care."

Nat's face was showing relief and happiness at my words. She no doubt recognized the subtext of what I was saying – I was only home because Nick forced me, and I had no intention of returning to a marriage with Ryan.

"Ok, so, Iris, you're here to let Ryan know about Dalilah, and fix your divorce, right? I mean, Ryan is entitled to joint custody, of course, and I don't mind helping him raise little Dalilah. She's the same age as little Christopher. You know what they say, it's just as easy to raise two as one," Natalie said in a rambling fashion.

Ryan was staring at me with those penetrating eyes. The depths in them were scary. I could read them so very well. They were saying that he wanted me back, and that he hoped that I didn't just come home because Nick forced me to make good on what I had done with our child.

I started to waver. Then I took a deep breath and said "No, Nat, actually I wanted to come home to see if there was any way possible for Ryan and I to find our way back to one another." Then I looked at Ryan, whose color was, once again, flooding back to his face. Addressing him, I said "I hope there isn't too much damage here. You're the love of my life."

At that he smiled, big. Nat gave me the look of death. "Iris, you can't do this. You can't just come in here after all this time and just snap your fingers and expect everything to be ok. You fucked him over, or did you forget that? Ryan is with me now, we have a child together, and you can't do this. And what were you going to do if Nick didn't drag you back here? You still would be out there, living your life, hiding Ryan's child from him…"

Natalie was droning on and on, but I tuned her out. Ryan did, too, apparently. Neither of us bothered to even engage her in conversation at all. We both just stared at each other.

Then he took my hands and kissed them tenderly. He kissed my forehead, and put his hand in my hair, inhaling deeply. I put my head on his chest, hearing his heart pounding. Dalilah, for her part, lay in her bassinet, gurgling and cooing.

Ryan looked at Nat. "I'm sorry, Nat. We both know that Christopher isn't mine. I haven't had the energy to do anything about it until now. But I'm calling Sheldon the first thing tomorrow morning, and I'm going to get a court order for a DNA test. Then you need to return to your husband."

"No," Nat said. "You can't get rid of me that easily. I know that this baby looks like Nate, but he also looks like me. And you, for that matter. The dark curly hair is all you. Blue eyes run in your family – look at Sarah and your father, and I have blue eyes as well. This baby is yours, I'm telling you."

"Ok, if he's mine, we'll deal with it. I won't leave him high and dry. I'm more responsible than that. Either way, though, I want you to patch things up with Nate. He loves you. I don't."

"I can't just go to Nate and ask him to raise your child. Your child belongs with you."

"I admit, it will put a crimp in my relationship with him, even more than it has already been damaged. But, we'll all get past this, I promise you." Then, he looked at me. "Iris, I can't tell you how thrilled I am that you want to come home. I'm not going to say that it's going to be easy for us – both of us have done something major to the other that is going to make it hard to trust. We're going to have to do some work on this relationship so that you can forgive me for Nat, and I can forgive you for hiding Dalilah from me. And don't think that I've forgotten that Nick had to force you to come back." He shook his head. "Nat does have a point, come to think of it. What would you have done if Nick hadn't been there at that coffee shop to force you to come back?"

"I admit, I wasn't ready," I said. "Not because I didn't want to come home. I did. I missed you terribly, every single minute of every single day. I used to pray to God to take care of you. I wanted you to be happy, even if it wasn't with me. I somehow thought that you could be happy with Nat and your child with her. Nick let me know that wasn't the case."

"So, if Nick didn't run into you..." Ryan said.

"I'm not sure, to be honest with you. I didn't want to face you and Nat together, and I knew that seeing you with her and your child would absolutely rip out my soul. And there was a part of me that thought that if you could find happiness with Nat and the baby, that would be enough for me. I would never be happy without you, but I could find some peace if I knew that you were happy."

"I'm not happy, Iris. I could never be happy without you, either. I hope that you're serious about coming home."

"I'm not going to jerk you around again, Ryan. I don't think that I could live without having you in my life in some sort of way."

Nat was standing there, watching this unfold, a pissed-off expression on her beautiful face. Christopher started screaming, but she just ignored him. It was like she was in some kind of trance.

"Nat, aren't you gonna attend to your child?" Ryan asked.

"Our child. Christopher is our child. Yes, I will attend to our child."

Turning to me, Ryan said "we can find our way back to each other. It's going to take a lot of work, but we can do it. Do you mind going to see Dr. Halder?"

I shuddered just a little. I was still uncomfortable with men in some ways - mainly because I didn't want to share my intimate secrets with them. With the exception of Ryan, of course. But I would do this for him.

So, he made an appointment with Dr. Halder for the next day.

Chapter Fifty

I stayed the night with Ryan and Nat, in our bed in our bedroom. The bed was still the only real furniture in the house, save for the furniture in Christopher and Nat's room. Dalilah slept peacefully between us. I still had to get up during the night to feed her, and I did so while sitting on the floor. It wasn't comfortable, and I had to rock my body back and forth, because the rocking motion was the only thing that could get her to sleep.

"I'm so sorry, Iris," Ryan said. "I guess I couldn't bring myself to decorate this home without you."

That touched me more than anything else, in a weird way.

Ryan continued, "if you are home for good, then I'll get the decorators here right away. I still want to realize our visions for the house."

"I am home for good, if you will have me."

Then, the next day, we went to see Dr. Halder, and Ryan called the decorators to come and start bringing the ordered furniture into the house. I dropped Dalilah off at my mother's house, although I felt guilty about this. My mother was in her late 70s, and caring for an infant was something that I knew she never thought she would have to do again. But I gave her some bottles of breast milk, and Dalilah's toys and blankets, and thanked God that she was a good child.

We got to Dr. Halder's office, and he greeted us warmly. "Iris. It's good to see you again. Ryan, you're looking well. Now, what can I do for you?"

I started. "I need to find a way to trust Ryan again after he had sex with another woman. Ryan needs to find a way to trust me again after I went to San Francisco and hid his child from him."

"Infidelity is a very serious issue," was all he said. Then he looked at Ryan. "What do you say to your wife about that?"

"Well, you know, Dr. Halder, I've talked to you about all that at great length. I can't seem to get Iris to believe me about the way it happened."

To this, I said "It's just so far-fetched. So daytime soap opera-ish. Nat is a beautiful woman, so it's just hard for me to believe that Ryan had to be in an altered state to be with her."

Dr. Halder said in response "that's the major problem here. Your lack of trust and belief in what your husband is telling you. You have to believe in your husband when he is telling you that he never would've been unfaithful if he wasn't in an altered state. Otherwise, it will be very difficult for you to trust him, and that would be toxic for your relationship."

Ryan was just looking at me with a pleading look in his eyes.

And I suddenly knew that what he was saying was the truth.

Why didn't I see that before? How could I have been so blind? And so stupid? To think that I was thisclose to screwing up the best thing that ever could've happened to me because I refused to believe Ryan's story…And, all at once, I wanted him in a way that I never wanted him before. He put his hand on mine, and I felt the old electric tingle make its way from my hand all the way up to my shoulder and down the other arm.

I looked him in the eye and said "I believe you."

His facial expression changed completely. He lit up at my words, his eyes getting bright and his smile taking on the mega-watt quality that I hadn't seen in so long. He squeezed my hand, and put his hand in my hair and stroked it.

Then I told Dr. Halder "it's a great thing that I now believe Ryan, but I did something hideous. I don't know how he can trust me again."

"What was this hideous act?"

"I covered up the fact that I was pregnant with his child when I divorced him. Then I immediately fled halfway across the country, to San Francisco. I only came back because his best friend made me."

"Ryan, what are your feelings about this?"

"I'm angry," he said. "And hurt. Betrayed. But, at the same time, I know that my wife has been through some of the worst traumas imaginable in the span of less than a year. I'm inclined to give her a break for that reason alone."

"Iris, tell me about why you would've done this to Ryan?"

"I was out of my mind, I guess. Kinda like when I went into the drug house. I'm sure Ryan told you about that?"

Dr. Halder nodded.

"I had a hard time coping. Things got so much better out in Beverly Hills. But Nat drove me out of my mind. And my hormones were raging, which didn't help things, I guess."

"The problem is, Iris, that you didn't come home on your own," Ryan said. "I can almost understand why you did what you did. Your thought processes have always been just a little bit left of center, which is one of the reasons why I love you so much. But why couldn't you come home on your own?" Ryan asked.

I shook my head. "I really don't know the answer to that question. I guess that I felt that I needed to keep running, because if I stopped, and confronted the true situation with you, Nat and your child – I felt that I would fall apart. Avoidance was always my greatest friend."

Dr. Halder said "Iris, you're saying that avoidance is your coping mechanism?"

"Sure," I said. "Isn't it that way for everybody?"

"That is human nature," Dr. Halder said. "But you seemed to have taken it to the extreme."

"What can I say, I raise avoidance to an art form."

"So, how can you confront the situation with Ryan and Natalie?" Dr. Halder asked.

Ryan said "she doesn't have to confront it. I'm getting a court order for a DNA test, and I have a feeling the baby isn't mine. Even if he is, I'm not going to let Natalie live in the house anymore. That house is mine and Iris' house. Getting Natalie out isn't going to be easy, but it's something that has to be done."

The session went on for the rest of the hour, but we both were feeling that it wasn't all that necessary, after all. We understood one another. We always had almost a psychic bond with each other, and this bond was something that evidently went haywire when I refused to believe Ryan's story.

When we got to the car, which was parked in the parking lot, I made my move. I straddled him, pushing him down and releasing the seat latch all at once. Neither of us spoke. I just ran my fingers through his hair, and we were kissing passionately. Just like old times. I ran my hand to the buttons of his shirt, feeling his chest. He had lost quite a bit of weight, but he was still firm in his pecs and abs. He kissed me back, running his hands through my hair, but not trying to put his hands anywhere else. So, I put his hand on my breast, as I lifted up my shirt. It was an uncomfortable position, as we were, unfortunately, in the Porsche, not the Escalade, but I wasn't thinking about that. I wasn't thinking about the steering wheel which was pinning my back, or the gear shifter which was squishing my leg. All I could think of was my beautiful, beautiful husband, and how much I wanted him badly.

So badly.

I unbuttoned his pants, and lifted up my skirt, pulling down my panties. He looked at me nervously and said "Are you sure about this, beautiful?"

I smiled at him using my nickname again. I secretly cringed every time he called Iris. I sighed and said "Yes. Yes. Yes," as I took his manhood and put it inside of me. I had a little bit of trouble, not for lack of lubrication, but because it had been so long since we made love. I released the seat fully, so that Ryan was completely lying down, as I rode him, coming to orgasm after orgasm. He tentatively put his hands on my breasts as he kissed me passionately, his lips running from my lips to my cheeks to my neck to my clavicle, and back again. There were people walking by, and I heard laughter, but I didn't care. There was only me and

Ryan in the world, nobody else. He consumed me like nobody else ever had before. I knew that nobody would ever consume me like that again. I didn't want it to ever stop, so I just kept riding him, even after I felt his hot cum inside me.

I finally was sated a little, so I climbed off of him and into the passenger seat. I looked at him - his thick hair was going in different directions and his shirt was still unbuttoned. My underwear was still on the floor of the car. He smiled at me and said "do you think that your mom will be ok with Dalilah for a few hours more?"

I nodded, getting on the phone and asking my mother if she could continue to watch our child for the rest of the afternoon. She reluctantly agreed.

We didn't go home, of course. Nat was still there. So, we got a suite at the Radisson, an upscale downtown hotel. As soon as we got into the room, Ryan pounced on me, his hands on my breasts as he stripped off my top. I unzipped my skirt, tossing it to the side of the bed, while pulling down his pants, then unbuttoned his shirt, pulling this off of him as well.

Although we got our clothes off in record time, the actual love-making did not have the same urgency as it did in the car. Ryan laid me down gently on the bed, looking into my eyes and stroking my hair before he started kissing me passionately. He worked his way down my neck, my breasts, my stomach, then started kissing my thighs. I sighed. This was one of my favorite parts, when he started to lick my thighs slowly. Then he started licking and sucking my genitals, very gently and smoothly, his hands running the length of my entire body. He teased me, bringing me to the precipice of an orgasm, then backing off, only to come back to that area a few minutes later. Briefly, the memory of

Andrew flashed in my brain, and I could feel my heart racing in panic and fear. But I willed myself to tamp it down, and concentrate on what my magnetic husband was doing. It felt amazing, and I finally exploded in a powerful orgasm.

Then he was on top of me, once again kissing my lips as he entered me slowly. I gasped a little. We had just made love in the car, but this was different. The action in the car was more like a release, a satisfaction of a need I suddenly had for him while we were talking to Dr. Halder. Once I realized that Ryan had been telling me the truth, I suddenly had to have him inside me. That was what the car lovemaking was. But this – this was just a pure expression of love. Of undying, unadulterated love. Of two people who would never stop having a need for one another, no matter what happened. It was obvious from the way that we touched one another, to the unspoken words that we conveyed with our eyes. As corny as it sounds, our lovemaking was the culmination of two souls that had a need to be together, and they finally were fused again, after being apart from one another for way too long. For hours, we were like this, me feeling him hard inside me, feeling his mouth all over me.

Then, after making love for hours in the bed, we moved to the bathtub. Ryan lit some candles as we soaked in the enormous Jacuzzi tub. He gently soaped me up with a sponge, laying behind me, then kissing my back and my neck. Some music was playing from the stereo in the room, and it was being piped into the bathroom. It was easy 70s music, which was one of my favorite genres. Barry Manilow, Neil Diamond, Carly Simon, The Carpenters, Christopher Cross, Bread, Air Supply, The Commodores, Kenny Rogers, David Gates, Dan Fogelberg

– I loved them all, and Ryan apparently made a CD featuring all of my favorite old-time artists. We hadn't really spoken in all this time, just letting our touch and our eyes do the communicating. We remained in the bathtub for hours, just relaxing and enjoying each other, and making love in the bubbles.

I finally was out of my reverie when I realized that it was 10 PM. We got the hotel room at 10 AM, after our appointment, and had been enjoying each other non-stop since then. And, as much as I wanted to continue throughout the night, as did he, there was a little matter of a baby who was at my elderly mother's house.

Both of us looked at each other and said, at the same time "Dalilah." Then we smiled.

As we made our way to his car, my legs felt like spaghetti. He held my hand, and I could feel the tingling coursing throughout my body as we touched. We were still quiet, neither of us wanting to break the spell. Finally, I spoke. "I hope Dalilah was ok at my mother's house."

"I'm sure she's fine, beautiful. Like we are, or will be, from now on."

We got to my mother's house, then picked up our daughter. "How was she?" I asked.

"Fine," my mother said. "A little unusual, though."

"What do you mean?"

"I swear to God, she said an actual word."

"Oh, come on, she's just over four months old. How can that be possible? What word did she say?"

"It sounded like grandma."

I made a face, then took Ryan's hand and led him up to the room where Dalilah was staying. She was in her crib, punching and kicking the air. Then she looked at me and clearly said "mama." Then looked at Ryan and said "dada."

Ryan and I looked at each other with a puzzled look. Then I gave her a stuffed bear, and she clearly said "bear."

What the hell? She was gurgling and cooing this morning. Then I thought back – it did seem that she was trying to form words for awhile now, but I'm ashamed to say that, with all the chaos going on, I really wasn't paying attention.

Ryan and I both just shook our heads, as I picked her up and put her in her car seat. "Bottle," she said. So I got a bottle out of the diaper bag, and she sucked on it hungrily.

Neither of us spoke about our unusual daughter in the back seat. It was just too weird. Then again, nothing would surprise me anymore about anything. There was always something strange that had been popping up – horrible strange things, but nice ones, too. Like having a less than five month old daughter who suddenly knew words.

And, when I got home with Ryan, I suddenly felt the urge to see his mother.

Chapter Fifty-One

It was a very peculiar situation at home. Nat and Christopher were still there. Ryan and I had not yet figured out how to get her gone. And Nat had announced to us that she was staying until the results of the DNA test was in, and, if the baby was Ryan's, she was going to stay with us indefinitely.

Ryan sighed. "Nat, you can't just be a squatter here. My life is with Iris. It always has been, it always will be, and you've always known that. Now, I really don't want to resort to calling the police and having you arrested for trespassing, but I also don't know what else I can do."

"Well, I'm not leaving," she said. "And it'll be such a nicer home with furniture in it, and a full fridge." Ryan and I had just gone to the store and stocked up on everything that we needed and more, and the furniture guys were going to be here the next day.

Quietly, while Nat was in the other room, I said to Ryan "This probably seems familiar to you."

"What do you mean?"

"You know. You, Nick and Alexis. Hamptons House."

"Ha ha. That was different, and you know that."

"Yeah. But why do I get the feeling that she wants that kind of situation here?"

"Guess again. Believe it or not, to my knowledge, Nat doesn't get into women."

"That's a shock. She's always been so touchy-feely with me."

"That's just the way she is."

"Ok, then, I stand corrected." Then I said "I need to go to the library today. I hope you don't mind."

"Fine. Leave me here alone with Stalky McStalker," he said, with a smile.

I nodded. "I'll be home in a few hours," I said. "I'm assuming you're okay with Dalilah?"

"Of course. Oh, and pick up some Chinese on the way home, huh? Orange chicken and egg rolls. And bring enough for Nat."

I nodded my head, and, as I turned around to leave, I saw him picking up Dalilah and looking at her with wonder in his eyes. She purposefully put her hand on his nose, and said "dada." He just shook his head.

I headed to the library, and quickly picked up a few books. Then I headed over to Maggie's group home, turning off my phone. I remembered that Ryan put a tagger on my phone. He usually doesn't use it for me, except when he had a feeling I was in danger.

I hoped against hope that I wasn't giving off the danger vibe this morning.

I got to the group home, which was a transitional living home for people who had been released from mental hospitals. Maggie was scheduled to live here for a few more months. She was supposed to be released after a year, but she had a mild relapse because her drugs were miscalculated, so she had to stay an extra six months.

The home was rambling, built during the turn of the century, with 10 bedrooms. Each of the bedrooms housed two people. The people in this house shared the common areas of the living room and kitchen, and there were three therapists living there full-time.

I entered her room, knocking on the open door.

"Iris!" she said. "What a nice surprise!" Then she gave me a big hug. "How's my favorite daughter-in-law?"

"Great. Couldn't be better." Which was actually true. After all I went through, having this nice lull was a slice of heaven.

We chatted for awhile, catching up with each other's lives. "I can't wait to get out of here and live out on my own," she was saying. "Ryan and Sarah are going to set me up in a nice condo downtown."

I nodded. Then I told her "Uh, Ryan and I have a daughter together."

She clapped her hands delightedly. "Do you have pictures?"

I showed her the pictures on my phone. She looked at me quizzically. "She looks so big. How come Ryan hasn't told me about her?" She looked very hurt.

Oh, how to explain all of that to her? "Actually, Maggie, he uh, he uh, just found out about her."

"Oh. Ryan told me that you two were divorced. I actually didn't know you were back. So, I guess that you had his daughter and didn't tell him about it?"

"Something like that." I immediately felt terrible. Maggie and I had always gotten along. Now she was looking at me suspiciously. "I've had a lot of things happen to me lately, and I just kinda went crazy for awhile," I said, then instantly regretted my choice of words. How could I refer to myself as crazy, when Maggie was a schizophrenic?

She just shrugged. "Who am I to judge? But I have a feeling that you are here for a reason."

"Yes. Our daughter is unusual."

"In what way?"

"She started saying words yesterday, and seems to know what these words are. She's just over four months old. So, I was wondering about Ryan. He's so modest, but I was wondering if that was something that he did as well."

"Of course. Ryan and Sarah both have off the charts IQs. They're both prodigies, too. Ryan was painting by the time he was two, and Sarah started playing the piano at the age of 3. Both of them were fluent speakers by their first birthday, and they both read entire books by their second birthday – Ryan read *The Wind in the Willows* before he turned two, and Sarah had finished *Charlotte's Web* before she had her second birthday. By the time Ryan was five, he was reading *A Tale of Two Cities*."

A Tale of Two Cities? I had trouble getting through that dense tome in high school. "I see. I suppose he was reading Dostoyevsky by age 6?"

"Age 7, actually. He read *The Brothers Karamazov* that year, and actually understood it all."

"So, Dalilah isn't really unusual in the Gallagher family?"

She shook her head. "They get their artistic bent from my side. They get their utter brilliance from their father."

"So what should I expect from her?"

"She's going to be a handful, I'll tell you that. But Ryan should know how to handle her. We kept him in school, in his own grades. That was what he wanted. He didn't want to skip any grades. But he always went to the very top schools, so they had excellent programs for him and others like him. There were quite a few pupils in his school that matched his brilliance, so he never felt like he was all that unusual."

I thought of my own high school. There was a gifted program, but probably nothing like what Ryan went through. I also imagined that his school was the type of school where the lessons were demanding for all the kids. I knew that Dalilah would also be going to the very best private school, so she should be challenged sufficiently.

We chatted some more. As I started to leave, Maggie gave me a hug, and said "Please bring my granddaughter to me the next time you come?"

I nodded. "I will. Please don't tell Ryan I visited you today. As I said, I only came here because I have the feeling that Ryan never would've told me this. He is never one to toot his own horn."

"Truer words were never spoken. I'm very glad you're back, by the way. I started to worry about my son after you divorced him."

"We aren't divorced. I mean, we were, but I lied on the petition, so it's pretty much void. All I have to do is file a motion with the judge to have it thrown out. I need to do that soon."

"At any rate, I'm very glad you're back with him. He loves you so much."

"And I, him."

When I got home, bearing the Chinese food that Ryan requested, I saw Ryan sitting on one of the orange crates, his head in his hands. Dalilah was in her bassinet next to him, saying random words. Nat and Christopher were also there in the dining room. Nat looked at me worriedly, and

Ryan immediately got up from his perch, and wrapped his arms around me.

Uh-oh. I turned off my phone, so now he's worried.

"Oh, thank God," he said.

"What? I've just been gone for a few hours."

He just held me and said nothing. I looked at Nat, who was biting a thumbnail, a worried expression on her face. I made a gesture to her to explain what was going on.

"Ryan talked to his dad while you were gone," she said.

"Is he ok?"

"He's fine. But he's been in touch with Andrew. He knows that you've told people that he was the one who attacked you."

"And?"

"And he wants to kill you."

Chapter Fifty-Two

I was feeling like I was Pauline now in *The Perils of Pauline*. Or Indiana Jones. Something was always happening to me so that my life was always being threatened somehow. Will she die from her Rochelle attack? Find out in the next installment. Then will she die from being a junkie in a drug house? You'll have to wait until next week. Then will she die at the hands of her obviously insane rapist? Duh, duh, duh!

I pushed Ryan away from me, and said "Is that all you're worried about?"

"What do you mean, is that all I'm worried about? A retired government assassin has your number, of course I'm worried about that," Ryan said. "And you should be, too."

"How did your father find out about this?"

"Let's just say he heard it from his associates. Andrew has become unhinged."

"Imagine that. A man who used to kill people for a living, becoming unhinged."

"Why are you taking this so lightly?" Ryan demanded.

"I guess because I'm getting used to this type of thing happening to me anymore. There's always something that's threatening me. Some bogey man. I'm tired of looking over my shoulder constantly for one person or another. Just finish me off, already."

Ryan looked stricken, then picked up Dalilah and handed her to me. She looked me right in the eye, grabbed my hair, and said "Mama."

"There," Ryan said. "There's your reason for living."

"Don't be silly," I said. "You and Dalilah both are my reason for living. That's not the point. It just seems that somebody is going to get me. It's like that movie *Final Destination* – I cheated death once, now it's gonna stalk me."

"Well, there's something I need for you to do. I need you to resume target practice. You need to get handier with your .45. I'll go with you, of course. I'll teach you how to handle your pistol. Then we need to get you a concealed carry permit."

"What, we're gonna take Dalilah there? She'll freak out."

"Nat has offered to watch her while we do this."

I looked at Nat, and she nodded. "I still like you, Iris, and I don't want anything bad to happen to you."

"I suppose that there isn't any way you'll take no for an answer on this?"

Ryan just shook his head.

I sighed. "Here we go again. Well, I suppose it can't do any harm. It's not like hiring some random guy to protect me. And I suppose if I'm going to be married to you – and I will be, I promise you I'm not going to leave again – I probably should know how to defend myself. It seems that will be a necessity from here on out."

"I'm sorry, beautiful, that it is a necessity. God knows, I have lived an f'd up life. It's caught up to you, and I can't tell you how sorry I am about that. But you need to be safe, and I can't be with you every minute of every day. Much as I would like to be. And I know that hiring another bodyguard would never go over with you. So you, my beautiful, need to be able to defend yourself."

I nodded. "Ok, then, let's go target shooting."

So that Saturday we got to the target range, which was a typical target range, with stalls and figures of men some fifty feet away. Ryan and I had our headphones on, and Ryan was showing me how to hit the targets. He cocked his pistol towards the figures, and bam! bam! bam! – he hit three bulls-eyes in a row.

"Now you try it."

I nervously cocked my gun, and tried to aim at the figure, but missed it entirely, the bullet landing somewhere to the right of the cardboard cut-out.

"I'm sorry, I guess I really don't know how to aim. That bad man taught me how to load the pistol and everything, but we really didn't get into aiming it. By the way, how did you get so good at this?"

"Lots of practice. You have to remember, I hung out with druggies and dealers for quite a few years in my early days. You have to be handy with a weapon when you're hanging with that crowd. Now, this is your very first time trying to target shoot, so you're just going to have to be patient with yourself."

Then he got behind me. "Here, you have to have the right stance. Feet shoulder-width apart. Now lean forward, and close your left eye. Concentrate. Now squeeze the trigger."

I did, and the bullets landed on the cardboard cut-out, still missing the figure entirely.

"That's better, beautiful. Keep practicing."

We practiced at the target range the entire day. Ryan was very handy with his gun, and, by the end of the day, I at least was shooting the figures about 50% of the time. I never did hit a bulls-eye, but Ryan was feeling more confident about my abilities by the end of the day.

The next step was getting a concealed carry permit. I first had to complete a firearms safety training course, which was a two-week expedited course that I would be attending for an hour a day. I completed that course, and made an application to the state. I received my certificate to carry, so I was able to carry my pistol with me everywhere I went. Through it all, Ryan and I went to the target range every day for two hours after he got off work, and, by the end of the two weeks, I was hitting the figures up to 75% of the time.

Ryan also got a concealed carry permit, and he also committed to packing 24 hours a day. He had already passed his safety training course, so he didn't have to do it again.

Meanwhile, Dalilah was amazing me more and more. She was learning new words every single day. She was parroting different words that she heard, and she appeared to have some type of cognizance about what they meant. Nat came in handy, actually, as she watched Dalilah while Ryan and I were busy at the target range. Ryan appeared to be surprised by Dalilah's progress, as well, but he was quite a bit less shocked than myself. He wouldn't ever tell me that he, himself, was a prodigy, of course.

"Dalilah is going to be a handful to raise. At least for

me. She's going to have more knowledge than me before she's five years old, at this rate," I said.

"Don't be silly, beautiful. Dalilah is extremely intelligent, of course, but so are you."

Yes, but she's a genius, and she gets that from you, not me.

This was also a stressful time. I was constantly looking over my shoulder, and Ryan was with me all the time, except when he was working. When he was working, I had to say that I was grateful for Nat's company. I didn't think that she was exactly handy with a gun, but I still felt a little bit protected. Just having somebody else around the house who was an adult was helpful for me. Never mind the fact that this particular adult was in love with my husband, and probably, secretly, wanted to off me herself. But Nat and I always got along, so it was kinda fun having her around. And, Nat was right – the house did look gorgeous now that we had all of our furniture in there. It was exactly like I had pictured it would be, so both Nat and I were much more comfortable in the house.

We were like sister wives, except that she never actually got to have sex with the husband.

I was the only one who did that.

And I did that often. My sex life with Ryan was going gangbusters. We were apart for so long, and, for so long, I was not able to be intimate with him at all. But, once I broke down the barriers in the Porsche that day, we pretty much had been going at it ever since. We made up for lost time, making love for hours every evening while Dalilah slept in the next room. I had the baby monitor on at all times, of course, and there were times that I had to interrupt the fun to attend to her, but it really wasn't a problem. We couldn't get enough of each other. We were like an addiction for each other.

I didn't know what Nat thought about it all. She had moved into the lower level when I arrived, and she hung out there, watching television and tending to her son while Ryan and I were in our bedroom, making love for hours on end. This was an odd situation, of course, and I wondered when, or if, she would just give up and return to her life in New York with Nate and her job at Goldman Sachs.

Chapter Fifty-Three

I might have been, once again, marked for death, but life had to go on.

And go on, it did.

We had dinner with Nick and Alexis one night, meeting at a steak house for dinner, with plans to have drinks afterwards. I actually hired a sitter for that particular occasion, not expecting Nat to watch Dalilah. I didn't really know how to explain how a child who was less than six months old was stringing together words. I figured that I should probably just tell the sitter beforehand.

"Mama and daddy go out?" Dalilah asked, watching us getting ready for our dinner.

"Yes, baby, mama and daddy are going out." I was feeling a pang leaving her with a strange person. This would be the first time that I would be leaving her with somebody unfamiliar. I had actually found Janelle through a nanny service, so I felt comforted knowing that I wasn't leaving Dalilah with some punk teenager who didn't know what the hell was going on. I was that punk teenager once, but that particular gig ended when the ladies for whom I babysat came home too drunk to take me home, and I ended up being driven home by one of the random guys they picked up at the bar. Once my mom found out about that, it was all she wrote. All she fucking wrote. Still, that was one of my favorite jobs – I put the kids to sleep around 9, and read *Sweet Valley High* books for the rest of the evening.

Talk about easy money.

But Dalilah would be much more challenging than that.

Her green eyes got big. As she grew, she resembled Ryan more and more. I really didn't see me in her all that much, although Ryan disagreed. "She looks just like you when she crinkles up her nose. You do that all the time," he said.

"NO," Dalilah said. "You stay here."

"Now, Dalilah, mama and daddy are going to see Uncle Nick and Aunt Alexis. You remember Uncle Nick, now, don't you?"

She made a face, but sat down in her play pen and played with her Etch-A-Sketch. She was learning how to work the controls pretty well, and she was creating little houses, flowers and animals with it.

The baby-sitter, Janelle, arrived at 6:30. "Oh, what a beautiful little girl," she said, rushing to the playpen. "How old is she again?"

"Around six months," I said.

At that, Dalilah said, looking right at Janelle, "Mama and daddy go out. You watch me?"

Janelle got an astounded look on her face.

"Yeah, about that," Ryan said. "Our daughter is special. Here," he said, giving Janelle some basic books. "These will keep her occupied for awhile."

"She reads?"

"Yes," I said. "Just basic books, like *Goodnight Moon*, but, yes, she can read a little."

"Special, indeed," Janelle said.

We both said goodbye to little Dalilah, then got into Ryan's Porsche. We hadn't actually taken this car in quite a while, traveling only in the Escalade or the Rivian, as it was very rare that we went anywhere without Dalilah. The exception to this, of course, was the target practice. This was continuing apace, and I was now able to hit the figures most of the time. But, even then, we took the Escalade or the Rivian. Not really sure why, that was just how it worked out.

We got to the restaurant, and Nick and Alexis were already there. They had apparently both been drinking for awhile. Nick stood up, and hugged and kissed Ryan on the cheek, then playfully punched my shoulder. "I'm so glad you guys could make it," he said.

"Us, too," Ryan said. "It's nice to get out of the house for some fun for once. You know how it is when you have a baby at home."

"Been there, done that, not doing it again," Nick said. "Right, Alexis?"

Alexis didn't say anything, just sipped her Cosmo.

"So, what's new?" Ryan asked, peering over the menu. He had his arm around me, and was absent-mindedly rubbing my neck while he spoke.

"Well, you aren't going to believe this, but..." Nick began.

"We found a guy," Alexis said. "We're Hamptoning with him."

"What? You got somebody living with you two?" Ryan asked.

"Well, he doesn't actually live with us," Nick said. "He's

married. But he goes on a lot of business trips," Nick said, air-quoting the words 'business trips,' "and he hangs out with us."

Alexis nodded. "His name is David. You should meet him sometime."

Ryan said nothing, just cocked a single eyebrow at Nick. "Looks like we better start drinking to catch up to you two. I have a feeling this is going to be a Daniel night."

"Don't worry," I said. "I'm still breast-feeding, remember? I'm not going to drink."

"Ok, then," Ryan said. "Bring on the scotch." At that, he signaled the waiter and ordered himself a Dewar's rocks and a sparkling water for me. I was off all caffeine and most sugar, as well, so I was always restricting myself to some kind of water.

"Now, tell me more about David," Ryan said. "And when did you two start getting into that?"

"You're jealous," Alexis said.

And, indeed, it seemed that Ryan *was* jealous. I wondered if he secretly wished that he could go back to that kind of carefree lifestyle, fooling around with Nick and Alexis both. Ryan had, to my knowledge, not had any kind of intimate contact with Nick since I met him, even though I told him that I would be fine with it if he did. I did catch them kissing that one time, though, and felt strangely titillated by it all. Now it seemed that Ryan was going to live vicariously through Nick and Alexis.

"David," Nick began, "is a former male model who now is one of the leading architects at my firm. That's where we met. Alexis and I had him over for dinner one night, and he was digging Alexis and me both. That's where it all began."

"Where have I been?" Ryan said.

"Raising a genius child, while trying to keep your wife

alive," Nick said. "Hey, I wanted to Hamptons with you guys, but apparently Iris isn't to into that."

I looked at Ryan quizzically. I didn't know that was ever a topic of discussion.

"No, Iris isn't into that. I'm not either these days. As you know, I only have eyes for my wife."

I sipped my water and said nothing. But I wondered if Ryan wasn't secretly wishing to have Nick stay with us, and do three-ways like in his college days.

"So, Iris, how are you doing?" Alexis asked me. "I've been meaning to call you. As you know, I've been through similar experiences."

I knew that. She went through similar experiences with Ryan's father, who raped her when she was young. And she knows all about drug addiction, too. But I didn't think that she had to go through losing her mind because Ryan impregnated another woman, then living with that other woman once she returned home.

I had to admit, if nothing else, my life was unique.

"I'm doing as well as could possibly be expected," I said. "On the upside, I've got a truly wonderful husband and baby girl. On the downside, I have a crazy guy who wants to kill me," I said, patting the pistol in my purse. "I guess it all balances out to neutral. Really great stuff, really bad stuff – they cancel each other out."

"Ryan said something about that. So, your rapist wants to kill you?" Alexis inquired.

"Yeah. Or so the story goes," I said, studying the menu. "I think I'm going to get the scallops, or maybe the seared tuna. What about you, Ryan?"

"The halibut is terrific here," he said.

Seeing Alexis' face, which had a rather dumb-founded expression, I explained "Ryan and I try to live as normal of a life as possible. I carry my pistol with me everywhere I go, so hopefully I can protect myself if something happens. And, really, after everything I've been through in this past year, very little fazes me anymore."

"That's a good attitude to have, I guess," Alexis said. "And you really have to be able to roll with the punches when you're married to Ryan. I knew that well myself."

I nodded.

"How is Dalilah?" Nick asked.

"Dalilah is a Gallagher," Ryan said.

"Meaning?"

"She's a prodigy. She's already stringing together words, reading rudimentary books, and drawing pictures on her Etch-A-Sketch and on the papers we give her."

Alexis looked down, tears in her eyes. "Sounds like Mia," she said.

Ryan looked sad, too, putting his hand on her hands.

I looked at Ryan. He never once mentioned that Mia was also a genius. He looked at his Scotch and said nothing.

Alexis was apparently drinking heavily, as she looked at Nick, then slapped him across the face. "You're a fucking bastard," she said.

"What the hell?" he asked.

"Been there, done that, not doing it again," she mocked him.

Nick said nothing, just turned to his drink, then started talking to us while Alexis glared at him. "Anyhow, so Dalilah is a genius, huh? Sounds like her father and aunt."

Alexis looked like she was about to haul off and hit him. Ryan and I just looked at her in mystification.

Then she stormed off without a word.

Nick rolled his eyes. "I'm remembering now why Alexis and I never really have gotten together before. She's fun in small doses, but, Christ, how did you put up with her all those years?"

"She on her meds?" Ryan asked.

"I have no idea. She's been acting strangely, really, ever since I told her that I'm going in for a snip and clip. She wants another baby. I don't."

"Why are you going to get a vasectomy?" Ryan asked.

"I have my kids. Granted, Rielle hasn't been too generous in letting me see them, but they're around, and they're enough for me. The O'Hara name will continue, and that's what counts," Nick said. "I can't go home tonight. I pretty much have to let Hurricane Alexis blow over. Do you mind if I crash with you guys tonight?"

Hmmm...maybe we can pawn him off on Nat?

Ryan looked at me skeptically. "Do you mind, beautiful?"

"Of course not. Mi casa, su casa, you know?"

We stayed at the restaurant for several hours, Ryan and Nick drinking Scotch, me drinking water. When we got home, I headed up to bed, after putting Dalilah down for the night. Ryan and Nick stayed up, talking in the living room. The baby monitor was on in Dalilah's room, but it also was on in the living room. I guess Ryan wasn't aware of this. So, I eavesdropped on their conversation.

Nick was talking. "God, you know, Ryan, I made fun of you when I met Iris. I'm starting to realize the logic in being with someone like her. Between Rielle and Alexis, I don't know who's crazier. They're hot, for sure, and well-bred, but cray. I'm getting it from both sides – Rielle is constantly calling, bitching and wanting something. Then Alexis is around, bitching and wanting something. I'm fucking exhausted."

"See, I told you Iris was special. You know, when she divorced me, I had to force her to take anything at all? Then she went out and got a job at the Whole Foods, instead of taking the money I gave her. Just goes to show how wrong my sister was."

"What? I thought Sarah and Iris get along?"

"They do, famously. But when I was first going to marry Iris, Sarah warned me to get a pre-nup. She thought that Iris would take me for everything. Turns out I was right – Iris wants me, not my money. And I love that about her more than anything else."

"Yeah. Perhaps I need to get out of the incestuous barrel I've been picking from and find somebody normal. Like Iris. Yeah, she went ape-shit for awhile, but who could blame her? That poor girl sure has gone through the mill in the past year or so."

"And is still going through it. She puts on a brave face, but I know she's scared. I've been calling my dad every day about Andrew. Dad has his people tracking him. Andrew hasn't made a move just yet, but my dad has told me that Andrew has become extremely unhinged. He's had some kind of a psychotic break. I never tell Iris about this, though. I don't want to freak her out even more."

"How are you holding up about it?"

"I don't show it, but I'm pretty goddamned freaked out myself. I know that I could take him, if it came to that. Andrew, before his apparent psychotic break, was cunning and ruthless. He had to be in that job. But if he's out there, acting like any other crazy person, I can outsmart him. I know crazy. I've been surrounded by crazy my entire life."

"You can't outsmart crazy. That's the whole point. People who got nothing to lose are the most dangerous of all. And, when you're truly crazy, you don't realize that you have shit to lose. Watch your ass, there, buddy. I don't want you getting hurt."

"He's not getting Iris. That's all I know. I would literally die for that woman."

"I know, buddy. Wish I could find a woman that I would give my life for."

"Let's change the subject. We've got Natalie living here. You ever think about that?"

"Nat and me? We tried that, remember?"

Good God, these people are incestuous. My head was spinning. Nick, Nat, Ryan, Alexis apparently have been on the love-go-round.

"Yeah, I know. But what can I do? She won't leave. Granted, the DNA results aren't in yet. They should be in next week. But she told me that she won't leave, even if it is proven that I'm not the father."

"Get a restraining order, and have her arrested for trespassing. Change the locks. One thing about Natalie – she won't Alexis you. She's still a sweet girl. Misguided, but sweet. She won't go ape and stalkery if you kick her out."

"Is it wrong that I feel badly for her? I mean, Iris has been absolutely phenomenal about Natalie being here. Believe it or not, I don't think that Iris minds her here. I don't think that Iris necessarily wants Nat to stay with us forever, but she also doesn't seem to be upset that Nat isn't leaving. But I feel sorry for Nat. She's always been like a sister to me."

"And you've always been her great love. You gotta figure out a way to get her gone. Besides, Nat almost cost you *your* great love. I mean, you were in an altered state when you guys slept together. She wasn't. She took advantage of you. That should piss you off enough to get tough with her."

"I know. I should be really angry with Nat, but it's hard to be mad at her. At any rate, I guess I'll figure something out once the DNA results are in. God forbid Christopher is my kid. That will more than screw everything up."

"You're too nice. That's always been your problem."

"Yeah. Some problem. Anyhow, what about that David guy?"

"I don't know. He's into Alexis, but he's into me, too. He's been kinda a regular three-way partner for about a month now. Do you ever think about joining us?"

"You and Alexis? Oh, hell no. Hell to the fucking no. As you said earlier, been there, done that, got the t-shirt, not doing it again."

"You ever think about me joining you and Iris?"

"All the time. All the time. Iris is pretty straight, though. She wouldn't be digging that at all."

I sighed. I knew that Ryan wanted Nick in our relationship. Ryan had never told me as much, but I always suspected. I wondered if I should offer to bring Nick in on a semi-regular basis. Good, God, though, what a crazy-quilt pattern those Harvard people have formed. Nate-Ryan-Nick-Nat. Ryan-Nick-Alexis. Hell, Alexis probably was with Nate a time or two as well. Anything is possible.

With that bunch, anything is *probable*.

"So, why don't you talk to her about it?" Nick asked.

"I don't want to push it. We just got back together not two months ago. She's going through a lot, too, with the Andrew threat. Also, I don't know if she's going to quite know what to do with our daughter. I have a feeling that Dalilah is going to outshine all of us. Iris isn't used to that, at least not as much as I am. Dalilah's going to be a handful for us."

"My talking about Dalilah is what set off Alexis. I dread the day that Alexis meets that child. She looks so much like Mia, it's scary. She acts just like her, too. Alexis is bound to go off the deep end. She never got over Mia, you know," Nick said.

"I didn't, either. That was probably the most devastated I've been, losing her. Dalilah seems like a miracle to me. Iris, too. Neither can entirely replace Mia, of course, but they've both gone a long way towards making me feel that life is worth living again."

Hearing him talk about Mia broke my heart, and made me feel guilty for listening in on their conversation. So, I turned off the baby monitor from the living room, and tried to sleep. The baby monitor from Dalilah's room was still audible, however, and I heard my little daughter breathing heavily in sleep. She spoke some garbled words, too. She was like her mother that way – I have always been told that I talk in my sleep pretty constantly. That was probably the only thing that she would get from me, though.

In looks and intelligence, she was clearly her father's daughter.

I couldn't sleep, though, so I knew that Ryan didn't come into our room until a couple of hours after I stopped listening in on their conversation. I had no idea what they were saying after I stopped listening, and probably didn't want to know. What I did know is that Ryan wanted Nick to get sexual with us, and didn't know how to ask me about it. While I was happy that he respected my feelings about this, I was also a little upset that he wanted that, and I didn't know if I could provide it. I wanted, more than anything, for him to be happy. I always tried to make him happy. Well, aside from the living in the drug house and taking his daughter without telling him that she existed. Yeah, those are pretty major transgressions. But I really wanted to make it all up to him, and be the best wife I could be.

"You awake?" Ryan asked, crawling into the bed next to me.

"Yar," I said.

He got undressed, and crawled under the covers with me. He started stroking my hair, and kissing my back and neck. I was also naked, and I could feel him behind me. He was completely hard, and he entered me without a word. I felt the familiar rush, the feeling of completeness and wholeness. His hands were on my breasts, and he moved inside me rhythmically. I orgasmed, and he also did shortly thereafter. He groaned, then put his head in my hair. I could feel his heart and his breathing, both of them also audible.

I turned around to look at him. I put my hand on his cheek, and stroked it. I wanted to address some of the things I was hearing downstairs, especially the Nick-being-with-us conversation. I also wanted to talk to him about Andrew and his psychotic break. Ryan had never told me about that. He hadn't even told me that he had been in contact with his father about Andrew. He wanted to protect me, and make sure that I didn't worry, but I was feeling that I was being left out of the loop about it. I wasn't liking that one bit. However, I couldn't bring it up. I was eavesdropping, as usual, and I wanted him to trust me. I wasn't at all sure that he would be able to trust me if he knew that I was invading his privacy like that.

He looked at me, smoothing my hair back. He kissed my forehead. Then he was kissing my lips, and I could feel his hardness again. He always had the shortest refractory period of anybody that I had ever known. He laid on his back, bringing me on top of him, and he was inside me again, with me riding him. I brought down my head, putting it on his chest. His body was coming back after his weight loss, and he was almost back to the pecs and abs of steel that he had before he started taking on the junkie look of the past few months. I put my hands on his shoulders and chest while I straddled him as he thrusted inside me. We were like this for a little while, then I crawled down so that my genitals were in his mouth, while I sucked his hardness in a 69 position. He groaned, then shot into my mouth almost immediately.

I crawled back into my original position next to him on the bed. I put my head on his chest as he stroked my hair. "I can't get enough of you," he said. "I mean, that was always true for me, but, since you've been back, it seems that I want to be inside you all the time. All the time. I don't know if it's because I feel like we need to make up for lost time or its-" Then he stopped.

I think I knew what was on his mind. He was afraid of losing me again. I didn't think that he was exactly afraid that I was going to run again, but, at the same time, I was sure that he felt that our happiness was always fleeting. We always had moments, days, weeks that were pure bliss. Then something awful would happen, and we would end up devastated. We always had to look over our shoulder for the next thing that fate would cook up for us. We could never just relax. So, it was unspoken between us that these blissful moments we had together had to be savored.

Because they might not last very long.

I said "I know, baby. I know you're scared. You put on a great front, but I have a feeling that you're more freaked about Andrew than you're letting on. I wish that there was some way to ease both of our minds." I paused for a few minutes, my head on his chest, listening to his heart. I played with his chest, then asked him "What's going on with that?"

He took a deep breath, then let it out slowly, like a

leaking balloon. "My father and I have been talking. My father has been keeping tabs on Andrew through some associates who know him. Andrew has been behaving extremely erratically. It seems that he is no longer the calculating man he was, but more...disorganized."

"Ok, so he's disorganized. It sounds like he is suffering from some kind of breakdown, maybe."

"Right. Andrew apparently doesn't shower much anymore, and..." His breathing started coming harder.

"And?"

He shook his head. "He has pictures in a room. Pictures of you. Of us. Like the *People* Magazine we were in. Our wedding notice. He took one of our wedding photos out of the house, and that's in the room, too. I'm sure you never noticed that it was missing. I did, though. I wondered what happened to it."

I just sat there, listening to him. This was getting creepier by the second, but I somehow didn't feel the white hot feeling of fear that I should've been feeling upon hearing all this.

"There's something else," he said.

"Oh?"

"Yeah. He labels the pictures. He labels them Cherry and Andrew."

"Cherry? Like the tree?"

"Cherry like his ex-wife. My father sent me a picture of her on my phone." At that, he got his phone and sent me the photo of Cherry, Andrew's ex-wife. I gasped a little. Button nose, freckles, red hair, roundish face, full lips. She was my doppelganger, if ever there was one.

"Ah," I said. "Now it all becomes clear. It's not me he wants to kill, it's her."

"That's the thing," Ryan said. "She's already dead."

"What? What happened to her?"

"She died of cancer a little over a month ago. My father thinks that her death is what caused Andrew to finally go off the deep end."

"Let me guess. Things between them did not end well."

"Of course," Ryan said. "Dirty divorce. She got custody of the kids, and took him for everything he had, just about. It was one of those things."

"And they got divorced when?"

"It was finalized in December of the year before last."

"Right around the time that he started protecting me."

"Yup," he said. "You got it."

The puzzle pieces were starting to come together nicely.

"So, she's dead. Yet he still wants to kill me?"

"Yeah. This is what my father has been able to piece together about this guy. Apparently, he started becoming unhinged right around the time that he was hired to protect you. Before that, there wasn't anything that was visibly amiss with him. Otherwise, he wouldn't have checked out, and my father would've hired somebody else for you," Ryan said, while I lay on his chest, his heart pounding in my ears. "Then, after he, uh-"

"Raped me," I said. "Go on, you can say it. I can take that word."

"Right," he said, and I could feel his muscles start to tense up as he talked about that incident. "Well, after that happened, Andrew started acting strangely. Not like now, but he started becoming paranoid acting. It's one of those things, though – because of what he used to do, he has a reason to be paranoid. You know the old joke – just because you're paranoid, doesn't mean that someone isn't out to get you."

I laughed a little, trying to break the tension.

"Then, after Cherry died, he apparently had a full-on psychotic break. He's been hallucinating, hearing voices, and he thinks that Cherry is still alive. He thinks that you're Cherry, now. He thinks that it was Cherry that he, uh, attacked, and that it was Cherry who told everybody about it."

My blood started to run cold. "So, he's crazy. Is that going to make it easier or harder for me to defend against?"

He drew a breath. "The good news is that he no longer has the ruthless, cold and calculating instinct that he had in his former job. The bad news is that crazy is, by its very nature, unpredictable. I could probably make chess moves with this guy in his normal state. Outsmart him. But the way he is now – who knows what's going to happen?"

"So, more difficult to defend against."

"Yeah. I've thought about..."

"What? You've thought about what?"

"Nothing. You wouldn't approve."

"Try me."

"I've thought about having a hit put on him."

I looked at his face.

He was dead serious.

"Huh," I said. "A hit." I thought about it for about five minutes, my head on his chest, him stroking my arm, neither of us saying anything. I finally said "not a bad idea. Not a bad idea at all."

"Really?" he said.

"Yeah. It sure would be nice to not have to worry about that shithead again." Then I immediately regretted my words. Shaking my head, I said "No, no, no. I take that back. I can't put you in danger like that. You might think that nothing will go wrong, but what if it does, and you spend the rest of your life in prison? No. no. no." If that happened, somebody would just have to finish me off. I didn't think I could survive a blow like that.

He sighed. "That actually was the reaction I was expecting from you. So, it's back to the drawing board. More target practice, and more looking over our shoulders constantly. The good news is, my father has tabs on him, so I know his movements for now."

I just nodded. "Hey, let's not talk about this anymore. It's getting too depressing. What's going on with Nick?"

"Nick is finding out what it is like to live with Alexis, unfortunately for him. He always knew that she was unstable, but he never really got to experience the full effect of it. She apparently is desperate for a child, and he wants a vasectomy. He might be staying here for a few days while he waits for her to cool off. I hope that's ok."

"Sure. Maybe he and Nat can get together and ride off into the sunset."

"No. Been there, done that. Nat and Nick don't get along. Not exactly sure why, but I think it has something to do with Nick hitting on Nate."

"Oh? What happened there?"

"Nate wasn't interested. Nick apparently was misreading the signals. At any rate, Nick and Nat have a sexual history as well, so when Nick made a move on Nate, Natalie was pretty upset about that. So was I, to be honest with you. Nick caused a lot of tension between himself, myself, and Nate for a long time with that stupid move."

"Maybe it's time that Nick moves on and finds somebody who doesn't know any of you guys."

"That's what I told him. He liked Alexis because he thought she understood him. She does understand him, but she's also demanding and wants her way. I just hope that she is stabilized and on her meds, otherwise, she's going to be coming over here. There's no room at the Inn over here, with us, Nick and Natalie staying here."

I took a deep breath. "Do you, uh, do you."

"Do I?"

"Do you want Nick to, uh, be with us sometimes? I mean, not all the time, but periodically?"

Ryan was quiet. He finally said "Yes. But I know that you're not comfortable with it, so I don't really want it for that reason. I would never do anything that might jeopardize us again. We just got back together."

It was my turn to be quiet. "I would do it. I want to make you happy."

At that, he kissed me passionately. "You make me happy. Just by being in my presence." He was hard again, and, as he entered me, he said "let me show you just how happy you make me." And, for the next few hours, this is what he did – showed me how happy I made him.

Chapter Fifty-Four

It was certainly interesting having Nick stay with us for those few days.

Interesting in a good way, for Nick was the one who finally got Nat out.

"Hey, Nat," Nick said. "What's taking so long for those DNA test results to come in?" Ryan had gotten the promised court order several months before, immediately after I moved back in.

She looked embarrassed. "I don't know. The wheels of justice turn slowly sometimes."

"Uh, huh." Then he looked at Ryan. "You believing this nonsense?"

It just occurred to Ryan, apparently, that the results should've already been in. Like myself, Ryan's mind had been 1,000 miles away from many important things, as we were focusing on Dalilah, my shooting ability, and finding out information about Andrew. "Yeah, Nat," Ryan said. "Maybe I need to call the judge and find out about that."

"Oh, alright. You caught me. The DNA letter actually

came in about a month and a half ago. I've been too nervous to look at it, so I didn't say anything."

Once again, it took Nick's bluntness to make things come about.

"Well Nat," Ryan said. "Let's see the letter. Come what may, things will be fine."

I really didn't believe that. Little Christopher looked like Nate, so I thought the results would show that Nate was the father, not Ryan, but if that wasn't the case, I didn't know how Ryan would handle it.

Let alone how I would handle it.

At that, Nat went to her room, and came back up with a letter in her hand. With shaking hands, she gave it to Ryan to open. He did so, unfolding the paper. Then he smiled a huge smile. "Ha. I knew it. I knew it from the start. Christopher is not my child."

Nat burst into tears. I think that she, herself, always knew as much, deep down. She just never wanted to admit to it.

"Well," Nick said. "Looks like you no longer have an excuse to stay here. Let me go downstairs with you and help you pack your bags."

Nat looked sorrowfully at Ryan and me. I went over to her, and put my arm around her. "It's going to be ok, Natalie," I said. "Your husband wants you back. Your child should be with his father. We'll always be friends, but I think it's time to call it a day."

"I'm so sorry, Iris," she said. "I really caused a lot of problems with my actions." Then she turned to Ryan. "I'm sorry to you, too, Ryan. I love you. I've always loved you. That's all I could see. But I hope that all of this will eventually blow over, and you and Iris can come and visit Nate and me sometime soon."

To this, Nick said "Yeah, they'll be getting right on that."

I shot Nick a look. He was so insensitive sometimes.

All the time, really.

"Shut up, Nick," Natalie said. "Ryan and Nate have been friends for a long time, and I hope they will always be friends."

"We will, Nat," Ryan said. "But you and Nate have a lot of patching up to do, so let's just say that we won't be seeing you guys anytime soon. Do you need transportation home?"

Nat nodded.

"Ok," Ryan said, calling Tim, his pilot. "Tim," Ryan said. "Can you charter a flight today, in about two hours or so?" Ryan paused. "Good, thank you." Then he turned to Nat. "Done." Then he called Daniel to come and pick her up to give her a ride to the airport.

At that, Natalie went downstairs to pack her bags to prepare to leave. She came back up, kissed all of us goodbye, then waited for Daniel to come and get her so he could take her to the airport. Daniel arrived after about a half an hour, and Natalie was gone. Just like that.

"Damn," Ryan said to Nick. "You certainly have a way of getting things done."

"You just gotta be firm and unwavering. Natalie's like Alexis in a lot of ways. They're both like children, and you need to treat them that way."

"Well, thanks," Ryan said. "I owe you one."

"Speaking of children," I said, hearing Dalilah calling for me through the baby monitor. I went upstairs to get her.

I came back downstairs with her, and she saw Nick and reached for him. "Uncle Nick," she said, as Nick took her from me. She put her little hand on Nick's nose and smiled.

He laughed back. "Wow, she is a Gallagher. A Whitney, really."

"Yes," Ryan said. "She's artistic and brilliant like my mother and father. But I see a lot of Iris in her as well." Indeed, it looked like her hair was going to be red, which was probably going to be the only major thing she inherited from me.

Nick sat down on a chair with Dalilah on his lap. He addressed both of us. "What can I do to help with this Andrew situation?" he asked.

"Let me talk to Iris alone, ok?"

"Sure," Nick said. "I'll be downstairs if you need me, ok?"

"Thanks, buddy," Ryan said. Nick headed, with Dalilah, to the downstairs area that housed the game room, the wine cellar and two bedrooms. Then Ryan addressed me. "I need to talk to you about something important."

"Ok," I said, already dreading this.

"I've been trying to find the best time to tell you this," he said, then hesitated slightly.

I started to feel the ice cold feeling of fear creep through my veins.

"Anyhow, I know this is probably the very worst time for this, but..."

"Go on."

"There's another trip I need to take for the bank. We're in merger talks with another bank headquartered in New York City. I'll be gone for a week."

"New York. That's great. It'll give you a chance to maybe see Nate and see if you guys can patch things up there."

"I thought about that. Nat doesn't know about this trip, of course, so I'm not sure that calling Nate while I'm there would be such a great idea. It might be too much of a distraction. But that isn't the point, here. The point is that I need to make sure you're safe while I'm gone. A bodyguard is out of the question, of course."

I suddenly knew what idea he had for me. "You want Nick to stay here while you're gone, don't you?"

"I was going to ask him, but only after I talked to you."

"Nick, is he trained like you are, with weapons and that?"

"Yeah. He's an excellent shot himself."

"Alexis won't care about this?"

"Alexis doesn't have a say. I don't think they're going to stay together anyhow."

I sighed. "If he'll do it, sure. What's Plan B, though?"

"I stay here. The problem with that is my job wouldn't exactly be happy with me about this. This is an important merger that we've been working on for awhile. But I can't leave unless I know you're in good hands. And Dalilah, too. Both of my girls have to be safe."

"Ok."

At that, Ryan went downstairs to get Nick.

"So, what's the big secret?" Nick asked upon coming up.

"I need to go out of town next week," Ryan said. "And I wanted to know if you could stay here with Iris and Dalilah."

"Sure," Nick said without hesitation. "Hell, it'll get me out of the house and away from Alexis' cray, so that's a bonus. But anything you need, buddy, you got it."

"Now, you have to know that there might be a time when you're going to have to face down Andrew. So you're going to have to be on high alert and packing all the time you're here."

"I know the drill," he said.

"Good," Ryan said.

I felt relieved that Nick could stay here with me, but I also felt a sense of sadness and loss that I would have to spend a week apart from Ryan. Ever since I'd been back, I'd felt a need to be with him always, so a week away would be horrible.

But I sucked it up, and prepared for Ryan's leaving and Nick's staying.

Chapter Fifty-Five

Ryan left on an early Monday morning, after making love to me several times. I tried to banish the thought that our lovemaking had an urgency because both of us were afraid that we wouldn't see each other again. But it was in the back of my mind. What if Andrew came for me that week, and I just never saw my beautiful husband again? Or my beautiful child? I wouldn't know differently, because I'd be dead. But, still, just the thought of not seeing him again frightened me.

Nick, for his part, chose to work from home that week on a drafting project. I was grateful to have somebody around, and the fact that he was handy with weapons was a definite bonus.

Not having Ryan around that week gave me a chance to focus all my energies on Dalilah, who was stringing together more words every day. At just under seven months old, she was talking better than an average 2-year-old, which was amazing to me.

"Daddy go away?" she asked, after Ryan kissed her goodbye and told her to be a good girl.

"Yes, baby, Daddy will be gone for a week. He'll be home Saturday." That was one good thing – he was only going to be gone for a business week, not a calendar week.

"Uncle Nick stay here?"

"Yes, Uncle Nick is staying here. Now, what would you like to do?"

"Draw," she said. "With paints."

I gave her some of her water colors, which were the kind used by elementary school children in the little white tray. I mixed up the water with the little disks in the tray, and gave Dalilah some art paper and a brush. I got a set for myself, and Dalilah and I lay on the floor, side by side, painting all morning long. Dalilah was becoming more sophisticated with her paintings and drawings – she was able to draw dogs, cats, birds, flowers, trees, houses and bumblebees. For my part, I was able to draw little stick figures, and I colored them in different colors. My houses and flowers were less sophisticated than my tiny daughter's, as were my dogs and cats.

One thing was for sure – Dalilah got her artistic bent from her father, not from me.

We worked quietly downstairs, while Nick was working in Ryan's office upstairs. I could hear him talking on the phone to clients, which gave me a sense of security, just knowing that somebody was around. I had to admit that I missed Nat, because she always kept me company while Ryan was at work. Now it was Nick's turn.

I wondered if there ever would come a time when I wouldn't need a babysitter anymore.

The first few days with Nick were fine. We started to become tentative friends, after having gotten off on the wrong foot when we first met, because Nick didn't think that I was good enough for Ryan. Not sophisticated enough, not worldly enough, and not attractive enough. He pretty much confirmed all my own insecurities with his attitude towards me in those days, so I really didn't like him.

However, I soon found out that he developed a newfound respect for me.

"You know, when I first met you, I have to admit that I didn't see it. I didn't see you and Ryan together at all," Nick said over a dinner of take-out pizza and beer. Nick apparently wasn't a cook like Ryan, and I, myself, was always too busy with Dalilah to cook.

"I know that," I said. "I heard you guys talking on the night you and I met."

"I mean, I was pissed when I found out that you took Dalilah from him and didn't tell him about her. Don't get me wrong. But Ryan told me that you didn't want a thing from him when you divorced him," Nick said with a shake of his head. "Every time I get another call from Rielle's lawyer, demanding more and more, I start thinking about the wisdom of finding a girl like you. Just down to earth, not pretentious, not in love with money and possessions."

"Well, thank you, Nick," I said, clinking my beer bottle with his. "I admit that I wasn't too fond of you, either, because I thought you were judging me. Ryan loves you, though, and you've always done so much for him. That means a lot to me, too. Just because Ryan means so much to me."

Nick and I bonded that week. We watched movies together in the evenings, finding that we shared a similar sense of humor. We both laughed until we cried at Chris Rock standup comedy and Monty Python movies. I showed him my favorite movie, *The Way We Were*, and, to my surprise, Nick teared up at the conclusion of that movie, even more than I did. He showed me one of his favorite movies, *The Departed*, and I was enthralled with this movie from beginning to end.

He was also great with Dalilah, playing with her in the evenings after he finished his work. He sat with her at our new baby grand piano, which arrived that week after being on back order for over a month. The enormous piano was the centerpiece of the living room, fitting in with the masculinity and dark colors of this room perfectly. It turned out that Nick was an excellent piano player, and he helped Dalilah put her chubby hands across the keys. I wondered if she would be musical as well as artistic. It did seem that she was understanding and appreciating the music.

Nick and I were becoming friends, at long last.

The week ended without incident, with Ryan arriving that Friday night on the red-eye. He got in around midnight, climbing into bed with me. I verbally acknowledged him in the bed, so that he would know that I wasn't sleeping, so he put his hands on my breasts and stomach, then got undressed and made passionate love to me. "I missed you," he said. "God, how much I missed you," he said while he thrust, his head buried in my shoulder. He quickly came, then rolled over and continued to stroke my body until he was hard again. He kissed me slowly and tenderly, and entered me again, without the urgency of the first lovemaking of the night. "I love you so much. So very much. I would die for you," he was saying. "I would die for you."

We made love like that, slowly, tenderly, leisurely, into the morning. The sun came up when we finally disentangled and tried to get caught up on some much-needed sleep.

Of course, Dalilah got up, herself, around 8 that morning, so it turned out I only had about three hours of sleep.

But it was well worth it.

Chapter Fifty-Six

I found out unpleasant news that week – Rochelle wasn't going to plead, so the trial was scheduled in a month. It had been over two years since the incident happened, and the trial should've gone several times, but, each time, there was some kind of continuance for one reason or another. I was also supposed to be deposed several times, but this kept getting put off as well. Now, finally, I was going to be deposed, and, since the trial was getting near, the media was becoming interested in the story as well.

I started getting phone calls from random media personnel, asking for some kind of comment. They were interested in not just the trial and the crime, but also my personal life – why I divorced Ryan, yet was still with him, and they also wanted information about our daughter. I politely told each person who called that I didn't have a comment, and I didn't watch any 24-hour news channels, so I had no idea if I was being discussed on the shows. I probably was, but I didn't want to stress out, so I didn't bother with watching these shows.

Yet, somehow, information was being filtered to these media people. Some of the messages on my voice mail referenced my drug abuse and rape, and my stint in rehab. I had no idea who was feeding the media this private information, but I would imagine it would be somebody with a bone to pick – probably Natalie, maybe Alexis. Alexis seemed to have given in to her dark side again, like when I first knew her. Only now, she wasn't hassling Ryan, she was hassling Nick. Nick was threatening to break up with her, but he confessed to Ryan that he couldn't cut the cord completely because "the sex was just too good."

"Yeah," Ryan said. "When she's manic, it usually is good. But the mania brings out all sorts of other goodies from her as well. Just wait. You'll be begging to leave in a matter of days."

Nick reported that Alexis was staying up for days on end, talking incessantly. She had also broken into an Hermés store because she wanted a bag from there after hours, and couldn't wait until the store opened. She left the money for the bag, $20,000, on the counter, but the surveillance video caught her and she was charged with trespassing and property damage. Nick also reported that David was coming around more and more, and he and Alexis would be going at it long after Nick had left the room. Nick wasn't sure how David could keep up with her, but Nick was happy to have a buffer there.

Ryan nodded. "This is all sounding very familiar. Just wait until she starts doing lines again. Just wait."

It wasn't a day before Nick was back, wanting to stay at our house again. "Alexis kicked me out, throwing all my stuff out on the lawn," Nick explained. "And it's my house! I need to stay here until she cools off."

"Get a restraining order," Ryan said. "Trust me, you're gonna need it."

I sighed. I was in the middle of examining the discovery documents in preparation of my deposition in the morning. I didn't need the distraction of Nick staying with us, especially as I knew that Alexis was probably going to be at our house as well.

"If you'll excuse me, I have to prepare for my deposition tomorrow," I said, going downstairs.

Not a half hour later, I heard Alexis upstairs, screaming at the top of her lungs. "Asshole," she screamed. "Or should I say assholes? You two are peas in a pod."

"Good to see you, too, Alexis," Ryan said.

"Good to see you too, Alexis," she mocked him. "What's good about it? Nick here just ran off, just ran off, leaving me to fend for myself with that sex maniac David. And, what about you, Ryan? You're so fucking pussy whipped that your stupid slut can do anything to you and you'll just take it. I'd like to see your reaction if I would've hid your daughter for as long as she did."

"Nick," Ryan said. "Remember what I told you?"

I felt for both of them up there, Ryan and Nick. I wondered what Alexis was really capable of when she got like this. I remembered the last time, when she revealed to me that Ryan was bisexual. What might come out of this tirade?

Then I heard "Holy fucking Christ!" It was Alexis. "Fuck, that's Mia with red hair." Then she started sobbing, loudly. "Mia, Mia, Mia," she repeated, over and over. "Oh my God, my baby. My baby. My baby."

Nick was talking next. "Alexis, you're going to have to leave." Leave it to Nick to be completely insensitive about

Alexis breaking down upon seeing little Dalilah, who was apparently the spitting image of Alexis and Ryan's child.

Then there was absolute bedlam in the living room. Dalilah started screaming and crying, Ryan started admonishing Alexis about scaring her, Alexis continued to howl, Nick continued to yell.

I went upstairs to try to straighten everything out. I found Alexis looking disheveled – her blonde hair was tangled and askew, her makeup was running down her blotchy face, and two of her fingernails were broken, while the others were long. She was dressed in a skimpy, filmy negligee that revealed all of her magnificent body, with no coat on, despite the fact that it was below thirty degrees outside. She had on one sock and no shoes. She had a frying pan in her hand, and was brandishing it like a weapon.

She saw me immediately, then came over to me and wrapped herself around me, frying pan still in hand, and sobbed into my shoulder. I looked over her shoulder at Ryan, who was watching Alexis with a half-amused, half-pissed, look on his face. Nick was looking at her with a one-hundred-percent pissed look on his face.

I wondered if the guys expected me to be the official Alexis caretaker for the evening.

I couldn't deal with that. I had enough on my mind as it was.

Alexis was like that for a good five minutes, clutching me hard while sobbing. Dalilah had calmed down, and was now like her father and Uncle Nick – her chubby hand was shoved in her mouth, and she was just staring at the circus sideshow known as Alexis. She was dressed in a blue Winnie the Pooh onesy, her little red curls rioting around her face. She was sitting on Nick's lap.

I finally had to extricate myself from the sobbing Alexis.

I got a better look at her, and it seemed that she wasn't quite in touch with reality. She had an expression that was one of extreme pain and fear – her beautiful mouth was quivering, her blue eyes were saucers, and her pupils were extremely dilated. She was looking at me, yet didn't really seem to see me. Her hands were trembling wildly.

"There, there, Alexis, why don't you have a seat?" I said, directing her to one of the chairs in the living room. She obeyed, and sat down, staring into space, her eyes glazed over in catatonia. I went to the kitchen to fix her a cup of hot chocolate. Ryan followed me in there.

"I'm so sorry, beautiful, about all this. I know that you have a stressful day ahead of you tomorrow, and you don't need this kind of bullshit occurring in this house."

"It's not a problem," I said, thinking that bullshit just came with the territory of being with him. "She needs back on her meds, obviously. So you better talk to her somehow. You were the one that she listened to the last time. I don't think Nick is equipped to deal with this."

"You're probably right," he said, with a sigh.

Before we got out of the kitchen, Alexis was back at it. She was screaming at Nick "You're an asshole, a goddamned asshole. I hate you," she screamed, then hauled off and whacked him with the frying pan in her hand. Nick caught the frying pan before it could smack him a second time, and grabbed it away from her.

This made her howl even more.

Ryan sighed, nodded at Nick, then disappeared briefly. He came back in a few minutes, a syringe in hand. He then tackled Alexis, overpowering her while Nick held her feet, and injected her while she screamed and kicked. In a few seconds, her screaming and kicking subsided, and she was passed out on the couch.

"It looks like she's going to have to be checked into the hospital," Ryan said, stating the obvious. "I doubt she'll go willingly, though. At any rate, we can't take her over there right now. We need to just let her sleep this off, then deal with it in the morning."

Nick just nodded, mute for once. Then he said "Holy Christ, how did you do it all those years?"

Ryan just smiled wryly and said "Now you know why I was so high all the time."

In the morning, Alexis woke up, and, surprisingly, she was lucid, and, even more surprisingly, she was willing to check herself into the hospital. "Yeah, sure," she said, when Ryan told her that he was taking her to an exclusive mental health facility for evaluation and treatment. She evidently wasn't manic anymore, but had swung down to depression, because she was laying on the couch, one arm draped over the side. "I don't really care what you do. My life is over, anyhow."

At that, Ryan called his work, and got her on her feet. Nick was on the other side of her, and they marched her out of the house and into Nick's car, which was parked in the driveway. Ryan immediately came back in, and gave me a big hug and kiss, and said "I'm so sorry about this, beautiful. I know that today is important to you, and I'm behind you all the way. I love you, more than you can ever know."

I just nodded. "Good luck with her," I said. Then went back into the house to wait for the sitter to arrive. Helena was from the same agency as the last girl, Janelle, and I went through the same drill about explaining about Dalilah and her specialness. Dalilah was sitting in her playpen, then looked at Helena and said "Mommy go to court. Daddy go to hospital. You watch me."

Helena looked at me "She's seven months old?"

"Yes," I said. "Here, give her these Winnie the Pooh books to read, and these puzzles to work," I said, giving the girl some of Dalilah's favorite little puzzles. "She'll be fine, she's a wonderful little girl."

"I guess so," Helena said. "Take care."

At that, I left for the courthouse for my deposition.

Chapter Fifty-Seven

I dreaded this deposition, for some reason. For one thing, I was going to the courthouse for the deposition. This is where Cindy wanted to hold it, in one of the courthouse conference rooms. This meant that I could not bring my gun with me, and I felt a little naked without it, to tell the truth.

There was also a matter of knowing what questions were in store for me. I knew that I had absolutely nothing to hide, but that the attorney was, no doubt, going to go on a fishing expedition with this. I would imagine that he was going to ask me all kinds of objectionable questions that would never be allowed in court, mainly to find out what my weaknesses would be.

How right I was with this assumption.

"Mrs. Gallagher," the attorney, Greg Schultz, began. The man was around 55, and he was an imposing figure at 6'5", and around 200 lbs. His thick hair was completely grey. He was dressed in a megadollar suit, much like what Ryan wears to his job, and his shoes were black and buffed to an impeccable sheen. Next to him was Rochelle, looking subdued in a dark suit with a silk orange shirt underneath. Her dark hair was pulled back in a severe bun, she had on glasses, and her teeth were fixed. "Mrs. Gallagher, I understand that you spent some time in a treatment facility just recently," he said.

The man was not beating around the bush.

"Objection," Cindy said for the record. "Lack of relevance. You may answer the question."

"Yes," I said.

"Why did you spend time in this treatment facility?"

Cindy renewed her objection, then directed me to answer.

"I had a drug addiction," was all I said. I wasn't going to give him more than what he asked, at any point. I was annoyed that he was going there, although I fully expected it. I also knew that none of these answers could be used on the record, because they weren't relevant to my mental state at the time of the attack. He was just trying to get me off-balance.

I was determined that he wouldn't succeed.

The deposition continued like this, with one objectionable question after another about my stay at the Beverly Hills Hospital, my divorce from Ryan, my rape, my drug addiction. All of these events were after Rochelle attacked me, so none of these events were in the least bit relevant to the matter at hand. Yet I had to dredge all this up. I was feeling more stressed, anxious and irritated with every question that I had to answer, and I knew that Schultz' strategy was to break me down mentally before he would ask me the relevant questions.

I was more liable to slip up that way.

I didn't care. I didn't have anything to hide, so he couldn't trip me up.

He had been asking questions for four hours, so Cindy called for a lunch break. I could tell that Schultz was none too happy about breaking, because he had me on the ropes, and was going to go for his knock-out punches soon.

"Can I take you to lunch?" Cindy asked.

I simply shook my head. "I'm going to stay here during the break, if you don't mind," I said. I had to compose myself, and the best way I knew how to do this would be to just contemplate in solitude.

At that, everybody left, including the court reporter. I stared out the window, feeling resentful that Ryan wasn't there with me. He was with his ex-wife and best friend, instead. Granted, said ex-wife was a mess, but so was I. I just didn't show it like Alexis did. I really needed him, even though he couldn't actually sit in on the deposition. I needed him in the waiting room, so I could see him during my breaks.

I then tried to call him, but the call went straight to voice-mail.

I closed my eyes, and took deep breaths. I tried my CBT exercises, because negative thoughts were crowding my headspace like no other time since I got back with Ryan. I started to feel a little bit better, then I started to meditate. I felt better still.

After lunch, the attorneys, Rochelle, and the court reporter crowded back into the room, and I felt ready to tackle the next round of questioning.

Schultz didn't waste time. "Mrs. Gallagher, did you have practice self-mutilation in your younger years?"

This time there was not an objection.

"Yes," I said.

Then there was a series of questions related to that, and to my prior suicide attempt. I answered all of these questions calmly, not meeting anybody's eyes. This was still so humiliating for me to talk about.

Then Schultz passed me a picture that was marked as Exhibit G, Exhibits A-F being various documents and pictures that I had to identify. I looked at the picture, and tried to make my face impassive.

"Mrs. Gallagher, is this you?"

The picture was me, completely nude and lying on a bed and posing. This was the picture taken on Spring Break around 13 years prior, during one of my many drunken escapades that week, by some random hookup.

Cindy registered her objection about the relevance of the photo.

I knew what Schultz was trying to do. He was trying to shake me up by my knowing that he had ahold of this photo, and he probably got it off the Internet. Which meant that I was right about my earlier suspicions – this humiliating photo was probably viral and making the rounds. I had consciously not followed my name or my case on the Internet, so I had no idea this photo was out there, although I suspected it.

"Yes, that's me," I said. "I looked good, didn't I?" I asked, looking him right in the eye.

I wasn't going to be intimidated by this jackass.

Cindy then objected to the lack of foundation for the photo.

I tried to compose my thoughts, but it was difficult to do. The presence of the photo had the desired effect for him, in that I felt that I was off my game now. I was prepared for the other questions that were asked.

I was not quite prepared for this.

Schultz smiled an enigmatic smile, then launched into a series of questions about the actual attack. In rapid fire manner, he asked question after question, and I was distracted to say the least. My mental defenses were worn down, and I felt confused.

"When did you arrive at Ms. Anderson's house?"

"I don't remember."

"When did Mr. Gallagher arrive there?"

"I don't remember."

"When did the police arrive?"

"I really don't remember. I was unconscious by then."

On and on and on it went, and I was in a fog by then. I didn't remember many details of the attack, anyhow, because of the coma. I only remember the searing pain of the torture she put me through.

I knew that, by the end of the day, I probably provided ample ammunition for their cause and their story.

I trudged home, feeling that I had been beat up in a fight. Before I left, Cindy told me that she would be scheduling Ryan's deposition next, so I knew that he would have to go through similar torture soon.

But when I got home, I discovered that what happened in that deposition room was not, by far, the worst thing to happen to me that day.

Andrew was standing in the living room, holding a screaming Dalilah.

Helena was nowhere to be found.

Chapter Fifty-Eight

RYAN

Alexis was pulling her bullshit again. I really needed to have some kind of sympathy for her, because I knew how much she has always struggled with her illness, but it was difficult sometimes. I hated to be selfish, but it always seemed to come at the very worst time.

Like the day my wife has to go in for her deposition.

"Where are we going?" Alexis asked from the backseat.

"To your house to get you some clothes, then to the treatment facility," I tell her.

"The same place I always go?"

"Yeah, that place."

She said nothing more, just looked out the window.

"I have to start meeting different people," Nick whispered. "Why do I always end up with such nutcases?"

"Come on, now, Nick, you've known Alexis for as long as I have. You have always known that she is unstable. Always. Yet, here you are, thinking that she's suddenly going to be this different person."

"Rielle is another one," Nick said. "I swear to God, that

woman has some kind of personality disorder. Like narcissism or something. She literally cannot see any point of view but her own."

"How are the settlement talks going?"

"They're not. She wants just about everything. The Lake Como house, the Mission Hills house, all the paintings, half of the money, everything. She's demanding $50,000 a month in child support, and $25,000 a month in alimony. That's on top of what she's demanding in the property settlement. I have no idea why she thinks she's entitled to all that. She's demanding well over half the property."

"What does your lawyer say?" I asked him, thinking again about how I had to force Iris to take a single penny from me.

My wife really is one of a kind.

"Pound sand. She wants everything because she's going to have primary custody of the kids. Not that I want that, either, but she's talking about me being unfit because I'm some kind of sex addict or something." Then he shrugged. "Eh, maybe she has a point. I have had a lot of partners of both sexes over the years."

I didn't say anything. My best friend is the biggest manwhore I knew, but he always had been. I didn't think that he was addicted so much as he just loved sex. A lot. I'd never been able to see him and Rielle together. She was so uptight - if you put a lump of coal up her ass, you would have a diamond in less than a year. Nick was the opposite of that. He was a sexual free spirit.

At least he always plays safe, which was important. One thing about Nick - he always, always, always used condoms. Or so he said.

We arrived at Nick and Alexis' house, which was soon

going to be just Nick's house. "Nick, go in there with her and make sure she gets dressed ok," I said. "And make sure she packs a bag with about a week's worth of clothing, shampoo, conditioner, toothbrush and whatever toiletries she needs."

"Sure," Nick said, getting Alexis out of the backseat of the car. "Come on, Alexis, let's go in and put some clothes on you and get a bag packed." He was talking to her like a child. I wondered if he was aware of this fact.

Nick and Alexis came back out not ten minutes later. Alexis was wearing jeans and a sweater and was carrying a bag. Her face was washed and her hair was brushed. She looked almost respectable.

"I want to die," Alexis was saying, after she got back in the car and we drove off. "I want to drive my car off of a bridge into the water and drown."

"You don't want to die," I said. "Your brain chemistry is out of wack again, but we're going to help you fix it." Again, I thought. Sometimes I thought that I'd be going through this with this woman for the rest of my life. I sure was glad that I was married to such an understanding woman, otherwise Alexis would become an enormous problem.

"What's the use?" Alexis asked. "I have no job, no babies and no husband."

"No job?" I asked, looking at Nick. Nick obviously knew about this, because his face registered no surprise. "What happened to your job?"

"They canned me after the Hermés incident," she said. "I haven't had the energy to find a new one."

I sighed. Alexis was a partner at one of the largest law firms in town. She was not independently wealthy, because her parents cut her off. She relied on her salary, which was substantial – a high six figure. I doubted she had a penny in savings, and I knew she didn't have any property. She ran through everything I gave her in the divorce to support her drug habit and her spending addiction.

I had no idea what she was going to do now for money.

I felt a feeling of dread, knowing that it would be a short period of time before she was going to start harassing me again to give her money and property - money and property that would end up going down the drain, just like all the rest of the money and property she used to have. Oh, well, she couldn't blackmail me again like she did before. The whole world already knew everything there was to know about me, so who cared anymore?

I turned to Nick. "Did you know about this?"

"Sure," he said. "I found out the day it happened."

"Why didn't you say anything?"

"I don't know, I guess I didn't see the relevance."

Sometimes Nick can be so obtuse.

Now was not the time to try to figure out what Alexis was going to do for money from here on out, although I was tempted to harangue her about it. I was not responsible for her anymore, but I knew that she would somehow, someway, make me take responsibility for her. If she couldn't blackmail me into it, she could certainly guilt me into it. Like she had the entire time I'd known her.

"Don't worry about me, Ryan," Alexis said. "I'm not going to be alive much longer."

I willed myself not to roll my eyes at that one. She had been saying that forever. Every time she spiraled into depression, she said that she doesn't have long to live. She always talked about offing herself as well. One day she might be like the boy who cried wolf, and I hoped not, because I didn't want that on my conscience. But I also knew that, as soon as her meds got straightened out again, she would be singing a different tune.

Like she always does.

Then she was crying. "Oh, God, I don't have anything. Nobody loves me. What I wouldn't give for you to love me again, Ryan."

Oh, lord, here we go. I looked at Nick, who shrugged.

"Alexis, you're not with me, you're with Nick," I said.

"Stop it," Nick said. "Don't remind her."

"Nick is nothing but a manwhore," she said.

Then the two of you are a match made in heaven.

The three of us finally arrived at our destination. The treatment facility was in a shady area, surrounded by trees and wildlife. It didn't compare to the place in Beverly Hills where I took Iris, and where I, myself, stayed after I had a drug addiction relapse. But it was the best place in town.

"I can't go here," she said. "You need to take me to a state hospital. I have no income and no insurance anymore."

I gritted my teeth and almost told her not to worry about it. Then I thought I should talk to Nick.

"Nick," I said. "What do you say we go halfsies on this?"

"Hey, you aren't in the middle of a messy divorce. I am. I'm not sure if I'm going to have anything more than a barrel to put around my ass after Rielle gets done with me."

"Why is it always me who has to bail her out?"

"Because nobody else will, buddy. Just you."

I looked at Alexis, feeling halfway tempted to turn the car around and take her to a state hospital, like she said. Then immediately felt guilty for thinking such a thing. I had the money and Alexis had been in my life since I was 13. I couldn't just leave her high and dry. I banished the thought that she has cost me literally millions over the years, with all her rehabs, drugs, rehabs, drugs, spending, gambling, rehabs, drugs, etc., etc.

"Charity begins at home," Nick said. "Charity begins at home."

"Well, we're gonna check her in, but I can't stay," I said. "Iris needs me. Today is very important for her."

"Iris is a big girl," Nick said. "She can take care of herself."

"Even so, I need to be there for her."

"You're a little obsessed with that girl," Nick said. "I mean, I can see why. She's refreshingly not a gold-digger, and for anybody in your position, that's important. But you almost get stalkery and overprotective with her."

"Of course, I'm protective of her. Good God, look at what she has gone through, all of which has been directly or indirectly attributable to me. Look at what she's still going through, with that maniac Andrew out there, literally gunning for her. So, yes, I'm protective of her. She's the love of my life and the mother of my child."

"Listen," Nick said. "I don't ask for much from you. I'm asking you this. Stay with me and Alexis today. I can't handle her alone. You're used to all of this. I'm not. Iris is fine. Alexis and I need you right now." Then he raised an eyebrow. The implication was clear – after all he had done for me over the years, I needed to step up to plate for him.

I couldn't argue with him. He was absolutely right. He hadn't asked much of me, and I couldn't count the number of times that he had been there for me. I owed him this much.

"Ok," I said.

"Don't be so enthusiastic about it, now," he said.

"Sorry, Nick. My mind is on other things right now. I guess I just resent always having to deal with Alexis like this.

I mean, I know she can't really help it. But I also fear that I'll never get away from it. Because, like you said, I'm the only one willing to help her. I mean, besides you."

"Yeah, but even I'm not going to foot her bills. No offense, but I'm not that close to her. Not like you, anyhow."

After we had our little talk, we approached Alexis, who was hanging around the outside of the facility.

"Don't worry, Alexis," I said. "I'll pay for your treatment."

She smiled. "Thank you," she said.

Then we all went inside.

We checked her in, then took a seat in the waiting room. Alexis just stared at the TV above her head, with no expression. Then she looked at me and said "I was just wondering, Ryan, what it would take for you to leave your silly wife."

"Now why would you ask that question?"

"No reason. I mean, she divorces you, she leaves you without a forwarding address, she has your child and doesn't tell you, and she doesn't come back until she's dragged back, kicking and screaming. I just think you deserve so much better."

"Listen, Alexis," I said between gritted teeth. "My relationship with Iris is nobody's business but our own. And today is not about me, it's about you."

She just shrugged and returned her attention to the television set. "I just think that if I did half the things she did, you would've kicked me to the curb," she said, her eyes still glued to the TV.

"Are you really that non self-aware?" I asked. I knew that I was taking the bait, but I couldn't help myself. "After all the lying, the cheating, the spending, the lying, the drugs, the cheating, the cheating, the cheating that you did to me over the years, and you have the gall to impugn my wife?"

For once, Nick was the sensitive one, as he said "Ryan, you're talking to a woman with a serious illness here. Maybe you need to be a little more circumspect."

"I know, I know," I said. "But I can't help myself." I looked over at Alexis and she had a little evil smile on her face.

I inwardly kicked myself for letting her goad me like that.

The doctor called Alexis' name. Alexis looked at Nick and me, and said "well, are you guys coming or not?"

We got out of our chairs and accompanied her into the doctor's office.

"Now," Dr. Wright said. "What seems to be the problem?"

Alexis looked at me. "Do you want to tell him?"

"Sure," I said. "Ms. Peters here is suffering from Bi-Polar I disorder. And she needs a medication adjustment."

I knew the drill by now.

The doctor looked at his chart. "Ok," he said. "We'll start you on a course of Geodan, Abilify and Lithium," he said as he scribbled a prescription. "Do you need to be admitted?"

"Well, I have had suicidal thoughts," she said.

"Do you have a plan?"

"Yes," she said. "When I go home, I want to take my car and drive it off a bridge."

"Ok," the doctor said. "And how serious are you about this, on a scale from one to ten?"

"A twenty," she said, looking him in the eye.

"Do you have any other acute symptoms?"

She looked at Nick. "Tell him," she said.

"She doesn't sleep much at all," Nick said. "I haven't seen her sleep for almost a week. She comes into my room at all hours of the night and turns on the light and the stereo, making sure that I can't sleep, either. She wants to have sex constantly, she has gotten violent, she has lost thousands of dollars at the casinos in just a few days, and she broke into an Hermés store to get a purse in the middle of the night."

"But I haven't done drugs," she said, proudly. "That's a major switch for me."

"Ok," the doctor said. "Sounds like you need to be admitted."

"Ya think?" Alexis said.

"Please return to the waiting room," he said. "We will call you when your bed opens up."

We all returned to the waiting room. "Whatta tool," Alexis said. "That doctor is a real ass."

I had no idea why the doctor was an ass in her mind and I didn't bother to ask.

"Well," Alexis said. "I'm going to lie down over here and get some sleep. Wake me when the doc calls my name." At that, she laid down across four chairs in the waiting room and promptly fell asleep.

I waited until I heard her breathing heavily before talking to Nick. "What is she going to do?" I asked. "She needs to work. She can't support herself otherwise."

"She didn't tell you the whole story about why she was fired," Nick said.

"Why don't you tell me?"

"You ever see the movie *Michael Clayton*?" he asked. "With George Clooney?"

"*Michael Clayton, Michael Clayton*," I said, trying to remember. "Yeah, I think I did see that. What about it?"

"Do you remember why the guy in that movie got fired?" he asked.

It suddenly dawned on me. "Oh, yeah. He stripped naked in a settlement conference or something."

"Bingo," Nick said.

"You mean she-"

"Let's just say that she was explicitly setting out to recreate that scene."

"Oh, shit," I said. "Crap. Now what?"

"Well, she can always apply for disability," he said. "Could you imagine? Alexis living on $800 a month or something? She makes half that in one billable hour for her firm."

I put my head in my hands. I saw my future, and it was going to involve taking care of my ex-wife.

Iris will not be happy about this.

"Anyhow," Nick was saying. "If she has to live on disability, she'll off herself for sure. Can't buy too many Fendi bags on $800 a month."

"What does she have left from the divorce settlement?" I asked, afraid to know the answer to that question.

"You're joking, right?" he asked. "How much did you give her?"

"$10 million and a Porsche," I said.

"And you guys were divorced, what, six years ago?"

"Something like that."

"Looks like she went through $10 million in the last six years. Because she ain't got two nickels to rub together. She still has the Porsche, though."

I groaned and stared at the ceiling. How did I get myself into these situations? How? And why didn't I get her a conservator when I divorced her?

I looked over at Alexis, who was talking in her sleep. "Stop, David," she said in a giggly tone. "You're so naughty."

I crossed my arms. There had to be a way that I could avoid being her guardian. But I knew that her parents had long since cut her off, and nobody else in her family would even talk to her. I was really her only family.

"So," I said. "Unless Alexis can get another high six-figure job, which seems unlikely, considering what she did, she's pretty much SOL." I said that as a statement, not as a question, because I knew the answer to that.

"Ryan, Alexis couldn't make ends meet on $750,000 a year, even with your $10 million settlement. Unless she can get stabilized for good, I don't know what to tell you."

I sighed. "Iris won't be happy about this."

"What does she care? You could give your entire fortune to Alexis, and she'd be just as happy. One thing about her, she really could care less about your money."

"I know," I said. "But she probably feels differently now that we have a daughter. A very special daughter who is going to need top schooling, which ain't cheap."

"She was working at the Whole Foods when she had that kid. Trust me, Iris isn't going to care that you're supporting your ex-wife."

"No, I can't do it," I said. "As you said, Alexis blew through $10 million in four years, while earning a salary between a half million and three-quarters of a million a year. She has nothing to show for it. If I have to support her, I'll be broke in no time."

"I'm quite sure you won't be broke. Hate to state the obvious, but your billionaire dad doesn't have that much time left. Which means that you and Sarah will soon have money that you will literally never be able to spend in your lifetimes."

"My dad is in remission," I said. "And I would appreciate it if you weren't so callous in talking about him."

"This is the same dad who fucked you up, and was indirectly responsible for your drug problems and your suicide attempts, right? The same dad who was a child molester and a rapist? That dad?"

"He's changed," I said.

"Whatever. Anyhow, when he dies, you can support 100 Alexises. Not saying that's what you should do. I'm just saying that you could do that if you wanted to."

"What choice do I have?" I asked. "I can't just let her go down the rabbit hole. Of course, I'm going to have to set up a conservatorship for her. I can't just let her have unlimited funds."

"Oh, Alexis on a budget," he said. "That'll be fun to see."

"You seem to be taking delight in all this."

He looked at me for a few minutes. "Yeah," he said. "I'm sorry, buddy. I shouldn't be such an asshole about this. I guess I'm just jealous of you."

"Why?" I asked.

"Your life is so together. You have your adorable genius, and a sweet wife who loves you for you, not your money. I have a crazy girlfriend, a rapacious soon-to-be-ex-wife, and two kids who are going to be turned against me by said soon-to-be-ex-wife. My life is a nightmare right now."

I sighed. "You know why I'm together," I said.

"I know. You met your soul mate."

"Well, yes," I said. "But also because I've been in counseling for eight years. You should try it."

"You're right. God knows I seem to need it."

"Come with me to meet Dr. Halder," I said. "I see him every week."

Nick looked at his hands, which were on his lap. "Ok,"

he said, without looking up. "I think I finally am admitting that I need help."

I smiled. "Hey, it could be worse," I said, motioning silently to the sleeping Alexis.

"True," he said with a grin.

Then Alexis woke up. "Oh, God," she said. "I was having a nightmare that I was broke and going into a mental hospital."

"Um," I said. "That wasn't a nightmare. Look around."

She looked around at her surroundings. Then looked at us. "Shit, that wasn't a dream?"

I just shook my head.

She started crying, then she started wailing, pounding her fist on the arm of the chair. "What am I going to do? What am I going to do? What am I going to do? How am I going to live?"

Nick looked at me, then motioned to her. I didn't make a move towards her, so he whispered "you going to commit to taking care of her or not?"

I shook my head. I wasn't going to make a decision like that with a proverbial gun to my head. "Alexis," I said. "You'll find another job."

"No, I won't!" she said. "I embezzled money from them, and they agreed not to press charges, because let's just say that I know a little too much about some of their billing practices. But no other firm will touch me now. Plus, I stripped naked in a settlement conference for one of our largest clients. Trust me, I won't find another job."

Then she put her head in her hands. "I might as well kill myself right now. I don't have a way to live anymore. I don't have a way to live." Then she was wailing again.

Nick looked at me, his eyebrows raised.

I calculated in my head how much it would take to keep

her in some kind of Alexis minimum standard. Would a quarter of a million a year do her? If the money was in a conservatorship? That would be about one-third her current salary.

She's just going to have to learn to budget like the rest of the world.

"Alexis," I said. "I'll take care of you. We'll get something worked out."

She raised her tear-streaked face to me. "You mean it?"

"Yes," I said, hoping that Iris wouldn't get upset at me for committing to this without asking her. "I mean I can't give you as much as your firm was giving you, but we can work something out."

Nick was looking at me and nodding. I shook my head back at him. *Iris is going to kill me for this.*

Alexis' face brightened. "Oh, thank God," she said. "I was thinking that I'd have to live off of social security disability or something. Could you imagine? One pair of shoes, and my monthly check would be gone."

Just what I didn't want to hear.

I did silent calculations in my head. *Let's see, Alexis is 33. She might live another fifty years. That would be around $12 million over the course of her lifetime. Yeah, that's doable.*

I turned on my phone and called Iris, but her phone went straight to voice-mail. Of course, she was in her deposition, and she couldn't have her phone on. I prayed that she would understand. But I knew she would. Like Nick said, Iris cared little about money. And this really isn't a lot of money, in the big scheme of things. Nick was also right that I would have more money than I would know what to do with after my father passed. So, what did I care?

Alexis' name was finally called. We went to the desk that did the bed assignments, and Alexis was given a bed number and a private code that people had to use to come and see her. She looked at us. "Do you guys mind staying with me for a few hours? I don't want to be alone."

"I really have to go and see my wife," I said. "Today's an important day for her."

Alexis gave me a look and hung her head. "Ok, then" she said. "I guess I'll see you later."

God, she knows how to manipulate me. She knew just how to push my buttons. "Ok, ok, I'll come and stay with you for a little while. But only for a little while, then I have to be shuffling off to Buffalo." I turned to Nick. "You're staying if I'm staying."

"Cool," he said. "Let's go."

At that, we got on the elevator and headed to her assigned floor. Then we went to her room, which was a private room that consisted of a hospital bed, a television and little else. Still, this place costed around $3,000 a day, more than the gorgeous drug-treatment place Iris stayed in. It's a crime, really, how much these mental health facilities charge, considering the paltry services they provide. Three hots and a cot costs more than all of the pampering and services that Iris received in Beverly Hills.

"Ryan," Alexis said. "I really hate to ask this, because I know you have a new wife and new baby at home. But could I stay with you guys just until I get stabilized?"

Oh, hell no. Hell to the no. "Alexis, that's not possible. You're pushing your luck, here. Iris won't be happy to know that I have agreed to support you, and she really won't be happy with your moving in with us. Besides, we just got rid of Natalie. No room at the Inn."

Alexis pouted. "Well, I can't stay with Nick, here. He didn't make sure that I was med compliant, which is why I had my relapse in the first place."

I looked at Nick. "What?" he said. "I'm not her babysitter."

"No," I said. "You're her enabler. You didn't think it was the least bit weird the way she was acting?"

"Hey," he said. "No offense, but you grew up around crazy. I didn't. I don't know the first thing about handling people with mental illnesses."

"I did not grow up around crazy. My mother left when I was very young, or did you forget that?"

"True, but your father wasn't exactly playing with all his marbles, either."

"Be that as it may, you still should've been paying more attention. You've always known about her illness."

"I'm not her babysitter," he repeated.

I sighed. I wasn't going to get anywhere with him.

"Well," Alexis said. "Can I stay with you three?"

Criminy. I thought about all the possibilities. Alexis used to leave the house with the door wide open. If she did that this time, the dogs could run away. And my daughter is going to wonder what the hell is going on with all these people coming and going from the house. I couldn't do that to her. And Iris...sweet Iris, with the infinite patience. Her patience could very well run out, and who could blame her?

I really hated being put on the spot like this.

"No," I said. "You're just going to have to go into a group home or something. I mean, come on, the last time you had a relapse, it took you more than a month to get stabilized. You're telling me that I have to ask my new wife if my ex-wife can stay with us for a month. I mean, really? Seriously?"

"Iris won't mind," she said sweetly. "I know that I give you a hard time about her, but she really is a sweet girl."

"Yeah," I said. "But you're asking me to let you stay

with us, when you know that you're going to be staying up for days, crying non-stop, talking incessantly, and running in and out of the house at all hours of the night. You get violent, too. Not to mention you have a bad habit of sneaking in drugs. I have a new daughter at home, as well. I don't know Alexis, it's not a good idea."

She pouted again. God, why does she put me in these predicaments? I helped her get stabilized the last time, but Iris and I had briefly broken up during that time, so Iris' feelings were not a factor.

Now they would be.

Iris comes first.

I finally just said "I'll talk to Iris when I get home."

"That's all I can ask," she said.

So, I thought to myself, I have to ask my wife if she doesn't mind if I basically adopt my ex-wife. Become her financial supporter and her caretaker.

Iris will love this. Just love it. She didn't sign on for my crazy life. She signed on to be with me, and, in return, I promised to love her and cherish her all the days of our lives. Our wedding vows didn't include her agreeing to live with my ex-wife, not to mention the fact that she lived with Natalie, who was the possible mother of my child.

She didn't sign on for any of this.

On the other hand, if somebody didn't take care of Alexis, she would never get stabilized, which would cause even more problems for everybody around her for a long time. And Nick had proved that he didn't want the responsibility for her.

To be fair, Nick had enough on his plate.

But so did I.

"Listen," Nick whispered. "If you don't take in Alexis,

then she's going to be out on the streets. She can't come back to my house. I'm pretty much done."

Great. Just great.

At that, I turned on the phone and tried to call Iris. Her phone went straight to voice-mail again. I looked at the clock – 4:30. She said her deposition was scheduled until 5. I turned the phone off again, and planned to call her again around 5.

But the three of us ended up watching a movie in the TV room, and I lost track of time. Before I knew it, it was 6 O'Clock. "Ok, Alexis," I said. "I really have to get home. I always eat dinner with my wife and daughter."

"Ok, then," she said. "I hope to see you both soon."

I nodded. "You're going to be ok," I said.

And, at that, Nick and I left Alexis' room and started for home.

Chapter Fifty-Nine

IRIS

I froze when I saw Andrew in my house, holding my screaming daughter. I was too much in shock, momentarily, to do much of anything. Then, a second or two later, I noticed that he had a gun in his left hand. He was holding Dalilah in his right arm. He looked at me with an impassive look, but he was massaging his gun. Then he narrowed his eyes.

How did he get in here? What about the dogs? Then I heard them barking in the backyard. Also, I set the alarm before I left the house this morning, I know I did. Didn't I? That didn't matter, the fact was that he is here and he had my daughter. With a gun in his hand. Crazy or no, I would imagine that he could cock his gun and kill Dalilah before I could take a single step towards him. Once again, my brain was able to think clearly, even in the face of the most unimaginable circumstance. I had been in such a situation before, with Rochelle, and my mind was also clear then. I knew the situation at hand would require me to think coherently, because if I did anything out of panic, my daughter was dead.

I knew it.

"Andrew, darling, it's so good to see you," I said.

"Cut the bullshit, Cherry. Who is this?" he asked, taking his gun and pointing it to the screaming Dalilah. I prayed she wouldn't start calling for me. I had to convince Andrew that Dalilah was somebody who was not my daughter. So far, she was only screaming and crying. *Please, baby, please do not say mama. Please don't say mama.*

"That's the neighbor's daughter," I said. "Her mother is Helena. What happened to her?"

"I sent her away," he said.

Away. I hoped her body wasn't in the house somewhere.

"Away, love? I have to get Dalilah back to her."

Dalilah started going m-m-m-m-m-m, while looking right at me. Andrew looked at her, then looked at me suspiciously.

"See, honey, she's calling for her mama. She's wondering where she is. I have to get her back to her mama," I said lightly.

"You're not going anywhere, you stupid fucking slut. I know what you did. You're gonna pay."

"Which thing, honey? What are you talking about?"

"You know. Where is he?"

"He?"

"Yeah, the guy you fucked before you left me. Where is he?" His face was getting redder by the second and he was shaking. His eyes were bugging out a little, and some spittle was on the corner of his mouth.

"Give me Dalilah and I'll tell you."

He just looked at me, his face contorted.

"Ok, fine, I won't tell you then. You can just guess."

"You will tell me right now!" he raged.

"Give me the baby, and I'll tell you everything you need to know. Otherwise, you'll never get to know where he is."

He looked at me, shaking, then handed me Dalilah. I had her in my arms, then I immediately felt the gun on the small of my back. I had to get out of this alive, or else she wouldn't survive, either. "Honey, I have to call Dalilah's father to come and get her, since you won't tell me where her mother is."

He nodded, then jabbed the gun further into my skin. "No funny business," he said.

I made my way over to my purse, with Dalilah screaming and pulling my hair, going m-m-m-m-m-m-m-m. Andrew's gun remained on the small of my back.

Should I try to call Ryan? His phone had been turned off all morning and afternoon, probably because the hospital wouldn't allow him to have it on. If I called him and his phone was turned off again, that would be my only chance to contact somebody to come and get our daughter. I would have blown my one chance to get her somewhere safe, because I doubted that Andrew would let me make more than one phone call.

I needed to get her someplace safe. If she was somewhere safe, then I could play more high-stakes gambling here. Otherwise, I would have to play everything completely conservatively, and that probably wouldn't work.

I had to get her somewhere safe if either of us was to have a chance.

Daniel. I called his number, silently praying. He answered on the second ring. "Daniel," I said, my voice breezy.

"Yeah, Iris, what do you need?" he asked.

"Come and get Dalilah, please."

Daniel knew better than to ask why. One thing about him, he was good at following orders without having lengthy explanations. That was part of his job description.

"I'll be right there," he said.

I smiled at Andrew. "Her father will be here in around 5 minutes. Then we can talk. Sorry, but it is difficult to have a conversation with a screaming brat in my arms." I hoped against hope that I was acting like his wife. I had no idea if she referred to children as brats, but my instinct was guiding me here.

He nodded. "Ok, but after her dad gets here, you're gonna give me answers."

Daniel arrived after the longest 5 minutes of my life. Andrew and I were in a staring contest, with him pointing the gun so that a bullet would hit both Dalilah and me if he were to fire. Dalilah was calming down. Crap! Now that she was calming, what would happen if she started screaming again when she went with Daniel? She knew Daniel, so maybe it would be ok. Her head was on my shoulder and she was sucking her thumb.

I saw Daniel drive up in Ryan's Jaguar. Andrew saw him, too, because he was looking out the window with me. "Get out there," Andrew said. "Don't let him come to the door. And I'm gonna know if you're tipping him off about me being in here, so if I see any kind of body language or facial expressions that tip me off that you're telling him about me, I will snipe all three of you in the driveway."

"Oh, please, why would I tell him about you?" Then I walked calmly out the door, and met Daniel, who was coming up the stairs to the porch. "Here you go," I said, giving my daughter to Daniel calmly. "Thanks for doing this."

"Sure, Iris. I'm assuming I'll get an explanation later?"

"You assume correctly," I said gaily. "Actually, my hubby and I just need some alone time, if you know what I mean," I said, winking.

He laughed. "Say no more," he said. To my relief, Dalilah didn't start screaming anew. She put her chubby arms around his neck, then looked back at me and waved. *It's as if she knows how to behave.* I thanked God again that Daniel and Dalilah knew one another, as Daniel made his way down the stairs into his car, my daughter in his arms.

I went back into the house, relieved that she was safe, yet devastated that this might be the last chance to see my daughter in this world.

Stop thinking like that. You're going to get out of this.

Andrew was standing there. Then, when I came in, he jerked me back into the kitchen. Again with the kitchen. What was it with him and kitchens?

"Sit down," he said, shoving me into one of the chairs around the breakfast table. "Now, you stupid slut, you're gonna give me answers. Then I'm gonna kill you."

I crossed my arms. "What answers? You gotta ask the questions, first."

"Why'd you have to fuck him?"

"Oh, honey, it had nothing to do with you. I love you, you know that."

That was the wrong thing to say. "Shut up, slut!" he screamed, then pistol whipped my face. "Quit lying to me!"

I was momentarily stunned, then bit my lip hard to try to suppress a scream of pain. "Ok, then. It does have to do with you. We weren't happy together, you know that," I said.

To my surprise, this answer appeared to please him more. "Why couldn't we go to counseling if you were so unhappy? Why'd you have to fuck somebody else, then take my children from me?" He was now on the verge of tears. "Why'd you do it, Cherry pie? Why?" Then he had his head in his hands, his gun still clutched tightly in one of them.

I was getting somewhere. This next answer was crucial. What was he looking for? What answers would appease him? I had a little bit of time to think about this next answer, because he was now crying.

"I'm sorry," I said. "We just grew apart, you and me."

"What about the kids?" he asked. "How could you just keep them from me? Did they get any of their birthday cards or gifts?"

Fuck. He was going to want me to call them by name. "Of course, they did," I said. "I'm not that much of a bitch."

"Alan, how'd he like the train set?"

"He loved it, of course. He played with it constantly."

He looked sad. Then, in a split second, he was raging again. "You fucking bitch! I should've been there to see him open that up!" He brought his gun back up to my head.

Then I heard voices outside the house. Ryan and Nick. They were kinda loud, so I could hear what they were saying. "I told you, buddy," Ryan was saying. "God, I dread talking to Iris about this."

"Yeah," Nick said. "Good luck with that. I gotta get going. I'll call you later, huh?"

Then Ryan was coming in the door.

Chapter Sixty

Ryan came in, saw the two of us, with Andrew's gun to my head, and he froze. I knew he also had to leave his weapon at home when he went to the hospital with Alexis and Nick, so he was just as helpless as I was when I came in the door. Ironic, all that training...

"Who are you?" Andrew asked.

Ryan was quick on his feet. He was able to cover the panic that he was no doubt feeling, the same feeling I had when I saw Andrew and Dalilah.

"I'm Ryan. What are you doing with Cherry, there?"

"I'm trying to find out who she was fucking before she left me."

"That's easy," Ryan said. "I'm the one she was fucking before she left you. And, let me tell you, she was good. The best I ever had, that's for goddamned sure."

I knew what he was trying to do, and I silently prayed it wouldn't work.

If Andrew kills him instead of me, I wouldn't be able to live.

Ryan continued. "It's me you want, not her. I was the one who convinced her to leave you. She wanted to stay, but I convinced her to leave. I told her to stop letting you see the kids, too."

"You," Andrew said. "I don't believe you. You're way too pretty for my wife. She never liked the pretty boys."

"What can I say," Ryan said in a cocky tone that I had never, ever heard from him. "She made the exception, you know?"

Andrew looked from me to Ryan, and back again. I shook my head violently. "That's not the guy. Like you said, I don't like 'em pretty like that. I like my men craggy and old. That's not the guy."

"Babe," Ryan said. "You don't have to protect me. The secret is out. Now, Andrew, it's me you want. You just let her go, and you can have me instead. She never would've left you if I didn't talk her into it. If it weren't for me, she would've stayed with you forever."

"No," I told Andrew. "I don't know this guy, I've never seen him in my life. Please believe me. I don't know him."

Andrew continued to look at me, then at Ryan, trying to decide who to believe.

"Come on, buddy," Ryan said. "I had to tap that ass. That sweet piece of ass. That's all she was to me."

That's what finally set Andrew off. "You asshole! Don't you dare disrespect my wife like that!"

What happened next went in slow motion, like when I was in a car accident. Andrew let go of me, then I reached into the drawer for a butcher knife, then plunged it into his back.

However, before I plunged the knife into his back, he shot Ryan.

Chapter Sixty-One

Somebody was screaming, but I didn't know who. My beautiful husband was lying on the floor. There was blood. So much blood. I desperately put my hands on his wound, and the screaming sound seemed to come from everywhere around me. There was another body next to me, but I didn't know who it was. I could only concentrate on my impotent hands, my bright red impotent hands that were desperately trying to stop the bleeding. I could hear an ambulance in the distance, screaming to a stop in front of our house.

Somebody was prying me off my husband. "Miss, you need to come with me," the person said. "Miss, please, you need to come with me."

"NO, NO, NO," the screaming voice said. "NO."

Then it was like I was floating above the room, watching myself, screaming and crying, being violently pulled off my husband while the ambulance workers loaded him onto a gurney. Somebody had his arms wrapped around me, and I beat into his chest while I writhed and cried. There were police in the room, too, then a yellow tape was brought out that clearly said the words "crime scene." I had a blanket wrapped around me by somebody, then I saw myself demanding to be taken in the ambulance with Ryan. Somebody else then escorted me out of the house, and I saw myself getting into a police car.

Then I was back in my body again. I was in the back of a squad car that was screaming down the street at a mad pace, the blanket still wrapped around me, and a feminine voice soothingly telling me to calm down. "Shhh," the voice said. "We're going to join your husband at the hospital. Everything's going to be ok."

No. It wasn't going to be ok. Nothing would ever be ok again. If my husband was dead, then I would be dead, too.

Not literally. I had to live for Dalilah.

But I would be as good as dead.

Next in the Illusions series

vinci-books.com/end-illusions

Everyone thinks he's a good guy, but he hasn't always been.

A near-death experience forces Ryan to confront his past. Now, making amends may be his only chance to win Iris back.

Turn the page for a free preview…

End of Illusions: Chapter One

IRIS

Your husband is dead. We're sorry, we did all we could, but there was too much internal bleeding.

I stared blankly at the doctor who was standing above me in a white coat, looking very serious. He had just appeared in the waiting room where I sat, alone, except for the female cop who was staying there with me. I guess that there was a fear that I would fall apart. I said nothing, just stared at the floor. I planned, in my head, the way that I would join him. Some way that wasn't too messy and wouldn't be too traumatizing for the people who loved me.

There was no way that I could live without him.

"I, I, I have to call somebody," I said in a monotone voice. I got out my phone, and proceeded to dial some numbers. They were random numbers. I had no idea about anybody's phone numbers at this point. There was just no way that I could possibly call anybody.

"Excuse me," I said. "I need to take this in the bathroom."

The doctor nodded, and the police woman looked at me sympathetically and shook her head.

On the way to the bathroom, I was thinking about finding a razor somewhere and slashing my wrists. Or busting into a drug storage room and swallowing a handful of whatever I could find.

Dead. There was no way this was true. My mind couldn't even start to comprehend it.

The image of Ryan lying on the floor, with blood squirting out from God-knows-where, was flashing through my mind like a neon sign that I just couldn't shut off. I took several clumps of hair in my hands, and pulled. I got into the bathroom, and started banging my head against the mirror, over and over again, and started screaming at the top of my lungs.

Then I collapsed.

End of Illusions: Chapter Two

I was woken up by a kindly gentleman who was gently nudging me in my chair. "Mrs. Gallagher. Mrs. Gallagher," the voice said, shaking me gently.

I looked at him. He was the man who just informed me about my husband's passing.

I just shook my head. Go away. I don't want to talk to you. Leave me alone.

"Mrs. Gallagher, I wanted to keep you updated on your husband's progress in surgery."

"My husband's progress in surgery? I don't understand."

"Your husband has been in surgery for the past 10 hours. You must have nodded off in your chair for a few minutes."

I was still foggy. Was this a dream? Or was I dreaming before? I prayed that this was the real scene, and that the other was just a horrible, horrible, horrible nightmare.

"Surgery?" I put my head in my hands. Why was it so

difficult to comprehend anything? I just shook my head. I felt the lady cop put her arm around my back.

"She's still in shock," she said. "Why don't you tell me what's going on with her husband, and I'll tell her when she's a bit more coherent?"

"Well, this has been a very delicate surgery, very touch and go. The bullet went through his abdomen and lodged near his spine. The spinal cord was not injured, but there is some swelling. Mr. Gallagher might be paralyzed for awhile, but hopefully that will only be temporary. He's still not out of the woods, but we are making progress."

"You hear that?" lady cop said. "Sounds like your husband is going to make it through surgery."

I nodded and said nothing. I had an Indian blanket wrapped around my shoulders, and I wrapped it around me tighter, clutching it for dear life.

"Do you mind if I look at your cell phone?" lady cop asked.

I just shook my head mutely, then pointed to my bag.

Lady cop dug through my bag and found my cell phone. "Now, Mrs. Gallagher, if you don't mind, I'd like to look through your contacts. Is there anybody on here that I can call to come and be with you?"

I nodded my head. "Nick. Call Nick."

Then she dialed the phone. "Hello," she said. "Is this Nick?...this is Officer Cecelia White....I'm sorry to wake you...Mrs. Gallagher is here at the Emergency Room at the hospital...she asked me to call you. Can you come and keep her company?..I'm sorry I didn't call earlier. Mrs. Gallagher has been in too much shock to give me permission to use her phone until just now....the doctor will have to explain... ok, see you then."

"He's on his way now, Mrs. Gallagher. He said that he'll be here in about 20 minutes or so."

I said nothing, just stared at the floor and wrapped my blanket around me even tighter.

Sometime after police lady got off the phone with Nick, I heard his familiar voice. "Hi, I'm Nick O'Hara. You must be Officer White."

"Good to meet you, Mr. O'Hara."

"What's going on?"

"The doctor will be out in a few more minutes."

"No, tell me now. What's going on?"

"Mr. Gallagher was shot. In front of Mrs. Gallagher. Mrs. Gallagher stabbed an intruder, but not before he shot Mr. Gallagher."

"Holy Christ." Then he was sitting right next to me, putting his arm around me. "Iris, Iris, are you there? Talk to me, Iris."

I looked at him, and then the tears started gushing. He wrapped his arms around me while I sobbed, my hands still clutching my blanket tightly. He gently put his hand in my hair, and I immediately felt comforted.

It felt just like Ryan's touch.

Then I remembered that Ryan was in surgery, and he might not make it, and, even if he does make it, he might be paralyzed.

"Shhhhh, Iris, it's going to be ok. Ryan's tough. He's survived this long, in the most messed up scenarios imaginable. Shhhhh, it's ok. It's going to be ok."

I just shook my head. "Dalilah," was all I said.

"Where is Dalilah?" he asked.

"Daniel. Daniel has her. Please call him, I need to see her."

At that, he whipped out his phone. "Daniel, it's Nick...I

know what time it is...you have Dalilah there...could you bring her to the hospital?...Ryan was shot..........he's in surgery.......good point." At that he looked at me. "Uh, Daniel's ok with watching her. I'm not sure if it's a good idea to have her here in the waiting room."

"Is she ok? I need to talk to her."

"Is Dalilah ok?" Nick asked. "She's sleeping? Of course, of course, it's like 4:30 in the morning."

I pleaded with Nick, tugging on his shirtsleeve "Dalilah doesn't have anything there. No diapers, no toys, no breast milk, no nothing. I just gave her to him without anything at all. Please tell him to go by the house and get what she needs. Everything is in her room. There's a diaper bag with everything she needs, and the fridge is full of bottled breast milk."

I was amazed at how much just having Nick here was helping clear up my mental fog.

Nick said "Iris says to go by the house and get Dalilah's things. A diaper bag in her room, bottled breast milk in the fridge and..." Then he looked at me. Addressing me he said "She got any favorite toys that Daniel should pick up?"

I nodded. "A Winnie the Pooh stuffed bear, her Etch-A-Sketch, and some puzzles. Everything's in her room."

Nick turned back to the phone "You get all that?....ok, great, thanks...bye."

Addressing me again, Nick said "Daniel's on his way back to the house, and he'll call if anything is going wrong. Right now, he said that it's not a problem to take care of her."

I nodded. "Thanks."

He sat down. "Now, do you feel like talking about what happened?"

I didn't feel that I could talk without breaking down and crying, so I just shook my head.

"Ok, then, I'll ask Cecelia." Cecelia had stepped out, and was back in the waiting room with us. She talked into the receiver on her shoulder.

"So, Officer White, what happened?"

"We arrived at 6:07 PM to the Gallagher household. A neighbor who was walking his dog by the house called 911 after hearing a gunshot go off. We arrived and Mr. Gallagher was lying on the floor after having been shot. Mrs. Gallagher was with him. We rushed Mr. Gallagher to the hospital, and trailed behind them in a squad car. Mr. Gallagher was brought into surgery at 6:17, and has been in there ever since."

"Crap," Nick said. It was like the news just now hit him. He went pale, and sat down next to me. He was shaking. He put his head in his hands, his entire body visibly quivering.

I couldn't comfort him the way that he comforted me. I still felt numb, like my limbs simply wouldn't move. I cursed myself silently for my impotence

We sat next to one another, silently, with Cecelia the lady cop still hanging around and talking into her receiver. I wondered why she was still there. Probably she wants to talk to Ryan when he gets out of surgery, but I wouldn't imagine that he would be in any shape to talk to anyone at that point.

Finally, Nick looked at me. "How are you holding up?"

I shrugged my shoulders and said nothing. I didn't want to talk. Dalilah was safe, and Ryan was still in surgery. There wasn't much more I could say at that point.

Then I was crying uncontrollably again. "Oh, Nick, what would happen if we lose him? I think that I would want to join him. I don't see myself living without him."

"Quit talking like that. We aren't going to lose him, so you don't have to worry about that. Now, stop. Just stop." But I saw his face, and it was clear that he, too, was afraid of what would happen to both of us if Ryan, God forbid, didn't make it out of surgery. He and Ryan had been friends since elementary school. His loss would be even more acutely felt than would mine.

To take my mind off of my horror, I decided to find out a little bit more about Ryan and Nick's friendship. "How did you and Ryan meet?" I asked him.

"It was kinda funny," he said. "It was in kindergarten. We didn't have home room together, or nothing, so we didn't see each other that much. But Ryan was on a tricycle, hogging it if I can recall, and I knocked him off it. He hit his head. I laughed at him, and he came after me. We got into a fight on the playground, and both of us ended up in the principal's office. We became friends waiting there for the principal to come out and scold us." He chuckled. "Both of us got in trouble at home, of course, him more than me. Goddamn, his dad sure was a bastard back then."

"What happened to Ryan?"

"He got beat, of course. But that was nothing new. He was always being beat by Benjamin. Maggie was just too much of an ethereal hippy to stand up to Benjamin and his tyrannical ways." He shook his head. "Poor Ryan. It seems that fate just never lets him catch a break. He meets you, the love of his life, but he can't be happy because something is always waiting in the wings to snatch it away."

"What about you? What's going on in your life?"

"Eh, same old same old. I'm just about ready to give Rielle every piece of property I own, in exchange for her leaving me the hell alone. It's not worth it. Love isn't worth it. No offense."

"Sometimes it is. Love. Sometimes it's worth it."

"Well, you guys got lucky in finding each other."

"Yeah. I just hope that…" I trailed off, not wanting to finish that sentence. To think that Ryan wouldn't make it through surgery was just too horrible.

"Listen, Ryan is a tough guy. He's in amazing shape. He's gonna pull through."

I just nodded my head mutely, then stared at my hands. I felt awful. This was yet more agony. Everything that had happened up until this point felt like the end of the world – Rochelle's attack, Andrew's rape, Natalie's pregnancy. It all chipped away at my soul, little by little. I bounced back after all of it, but there was a part of me that felt like I was permanently damaged.

Now this. This was far worse than anything else that had happened. Would I recover if he doesn't make it? Would I want to? Would I be able to get out of bed in the morning without seeing his beautiful face? What would happen to Dalilah if I just fall apart? What would happen to Dalilah if I didn't make it either?

She would be an orphan.

"Uh, Nick, I hate to bring this up. But, with Ryan in there, it is a reminder that life might be fleeting. If he doesn't make it, God forbid, and something happens to me – would you take Dalilah?"

Nick just stared at me. "Don't bring this up now. Nothing is going to happen to either one of you. Now stop it. Stop with the fatalistic bullshit."

I sighed. Who would take Dalilah? My parents were way too old, my sister way too unstable. Nick was so good with her - he would be the obvious choice. But he was right, I shouldn't be talking like this. It would just jinx everything.

We sat in silence some more, and were sitting there quietly like that when the doctor came out into the waiting room. His face was non-committal. My heart was in my throat, trying to read his expression.

"We're through with surgery," he said. "Your husband has been taken to the ICU."

I started hyperventilating and shaking all over. I took Nick's hand and gripped it tightly.

"However, there is still a great deal of swelling around the spinal cord. Hopefully when the swelling goes down, your husband will regain use of his lower extremities. But, for now, Mr. Gallagher is paralyzed from the waist down."

"But he's alive? He, he, he's going to make it?" I gripped Nick's hand even tighter.

"Barring any kind of further issue, such as infection or an embolism, there is a good chance that your husband will be able to go home in a matter of weeks."

At that, Nick and I hugged each other tightly. We both were shaking, and I was crying uncontrollably again.

"When, when, when can I see him?" I asked.

"He's in the ICU. You can see him now, but he's not conscious."

"Can Nick come too?"

"I'm terribly sorry. Only members of the immediate family can see him right now."

I felt awful about that. If ever there was somebody who should be considered family to Ryan, it was Nick.

I looked at Nick, who looked pissed. But he nodded at me as I got up out of my chair to follow the doctor into the ICU.

Ryan was lying in the hospital bed, hooked up to a variety of scary-looking machines. His vitals seemed to be doing well, though, as I noticed that his heart rate was a steady 54 bpm, and his blood pressure was 105/64. He wasn't on a ventilator. He appeared to be resting comfortably.

I went over to the bed, and took his hand. I smiled. "My turn now, huh? You were by my side 24/7 when I was recovering from Rochelle's attack, now it's my turn to be there for you. I hope that you can hear me. I love you more than I ever thought possible. I love you, Ryan Gallagher. You're a part of me. And I'm going to help you get through this, just like you helped me get through Rochelle's attack. We're a team now."

I smoothed back his dark hair, and touched his face. His skin felt cool and clammy, which somewhat startled me. He also looked deathly pale. I so wanted him to open those beautiful eyes and let me drown in their depths, as was usual. But he just laid there, breathing in and out laboriously. A nurse stood by with a chart, ready to come and take his vitals.

I sat there for as long as I could, just talking away to him. I couldn't stop touching him. I thought that I would never again be able to touch him, never again be able to stroke him. Never again be able to run my fingers through his amazing mane. I was eternally grateful that I was given a second chance with him.

Finally, visiting hours were over. A nurse gently came up to me, putting her hands on my shoulders. "Mrs. Gallagher, visiting hours are over," she said. "Let me help you back to the waiting room."

I touched my fingers to my lips one last time, and placed them on his cheek. "I love you," I told him. "I love you."

I got back, and Nick was still there, reading something on his iPhone. He looked up at me. "How is he?"

"Resting comfortably," I said. "Thank God. What time is it? I'm starving."

"It's just about 10 o'clock. Ryan was in surgery for some 14 hours."

"Let's get breakfast, huh?"

End of Illusions: Chapter Three

Nick and I left the hospital and headed out to a local Denny's. I dug into my scrambled eggs and bacon hungrily. I had no idea why I was so famished. I guess because I hadn't eaten since…I couldn't remember. I skipped lunch because of the stress of the deposition, then, of course, didn't have dinner because, well, Andrew was there waiting for me when I got home from the courthouse.

Nick, for his part, got a Grand Slam with everything – bacon, eggs, hashed browns, pancakes and juice. Looking at his lean frame, I wondered where he put everything.

I didn't feel like talking still. I was completely wrapped up in my own head.

"How are you holding up?" Nick asked.

"I don't really know. I need to process everything, and it's just impossible right now. Just impossible. It doesn't even seem real. But Ryan made it through surgery, that's what's most important." I didn't want to think about Derrick Thomas, the defensive star for the Kansas City Chiefs, who made it through his surgery, was paralyzed, and died not a month later from an embolism, which was somewhat common in paralyzed patients. I also didn't want to entertain the possibility that Ryan might acquire a drug resistant infection and not make it out of the hospital. Right now, I had to concentrate on the fact that he was alive. He wasn't out of the woods, but he wasn't dead, either.

"Do you want to tell me what happened?"

At first I shook my head, staring at my shaking hands that were gripping my glass of water. I wanted to throw up.

But Nick just stared at me, not talking. He didn't try to fill the silence, so I hesitantly began my story.

"Andrew, he was uh, he was in my house. He was in my house, holding, holding, uh, Dalilah. He had, uh, a, a, g-g-g-un." Now I was trembling wildly. "He had a gun, and he thought that I was his ex-wife, Cherry. Cherry. She-she-she's dead, Cherry, she's dead. Dead. He thought I was her, and he-he-he-he threatened me. As her. He threatened me, thinking I was her. And Ryan came in and s-s-sacrificed himself for me. He made it so that Andrew wanted to kill him, not me."

"I'm not sure I'm following you."

"Ryan came in, and he basically told A-A-A-ndrew th-th-at Andrew wanted him, not me. Cherry was cheating on A-A-An, the bad man, and the bad man wanted to kill me, because he thought I was Cherry. Ryan came in and told the bad man that he-he-he was the one who was cheating with Cherry, so the bad man wanted him, not me."

Somehow, someway, Nick managed to follow the story, even with my stuttering and stumbling around. "So, cray-cray Andrew came in, thought you were his ex-wife, threatened you because he thought that you were cheating on him with somebody, and Ryan came in and posed as that somebody so that Andrew would kill him and not you?"

I nodded. "You managed to understand perfectly." Nick was apparently no dummy.

Nick just shook his head. "He said that he would give his life for you. I guess that he meant it."

I just nodded my head, then reacted to his statement several minutes later. "Uh, he said he would give his life for me?"

"Several times. It's probably 10% his guilt over putting you in those situations and 90% that boy's overwhelming love for you." He shook his head. "I've never met a woman that I felt that strongly for. Ever. I couldn't imagine taking a bullet for Rielle or Alexis. For my kids, sure, definitely. Would take 100 bullets for them. But the women in my life? Not a chance."

I felt badly for him, never experiencing that kind of unconditional love. Then I looked at my glass again. "I'd give my life for him as well. I love him so much, Nick. I'm still so scared about what might happen with him. He's not out of the woods yet. And he might be paralyzed. How will he deal with that?"

Nick just shook his head. "Listen, Iris, I don't think that you know Ryan as well as you might think. How much he has been through. You know the surface stuff about what happened, but you don't know the deeper stuff about him. How he thinks. What he has seen and done. Trust, he has been through far worse than not being able to have the use of his legs for a few months. Hell, he's been through far worse than not being able to have the use of his legs permanently. He's a tough guy. He'll get through this, like he has gotten through everything before."

I wondered what he meant by his words. That I didn't know the whole story of his life before me. I guess that I only knew the "highlights" – or low-lights, really. Nick had known Ryan virtually Ryan's entire life, so he knew Ryan better than anyone.

"I guess I don't understand," I said. "What do you mean that I don't know everything about Ryan's past?"

"You do," he said. "In a sense. It's like this – you like a certain band because of what you hear on the radio. Like Muse – you like them, right? Or the Silver Sun Pickups?"

"Yes, yes, of course," I said. Those were two of my favorite bands.

"What if all you knew about the Silver Sun Pickups was Lazy Eye? Or all you knew about Muse was Uprising or Resistance? Or, for that matter, all you knew about any band was their hits? You may think that you love Bruno Mars, but if you don't listen to him cover to cover, then you don't really know him."

"So, basically, I've gotten to know Ryan through his greatest hits, so to speak?"

"Yeah, something like that. All those other songs, the B sides and the unreleased, they all go into an artist's repertoire, but most people only know the bands by what they hear on the radio. Sometimes the deeper cuts are the most important ones of all."

"Well, we're here, talking. Maybe you can clue me in on some of the deeper cuts, so to speak."

Nick shook his head. "I'm not sure how much Ryan wants you to know. He's a complex guy. He has a dark side that he has managed to control for many years, and it doesn't entirely have to do with his drug use."

I nodded, encouraging him to go on.

"You might think that, because he's rich, he would just have access to whatever he wants, whenever he wants. Which is generally true, but there were times when he went off the grid, just like you did. I mean, not for weeks at a time, but he would hang out with some rough characters for days. Drug dealers, underworld guys, wrong-track junkies. He stayed in school through a combination of Alexis' charms and his father's money - otherwise he would've been thrown out for missing too many classes. Still, he always managed to get straight As. A lot of guys hated him for that reason alone."

"Alexis' charms?"

"Yeah. She's pretty talented in certain ways. She managed to wrap most of the Deans around her little finger. Professors, too. Ryan's absences were largely overlooked. Didn't hurt that Benjamin was one of the college's greatest benefactors."

"Why did he hang out with those types of guys? I mean, he's rich, he could just get his drugs through some kind of safe connection, right?"

"Yeah," Nick said. "But the guy had a death wish. Besides, Nate and I were constantly on his ass about quitting. Interventions, rehab, more interventions. I even restrained him for a three day period, like in that movie The Basketball Diaries. Had a puke bucket by the side of the bed, and I handcuffed him while he detoxed. I never had seen him so enraged as he was for those three days, then, when that was over, he disappeared for several days and ended up getting shot."

I examined my eggs and said little. I somehow knew all of what Nick was telling me about his friend.

"That shot, and another time he was shot weren't life-threatening – these shots were in the shoulder and the leg. He used to get involved with turf wars, so he was locked in a car trunk for two days, while the dealers threatened to set the car on fire. As I said," Nick said, shaking his head, "you may have an image of a rich kid getting his drugs the Upper West Side pristine way, but that's not how it was."

"How did he get away from all that?" I knew Ryan so well, yet I still didn't know the answer to this question of how he finally walked away from his drug addiction after being so heavily involved in it for so many years.

"It was him being locked in a car trunk that did it. He suddenly realized that he wanted to live, because he was so close to dying, with those thugs outside the trunk, threatening to douse the car in gasoline and light a match. They tormented him like that the whole time he was in there, but they really weren't serious. They just wanted to scare him. After all, the trunk had air holes in it, so they really didn't want to kill him. After he got out of that, he decided to seek intensive therapy. It took years for him to feel somewhat normal, but he finally started to come out of his dark place."

"So, he's survived some pretty tough situations, even more than I even knew about."

"Yeah. And he'll survive this, come what may. I honestly think that he's so happy to be alive, after all he went through, that, whatever his life throws at him, he takes it, because he's still above ground, instead of below it."

"That's certainly a good way to approach life."

"What about you? How will you handle it if Ryan is confined to a wheelchair, with a catheter and colostomy bag?"

"In sickness and in health, remember? No way I would cut and run. No.way."

Nick shook his head. "Easier said than done. There's going to be an emotional fallout. He might survive it, but that doesn't mean that he won't return to a dark place. He's difficult to handle when he gets severely depressed. Fair warning."

"We'll get through it. As you said, as long as he's breathing and not pushing daisies, then there isn't a thing that we can't handle together. Besides, look at all we've been through already. God knows that we've been tested, but we always come out stronger."

We ate a little bit more, then got a dessert to share. A fudge brownie sundae.

"Let's change the subject, shall we?" I asked. "There's no point in speculating about how much of a basket case Ryan will be, or myself, for that matter. Let's talk about you. What's going on with you and Alexis?"

"I thought we wanted to avoid depressing subjects," Nick said, his eyebrow raised. "Anyhow, she's in a treatment facility again. A familiar place for her. She's lost her job, and, I might as well tell you, because Ryan will at some point, but, Ryan's going to have to financially support her for the time being."

"The time being?"

"Yeah. As in, probably for the rest of Alexis' life."

"I see," I said. "Why is that?"

"Alexis has become unemployable."

"What does that mean?"

"She's done so much crazy shit that she probably won't be able to find another job. And, since she's broke, Ryan is the only game in town for her."

"How is she broke? I thought she was rich?"

"Her family is loaded. She, herself, was doing well because her job paid her anywhere from a half million to three-quarters of a million a year – it depended upon her bonuses year to year. Her family has long since cut her off, her job has fired her, and she has so many debts that any severance package she gets is going to be gone. Ryan has to support her."

I felt my mouth flatten out in a grimace, but I shrugged my shoulders. "Oh, well," I said. "If the worst thing that happens to us is that Ryan supports his mentally ill ex-wife, then I'd say we're doing pretty damned good."

Nick smiled. "I knew you would say something like that."

"Bi-polar disorder sucks," I said. "I wouldn't wish it on my worst enemy. Ryan is a great guy for doing that for her, to tell you the truth."

I noticed something different flashing in Nick's eyes, and it made me feel uncomfortable. There was a hint of the feelings that I got from Ryan. When I drowned in the depths of Ryan's eyes, and there was a look of overwhelming love for me, I saw, just a split flicker, of the same look in Nick's eyes.

I drew a breath, hoping that I only imagined it.

I tapped my glass impatiently and looked at my watch. "Uh, do you have to be somewhere today? I mean, it is a work day."

"No, I'm ok. I'm a partner, I can take off when I want, as long as I get my work done. As long as there are no meetings or anything going on."

"Must be nice," I said, still feeling that I needed to be somewhere. My entire life, I always had to be somewhere during the day, it seemed. It was still strange trying to adjust to the feeling that I literally didn't have to be anywhere at all. Except, of course, I had to pick up Dalilah.

"Listen, Iris," Nick said. "You're going to have to be at the hospital a lot. I don't have any major meetings coming up this month, so I can work from home. I need a breather from the Alexis situation. Maybe I could come and stay at your house and take care of Dalilah while you stay with Ryan?"

I looked at him, feeling my mouth gape open. This was arrogant, insensitive Nick? Sacrificing his time to watch my daughter while I tended to my husband in the hospital?

I suddenly started to understand why Ryan felt so strongly for the guy.

"That's wonderful for you to offer," I started. "But I can't ask you-"

"Don't be stupid. I want to do it. Somebody's going to have to watch her, because she can't be hanging around the hospital with you. I'm pretty good with kids, and she trusts me. This is going to be a weird enough time for her without her having to be in the care of a stranger."

"If you're sure…"

"Done."

"Well, ok, then. There is one thing, though."

"What's that?"

"I'm not at all sure I can return home. I mean, last I knew, the place was marked as a crime scene. I think…" Then I shuddered, not wanting to remember the fact that there was a dead body in the living room, the last I knew.

At least, I assumed that Andrew died.

That was my hope, anyhow.

Nick seemed to know the dilemma. "Of course. Andrew died in that house, presumably. And Ryan almost died. Not sure how that works, as far as how long the house will be inaccessible. You and Dalilah might have to stay with me."

Grab your copy…
vinci-books.com/deeper-illusions

www.ingramcontent.com/pod-product-compliance
Ingram Content Group UK Ltd.
Pitfield, Milton Keynes, MK11 3LW, UK
UKHW040625161125
465103UK00004B/93